I hope you enjoy!

All my warmest wishes,

Kresley Cole

BOOKS BY KRESLEY COLE

The Immortals After Dark Series

The Warlord Wants Forever
A Hunger Like No Other
No Rest for the Wicked
Wicked Deeds on a Winter's Night
Dark Needs at Night's Edge
Dark Desires After Dusk
Kiss of a Demon King
Deep Kiss of Winter
Pleasure of a Dark Prince
Demon from the Dark
Dreams of a Dark Warrior
Lothaire
Shadow's Claim
MacRieve
Dark Skye
Sweet Ruin
Shadow's Seduction
Wicked Abyss
Munro
The Witch Queen of Halloween

The Game Maker Series

The Professional
The Master
The Player

The Arcana Chronicles

Poison Princess
Endless Knight
Dead of Winter
Day Zero
Arcana Rsing
The Dark Calling
From the Grave

The MacCarrick Brothers Series

If You Dare
If You Desire
If You Deceive

The Sutherland Series

The Captain
The Price

KRESLEY COLE

SHADOW'S HEART

VALKYRIE PRESS

New York • Dacia • Sorselan • New Orleans

Valkyrie Press
228 Park Ave S #11599
New York, NY 10003

Copyright © 2025 by Kresley Cole
ISBN 979-8-9893762-4-7
ISBN 979-8-9893762-5-4
ISBN 979-8-9893762-3-0 (ebook)
Published in the United States of America.

The Lore

". . . and those sentient creatures that are not human shall secretly coexist with man."

- Most are immortal and can regenerate from injuries, killed only by mystical fire or decapitation.

The Sept of Sorceri

"Forever covet others' powers, dueling to seize more—or, more darkly, stealing another's sorcery."

- Born with one innate or root power, considered their soul. If they lose it, they become slaves to their own kind called *Inferi*.

The Vampires

- Some can harvest a victim's memories by drinking blood straight from their flesh. Biting too many or drinking a being to death can make a vampire grow red-eyed and crazed, a condition known as *bloodlust*.

- Can teleport, also known as *tracing.*

- Three vampire factions exist: the Forbearer Army (turned humans), the Horde (red-eyed flesh-takers), and the Dacians (long thought to be mythical). . . .

The Dacians

"Whispered to have vast intellects and stony hearts, the vampires of legend observe the Lore with dispassionate eyes. Cursed with unending strife until the House of Old rises."

- Stronger and faster than other vampires, with esoteric abilities.

- Dacia's closed kingdom, the Realm of Blood and Mist, is hidden within a hollowed-out mountain range.

- The Daciano royal family traditionally consisted of five houses, each with a sacred duty to the realm.

Primordial

"The mightiest of all immortals."

- The firstborn—or the oldest surviving—of a species.

The Møriør

"The bringers of doom . . ."

- An alliance of primordials led by Orion the Undoing.

- Have journeyed to the mortal realm to conquer the Lore.

The Accession

"And a time shall come when all immortal beings in the Lore must fight and destroy each other."

- A mystical checks-and-balances system for an ever-growing population of immortals.

- Occurs every five hundred years. Or right now . . .

SHADOW'S HEART

Revenge is like a journey across a sun-scorched desert. If you don't know what you're doing in those burning dunes, they will swallow you whole.

—Adham "Silt" Harea,
Sorceri King of Sand

You tell me much when you tell me little.

—Kosmina "Mina" Daciano,
Princess of Dacia, the Realm of Blood and Mist

WANTED!

Dead or Alive
Silt Harea
Murderer, cannibal, oath breaker, invoker of dark rites,
and fugitive from the law
Last seen: The Plane of Lost Years
Reward: Forty dragon-gold coins
Offered by the Gaolers

REWARD:

Missing!
Name: Princess Kosmina Daciano
Species: Vampire
Hair: Long, light blond
Eyes: Blue
Height: 5'5"
Last seen: New Orleans riverfront, setting of the hunter's
moon
Reward: Fathomless
Offered by King Lothaire, the Enemy of Old

ONE

Outside of New Orleans

Mina had once sneaked a peek at explicit illustrations of satyrs and concluded their anatomy *must* be exaggerated.

Not so!

As those creatures chased laughing nymphs through the forest, their pendulous penises bobbed along like jaunty walking sticks.

Once Mina caught her mortified breath, she turned to King Lothaire, who stood within her camouflaging mist. "Uncle, th-this is obscene!" She blushed furiously.

"You've never seen a forest lech at full tilt?" He gazed at them with amusement, the fiery red of his eyes a striking contrast to his pale skin and light-blond hair. "The Lore teems with them."

"No, I haven't. Not in real life, anyway," she hastily added to avoid the lie. A handful of other types of Loreans made their home in the vampiric kingdom of Dacia, but not a *forest lech*. "I've never seen most of this outside of a book."

When Lothaire had first teleported her to the edge of this forest, she'd gazed up at the wide-open sky. "Stars," she'd whispered in awe.

For all her life, Dacia's cavern ceiling—the stone sky—had obscured her vision of them. She'd also encountered woods for the first time and a breeze. As it caressed her face, unfamiliar scents had teased her senses and tree limbs had danced, their tiny green sails catching the wind.

Everything was as wondrous as she'd dreamed.

Well, except for the satyr penises.

"I'm surprised you haven't sneaked outside of the kingdom before," Lothaire said, his tone making it seem as if *everyone* had.

Everyone but her. "Not once." No matter how much she'd longed to.

"You've been so sheltered it borders on criminal." Mina's family all equated *sheltered* with *safe*. "Is it any wonder that you're shy? Your brother and uncles have turned you into a potential killing machine—nigh unbeatable in the training yard—who all but faints at the odd curse word or stray satyr erection."

She . . . didn't disagree. While her skill with a sword was her secret pride, shyness was her not-so-secret shame.

More nymphs gamboled by, nearly running through her mist. Within this cloud, she and Lothaire were as indistinct as air, just as unseen, and their voices unheard.

The half-dressed nymphs melded into trees, hiding from the lusty satyrs. In her studies, Mina had read about those female immortals. They were said to take lovers indiscriminately and live only for revelry and . . . and orgies!

Mina blushed more, burning through her body's store of blood. "Uncle, where have you taken me? What is my mission?" For months, he'd hinted about sending her into the mortal realm for an important assignment, something to do with the nymphs.

Was Dacian security at risk? Perhaps one of them had garnered secrets Lothaire wanted neutralized.

"We're near the Tree of Delight, outside of New Orleans.

It's a supernaturally gigantic tree that houses droves of Dryads—tree nymphs. You will observe and learn from them."

"Learn? From nymphs, Uncle?" Lothaire was her distant relation, but she called him uncle out of kinship and considered him an *erratic* loved one. She dared to ask him, "Am I here because the shock of a bashful female will amuse you?"

"Likely." His irises gleamed in the night like a full-blooded Horde vampire's. Though Dacian law forbade drinking from the flesh, Lothaire had lived among the Horde and delighted in such a taboo. He'd harvested his victims' memories until his eyes had turned red and he teetered on the tipping point of total madness. "Do not leave your post until I summon you. That is an order from your king," he said, his voice ringing with finality.

"B-but if I can't trace back each day, how will I get blood?" In Dacia, fountains of it bubbled, for all to take their fill.

"I've made arrangements with Loa the Commercenary. Her emporium is near the French Quarter, which you can locate by following the sound of mortal merriment and the scent of intoxicants. She's agreed to put a jug on her back porch for any thirsty Dacians who might wander along."

Like a stray cat? The humiliation! Mina's first trip to the mortal world, dreamed about for so long, was a mere joke to the callous Lothaire. Dacia's newly installed regent had been full of dark surprises.

"Return to the kingdom only if an emergency arises," he said. "If you don't want to disgrace yourself thusly, and you're still in trouble, go to Loa for help."

"M-maybe we should rethink this plan. After all, Mirceo forbade me to leave." Her brother had informed her, *Mark my words, Kosmina Daciano, you will not be leaving this kingdom for centuries to come.* Spoken with all the breathtaking confidence of a Dacian prince.

Yet he was away, pursuing his mate, a death demon named Caspion who'd proved reluctant to settle down with a rake like Mirceo. Though her brother could be gone for weeks, she'd written him a missive to smooth things over just in case. But the fact remained . . . "If he discovers I'm gone, he will be livid."

"So?"

So.

Such a simple word. Mina had expressed worries, and Lothaire had circumvented them—with two little letters and attitude.

Then she frowned. "Why cast me adrift here?" She'd never been near a boat, but she liked nautical references. "Why does this matter to you?"

"Because you're so socially inept that seeing you in my court pains me."

As his words reverberated through her, blood tears threatened. "Oh."

A natural-born vampire like Lothaire couldn't lie without the *rána* burning his throat; he'd shown no discomfort.

I pain him. Her pride stung with its own pain because she could see his point.

Mina's confidence was forever at odds with her shyness, so much so that she'd settled into an unshakable *awkwardness.* And despite all the training her brother and uncles had provided in combat and scholastics, none of them had helped her grow into vampire womanhood.

"I see." She stifled her hurt, wondering for the millionth time why she never lacked boldness in the training yard—only everywhere else. "My apologies for your discomfort." *Do I make others feel the same? Do Dacian subjects laugh behind my back?*

Lothaire added, "I'm also sending you away because I've seen where your heart has landed. Your infatuation is not acceptable."

She gasped. "You know?" She called her crush the Ideal because he would be perfect for her. Or nearly so.

Broad shoulders. Ruffled blond hair. Clear blue eyes.

Lothaire arched his brows. "Of course I know. Dacians are keen observers, are we not? You blush and stammer whenever Kristoff so much as gazes in your direction."

"I-I do that with almost everyone, especially those not related to me!" Kristoff the Gravewalker was the half brother of Lothaire, but he shared no blood with Mina.

"He's not for you. Nïx has already foretold his Bride, and you didn't make his heart beat."

Yet. And Nïx lied about all sorts of things.

"Besides, Kristoff is likely soon to be dead." Mina knew Lothaire debated killing him for political reasons. For now, Lothaire's queen had held her mate in check. "By the time you're finished with the nymphs, you'll be wiser and emboldened—and you won't think he's good enough for you."

Doubtful! "Uncle, p-please! Another mission would better suit me. *Any* mission."

Ignoring her, he strode deeper into the forest, and she had no choice but to follow. In the distance, she spied a giant oak tree towering hundreds of feet in the air, with windows and balconies throughout the trunk. String lanterns lit the enormous branches. Loreans thronged it.

As the sounds of the crowd grew louder, Mina's hand found her sword out of habit. This weapon had been handed down by her mother, who'd inherited it from her own.

"Ah-ah. No engagement. Only observation." Lothaire eyed her. "Why are you not falling over yourself for this opportunity? Your mist will protect you from attackers and the vampire plague, and you'll have blood whenever you need it. You would have to *try* to fuck this up."

"Language, Uncle!" Her tone was pleading. "And what about the sun?"

He blinked. "Oh. That. Though you are abysmally young, your mist should protect you."

Should? She'd trained with her mist since she was a vampling, but she couldn't maintain it indefinitely.

"Do a good job, learn the Lore, and perhaps I will decree you Dacia's first ambassador to this otherlanders' realm once I open up the kingdom."

What an honor that would be! "Do you really mean it?"

"No."

Crestfallen, she said, "Mirceo and my uncles believe you are cruel. I've defended you, saying you were misunderstood." She gazed up at him. "Who was right?"

He grinned, flashing fangs. "All of you were."

Movement drew her attention. A trio of satyrs had begun grinding against a trio of oaks. "Th-this is . . . is tree fornication!"

"Aren't they inventive little perverts?" He chuckled as if charmed. "They're always up for a Lore-gy. Puns intended."

Then she realized the nymphs had become one with the trees, fading just below the surface of the trunks to allow the satyrs to mate them like this.

Such a place is not for me. Mina gaped in blushing bewilderment, her heart racing. Once she'd recovered speech, she said, "I-I was hasty to leave Dacia. Logic says I will enjoy only a poor outcome in this realm."

Of course Lothaire heard her thundering heart. Just before he abandoned her, he said, "You fear this world? You're a Daciano, girl. All the worlds should fear you."

And then she was alone.

Fine sentiment, she mused as the nymphs and satyrs finished with a crescendo that shook acorns from the branches.

Scandalized, Mina hastened away toward the Tree of Delight, her eyes going even wider at the scenes there. A menagerie of species partook in raw debauchery.

Yes, a fine sentiment, Lothaire. But how could Mina maintain her protective mist if she fainted from embarrassment?

She'd just had that thought when she beheld her first centaur at "full tilt," and the satyr appendages became a distant memory. . . .

TWO

Poly, the Plane of Lost Years (Maybe)

Silt's bed—normally filled with soft concubines—felt cold and hard. And his arms hurt.

He dimly heard two voices. Males? In his lair?

Not possible.

He wanted to wake. Couldn't. His head swam. So he inwardly shrugged and relaxed into opium's embrace once more—*float away, Silt*—to return to his dream of an oasis.

Waves of sand crested in front of the sun, a golden backdrop to a pool of azure water. This wasn't merely a dream, but a memory. And over his thousands of years of life, he'd ached to return to that one idyllic moment in time.

Yet here he was, trapped within his lair, a pyramidal fortress that was both his pride and his exile. As a fugitive from the Gaolers, he could never leave this place.

Outside, a sandstorm raged, while the monsters guarding his keep slithered and skulked along the exterior walls. Inside Silt's bedchamber, a dozen concubines slept all around him, while his giant scorpion Sequara curled up beside the hearth. Firelight glinted off the shelves of Silt's revenge trophies: everything from stolen crowns to sacred treasures. The smoke of opium—his beloved *dragon's breath*—hung heavy in the air.

He assumed all these details of his home were true. His senses were so blunted he wasn't aware of his surroundings. Except this bed. *Cold? Hard?*

No, *float.*

Anything outside of floating brought pain. Earlier, when he'd drifted away from reality, hadn't he vaguely heard his concubines discussing him?

"He smoked enough to incapacitate a troll." Easily.

"No wonder he can't stay hard." His face had flushed even in his daze.

"It's like he's imbibing to avoid us." A truer statement had never been spoken. *"Oh well. So sad."*

Laughter had pealed all around.

Revenge, his true mistress, had bade him to wake and deal with these females, throwing them all out into the sandstorm.

No slight unpunished. No affront unreturned. Over the millennia of his life, he'd meted retribution so savagely that humans had considered him a vengeance god.

Revenge and sand had become intertwined, deserts emblematic of how unforgiving and lethal he'd been.

Yet now he remained sprawled naked on the bed, his godhood a distant memory. Maybe it was time to back off his habit.

Smoke whispered, *You belong to me.*

He did. Earlier, when his erection had waned, he hadn't missed it—

A threat shivered in the air. Those male voices pierced the veil of floating once more. Though the Gaolers couldn't enter Poly—he didn't know why—they posted bounties for hunters who could, and he was worth forty pieces of priceless dragon's gold.

Had someone come to collect?

Impossible. Silt's physical and mystical boundaries had kept intruders out of his pyramid for more than half a millennium. Scores of hunters had arrived to claim the Gaolers' bounty, and they'd all been eaten alive.

No more denying it; Silt wasn't in his bed. He lay on what felt like a cold, dirty street. He struggled to rise, finally managing to sit upright. His head swirled. "Where'm I?" Had someone dressed him in his pants?

He opened his eyes, his vision blurring. "The hell's going on?" Adrenaline surged, clearing his sight. Two males stood before him, a black-haired vampire with clear eyes and a blond demon with horns. "Who're you?" *The fuck is happening? Am I shackled?*

Seeming apologetic, the vampire said, "I'm Mirceo Daciano. My mate and I have captured you for the bounty. No hard feelings." These two hunters had breached Silt's every defensive measure to abduct him!

Daciano? This Mirceo must be a Dacian, a super vampire. Supposed to be a myth.

When Silt's breaths condensed, his gaze darted around to find that his nightmares had arrived. The Gaolers. Like rotted horsemen of the apocalypse.

The four had tattooed their faces to resemble skulls, but over the millennia, their regeneration had slowed, their skin peeling from the bone, their eyeballs shriveling to nothing.

These silent enforcers took lawbreakers to a dimension from which there was no return: *Nightside.* After all these eons of dreading his delivery to hell . . .

It was about to happen.

"Can't be. No!" Silt thrashed against his shackles, calling forth the emergency sand he always kept in his pocket, but the shackles neutralized his already withered sorcery. "I'll kill you two for this! I'll destroy anything you care about and murder anyone you love." Lips drawn back from his teeth, he hissed, "I'll replace the blood in your veins with sand!" Revenge roused inside him like a dragon stretching its scales after slumber, ready to lay waste to *everything*.

"Note to self"—the vampire tapped his temple—"beware of the Sandman."

One of the Gaolers dropped a clinking coin bag at the demon's feet. Transaction complete. Nothing remained but to deliver Silt to hell.

With a wave of that Gaoler's hand, Silt's consciousness dimmed, but he fought it. He caught Mirceo's gaze a final time and mouthed, *You're a dead man.*

THREE

Outside of New Orleans
Eve of the Hunter's Moon

Surrounded by her mist, Mina strolled the forest near the Tree of Delight for a last time. After weeks of observing, her mission was complete. Lothaire had left a message at Loa's for Mina to report to court upon the setting of tonight's moon.

She agreed it was time. She'd observed all she'd needed to at the Tree, without a single fainting spell (though it'd been touch and go in the beginning). Nor had her brother come storming this place to drag her home. He must still be working to win over Caspion.

As she wove around spears of moonlight, Mina recalled the letter she'd written back in Dacia, informing Mirceo of her upcoming adventure: *I can't wait to behold the otherlanders' world—the splendor of its natural beauty and the nobility of its peoples.*

She'd witnessed sex, sex, and more sex. Yet her initial titillation had dulled. Every scene blurred into the same aspects.

Arousal. Friction. Outcome.

Yawn.

Even the wild gaiety bored her. At one point tonight, too many party-goers had crowded onto one side of the great oak, and the tree had shifted, roots lifting from the ground.

Mina too had shifted.

Unlike that tree, Mina couldn't count on a coven of drunken witches arriving to repair her. Everything she thought she'd known about the nymphs, this realm, and herself had been turned upside down.

Lothaire had been right about one thing: observing these females—audacious immortals in charge of themselves and their world—had changed her, *inspiring* her.

What if she could set boundaries and navigate the course of her own life? She blushed just thinking about the possibility of telling her family that she'd like to leave the kingdom again in search of adventure.

She wasn't ready to return to her staid life in Castle Dacia, where her awkwardness had manifested. Sometimes, she wondered if her shyness had to do with living in the shadows of so many talented, powerful family members. Had Mina—a vampire—been starving for a moment in the sun?

Laughter sounded from a clearing amid the trees. Then sighs. Usually that forest clearing was quiet. She'd heard the nymphs whisper that it belonged to the fey folk and was off-limits.

Cocooned in her mist, Mina floated toward the sounds, coming across a pair of unclothed lovers, a fey male and female. They weren't partaking in yawn-worthy debauchery.

Just the opposite.

Rapt, she watched a scene out of dreams unfold—a communion bathed in moonbeams. She should leave them to their tender caresses and adoring gazes. Yet she couldn't pull herself away, sensing she'd climbed a precipice and now would be rewarded with an outlook she'd never experienced.

Her sense was right. With murmured words of promise, these two beings became one, as if through *alchemy*. Her mind opened to receive this epiphany. Blood tears welled, and she finally understood . . .

Everything.

Divinity in this realm existed. *And it's called lovemaking. . . .*

Once the couple finished their communion, they caught their breath and exchanged more of those caresses. Then they dressed and meandered away hand in hand, the bond between them seeming to thrum and glow.

Mina breathed, *"Alchemy,"* and gazed after them as they disappeared into the night. Like watching a current of mist surrender to a breeze—

Mist. Hers was gone. She'd been so enthralled that she'd lost track of her camouflage.

She inhaled a breath to concentrate and pictured herself as intangible. Before her form could fade and mist stretch outward from her, claws dug into her upper arm!

"You're a female!" a red-eyed vampire cried beside her, spraying spittle. "I saw you appear out of the fog."

"Unhand me at once." Zero hesitation hindered her words to this opponent. He was a Horde vampire, and judging by his eyes, he was well on his way to bloodlust from drinking and killing others.

"Never!" Expression crazed, he dismissed her wishes without a care. "You're coming with me."

She tried to trace from his grip; his hold was unbreakable. She might be a Dacian, but she was young, and bloodlust made him strong. As her hand dipped to her sword, she said, "No. I am not."

"A female vampire! What a prize you are. The Horde will

give you a welcome you'll never forget." When he started to trace her to her "welcome," Mina's sword flashed out.

He frowned. His frown deepened as his head slid from his severed neck to tumble to the ground. His body collapsed, his claws digging into her arm. Five wounds sliced her shirt and skin.

She told the severed head, "I said *no.*"

Bold words, yet she felt hollow inside. This was her first kill. Though she'd had no choice and she'd trained for just such a scenario, no logical warrior enjoyed killing.

As she scanned for more threats, she attempted to produce her mist again. Not a wisp appeared. Maybe she had drained her ability, relying on it for weeks. Would more vampires come?

Realization sank in. She'd broken the most unbreakable law of Dacia: *Forever to observe, never to engage.* She would have to confess her crime in front of the court.

Though she wasn't supposed to leave her post for hours more, under the circumstances she bade this place good-bye, then teleported home.

She moved not an inch. *Huh?*

Another attempt to reach home. Nothing. Yet when she traced across the forest, she disappeared and appeared as usual.

So Dacia's mystical boundary—which kept the realm safe and hidden—was rejecting her. She and her brother were considered the heart of the kingdom; for what reason would her home deny her return?

Suspicion took hold as she peered down at her injured arm. A red-eyed vampire had clawed her. Now her mist didn't work, and Dacia's boundary was rejecting her. . . .

Many Horde males were silent carriers of a malady, unaffected by it while spreading it to females. No female vampires existed outside the safety of Dacia for a reason.

She stared at her new wounds. They weren't regenerating,

actually looked worse. *Gods above and below, I have . . . the plague.* She swallowed past the lump in her throat.

In shock, she recalled one of her last exchanges with Mirceo before he'd left:

"Brother, I feel like I'm slowly dying in Dacia."

"As opposed to quickly dying out there?"

How quickly? He'd warned her of this. Even Lothaire had mentioned it. Calamities didn't get much graver than this.

She needed to send a message to Dacia. Loa could help! Yes, with the assistance of her family, Mina could figure out how to fix her predicament. She teleported to the Commercenary's emporium. During the few times Mina had swallowed her pride to go swallow cold blood, the store had been open all through the night.

She arrived to find the lights off, the shutters drawn. *What is happening?* She darted her gaze around. Where to go? What to do?

Mina was friendless, cut off from her family, and cursed with sickness. Her arm hurt worse, and her body felt heated.

She'd read about the plague in an obscure text in Dacia's library. The author had speculated that, while the illness wasn't lethal in itself, females grew red-eyed and frenzied to drink others. The Horde had been forced to eradicate them once they'd grown "rabid for blood," killing everything in sight, from their own mates and offspring to entire mortal outposts.

Insatiable and insensible—as far from a logical Dacian as could be. *I'd rather die.*

With consternation, she gazed up at the amber hunter's moon. Before tonight, she'd never seen a full one. The sight of it had mesmerized her, the globe abundant with power, like a female readying for birth.

Now it appeared indifferent as she rocked on her feet and

the sky spun and spun. . . .

Her hand found her sword, and the sky stopped. Mina was also strong and capable. She would find Loa, then return to Dacia. Somehow she would discover a cure. Only a brave, rational female could navigate such a fate.

Straightening her shoulders, she struck out onto the streets of New Orleans to locate her ally.

As she passed tourist haunts and taverns, she forced herself to slow her pace. A distant fey ancestor had graced her with abundant speed—and pointed ears—but Mina needed to blend in. Mortals packed the French Quarter; some of them were even sober.

The few lucid ones stopped and stared at her: a female with a sword and a slashed and bloody sleeve. When she came upon a closed clothing shop, she paused to view the wares in the window and decided on a quick detour.

Tracing inside, she surveyed the offerings. Every shirt was printed with some brow-raising message, so she changed into the least offensive one in a long-sleeved version, then kept moving. . . .

For hours as she searched for Loa or a friendly-looking Lorean, the moon followed her, arcing across the sky.

Keeping her gaze alert, Mina hastened past the other immortals she encountered in the Lore-rich city. Most were demons—some demonarchies were good, but many weren't. *Best not to risk an encounter.*

She turned another corner to find four tall, muscular males heading down the street in her direction. They sang a melodic song, their accents a rumbling burr. When they caught sight of her scouting an alleyway, they all froze.

One with a scar on his face murmured, "A leech on the hunt, with her eyes flickering from red to blue as we speak."

Flickering red? Was the plague marking her appearance in

mere hours? She'd just turned fully immortal this year, hadn't built up centuries of Lorean strength.

Another added, "Female or no', those eyes mean you've got to go. Shame; I'm a fan of your shirt."

She glanced down at the words emblazoned across her chest and grumbled, "It was the only one without curse words."

Their claws and fangs lengthened, their eyes turning ice blue. Werewolves! Natural-born enemies of Horde vampires, they were the strongest sentient creatures in the Lore.

As an enemy of the Horde herself, she agreed with their mission. "I'm not a Horde vampire," she said in a ringing voice to her new opponents, her training-yard boldness in full force.

That scarred Lykae, the presumed alpha among them, said, "You're hunting humans in our territory during the night of a full moon? Death wish, lass? We can oblige."

"I'm not hunting. I mean, I am in a way. I'm searching for someone." When they edged closer, she considered brandishing her sword but decided against a slaughter of wolves. "I don't want to hurt you gentlemen."

They shared a laugh.

"Do you no'?" the leader said. "That's no' been our experience with your kind. Doona make this harder than it needs to be. Now, lads!"

They sprang as one with claws bared; she evaded their grasp, tracing across the Quarter to leave them far behind. Frustrated howls rang out from miles away, but she knew they'd be prowling for her throughout this maze of streets for the rest of the night.

Press on, Mina. Her steps led her down to the waterfront. Along the churning Mississippi, she found a trio of females who smelled like water nymphs. "You there!" Mina called. "Are you Loreans?"

Wary nods.

One asked, "Are you a vampire? Haven't seen a female vamp in centuries."

"I am," Mina said without shyness, though these nymphs were no foes. Maybe her time observing their sisters had truly emboldened her. Or maybe the entire world had just become one big training yard—where everyone was an opponent. Her arm ached, signaling another possibility: the rabidity of the plague already affected her. "Do you know where Loa might be?"

"Yeah, she's meeting with a Valkyrie at Cemetery Number Three, *not* Number One."

"Can you provide directions?"

"Just follow the scent of lightning and bat. . . ." The nymph trailed off. Then in a burst of speech she exclaimed: "Whoa oh my gods your eyes flickered really red did you just cop a look at my neck?"

"Actually, no, I don't drink from others."

In unison, they all screamed, "Bloodlust!" They fled into the river, becoming one with it.

"I would never hurt you—" Mina's hands flew to her neck as the *rána* scalded her throat. Because she *would* hurt them? Gasping, she said, "I would never . . . consciously want . . . to hurt you." At last, the burn eased, but disbelief gripped her.

This is happening. I've been afflicted. If she couldn't get help, she would become a monster. *Focus, Mina. Follow your new lead.*

With no time to waste, she sorted scents and homed in on a trail of concentrated lightning. As she followed it over miles, the streets grew darker, the mortals fewer in number.

Ominous pressure settled over the area as some kind of supernatural force closed in. Though she was a vampire, typically the hunter in the night, she felt decidedly *hunted.* Her hand rested on the hilt of her sword as the tiny hairs on her nape rose and her breaths condensed in puffs of smoke.

An inebriated human paused at a nearby lamppost to throw up. Vomit spewed—then slowed until it hung suspended in the air. All around her time stopped.

A time freeze? She'd read about these! She drew her sword, her pointed ears twitching.

Four spectral males materialized atop eerie steeds not twenty feet from her. Clad in ragged black cloaks, they resembled decomposing reapers. Their eye sockets were empty, but they gazed right at her.

One's head dipped. Was he "looking" at the clawed arm she'd concealed?

Comprehension. *These creatures have arrived for me, a plagued vampire.* Maybe the Horde hadn't killed off their own females. Maybe these reapers had.

Mina sensed that tracing wouldn't help her escape them. No more running. She raised her sword and gave them fair warning: "Continue on your way, sirs, or I will be forced to hurt you."

One waved his rotting hand.

Her sword and scabbard disappeared. She could still defend herself, had trained all her life for this. "You won't take me without a fight!" She assumed a strike pose, readying to rain hell on these villains.

Another wave of that reaper's hand; Mina's body went from strike pose to limp. Her face met the ground, and her thoughts faded to nothing.

FOUR

Nightside

The only thing that could make hell worse? Withdrawal. It hit Silt hard and fast.

The Gaolers had forced him to Nightside, dumping him in a mountain cave surrounded by plains of fire. They'd removed his shackles, then disappeared. Silt had no food, no water, not even boots. He'd been delivered to hell with only a pair of breeches. He heaved, barely tamping down the contents of his stomach.

When he'd first awakened here, he'd limped to the entrance of the cave, surveying the landscape in disbelief. This elevation offered a view of a floodplain spreading in all directions below. A distant volcano spewed rivers of lava across it.

No stars or moon lit the sky, which was just a dome of black. As Silt's gaze swept the horizon, the impulse to say *fuck it all* had taken him by surprise.

But vengeance gave him a reason to fight. He would get free of this place and make those hunters pay. Every second of this agony could be laid at their feet, especially the Dacian's.

Silt tried to recall anything he'd ever heard about those "mythical" vampires. They lived inside some hidden mountain range kept protected by magic. Stronger and faster than Horde vampires, they were said to worship cold intellects with their cold hearts.

An unusual Dacian skill might explain how the hunters had gotten past Silt's barriers. But what had they done to Sequara? The scorpion would have given her life to protect Silt.

They must have slain her.

His eyes slid shut, his head falling back against the cave wall. Centuries ago at a bazaar, he'd bought the stingerling on the promise that she would grow no more than fifty pounds in weight. Three thousand pounds later . . .

He'd cherished her. Now she was gone.

Silt would avenge her—and himself. Yet how? Surprisingly, his sorcery wasn't bound in this realm, but he sensed no deposits of sand here. All he had was the handful in his pocket. When he tried to connect with those grains, his weakened magic sputtered—

His breaths condensed again. The Gaolers were returning! Boiling with hatred, he tensed to attack . . . but was frozen in place. . . .

When his movements were restored and his breaths cleared, a female lay unconscious on the cave floor across from him. The Gaolers had entered, dumped her, then left, without Silt seeing a thing.

Fucking despise them! Impotent fury pumped inside him with the force of a drug.

Gritting his teeth, he assessed the new prisoner. The female's long blond hair was loose, her features comely. Though she had dark circles under her eyes, she was attractive, in a pale and bloodless way. Pointed ears indicated she was fey, yet the hint of fangs he spied through her parted lips suggested vampire.

He hadn't seen a female one in memory. He'd never felt

much animosity toward that species, but now . . .

Resentment seethed.

He could easily guess what crime had landed her here. His research on this place and the Gaolers had revealed that most of their captures were immortals who hunted humans.

She moaned and rolled onto her back. She wore loose-fitting pants, sturdy boots, and a novelty T-shirt that read: *Braless Babes on Bourbon Street!*

A rallying cry he could get behind. He was a typical male; his resentment toward her lessened a touch, and curiosity urged him to go investigate her. His quaking body made him rethink such an ambitious plan.

He'd only ever experienced these bone-racking shudders and nausea during his sole attempt to quit dragon's breath hundreds of years ago. So he waited for her to wake, as what must have been hours passed by. Never taking his gaze off her face, he was watching when her eyes flashed open.

Her peculiar irises shifted from violet to reddish-purple. Reddened eyes. A maneater.

"Who are you?" With full alertness, she swept to her feet. "Where am I?"

Even in his state, he noted she was fair of form, with pert breasts, a narrow waist, and shapely hips. The draped material of her pants clung to long, toned legs. "I'm Silt Harea, the King of Sand, a sorcerer without equal." Two out of three were true.

Her gaze dipped to his tattooed chest, and her cheeks heated. "For how long was I unconscious, sorcerer?"

Her imperious tone irritated him, and her accent reminded him of something he couldn't quite place. "Hours. Centuries. Who knows? Time doesn't matter anymore." He attempted to control his shaking, but shudders racked him.

Nightside. He was actually here. *In hell.*

"What's nightside?"

He must've spoken aloud. Brain recoiling with horror, he muttered, "Immortal jail."

"It's always a jail, isn't it? My uncle escaped from one not long ago. Though humans ran that one."

"Immortals must be contained." *But not* me.

"Not me," she said, echoing his thoughts. She turned her attention to the opening of the cave. "When will the sun rise in this place?"

"It won't." *The dead have no need of light.*

"So Nightside comes by its name naturally. Well, at least there's that."

He started sweating as more dragon's breath left his body; it was all but flipping tables inside him on its way out. "Can you teleport, vampire?"

She shook her head, and a tendril tumbled over her forehead. She tucked it behind a pointed ear. "I just tried. My tracing doesn't work here."

Of course it wouldn't. This prison realm would be mystically protected against such an easy escape. Nightside offered *no* escape. Which was why Silt had dreaded this day so much.

She asked, "What were those repulsive beings that forced me here?"

"The Gaolers, demigod enforcers. Those phantasms imprison anyone who breaks the laws of the Lore. With eyes like yours, it's clear how you earned your way here." Had her purplish irises been blue before the redness set in? "Your crime is stamped upon your face."

"Is it, then?"

Bloodlust. If a vampire drained too many victims to the quick, his or her mind would turn soft, eyes reddening. In time, they would lose all their faculties.

Silt tried to imagine this creature dragging down prey. Dragging *him* down. As he waited for revulsion to hit, he asked, "How old are you?"

"Twenty-two."

"So young." *This tender little leech has been busy.*

"And your age, sorcerer?"

"Millennia." Taken with the lost years of Poly, he'd been alive for eons.

"Do you remember how you got here? Did they force you through a gateway? Have you seen anyone else?"

Her accent pinged some memory in his subconscious, but he struggled to dredge it up. "Two bounty hunters captured me and turned me over to the Gaolers." He ran a forearm over his brow to mop sweat. "Those four delivered me here."

As he choked back vomit, she turned her exploration to the rest of the cave, searching for a gateway that didn't exist. "Then there must be a portal."

For them. Silt's research indicated Nightside was a sealed dimension that only the Gaolers could access. Throughout the ages, he'd posted steep rewards for information about any immortal who'd escaped. Zero takers.

She investigated the walls, scenting every cranny. The vampire was one among the predator class of Loreans; her senses would outstrip his, despite her young age. She tugged at jutting rocks with mounting impatience. "The Gaolers stop time, don't they? If they possess such a power, how can they be fought?"

"They can't be."

She flicked a dismissive hand at him. "Well, not by you, obviously."

Leech! He parted his lips to curse her but only heaved again.

When she headed to the entrance of the cave, he expected

her shoulders to slump at the sight on the horizon. Instead, she straightened them. Raising her face, she inhaled the air. Then she turned back to him with a look of disgust. "I thought Sorceri kept themselves up better than this. Yet there's no denying the stench."

"The stench of what?" He sniffed himself. *Smelled worse.*

Eyes cutting, she enunciated the word: "Dissolution."

He didn't deny it, wouldn't even if he could. Between all his vices, he'd reached oblivion every night. For lifetimes.

She continued, "You've achieved a robust bouquet: wine, women, and drugs, with threads of general decay."

"And you, maneater, smell like bloodlust, so pot and kettle and all that." Another lie. Her delicate scent was mist mixed with woman, and it addled his brain like opium.

"Any other talents you'd care to declare before I leave you behind like dross?"

I possess a secondary Sorceri power that everyone always forgets about. "And where will you go?"

"Behind this cave, I scent nothing. It must be the edge of the realm. So I will go forward and search past that distant volcano."

"How will you cross the floodplain? There must be a hundred miles of lava rivers." Earlier, he'd watched as some cooled, leaving open paths, but then another river would pour in. The constantly changing labyrinth would incinerate any misstep. "You'll get burned alive."

"Not if I'm very lucky. And very fast."

"That volcano could be spewing lava on the other side as well."

"Possibly. But what other option is there? Surrender in this dismal cave without even a fight?"

Fuck it all. For millennia, he'd endured his existence as weariness seeped into him like saltwater poisoning a spring. *Why* had he endured?

She narrowed her gaze. "Have you no one awaiting you, sorcerer?"

His concubines cared only about gold, extracting it from him like prospectors stripping ore from a mine. "I told you that escape is impossible."

"I should take your word—a sick Lorean I just met—for that? Remember, my uncle recently escaped from an *inescapable* jail. I like my odds, sorcerer."

She had grit, he'd give her that. "What's your name?"

"I am Princess Kosmina."

Royalty. His dislike deepened. For ages, he'd been prey to the powerful. "Of what realm?"

"Dacia."

The connection he'd struggled to make fired in his mind like a zap of electricity. She was a princess of Dacia; Mirceo's last name was Daciano. Their accents were alike. "Any relation to Mirceo?" he asked, as his faithful companion Revenge helped him lever his frame to his feet, helped him swallow back nausea.

She frowned. "He's my brother."

Brother. A blood relation to the male Silt had sworn to kill was trapped with him in Nightside. Gullible immortals might have pondered the coincidence; the rest knew that dark players were forever causing mayhem. Especially during an Accession.

She asked, "Do you know him?"

Silt nodded slowly.

"Then you know he will do anything in his power to reach me here. If I don't escape first."

Though Silt's parents had held no love for him, some families shared devotion and would stop at nothing to rescue one another. Ramifications hit. These Dacians must possess abilities unknown to him—or the Gaolers. Perhaps an incursion into

Nightside was possible for Mirceo. *And I'll be waiting with that fucker's sister, the ultimate leverage.*

As always, Revenge was there for him.

The vampire canted her head at Silt. "You're not friends with Mirceo. Just the opposite."

He should lie. Falsehoods spilled easily from his tongue, and vampires rarely expected them since they were incapable of lying. But half out of his head with pain, he grated, "*I* am the one who brought you here."

FIVE

What are you talking about?" Mina asked the weird sorcerer. She didn't believe that he—a prisoner clearly in the grips of some kind of withdrawal—had worked with the Gaolers to capture her. Which meant he was insane.

Makes sense. She'd read that Sorceri were often paranoid and delusional. Even Bettina, her Uncle Trehan's new sorceress Bride, had admitted the rumors about her kind were largely true.

"Did you use some kind of magic against me?" Mina demanded of this one. Normally she wouldn't be able to speak to an unknown male, much less a half-dressed one, but he was a foe. She boldly scanned his muscle-packed build and the strange tattoos across his broad chest as she would size up someone in the yard.

He was nearly seven feet tall with longish, tangled black hair and what could only be road grime all over his sunken cheeks. A roughhewn metal cuff circled his wrist. His haggard appearance marred what might have been a jot of attractiveness. She thought he had amber-colored irises. Hard to tell since his eyes were so bloodshot.

I'm one to talk about reddened eyes.

"Did sorcery bring you to me? Or fate?" His laugh was a mean sound. "It doesn't matter. My will has been done. You've been offered up for punishment, and I accept the tribute!"

"Explain yourself."

"Mirceo Daciano is the reason I'm here. He and an accomplice breached my stronghold and turned me over to the Gaolers for gold."

An accomplice? The sorcerer must be talking about Mirceo's fated one, Caspion, who was a bounty hunter by trade. Had her brother, always ready for a lark, led a hunt with the demon?

"And then, all of a sudden, *you* arrived in Nightside—Mirceo's bloodthirsty sister."

This male had just assumed she'd been drinking from others. Typical paranoid sorcerer. She raised her chin. "Weakhold."

"What?"

"If my brother plucked you from your 'stronghold' like a feather from the ground, it doesn't sound so *strong* to me. Probably didn't help that you were intoxicated. I'm pleased he got gold for your capture"—she tapped her chin with a considering look—"but I can't see that he earned it."

Face a mask of hate, Silt lurched closer. "I'm going to enjoy this. I vow to the Lore that I will kill Mirceo Daciano. And you're the bait I'll use to lure him in."

Her lips parted. "Madman! You're playing with forces you don't understand. That's an unbreakable vow." Though her brother was more than a match for this sickened magician, a vow to the Lore could push Silt to supernatural heights of focus and lethality. And he could never stop until the deed was done.

Which meant Mina wouldn't rest until she'd vanquished this sorcerer, removing the threat. She reached for her sword, grasping only air.

Silt didn't seem to hear her. "Here you are, in my clutches. Here in hell, for me to torment. After I've meted revenge, maybe I'll dine on you as you've dined on so many."

Insane! When his palms glowed with unknown powers, aggression urged her, *Attack!* Logic dictated escape. She decided to split the difference. "Come and get me, Silt."

He lunged for her. Mina sprinted left, quick as a blur.

When he unsteadily pivoted his big build, she sprang to the right. He lurched around to snatch her—

She bounded up the cave wall. Shoving off for momentum, she twisted in midair to hit his knee with both of her boots.

Crack!

"Ahh! Leech!"

She darted away as he labored to grab her. "Too easy, sorcerer." Like a hawk dive-bombing a blindfolded bear.

His palms sparked light, dampening her sense of victory. A Sorceri king meant he was an alpha among his kind. Until she figured out the extent of his abilities, she should probably run.

Whirling around, she sprinted out of the cave. All she had to do was make it to the lava field she'd spied. Despite his age, Silt could never match her speed through that maze of flames, not in his condition.

Limping after her on bare feet, he yelled, "I will catch you!"

She yelled back, "Better hope not!" She ran down a winding path flanked by charred boulders, swiftly putting distance between them. With each mile closer to that maze, the temperature increased, wind gusts carrying acrid heat.

As she sped over jagged terrain, Mina formulated four goals.

Evade the sorcerer's immediate threat. Escape this place. Find a cure. Whenever the opportunity arises, kill Silt Harea. Once she had recovered her equilibrium here, she would strike, taking his long life.

Anything for her brother. Though Mirceo was arrogant at times, he was also steadfast and loving. He'd raised her, sacrificing everything to keep her safe within the perilous halls of Castle Dacia. Now she could finally return the favor.

As Mina ran, her mind turned to the past, to a night in the Castellan wing, when she'd been four and her brother had been sixteen. . . .

Mirceo tucked her into her warm bed, saying, "Sweet dreams, Mina."

But she took his hand to stay him. "Wait. Brother, why do we have no parents?"

He tried for a smile, yet it didn't reach his gray eyes. "You know why. They perished—our mother, just one year ago." He'd sat on the side of Mina's bed and smoothed her hair behind her ear. "We are the last of the House of Castellan."

"But our parents were immortal and out of danger of falling ill. What could have killed them?" She had heard servants whisper that other members of the extended royal family had murdered them, leaving two orphans—the young scion of a once mighty house and the vampling princess.

Mirceo's brows drew together as he tried to hide his sorrow. Voice gruff, he said, "We'll talk more about our parents when you are older."

Older. "Will we live to adulthood?" The servants had speculated against that possibility.

"Of course we will!" Mirceo pinned her gaze with his own, communicating his boundless love. "I will keep you safe. Little sister, I will always take care of you."

Before she'd drifted off, Mina had asked him one last question that had clearly stumped him, one he'd left unanswered—

Her recollection faded away once she reached the edge of

the vast lava field. In the dark, the volcano and its rivers resembled a monster with burning veins; to survive in this place, she must reach its heart and then beyond.

Which path looked least deadly? The gusts cooled some of the lava to form a blackened skin, so a blocked path might yet open. But how thick was each skin? She toed a rock, and it crumbled to reveal a piping center.

She attempted her mist again but couldn't produce even a wisp. When she needed her abilities most, the plague had stifled her mist, and this prison had bound her tracing.

The sorcerer limped into view, surprising her with his speed. The sweating brute must've run headlong after her. "You're going to get killed out there."

"Better than you *dining* on me. I'd rather burn to death."

"I don't know—we might've worked out something meaningful."

Ugh. When he shifted on his feet, she said, "Poor sorcerer, did my brother not give you a chance to grab your boots? You must already be feeling the heat."

Fury flashed in his bloodshot gaze. "I was raised to cross hot sand with my feet bare. Doesn't mean I like to feel the burn. Do not enter that field."

"Protective of your *bait?*" His vow would compel him to keep her in sight. She'd heard horror stories about the type of oath he'd made. There was no way to reverse or resist it. Because of such a vow, Lothaire had nearly destroyed his queen's soul.

The sorcerer said, "I know much about this realm. If you make it past these flames, you'll meet the undead. Legions of them live here. You have no hope without me." His palms flickered again. "*I* might keep you alive for a time."

"I run now, but I won't always. Your vow means you're a dead man. With luck, I'll watch you fall to these flames."

No more delaying. She turned from him to the labyrinth. *Focus. Calm. Reason.*

This was simply another world and another adventure. She hadn't chosen this challenge, but she would meet it nonetheless.

She leapt down into a flaming gauntlet and reminded herself, *All the worlds should fear me.*

The vampire sprinted away from him so quickly that she must have fey blood. Explained the ears.

Before he had even decided to, Silt doggedly followed between runnels of lava flow. Every footfall was agony, and not just from the heat or his new knee injury. Withdrawal intensified with the force of a sandstorm.

Sweat dripped from his forehead to sting his eyes. He tasted the salt as he heaved air thick with smoke and sulfur. Rocks shredded the soles of his feet, blood trailing him in the soot.

How had he come to this? *Stumbling about like a sickly human.* Ironic. He'd sought out smoke for so long; now clouds of it seared his eyes and lungs.

But his need for revenge drove him to pursue her. Over eons, Silt had been an acolyte of retribution. Once harmed, one harmed in turn. Once tricked, one tricked. Spreading downward, that chain of pain forged on with iron certainty.

After he'd accepted that he would never have a family, the chain had begun to resemble ancestry to him, and he revered it. Mirceo Daciano and his sister were cursed to become new links.

No match for the vampire's speed for now, Silt kept her in sight as she made steady headway. Unlike him, she was a study of focus as she dodged the red rapids. Whenever lava cornered her, she would pump her arms, gather more of that mind-blowing velocity, and vault across flames.

Though Silt had often been in life-threatening predicaments, he'd always brushed them off. Now anxiety filled him as he watched her. No wonder he'd only tried to quit opium once before. His hands shook, his heart pounding. And he couldn't drag his gaze off that vampire.

As if *she* were the source of his tension.

Concentrate, Silt. He staggered up a rise; the crust cracked beneath one foot. Just before he sank to his calf in lava, he gave a yell and sprang forward. Back on firmer ground, he squinted to lock his sights on her once more.

This was the stupidest thing he'd ever done, other than breaking the laws of the Lore in the first place. Setting oneself up as a deity for mortals to worship had ensured punishment. *How far from godhood I've fallen. . . .*

The vampire suddenly jerked her head right, focusing on something.

Miles away, lava surrounded three other prisoners. They waved their arms and screamed for help as flames lapped at their boots. Their guises flickered from mortal to animal and back. Shifters. They'd probably preyed on humans to earn their way here.

Kosmina slowed, a smudge of soot on her face. Did she appear sympathetic toward the trio? More likely, she dreamed about their blood. At her age, she must be thirsty after these hours of exertion.

He called, "Your dinner's about to be well-done!"

She flashed him a look of rancor. After a beat, she pressed on. As the shifters' screams followed her, she stiffened but didn't slow. . . .

For what must have been hours more, Silt labored his way onward. Sweat coated him, his body shedding toxins as his strength dwindled. Lucky breaks and near misses intermingled with misery.

At last the end was in sight, a sole path that led straight to high ground. *Thank sand!* Ahead of him, the princess closed in on their salvation, and he wasn't too far behind.

Yet then a belch of lava pumped from the nearby volcano, cutting them off. She would be forced to run back in his direction, and he blocked her only path.

When she twirled around to face him, Silt opened his arms and sneered, "Come to sorcerer."

SIX

That villain thinks he's got me. The path between flames was too narrow for Mina to skirt him, so logic dictated a full-bore assault.

He had to be taken down anyway, and the lava hadn't done her work for her.

Brace, fiend. Here I come. Over these last hours, the plague had continued to take hold. Her arm wound had worsened, her aggression increasing.

She didn't slow, just picked up speed. By the way he frowned at her eyes, they must be reddening even more. *Fear me. All the worlds should.* And that had been *before* her affliction.

She feinted again, as if she were going to dart past him—

At the last second, she barreled straight into him with unexpected strength, sending him flying backward.

Air whooshed from his lungs, surprise on his face. Training took over, and she flung her head down to snap her forehead against his nose.

Crack!

"Fucking leech!" He grabbed her shoulders, looking like

he'd toss her into the lava. So she grabbed his shoulders as well. *Where I go, you go.*

Their position—her straddling him, each clutching the other—seemed to register with them at the same moment. His eyes narrowed; hers widened.

Then her attention dipped to his jugular nestled along rigid neck muscles. It pulsed with a dinner bell's tempo. Mina's fangs—never needed before—sharpened for the first time to answer that call.

When he stiffened beneath her, she wrenched her gaze to his face.

"Are you a mad one, then?" His expression was one of bemused fascination, his heartbeat a repeating thunderclap in her plagued mind.

"Maybe I am!" She could see the appeal. Lothaire had zero cares; Mina had all cares. *I shed them.*

Lava surrounded her and the sorcerer. Between them was sweat, pumping hearts, and that pulsing jugular. They were in hell, about to be kissed by its flames, and maybe they both belonged here.

"Look at you," he grated. "You want my blood so badly you can all but taste it. "

Dacians don't drink from others!

Yet that was no longer true.

She rubbed her tongue over a fang, enjoying the new contrast of sharp and tender. *Am I already turning into a monster?*

"Try to bite me, leech, and see where that gets you."

The cruelty in his voice brought her back to reality. She snapped her fangs at him and snatched her knee up between his legs. His sound of pain was a cough mixed with a groan.

As if she hadn't just unmanned him, he flipped her onto her back, pinning her arms. She thrashed but couldn't shake him.

He stared at her lips the way she'd stared at his neck. Hungrily. Was he about to . . . to *kiss* her? Lava neared! Despite the threats all around—despite *him*—her traitorous body stilled beneath his.

Eyes glazed, he leaned down . . .

She scented burning hair, realized it was hers. "Stop! You're going to get us both killed!"

He shook his head hard, then swept his gaze around them. "You're coming with me." Keeping her wrists in hand, he lumbered to his feet, dragging Mina to hers.

A fast-flowing stream of lava blocked the way they'd come. Pulling her along with him, he twisted around for an alternative. Pools of fire circled them, too wide for even an immortal to leap over.

Trapped.

Over his lifetime, Silt had imagined his demise in myriad lights. But he'd never pictured himself burning to death while semihard for a predator princess who'd just introduced her knee to his balls. "I told you we couldn't cross this, maneater." No surprise; they were fucked.

When he released the vampire, her gaze darted. "Do something then, oh great King of Sand. Use your sorcery! Sand extinguishes fire."

Not a mere pocketful of it! "There's no sand in this realm. I'm picking up ash, marble, and obsidian—nothing to help me." At the height of his powers, he could have disintegrated rock into grains. Not now.

Silt had no gear, no power of flight or levitation. Unless . . .

Swiping sweat from his eyes, he snagged the sand from his pocket and called on his sorcery. Sputtering light emerged from his palms, a measure of how little power remained on tap. Most immortals grew stronger with age, but his abilities had waned from disuse and his unnatural appetites.

Lava shot toward his feet, singeing his skin. Another nearby dam of rock gave way, more lava racing for them.

"Sorcerer, whatever you're planning, begin *now*."

Do this, or die, Silt.

Simple.

He straightened his shoulders and made another attempt to connect with the grains. His palms brightened a shade. *Good enough!* Clenching his jaw, he shoved both of his hands forward. The sand straggled into the air, then dropped into the shape of a sparse platform.

Would it be enough to hold him? Maybe.

Her as well? Doubtful.

"Now what?" she asked. "Is this supposed to be a party trick or an escape? I'm confused."

"Will you shut up?" Survival argued against revenge. Revenge won, and he snared the vampire and hurried atop the sand, his free arm pinwheeling for balance. A heartbeat from failure, the platform scarcely supported them. Just below it, lava bubbled where they'd just been standing.

She murmured, "This idea is logical. Make it work."

Easier said. He'd once relocated entire deserts. Now he struggled to control a handful of sand.

Then he glanced down at the vampire.

Time felt momentous—his dream of an oasis hitting his consciousness like a sledgehammer. Keeping his gaze on her, he urged his power on.

The platform jerked forward in fits. Flames beneath him heated the grit, cauterizing his sliced feet. He bit back a yell.

"Focus," she said in a soothing tone. "We're almost there."

He held her gaze as he would a lifeline, inching them toward a raised rock plateau. With a last burst of sorcery, he maneuvered them to safety—just as his sand collapsed. Keeping her pinned against him, he dropped to his knees and sucked in air.

By all the gods, he'd done it! He'd gone so long without accomplishing anything that he'd forgotten the satisfaction. The hedonist in him craved more of this feeling. Silt frowned. Had he once been driven?

After centuries of oblivion, I have no idea who or what I am.

The vampire cast him a wary look with her cheeks flushed. The little leech was as beautiful as she was bloodthirsty. Even her curious irises couldn't mar her looks. Beside him, her trembling body was all curves and promises.

The intensity of his arousal shocked him. As before, her lips called to him.

Yet rumbling sounded, tremors vibrating his knees.

He loosened his grip for a split second. Which was all she needed to spring away—just as a geyser burst from the ground beneath him.

SEVEN

Dacia

When Lothaire moved a piece on one of the four-dimensional chessboards before him, Kristoff sensed his impending loss.

Again.

"We've been playing nightly for months," he said. "How much longer will we do this?" Lothaire had information he needed but wouldn't give it until Kristoff beat him in three successive games.

"Until I bore of defeating you." Lothaire's red gaze gleamed in the lamplight of the villa balcony.

Kristoff had always longed for family; his half brother left much to be desired. He stared at the pieces, hating the sight of them. Every night the two played, Lothaire delighted in saying "Checkmate" over and over.

If Kristoff ever managed to sleep during the day, he dreamed of his losses, that word exploding in his head.

Still. Something told him tonight would be different. For the first time in months, he felt the call of fate. Could destiny find him in a hidden kingdom?

Or will I win at last?

Maybe he would reach his limit and attack the much stronger Lothaire. Then Kristoff would be dead—the ultimate call of fate.

Lothaire sipped his bloodmead from a crystal goblet. "But then, I don't bore easily." Playing with others' lives amused him.

Kristoff bit out, "You truly are a son of a bitch."

"Careful, brother. No one calls my mother, the great Princess Ivana, a bitch. You get one warning."

The heir to the Dacian throne, Ivana had left this realm behind after losing her heart to Stefanovich, Lothaire and Kristoff's father, the king of the Vampire Horde. Lothaire's early childhood had been spent in the shadow of Stefanovich, whom he would eventually murder, and their uncle Demestriu, who would steal the throne after that assassination. *With family like this* . . . "And if I'm not careful, then what? You'll finally execute me?" He didn't only lose at chess; he was losing patience with these games. At first, Kristoff had attempted to manipulate him, as Lothaire did with the complex puzzles he enjoyed solving, but his half brother was uncannily brilliant.

"Do recall that you are free to leave your castle-view villa at any time." Though he'd initially abducted Kristoff, Lothaire had since offered freedom.

But should Kristoff leave, Dacia's mystical boundary would prevent an otherlander like him from returning. "You know I'll never forfeit my access to you."

An oracle had revealed that Furie—the half-Fury, half-Valkyrie queen of the Valkyries—was Kristoff's Bride. But Lothaire, on Demestriu's royal order, had chained her to the bottom of the ocean more than half a century ago.

Only Demestriu and Lothaire had known that location; Demestriu had since perished. "Tell me where Furie is, and then you can set off to rescue your missing niece." Kosmina, the painfully shy swordswoman, had always been kind to Kristoff.

Lothaire waved that away. "She's more of a distant cousin. She only calls me uncle because she adores me." He sighed. "More and more Loreans foolishly do."

"A member of your family is in jeopardy." Rumors of a red-eyed female vampire in New Orleans had reached even this realm, along with suspicions that the Gaolers had taken her. "You behave as if you're all-powerful, yet you won't undertake a search?"

Lothaire grandly said, "I did post a reward for her. And more, I will actually pay it. Does that count for nothing? In any case, all her other uncles are out searching. And Mirspion makes strides to find her." Mirceo and Caspion? "Their forays against the Gaolers aren't *un*inspired, their ideas *un*sound. They might rescue her."

Kristoff had heard of the new pair's exploits. Not for the first time, he wished for such a family bond. He hesitated, then positioned his rook.

Lothaire chuckled. "You won't save your Bride with moves like that."

Kristoff's claws bit into his palms until blood dripped. His destined Bride, the one who would awaken his dormant vampire heart, currently drowned somewhere. For six decades, she'd died, only for her immortality to resurrect her.

The urge to attack Lothaire burned inside him, but immortals grew more powerful with each passing year. Kristoff wasn't even a third of his half brother's age. If he snapped, then both he and Furie would be lost forever.

"I scent your blood." Lothaire's amusement deepened. "You're not deficient intellectually. You simply can't concentrate. Playing you isn't even sporting. Luckily, I'm not sporting." He moved a piece, his strategy unfathomable.

"Why are you doing this to me? I would have welcomed a brother."

"We are each an obstacle to the other. I will never give up the fight for our father's crown, and neither will you. Even though the Horde wants neither of us."

Lothaire was illegitimate, and Kristoff had forbidden his clear-eyed Forbearer army to take blood straight from the flesh. He didn't hold the vampiric Thirst sacred, so the Horde refused to accept him.

Lothaire considered the boards, absently saying, "Their wants won't matter when I use the Dacian army to subjugate them."

"This mythical place isn't enough for you?" After Lothaire's mother had been assassinated—the details of which were vague—this great kingdom had descended into deadly intrigues for the crown. Three millennia later, the remaining Dacian royals had sought out Lothaire to rule and quash those feuds. "To service your greed, you must have my crown as well?"

"No, it isn't, and yes, I must."

"Then why keep me alive?"

"I can always murder my foes, but I can't ever bring them back," Lothaire said, sounding deceptively reasonable. "And you interest me. You needed an army, so you created one, stalking mortal battlefields to turn dying soldiers into vampires." That was how Kristoff had earned the moniker of Gravewalker. "I've seen less impressive stunts." The closest Lothaire would ever come to a compliment.

"I assembled an army of vampires, and you assembled one of memories."

Lothaire inclined his head. Seeking knowledge, he'd drunk everyone from wizards to warriors, storing their experiences. "But you lack a killer's instinct. Probably just as well, since I could see you turning into a brutal despot like our father. That's why it's in my best interest to keep you from Furie, a warrior with a supreme killer instinct. Should you be able to tame her—questionable—she would be your greatest asset. Just as Lizvetta is mine." Elizabeth, his queen, was a former mortal, turned into a vampire with a wishgiver ring.

Having been raised by humans himself, Kristoff was partial to her. During their first real meeting, she'd clapped him on the back and said, "Hey, you, we're gonna be fast friends, just you wait. And call me Ellie! Everybody does, except for this chucklehead." She'd hiked a thumb at Lothaire, who'd appeared charmed.

The kindly new vampire had promised to use all her influence with Lothaire to help him. "Are you implying that you *tamed* Ellie?"

"My spirited queen? Heavens forfend. There's no taming such a force. Even now we are at odds, and I fear she will wear me down. . . ."

Perhaps Ellie's efforts were paying off!

"She talks of offspring."

Disguising his disappointment, Kristoff asked, "Would that be so bad?"

"I am concerned about her safety. She is a newly minted vampire, transformed by unusual means. We simply can't know what might happen."

Lothaire was a true enigma. Just when Kristoff deemed him the most selfish narcissist in the Lore, he would reveal a different side to himself.

"And I don't want to share Lizvetta with some mewling brat. All her attention and focus should be on *me*. Everyone's focus should be."

Kristoff exhaled. No. Just a selfish narcissist. He made another move, which earned him an eye roll from Lothaire.

"*Clearly* your best bet is to sign my new ledger." Lothaire was infamous for assisting Loreans in dire circumstances—for a price. He coerced them to sign his ledger with a vow to do anything he desired.

"The first thing you'll demand of me is to relinquish my crown!"

"Yes. But *your* greed demands you get the crown *and* the girl. Alas, your chess ability doesn't support your aspirations."

The Horde crown was Kristoff's birthright. Furie too was his by right. "You expect me to sell my soul to you."

"I do. And should you ever make this sacrifice for your mate, perhaps I'll refrain from telling her that I offered to help you months ago, all for a mere signature. How many times has she died and revived since then? Her Fury blood feeds on retribution. Tell me, little brother, each time she resurrects, do you think she dreams of air? Or *fire?*" Lothaire moved his queen. "Ah, and there's the scent of blood again."

"I couldn't hate you more."

"Because you know I'm right. As much as it pains me to say this, we are alike in some ways."

Kristoff sat back in his chair. "We are *nothing* alike."

"You'll see. One day, you'll see it. Now, back to the game."

Choking down outrage, he countered Lothaire's move. A grandfather clock ticked somewhere in the villa as they plied gambits. Out in the kingdom, blood fountains bubbled. A dog barked. A babe woke from slumber with a cry.

Concentrate, Kristoff. He'd stumbled onto a potential play. Was a win to happen at last? They traded more moves. "I will defeat you."

"Perhaps." Lothaire repositioned his queen. "But not tonight. *Checkmate.*"

That word.

Kristoff's vision swarmed. He'd wondered how long he could go before he attacked Lothaire in a blind rage. *Tonight. I made it till now.* The call of fate was murder.

He tensed to vault over the table—

"Look at you two," a female said as she sauntered onto the balcony. "The very picture of brotherly love."

Kristoff inhaled for control, because Nïx the Ever-Knowing had just waltzed into Lothaire's mystically protected kingdom.

The oldest Valkyrie and most powerful oracle alive carried a fluttering bat and a satchel that was bigger than she was. Fresh blood covered her. She was barefoot, her mane of tangled hair sticking out on end. As she gazed fondly at Lothaire and Kristoff, her amber eyes flickered silver with emotion—and more than a touch of madness.

Lothaire raised his brows at her appearance. "What have you gotten into now, Phenïx?"

"*Havoc*," she breathed, "wrought with a cheery smile and a Garfield plushie. Everything for the coming LoreWar this Accession." Grunting with effort, she hoisted her bag and dumped what looked like a massive heart onto the chess table. *Thump.* "That needs to air out." The heart sparked with tiny flames and appeared iridescent in the lamplight.

When its weight collapsed the table, she shrugged and addressed the bat: "Bertil, do not let me forget that organ. The fate of all the worlds depends on it."

Bertil screeched, then proceeded to suck blood from her drenched T-shirt. It read: *Total Eclipse.*

"Where did you get the heart, Valkyrie?" Lothaire asked, as if inquiring about a new accessory. "Looks like a dragon's to me."

"We stole it, during a rumble at a drive-in. Backed by allies, I struck a decisive blow to our enemy the Møriør. Everyone says I'm too loopy to be an effective leader. Everyone says I'm past my prime, but I showed th—oh my gods, Lothaire, what is a giant heart doing on this balcony? Yuck! Isn't that a health-code violation? You need to throw it away."

Lothaire gazed at her with surprising tenderness. "We'll get you cleaned up and rested, Phenïx," he crooned. "It must be naptime."

"Naptime? Who has time? *What* is time? The one-eyed sorcerer waits for no soothsayer. I have no time for time."

Kristoff grated, "Your sister Furie is certainly out of it." This Valkyrie must know where she was. Yet Nïx had once told Kristoff that *he* was meant to find and save her.

Now that Demestriu had been eliminated by an unlikely assassin, Kristoff's only leads were this crazed Valkyrie or his equally crazed half brother.

She frowned at Kristoff, her gaze gone distant. "I'm sure I saw Furie just a minute ago. Surely."

When he parted his lips to grill her, Lothaire snapped, "Not now, Gravewalker."

Nïx blinked back to the present. "I can't stay long. I'm only here for a quick delivery"—she pulled from her back pocket a leather-bound journal that reeked of witchcraft—"of stolen goods."

EIGHT

Nightside

Mina gaped as the sorcerer blasted into the air atop a jet of water. She'd just been marveling that they'd survived the fire field—and that the triumphant glint in his eyes was weirdly arousing—then *geyser*.

When he came crashing down onto hard stone, the impact knocked the breath from him; she swore residual opium smoke puffed from his lungs.

He spat steaming water. More sloshed from his leather pants and sluiced from his hair, cascading over blistered skin.

She gave a laugh. "You stunk so bad, even Nightside took exception!" The geyser had scalded him clean of that dissolute smell, and he no longer sweated out drugs. She detected a thread of his innate scent, and it was . . . nice.

His lowering expression made her laugh again. As he maneuvered himself to sit against a boulder, gusts of wind whipped across the rise, wicking away the moisture from his abused skin.

He'd be out of commission for a while, but not enough for her to take his head without a sword. Pity. Which meant she should concentrate on her escape.

Time was running out for Mina. She recalled her temptation to bite his jugular—clearly the plague's work. It was already influencing her behavior, eroding her logic.

And that wasn't her only concern. Once Mirceo discovered Lothaire had sent her away from Dacia and lost her, he might attack the much stronger king. Then Lothaire would relish the chance to do to Mirceo what he'd done to her uncle Viktor: beat him beyond recognition.

If Mirceo somehow kept his cool and realized where she was, he might provoke a Gaoler capture by appearing in front of a mass of humans. Or worse, his thoughts could turn to a perilous alternative, a ring that granted wishes. For a price.

If anyone was going to use that wishgiver, it'd be Mina. *I've got to get free of Nightside and save my brother from himself.*

Mind on the task ahead, she investigated the area. High ledges and stacks of seared boulders surrounded them, with only one outlet, a natural path.

Her gaze jerked up when a disturbing scent reached her from a distance. Something immortal but . . . dead. Undead.

Nightside's stakes are real, she thought, the screams of those burning shifters echoing in her mind. Yet she had to push on. "Thanks for the ride, sorcerer, but this is where we part ways."

"Even after I saved your life?"

"You told me I wouldn't be here if not for you."

His brows drew together, as if he was trying to recall his words. Then he said, "You already scent the undead, don't you? Nightside is their realm. Ghouls, wendigos, and revenants originated from here." She'd read about each species in her studies. "You'll face them all. At least *I* would keep you alive for a time and protect you from them."

"I've witnessed your powers. You couldn't protect me in a

sandbox. Good-bye for now, Silt Harea."

"I will find you. It's as good as done."

"Better hope I don't lay hands on a weapon before then."

As she hastened away, he yelled, "Coming for you, little leech!"

She yelled back, "I like my odds, sorcerer!"

As she gained elevation on the path, rain began to fall. Fresh water? Her fortunes were turning! After all, during her studies with her uncle Trehan, she'd read of otherland realms that rained acid under a constant sun.

She quickened her pace, wondering how her Dacian uncles would take the news of her disappearance. Though they all resembled each other with their black hair and tall builds, their personalities varied wildly.

Trehan was methodical but fierce, a book-loving master of weapons. Brash Viktor was a military genius who hungered for a war that would never come to a hidden kingdom. And Stelian, the sentinel of Dacia's stone borders? He sipped his ever-present bloodmead flask to disguise his hidden depths.

While Mirceo had raised her, these males had also shaped who she was today. She knew what they would do once they discovered she'd gone missing: *raze all the worlds to find me.* They could appear here at any moment. . . .

Her optimism faded when she reached a cliff. Below her spread an apocalyptic landscape of burned forest and drifting fog. Petrified trees jutted from ash, twisted remnants of a more verdant time.

Lava from another vent must have overtaken a swampy forest. She didn't know how trees had grown without sun, but then, not every plane was bound by the rules of the mortal realm.

Gnawed bones dotted the area, evidence of a hunting ground. Through the rain, movement caught her eye, figures winding around trunks in the distance.

Wendigos. They had haggard bodies with stringy hair and claws like daggers. Fangs and orange-red eyes dominated their elongated faces.

Were her reddening eyes like theirs? A warning?

More movement. Half a dozen immortal prisoners were sprinting through the ash, attempting to outpace those beasts.

From her vantage, Mina spied a wendigo leap dozens of feet into the air above the fog bank to land on a male—who'd never seen it coming. His screams rang out.

As with ghouls, a wendigo's single bite or scratch could transform a Lorean. Since the catalyst for a species change was always death, that meant undead contagion could kill even an immortal.

While ghouls were driven by an uncontrollable need to infect others, wendigos simply wanted to eat other beings, would unearth corpses to dine on in times of scarcity.

A pack of those corpse-eaters descended on the felled male. He wouldn't likely resurrect; wendigos didn't often leave enough of a victim's body to revive.

Another scream; two out of six immortals had fallen. She was tempted to help the remaining ones, but she had no weapon. Besides, they could be as evil as Silt the Crazy Sorcerer, imprisoned here for a reason.

Cold logic, cold heart, Mina.

As the last four struggled through the fray, she used her speed to get around and ahead of them, allowing those Lorean deaths to provide a distraction.

"I'm looking for a female vampire," Silt told a lion shifter curled up in the middle of a wendigo hunting ground.

"Be careful what you wish for," the male said weakly. Why was his voice muffled?

"Have you seen her?" When Silt had made a tactical detour to acquire weapons, he'd lost her trail. Though he'd once been a gifted hunter, the rain had erased her tracks in this ashy quagmire. "Answer me."

"Go suck your own tail."

Like a flash, Silt had one of his new makeshift swords under the male's chin. "Do not cross me." He pressed the sword harder, glad he'd taken the time to rush back into the fire field to pluck two lengths of crystal as weapons. "Did you see a vampire?"

"She did this!" The shifter opened his mouth and pointed to the missing top row of teeth and fangs. "That leech pummeled me to the ground, booted me in the face, and stole my belt!"

"Sounds like she made off with your balls too?" Silt's lips curved, though he hadn't fared much better against her. She'd broken his nose, busted his own balls, and cracked his knee. "Did she drink you when you were down?" Either she would benefit from this creature's blood, or the wendigos would. Silt searched for the telltale bite marks, but the male's coat concealed his neck.

"No, she didn't feed. Just booted me—for no reason whatsoever!"

Blood for the taking, and she passed it up? "Where did she go?"

"Dizzy after that. I think she headed toward that rise in the distance. We're all headed there."

"From where?"

"From the cave. Everyone starts in the same cave."

As suspected.

Half-delirious, the shifter said, "The Gaolers warned me in dreams . . . but human flesh calls to me." His pupils swelled to larger slits. "Mortals are so tender. I can't resist devouring them."

Silt punched him, knocking him unconscious, a death

sentence in this field. He dropped down to filch the shifter's boots, surprised they fit. Then he peeled off the leather coat from the male's lax body. The cut was too tight but might stretch. He ripped strips from the shifter's shirt to knot around the ends of his swords for handles.

Provisioned, he'd just started forward when he sensed wendigos behind him. He whirled around to find eyes burning with hunger. Gore stamped their revolting faces.

Opportunistic feeders would take the easy meat first. Weapons raised, Silt eased away from the shifter.

The wendigos pounced on the unconscious male with a ferocity that would have surprised even a predator like him.

As the pack started their feeding frenzy, Silt hastened away through the sludge.

The shifter woke in time for hell, his screams carrying over the desolate landscape.

Then more howls sounded in the distance. Ignoring the pain in his exhausted body, Silt ran headlong.

Another pack was on the scent of prey, heading away from him. His bet: *They hunt a female vampire.*

NINE

They've got me in their sights.

Those other immortals had fallen quickly, leaving Mina as the next target.

She plowed through the mud, that pack steadily pursuing. She was fast, but the wendigos moved across the sucking muck with ease. How close were they? The intermittent rain hindered her senses.

If she died in this place, Mirceo would blame himself for not being there for her, forgetting all his years as her determined protector.

And if Silt escaped this place, he'd be a threat to Mirceo as long as he lived. She simply refused to die before she struck down that sorcerer.

As miles passed beneath her feet, her thoughts turned to Kristoff. Why hadn't she been able to speak to him when she'd had the chance? She recalled bringing a prized bottle of bloodmead to his villa. He'd accepted the gift with thanks and absently said, "You look well tonight, princess." She'd stuttered some harebrained reply, almost passed out, then fled.

Now she imagined brave Kristoff storming this realm to rescue her, taking her into his arms. Having faced so many perils, she would have no time for shyness. Instead of stammering, she would clutch his shoulders and command him, "Kiss me, Gravewalker."

Interrupting her reverie, howls sounded from . . . *in front of her?*

She drew up short.

More wendigos approached from ahead. Those creatures had surrounded her? At least twenty of them grew visible through the sheets of rain. They hissed and bared their fangs as they loped closer.

She readied her weapon—that lion shifter's belt strapped around a large rock—and entered the fray. Swinging her sling, she landed a hit against one's temple, and a satisfying *crack* sounded. Brain matter and brown blood oozed.

Though years of training should guide her moves, the plague was like a fire in her, sending her aggression raging.

Using her speed to dart around swiping claws, she landed another blow. Another. Soon five wendigos lay twitching on the ground. Yet then the belt tangled around one's throat. She abandoned her sling to leap atop the creature's shoulders, dodging claws as she twisted its head free. The decapitated body stood for long moments. . . .

From her shoulder perch, she spied Silt rushing toward her with two weapons drawn. She met gazes with him. As she surfed the wendigo body to the ground, she whipped its gory head at the sorcerer.

Four wendigos sprang for him at the same time, distracting him; he felled the creatures, and the head struck him in the face.

"Godsdamn it, leech!" He swiped a forearm over his cheek. "I'm here to help you." Was revenge that important to him? *Idiot.*

He slashed his way through even more wendigos to reach her. The weapons he carried were lengths of crystal, resembling obsidian, but obviously much stronger. He'd also sourced boots and a jacket.

The wendigos that had been closing in on her turned to him, giving her a moment to catch her breath and grudgingly admire the sorcerer's skill. When two charged him, he feinted to his left and swung his sword right. He beheaded the pair with a single strike!

He looked worlds away from the sick sorcerer of before. He'd tied back his hair with a strip of leather, revealing all his face, now clean of road grime. His color had returned, which for him was deeply tanned skin.

Pronounced jawline. Aquiline nose. His lips, no longer thinned with misery, appeared chiseled with a sculptor's care. His eyes had cleared, the golden-hued irises vivid.

The more skill he demonstrated, the more concern she felt for Mirceo. This immortal male—with all his millennia of strength and speed—was a true threat.

Another wendigo leapt for her, breaking her stare, so she used her own speed to get the drop on it and twist off its head as well. As long as she had one . . . She hurled it at Silt as he pivoted to evade another one's claws.

The head struck him in the shoulder. His lips drew back from his teeth. "Will you desist?"

"No!" Yet then dozens more wendigos loped closer, heeding the others' howls. Her target shifted from Silt to the baying pack. A single sorcerer and an unarmed vampire couldn't fight off this many. "Give me one of your weapons!"

He laughed. "Get fucked, leech."

She gasped at his language. "I'm serious! I've trained all my life."

"All of your two decades? Just stay behind me."

A claw whistled inches from her face. She booted the creature's leg, cracking its femur. "I won't target you again until this threat has passed."

Seeming to judge her truthfulness—as if she could lie!—he finally said, "I hope you're as good as you let on." He tossed one of the crystal blades to her.

Testing the weight with a flourish, she recalled her uncle Viktor's words: *Wielding a sword is so comforting to Mina that it might as well be a shield.* Though hideous wendigos bore down on them, she laughed. "Ah, sorcerer, I'm much better than I let on."

He frowned, as if he couldn't quite make sense of her.

Laughter fading, she inhaled for focus and began. She felled the closest one with a swift strike, then another. A third. During a brief lull, she spared a glance at the sorcerer.

When a pair charged him, he halved one with his sword's downswing—then dissected another on the upswing.

Mina continued dropping foes, but her attention kept drifting to the sorcerer. The male she'd viewed as a pitiable magician was actually a warrior. Between the edges of his new trench coat, his skin sheened, his muscles swelling even more. His tattoos moved with mesmeric intensity.

She felt . . . attraction.

Now? For *him*? It must be the plague madness taking root!

Focus, Mina. When she decapitated another wendigo, its head somersaulted in Silt's direction. He sent it flying with the flat of his weapon, then glowered at her.

"That one was accidental!"

Onward she and the sorcerer fought. Her weapon struck bone; his struck bone—*clanging, clanging*. Martial harmony.

Four larger wendigos surrounded her. She ducked under claw strikes, using her speed to confuse the creatures. Her weapon alleviated their bafflement forever.

When Silt halved the body of a giant one, his gaze found hers and awareness simmered between them—a pair of immortals impressed with one another.

Soon only two corpse-eaters remained. "You want the honors?" Silt asked, sharing foes, a polite gesture.

"Delighted." With a grin, she sped between the wendigos, twirling with her sword outstretched. Heads tumbled as their bodies collapsed.

Never slowing her momentum, she raced forward to attack the sorcerer.

"The hell?" He blocked with wicked strength. Then a second time.

Stalemate. Out of breath, they circled each other.

"I just saved your life—again—and this is how you thank me?"

"The threat has passed, so I reacquired my former target. Besides, you only saved your bait. I don't want to be *kept alive for a time*."

His lips curled, and he didn't deny it. "You didn't overstate your talents with a blade."

"You didn't hint of yours," Mina said, proud of her banter.

"But I'm going to want my sword back." He must be feeling better; he assessed her figure with a slow perusal.

The flare of interest in a male's gaze should have mortified her. She felt her old awkwardness surging. Fury, plague, and the heat of battle helped her stifle it. "Indeed? Come and get it."

"Your eyes are even redder. You're as much of a maneater as that shifter you attacked."

"He pounced first," she said, beginning to explain. But letting this sorcerer assume she was a terror made sense. "And so he paid."

When more howls rang out from behind them, indicating a number that would dwarf this one, Silt said, "That pack will swell as long as we're in their territory."

She'd spotted a rise several dozen miles away. Higher ground out of this muck should give her an advantage. "You and I will resume this at a later time." She whirled around and sprinted.

But the sorcerer was right on her heels.

TEN

Save your murderous looks," Silt told the vampire as they slogged over soggy ground. "I go where you go."

Her glare deepened, though she never slowed. "What's your plan now?"

"Make sure I'm beside you in case Mirceo somehow shows up here. He might actually do it, using whatever arcane powers he used to breach my home's defenses. I doubt his demon friend could've managed that on his own." Scores of demons had tried and paid for their folly. "And then when Mirceo arrives, I'll strike."

Lips thinned, she said, "You blame him for your plight? Why not blame the Gaolers? Or by that chain of reasoning, blame yourself for breaking the laws of the Lore!"

The Gaolers had warned Silt not to use his sorcery in front of humans. But after he'd been robbed of his abilities—enslaved, then preyed upon as a child and young man—his lust for power had overwhelmed him. "You're one to talk about broken laws, maneater," he pointed out. "And of course I blame your brother. I've survived as long as I have because of my reputation. Mirceo has undermined it. Until I behead him, every immortal from here to the Elserealms will consider me an open target. That's the way the Lore works."

"You confound me. You seem to believe you can easily defeat Mirceo—who is an expert swordsman—yet not defeat any other foe."

Silt sped through a puddle, splashing mud. "You must think I can defeat him as well."

"I know that vow of yours will strengthen the resolve of a man otherwise lacking in it." She eyed him for a strike, would cut his throat without so much as blinking. "And there will be zero chance of a conflict after you're dead."

"Try it, leech. Make this interesting."

"You won't see me coming." Had her gaze dipped to his neck?

With each step across this wasteland, his hunger increased. Her thirst must be burgeoning like a tidal wave. "When was the last time you drank?"

She hurdled a large rock. "Why do you care?"

"You just clocked my throat." He recalled the way she'd stared at his neck in the lava field, that dark thirst. Now he pictured her slowly piercing him, sucking on his flesh. He imagined her afterward, warm and sated from his body, licking her lips. . . .

Despite their circumstances, his cock stirred. He'd never been bitten, but if he'd come across a comely vampire, would he have allowed her to feed? Back in the day—or, rather, a few days ago—he would've tried almost anything to shed his worlds-weariness.

His perversions shouldn't surprise him. His very name meant dirt and adulteration.

She said, "I have no intention of drinking you. I've never

been intoxicated, won't start now. Which means your befouled blood is off the menu."

Of all the words. Over the ages, he'd been known as Silt the Befouler. "Why didn't you drink the shifter you attacked back there? He wasn't intoxicated."

"I'm thirsty. I'm *really* thirsty. But I'm not at a point where he—or you—would prove appetizing enough."

Silt hadn't particularly wanted to strengthen this vampire, but her turning her nose up at his blood rankled. "At your age, you probably need blood every night. You'll beg for mine before long. No other food exists on this plane." Vampires could eat food if pressed, but nothing satisfied them like blood.

"I don't believe that. If our captors intended for us to starve, then why not just kill us? They're called the Gaolers, not the Executioners. There must be a higher purpose to this place. I continue my exercise in survival to discover it. And all the while, I'll search for an escape and an opportunity to kill you. Fortunately, I can concentrate on many things at once."

Her points weren't lost on him, but he found himself preoccupied with her blood drinking: "With eyes like yours, you must not have been so discerning about your victims before. The Gaolers would have sent you warning dreams of this place, but you continued preying on others." As that shifter had done. Had Kosmina found human throats *tender*? For some reason, the idea enraged Silt.

"Seems you've got me all figured out. And what crime did the great King of Sand commit to end up here?"

"Millennia ago, I set myself up as a god among humans. After a show of my stunning sorcery, they fell to their knees and showered me with riches and adulation."

"At your advanced age, you should know better than to reveal yourself to humans."

Everyone in the Lore knew this. "Apparently, the guideline about not revealing ourselves is more of a rule." He'd paid those warning dreams no heed, until they'd stopped. Then he'd sensed the Gaolers were coming for him, so he'd become a fugitive.

"If you're so powerful—worthy of worship even!—then use your *stunning* sorcery to fend off the wendigos trailing us."

He swiped rain from his face. "I told you. No sand here."

"Why would it be so difficult to come by?"

"It's rock broken down by physical processes, which takes untold energy over eons. For all we know, Nightside only recently developed rain and wind."

As she ran beside him, she canted her head. "You're not like the sorcerers I've read about with their impeccable clothes, masks, and glib words."

He sidled around a petrified stump. "Not glib."

"You don't say."

"What else do you think you know about Sorceri?"

As if reciting some text, she said, "Your kind are isolated creatures, prone to revelry and paranoia. Historically, you wore masks to discomfit enemies and armor to protect your bodies. You are obsessed with gold and eschew meat."

He grunted.

"You can't deny any of it, can you?"

"Of course I can. I eat meat."

Eye roll. "One of my uncles recently found his Bride in a sorceress, and she confirmed everything I've read, saying Sorceri often enchant themselves with their own ills."

Though true, Silt said, "Condolences to him. Sounds like your uncle got saddled with a killjoy."

"They're ecstatic together, thank you." With an analytical expression, Kosmina observed, "You don't look like a reveler. You must have been very active before you froze into your immortality."

I was forced to be active. In his youth, he'd stayed just ahead of the tip of the whip. "I built many things. Homes, temples, castles." He'd been good at it, seeing all the engineering angles, appreciating them. "And then I used my knowledge to fortify my stronghold, routinely updating my defenses." Until he'd grown so weary of the monotony that he'd almost hoped for capture. *Just end the suspense.*

Smoking had obliged where enemies hadn't.

"Your weakhold," Kosmina repeated. "A pup of a vampire outwitted you. And now you have to kill him, or else other boogeymen will slink up behind you or something? The details don't add up."

He scowled. "My bounty was the longest-standing in the Lore for a reason—it was the most dangerous. To guard my holding, I let a pack of a hundred wendigos, like the ones back there"—he pointed over his shoulder—"patrol my valley. Past that was a field protected against tracing vampires and demons, one filled with ravenous, subterranean gulgs. *Past them*, two sand scyllas with esoteric powers nested at the base of the structure, their tentacles forever combing the walls. I inscribed the bricks with spells to repel break-ins and teleportation." The scyllas alone had been worth their weight in Sorceri gold. "So how did your brother get past measures that foiled so many other hunters? You know, don't you?"

She just smiled, irritating him the way sand in a shoe might irritate others.

"Why would he become a bounty hunter anyway? A prince like him wouldn't need money."

Her smile widened, displaying flawless teeth and two tiny fangs. "This fact is going to sting, but . . . he is *not* a bounty hunter. I'm fairly certain you were his first job."

That fact stung like scorpion venom. As Silt dug for

patience, lightning forked out over the sky and a strong wind gusted to pelt them with stinging rain.

Most people kept their heads down against the elements. The princess raised her face, as if the weather were an enemy she'd decided to defeat. And so he kept his head up to watch her.

Irritating, frustrating female.

When the ground rumbled in a series of small quakes, she said, "There's a lot of seismic activity here. Unless one of your subterranean gulgs is beneath us."

Silt ran a palm over his mouth, a suspicion arising. *I prefer the gulgs.* Volcanoes, geysers, and quakes hinted at dimensional instability. Some realms convulsed in the beginning, some toward the end. Despite a lack of weathering, Nightside had existed for ages. *There might be a clock on my escape.*

"Whatever it is, I'll face it." To herself, she added, "Adversity builds mettle."

Who the hell was this vamp? At times, she seemed far wiser than her scant years. Other times, vulnerable and impressionable. Was she innocent? He believed so, her shirt's message notwithstanding.

He cast her a considering look, again struck by her beauty, even with her wan skin and the strain in her feminine features.

While his concubines varied—he had no preferred type— he'd never bedded a fey-looking vampire before. Nor had he slept with sexually innocent females. Maybe he should make an exception for revenge.

No hardship there. Her wet T-shirt clung to plump breasts that bounced as she ran, captivating him. She was, in fact, a *braless babe*. He imagined plucking that shirt off and covering those mounds with his roughened palms, gripping her as he leaned down to suck—

"Tell me more about our jail," she said, rousing him from his fantasies.

"Jail?"

She pursed her lips as if she'd detected the direction of his thoughts. "If this is the origin realm for all undead creatures, then they must have escaped Nightside. How else would their contagion exist in the mortal world?"

"I see the wheels turning. You think that proves there's a way out, maybe a portal or a rift. But if an escape once existed, the Gaolers sealed it. Otherwise, these beasts would have flooded the humans' realm."

She frowned at him. "How do you know so much about this place anyway?"

"Before I resigned myself to exile, I tracked down every rumor of Nightside and its wardens to uncover weaknesses. I talked to mystics who'd had visions of this place. I questioned others experiencing the same dreams I had—before they were collected, one by one." Only those in Poly eluded the Gaolers' reach.

"What would you do if you somehow escape before I kill you? Won't you be recaptured? At least Dacia will provide me some protection."

"If an escape existed, I would return to Poly and work on my defenses." The prospect of more exile there made him queasy. "The Gaolers won't enter that realm. No one knows why."

"I read it's unforgiving there."

"Just as bad as this realm, yet freezing too." But unlike Nightside, sand covered it.

She cocked her head, listening for the wendigos over the now pounding rain and wind. Did they already near?

Silt told her, "You were seeking a purpose for our imprisonment? Maybe Nightside is a menagerie of undead creatures, and *we* are the food." At her disbelieving look, he said, "In the Lore? Why not?"

The prospect didn't faze her for long. "This isn't the end of my story. I won't consider the battle lost till I've no more moves open to me."

"Are you never daunted?"

She raised the makeshift sword he'd foolishly given her. "As long as I have a weapon, I will find my way."

She continued to prove cool in a crisis. If he were honest—he wasn't—he'd admit a growing fascination with this vampire that warred with his irritation. He might have to continue on with her just to satisfy his curiosity.

Then he recalled where he was and who'd put him here. As he was tortured in this realm, so too would he torture. *Pain is a chain.* His fascination vanished as if swallowed by sand.

She cast a glance over her shoulder, tension stealing through her. "They're coming."

Revenge took a backseat to survival. "If we're lucky, we can get to higher ground before they catch us," he said, wishing he believed his words as readily as she seemed to.

ELEVEN

Mina and the sorcerer had *not* made it to higher ground before an army of corpse-eaters closed in on them. Not by leagues.

Whenever smaller bands of them advanced, she and Silt had battled them back, then run headlong. As night bled into night, a cycle of survival emerged: battling then running. The two of them weakened without food or rest. And all the while, the number grew behind them.

"Sorcerer, we're almost there!" At last the terrain changed, growing less mucky. They'd be able to gain more of a lead.

Fatigue marked his face as he nodded. "Push hard, vampire."

Using the last of her reserves, she did. Only adrenaline fueled her now. As she scrabbled over rocks, her legs felt boneless, and her injured arm ached.

A trail between boulders appeared not a second too soon. "This leads to a cave entrance. We can defend it."

He grabbed her elbow, helping her along. "It'll give us a shot."

Throughout these nights, the rhythm she'd experienced

with him during their first skirmish had only deepened. After learning each other's moves, they each knew when to duck, when to assist, and when to get out of the way.

And he'd always ensured she was in a prime fighting position, taking the soggier ground, protecting his bait.

Reluctantly she'd noted the set of his masculine jaw as he concentrated and his slight grins after particularly gruesome kills. She'd noted the way he seemed to trust her own expertise whenever she'd suggested a charge or a defense.

The thought had struck her: *For a female like me who is fascinated by combat, he is . . . attractive.* She'd had to remain on guard against wendigos, against him, and against that peculiar attraction—a multifront war that had exhausted her.

Howls sounded, even closer. "How are they gaining so quickly?" She darted a glance over her shoulder, shocked by their proximity. Was something spurring them? They dogged Mina and Silt's heels.

"Go, go!" Silt shoved her forward just as one vaulted for him.

Its knifelike claws sliced through the sorcerer's coat!

"Fight!" He and Mina whirled around yet again, weapons flashing out. Flying heads should have deterred the others, but they never did. Dodging strikes and dropping bodies, she and Silt backed toward the cave.

Yet then the wendigos abruptly stopped. They swiped those dagger claws but wouldn't advance up the trail.

She murmured, "It's like there's an imaginary line they won't cross. You may not understand that concept."

"Heh. They fear something behind us. Something in that mountain." Yet he continued in that direction.

"We're going in? If they fear something, perhaps we should be cautious." That was why the creatures had sped up—they'd known their capture window was shrinking.

"We can't stay here," he said. "Sooner or later, the sight of us will spur their hunger beyond their fear."

"Heading into a murky cave with a devious sorcerer to face yet another threat? Why not? I suppose you might be the lesser of many evils." She wiped her sword clean on the sole of her boot. "*Lesser* fits."

His gaze narrowed. "You think you're so elevated, princess. I should have left you behind a hundred times."

"Yes, you should have." They entered the cave, their steps echoing. "My commitment to killing you has only strengthened."

He waved that away. "What can you see, maneater?" He'd continued to rely on her senses.

The sounds of dripping water pinged in different directions from miles within. "This isn't just a shallow cave. It's an ongoing cavern system with a multitude of branches." She cocked her head back in the direction of the wendigos. "The pack remains outside."

"Do you detect any danger ahead?"

She raised her face and inhaled. "I'm picking up a scent: the remnants of some sort of creature. But I've never encountered it before."

"Can you hear a heartbeat?"

"No, and I can usually pick that up from far away. I hear no movement whatsoever." She shrugged, then winced at the growing pain in her arm. Her normal regeneration hadn't had any effect on those slashes.

Nights of fighting rabid creatures brought her own transformation into sharp relief. How long did she have before she lost herself?

The sorcerer continued in, and she joined him. Meandering deeper, they found a collection of decaying logs, littered with bones.

He shuffled the bones with his boot. "Looks like an old nest of a basilisk, a dragon. That must be what spooked the wendigos. But I wager it's long dead."

She'd read about basilisks, had seen sketches of majestic dragons with golden eyes and iridescent scales. "You're probably right. I don't detect any fresh kills." She glanced up sharply. "The only blood I smell is yours." He must have sweated out all those pollutants—because his blood was *sublime*. Then she recalled that wendigo slicing his coat. "Sorcerer, were you scratched?"

TWELVE

Though Silt had traveled through life united with no one, he'd experienced a camaraderie with the leech. Surprisingly for a princess, she'd never complained, giving as much effort as he had. Now he could almost pretend she actually cared about him. "No, I wasn't scratched. The grip of my improvised sword sliced my fingers. I'll heal quickly."

"Good," she said with obvious relief, before adding in a cutting tone, "As if I'd need another reason to kill you."

No, she hadn't complained, but her insults continued. So did his: "The only one of us who'll ever be a maneater is you."

"You are a wretched excuse for a . . ." She trailed off, her gaze locking on the flow of blood dripping from his hand.

"It looks good, doesn't it? You've gone at least three nights without drinking. I bet you'd suck my body as dry as a desert right now." He was exhausted. Starving. Fuming. And now . . . his wayward cock stiffened? "I predicted you'd beg. The words are on your lips."

She bit out, "Never."

What is so wrong with me? A thirsty leech wouldn't even tap him! Her continued refusal made him wonder if she might have another reason for her reddened eyes. Female vampires were rare in the Lore because of the plague; was that the cause of her crimson gaze?

He discounted the idea. A sickened, twentysomething vampire couldn't have fought as long as she had without dropping. No, she was simply refusing *him*.

Silt's ego didn't like that. "Never?" He moved in, lowering his voice to say, "Because you know that once you tasted me, you'll always hunger for me." He raised his dripping hand. "I could make you a slave for this."

Her cheeks heated to a warm rose color. *That must've cost her some blood.* Her gaze, trying valiantly not to dart to his hand, had reddened even more. Those eyes signaled danger in every fiber of his sorcerer's body, yet his cock was hard as stone.

She licked her full lips, and his length *strained* for them. If she noticed, she didn't let on. "You have no real sorcery, but you don't fear what I could do to you?"

"Not at all." Fear it? *Do your worst.* A dozen concubines hadn't been able to arouse him. Yet his body reacted to this leech with raw intensity.

Nothing special about this female; the drugs had simply deadened his drive before. Of course. Free of his pipe, he was back to desiring once more. And what he desired was to have this princess bite him. He imagined feeding his member between those lips, her tongue greeting him. Her *fangs* greeting him . . .

Sand almighty. As a male who'd chased down every pleasure, had he been missing out on blood play? Two thoughts arose in rapid succession:

You're reacting this way only because there is *something special about her.*

No. Shut the fuck up.

The last thing he needed to do was let down his guard with Mirceo Daciano's sister—a female who'd been doomed by her crimes against the Lore, by the Gaolers' punishment, and by Silt's plans for revenge.

Magic.

Within the sorcerer's blood, Mina scented life, power, and so much *magic.*

She'd bet one drop would fuel her like a thousand Dacian blood fountains—and he was brimming with that nectar! The heady scent of it threaded through her, seeming to take root in her very heart. Had she ever felt so euphoric?

She wasn't the only one affected. His pupils were blown. Though the irises of most immortals changed shades with sharp emotions, his didn't. They glowed and shimmered like gold dust. Within his muscled chest, his heartbeat thundered, awakening her every predator instinct.

Why was his heart working so hard? Where was all that blood being pumped? Her attention descended his torso, past his navel to the trail of hair leading down. Below the low-slung waist of his pants, his penis stretched to his hip, visibly pulsating.

Mouthwatering. The organ of his pleasure just happened to be filled with his magical blood. It beckoned her to taboo's front door, and her fangs sharpened again. With her tongue, she tested their little edges, their achiness.

His deep voice washed over her: "Like what you see?"
I want to pierce your manhood and drink you while you roar.
The seductive sorcerer murmured, "Take a sip, princess."
From his fingers, his neck, or . . . *there?*
Yes, yes, yes!
"Your vampire instincts demand it. And I've decided I want

to experience those fangs of yours buried deep into my skin."

They'd never throbbed like this, as much as her pebbled nipples. She imagined his skin closing around her fangs, milking them of sensation.

Inner shake. She almost told him that no Dacian would lower themselves to consume blood from the flesh, but that wasn't true anymore. Still, drinking from a source wasn't something a proper princess like her would ever consider! She met his gaze. "If I took your blood directly from your body, I would harvest your memories." His thousands of years' worth of them would surely send her straight into madness. "I'll dream your past when I sleep. Are you ready for that?"

A shadow crossed his face. Then his lips curled into a cocky grin, revealing even white teeth. "I think my sorcerer's blood is potent. It'll ruin you for all others, maneater."

Stop staring at his sexy grin! "You want me to drink you because you think it will gratify you as well."

"In so many words."

Out of the corner of her eye, she saw his member pulse even harder. *Gods above and below.* At the Tree of Delight, she'd seen males in this state. Fantasies bloomed of this sorcerer participating in some of the acts she'd witnessed—participating with *her*. The scenes she'd deemed yawn-worthy took on a lascivious bent. Her breaths shallowed even more, and her skin grew flushed all over.

She'd never reacted this way while staring longingly at Kristoff. This bruiser of a sorcerer was a world away from the sophisticated vampire king, but only Silt conjured wicked scenarios in her mind.

Mina pictured him crazed for release, gripping her body. *Entering* it. Thrusting between her thighs until she soaked his rod in her climax. Would he bellow against her neck when his own lust spilled over inside her . . . ?

She blushed as if he could hear her musings.

"I don't understand you." He scrubbed a hand over his mouth. "One minute you're throwing heads at me, the next you're blushing like a demure virgin. So is my gratification on the table? I mean, why else would you mention it?"

She yearned to share pleasure as much as the next immortal female, but after witnessing that couple in the moonlit clearing, she knew she would need affection and trust to fully enjoy it. She didn't want mere sex; she wanted everything. *I crave the divine.* This sorcerer wasn't even in the realm of possibility. "It's not on the table, no more than my drinking your blood is."

"Such scruples. Do you think I'm not good enough?"

"Or maybe it has something to do with the fact that you're sworn to kill the last of my immediate family!" Saying the words aloud reminded her of what a villain he was, snuffing her arousal like a candle.

Good. Arousal thwarted reason. She'd seen it happen again and again at the Tree. Would she forget the lessons she'd learned? Shame swept over her, and with it came fatigue as she'd never known. Thirst only worsened her weariness and confusion.

This sorcerer had protected her, but he'd acted for nefarious reasons. The mental wear of being near someone like him affected her as much as fighting wendigos.

Seeming to make a decision about her, he said, "We need to keep moving anyway."

"Agreed," she said, and they forayed deeper into a black-hole gloom.

THIRTEEN

The vampire's shivering intensified, her steps swerving.

She and Silt were both soaked and had been for days. They'd fought through that sludge without rest, even though younger immortals needed sleep every night. How was she still standing?

When they came upon another abandoned basilisk nest, words left his lips: "I can make a fire out of those logs. Do you want to stop here for a break?"

She eyed him warily. "Warmth sounds good."

Silt collected wood, pondering his impulse to provide her heat. But he was exhausted and chilled too.

When he crouched to place kindling, she watched him work. "Your withdrawal symptoms seem to have subsided."

"Largely." But the hunger for opium remained. Would it always?

"You're . . . different now. I noticed it when you showed up at that first wendigo fray."

"Different how?"

"Well, your eyes aren't crazed, and you haven't mentioned

cannibalism since the cave." At his blank look, she said, "Do you not remember your behavior? You told me you'd dine on me."

Cannibalism had always been a favored threat of his—seemed to unnerve enemies more than a threat to smother them in sand. It'd even been listed on his wanted poster. "I remember you cracking my knee in that cave. Without food or rest, I still haven't regenerated all the way."

She hiked one slim shoulder, all but telling him she'd do it again. Harder.

In minutes, he'd wrought flame from friction, and a fire roared. Hidden drafts carried the smoke from the area as he and the vampire sat on the stony ground.

Keeping her weapon close, she raised her delicate hands to the warmth. "For how long have you overly imbibed?"

"Centuries upon centuries." He'd quit that one time to see if he could defeat his weakness and discovered he couldn't. Why hadn't he tried more?

Again the thought struck him: *I have no idea who or what I am.* He was so unfamiliar with *Silt Harea* that he felt like a stranger lived inside him. "I needed something to pass the nights."

"Couldn't you have mustered a hobby in all that time?" She reminded him of a mirror positioned in the sun, blinding him with glaring light.

"I'd rather be addicted to opium than to blood. When I quit, I'll have no lingering effects in my immortal body. But your habit will muddle your mind."

"If you're the King of Sand, then why did you struggle to control a handful of it? You say you'll have no lingering effect, but I think you're paying for your excesses."

Losing his sand control in front of this female embarrassed him more than losing his cock control in front of a harem had. "Sorcery renews. Nothing can stamp it out." Probably not.

Without his pipe, he could rebuild his store of power.

"How did you get started with opium anyway?" The growing firelight illuminated the red of her eyes, making him wonder how this princess had gotten her own start. Hunger? Or lust?

He frowned to find his hands clenched. Releasing his grip, he said, "I first tried it in Mesopotamia. They called it *hulgil*, the joy plant." It hadn't enthralled him though—not until he'd been condemned.

"If you escaped Nightside, would you return to it?"

The question of questions. Could he shake its grip for good? "I would prefer not to."

Her gaze flicked over his face, assessing his truthfulness. "How does your family feel about your habit?"

"I have none." *Good riddance.*

"No one you care for back in Poly?"

"Not a soul." Sequara had been the closest thing he'd had to a confidante. "Sorceri are a solitary species."

"Solitary? I detected various perfumes on your skin. No fewer than twelve."

He relaxed back against the cool cavern wall. "I had females in my stronghold." He hadn't set out to have such a large harem, but he hadn't been motivated enough to do something about it.

"You lived with others, but you told me you have no one you care about."

"Both can be true." He'd warned them at the outset, "If you develop feelings for me, they will go unanswered."

Kosmina cast him a look of confusion. She didn't seem surprised to learn that he'd lived with many women, just that he hadn't given a damn about any of them.

Defensive, he said, "They fleeced me out of a hoard of gold." A couple of years ago, he'd awakened from a stupor to find one of his vaults emptied and the lot of them working together to crack the others, which was probably why so many had wanted a position inside his home. He pictured them sending out the word: *We've got a live one, ladies!*

Their actions might have hurt if he'd felt anything for them at all—and if he hadn't had more gold hidden away in other worlds.

"Could you be as happy with one woman as you were with a dozen?" the princess asked, her interest soothing his ego a touch.

"My experiences weren't enhanced by the number." If he were honest—that word again—he'd say the opposite.

"With so many females involved, you must have fathered countless children in all your years."

"No. This cuff I wear"—he pulled up the sleeve of his stolen coat to display it—"is bespelled to prevent that." All the females he'd bedded had insisted upon the cuff.

In a haze, hadn't he once heard his concubines agreeing that he'd make an awful father?

"I suppose after you were sentenced to this place, bonding with another wouldn't be fair," the vampire said. "But do you not wish to share your life with someone?"

"Perhaps that's easier said than done." In a rare bout of sincerity, he admitted, "I haven't always been what you'd call a catch."

"Yes. I can see that." Irritating woman! He parted his lips to deliver a setdown, but she said, "Your moods shift like the sands you favor. Are you always so changeable?"

I don't know! "I've heard no complaints about my moods."

"Weren't your companions paid not to complain?" she pointed out, the mirror shining her light.

His jaw clenched. "And what about you? Any family besides Mirceo?" That prick.

"My parents died when I was young. Mirceo raised me, though he was just a boy." She eyed Silt. "He is still incredibly young to be targeted for one folly."

"One folly?" Silt gave a mirthless laugh. "I'm likely going to die here, sweet. And so are you."

"Perhaps. Yet the only way you can get revenge is if you *don't* die here. So your logic is flawed. But convincing you of that doesn't matter when you've made your reckless vow."

He started to explain what revenge meant to him—without it, he would have perished as a child—but she would never understand. She was only experiencing powerlessness for the first time.

Besides, he owed her nothing. He fell silent, staring into the flames, fielding the memories that surfaced. Without dragon's breath to deaden the past, recollections sparked like this fire.

In time, her shivering eased. Gaze alight with curiosity, she said, "I once read about a sorceress who uses mountains as weapons. Portia, the Queen of Stone. Are her powers similar to yours?"

He welcomed the distraction of more conversation. "Yes, in theory." He and Portia had joined forces a couple of times in the past. He'd taught her how to make tornadoes out of boulders. "We both control stone at different sizes. *Sand* describes a size— it's just a grain of infinite types of stone. Silt is smaller, and pebbles are larger. Portia can't control the finest sand, and I can't control pebbles—or mountains."

Despite his nickname, silt wasn't his favorite medium. Pure quartz sand was a silken luxury for his sorcery. Or, rather, it used to be. He dug into his pocket, stunned by how disconnected from it he felt—as if his fingertips had disappeared.

"If you've always had this power, why are you so adept with a weapon?"

Incisive female. *Because I haven't always had this power.* "I trained with all manner of weapons, sand among them."

"How did you get these?" She gestured to the makeshift sword she kept nearby.

"From a rare growth of crystal near the fire field. I don't know the name of it outside of my native tongue, but in old Sorselan, we call it *justale-ko.*"

"Sorselan? That's also the name of the Sorceri origin realm. I wanted to read some of its history, but even Dacia's great library contained no information on it."

Then you wanted to read my *history.* He'd shaped that dimension like sand, and when he'd released his hold, it had collapsed just as easily. "I was born there. It's a desert land with scarce resources, but the dunes carry gold, which made it sacred to my kind."

"Describe a desert to me. I've only seen illustrations."

How could he possibly? Yet just those three words—*describe a desert*—sent him back to a time long ago, when he'd been six years old on a grand adventure across a sea of sand.

As if he were there, Silt recounted some of the details of that day: "The sun glares down, burning like a white flame. The sand hisses at it, begging for mercy, but it's indifferent. The dunes swell and break as they dance with the wind." Awash in memories, he murmured, "The sand is never-ending; I witness everything in it. Every color. Every shape. I see infinity. Death. Life."

But then his connection to it had been broken by those he'd loved best.

"The way you describe sand beneath the sun," she said with a hint of humor, "is probably how I would react in a similar situation."

Blinking back to the present, he said, "Hissing? Maybe. Begging for mercy? From what I've seen of you, princess, I highly doubt that."

The tips of her pointed ears heated. The fey had sensitive ears. Would hers be? "Still, I hope I live long enough to behold a desert. Perhaps one day. Or rather, night."

A doubtful prospect. *You're probably going to die here. Soon.* A charitable impulse made him say, "The desert at night is a wondrous sight, especially under a full moon. You would like it."

She tilted her head, seeming bemused by him. "I also read that the realm of Sorselan was lost. Is that true?"

"Yes. When its last ruler"—*me*—"left for distant lands, that dimension fell into chaos. Sorcery theft was so rife, everyone scattered to the winds. And they've remained solitary since."

"Do you miss it?"

Desperately. "On occasion."

"How do you steal sorcery?"

"Find one of our kind who's inebriated, weakened from exhaustion, or mindless from sex, then pluck the unguarded ability like a thread. Sorceri are always probing to see if another's magic is locked down—an aggression if caught. Also, murdering another Sorceri will net you some powers."

"Speaking from experience?"

"I've never stolen another's power." Much. He knew brethren with scores of them, didn't understand how they kept up with them all. He'd taken only one other ability, allowing little else to distract him from protecting his sand.

"Have you had *yours* stolen?"

He forced himself to appear casual, to keep his heartbeat steady. "That would be a humiliation without equal, one I have not suffered." Not since he'd been a boy. "We consider a root power, the one we're born with, our soul. When another takes it . . ." *Hope is lost. Pride is lost.*

"Then a Sorceri becomes an Inferi."

That hated word. It harkened shame, made bile churn even now. "Yes." He sometimes disbelieved that he'd once been an . . . Inferi, that he'd lived with that barren emptiness. "So we guard our root power with ruthless determination," he said, fighting the urge to trace his tattoos.

Fortunately Revenge had been there to keep Silt warm when he'd huddled hungry and alone in the cold desert nights. Revenge had nursed him through the outrages of slavery. She'd made sure he could handle a sword to enact her plans, and she'd promised him purpose.

In return, all he'd had to do was keep the chain going. He'd honored that contract, until opium had taken her place. . . .

He glanced up to see Kosmina's analytical expression. "Will we speculate on each other at every moment of this journey?" he asked. "Without blood, I'm surprised you have the energy for it. You grow weaker by the moment." He might've spared some pity for his maneater, if he'd had any left in him.

She straightened her shoulders. "I do grow weaker. I'll have to dig deeper and fight harder."

No one could be as dauntless as she acted. Eventually she would hit her limit and revert to form: a spoiled princess using others for blood and damn the consequences. "You must miss a steady supply of victims." Then he frowned as a thought occurred. "Why are your brother's eyes clear?"

Her expression grew frosty. "Mirceo is an off-limits topic for you." Her steely words were undercut by a muffled yawn.

That yawn made her look vulnerable and called to some unfamiliar emotion inside him. Was this . . . protectiveness? He turned the idea over in his mind, could remember feeling it once for his parents.

Defending Kosmina over these nights must have done a number on his head. *Shake it off, Silt.* Yet when he took in her heavy lids as she struggled to stay awake, words left his lips: "Sleep, vampire. I won't hurt you."

She made a scoffing sound.

"We can call a truce for the night, and I'll keep watch for any bold wendigos."

"Truce? You've vowed to use me to hurt Mirceo."

"That's not true." At her look, he amended: "Well, yes, of course I will murder Mirceo. But I'm not *compelled* to use you."

"And how can I trust the word of an evil sorcerer?"

"The same way I can trust the word of a parched maneater. We'll each make a vow to the Lore not to harm the other in this cave."

"Only an idiot would make that kind of a vow. They often end in ruin."

Most immortals refused to make them because those oaths had a way of backfiring and were binding until death. Few could predict the perils of being constrained so totally. "Have it your way. We'll both stay on guard and rest not an instant. But you're looking done in. So cold . . . tired . . . *thirsty*. At your age, you must need to sleep every night. I'll bet you're wishing you'd drunk my blood now."

"Will you let it go? I don't have to listen to this. I can leave."

"And I'll follow. I won't let you out of my sight, leech."

She rubbed her temples. "You saved my life, almost as if you cared, and all the while, you're plotting to kill the one I love best in the world."

Yes. Which must be fucking with her mind. Good. "You'll sleep. And then you'll discover that if I wanted to harm you, I wouldn't have to wait until you were vulnerable. You're *always* vulnerable." The thought of hurting her made his gut tighten with something like anxiety. No, no. It must be the last of the opium leaving his system.

"So reassuring."

When her shivering resumed—this time from obvious exhaustion—that unwanted protectiveness returned. "Fine. I alone will make a vow. I vow to the Lore not to harm you while you sleep tonight."

Almost against her will, tension ebbed from her, her lids growing even heavier. "I will rest a moment. Then we must push on." She curled up on the cave floor. In moments, she was asleep.

Even breaths. Parted lips. A lock of blond hair teased her cheek.

She was a ruthless warrior, yet fragile. At times tonight, she'd spoken as if she'd forgotten their animosity, reminding him of a rose opening in the desert, not knowing that the harsh sands would soon destroy it.

Had their trials together softened him toward her? A touch. But it wouldn't save her. It wouldn't save her brother.

Silt pulled the sand from his pocket, whirling it above his palm with difficulty. He was still tapped out by that platform from days ago. His sorcery sputtered and he grimaced, pocketing the grains once more. He'd blamed others for severing his bond to sand, but he'd done it to himself as well—with every lungful of smoke.

He thought of that lion shifter addicted to the taste of mortal flesh. Was Silt any different with his pipe? He'd surrendered to its spell without even a fight.

He returned his attention to the mysterious vampire. She would've fought.

Silt's gaze traced over her finespun features. He'd noted her beauty upon first seeing her, but after beholding her in battle, a part of him found her . . . glorious.

He could watch her sleeping for lifetimes as the firelight danced over her ethereal face. Judging by her shifting expressions, her clever mind supplied a rich dream life. When a weak quake rumbled the cave, she frowned but didn't wake.

Shame she was related to a male Silt would soon destroy.

Still, watching her like this relaxed him. And with that ease, hazy recollections arose from the night of his capture. Though he'd been passed out, he must have absorbed memories as if through diffusion.

He recalled Mirceo battling Sequara. As suspected, the vampire had slain her as she'd defended Silt. He briefly closed his eyes. He'd always known she would die for him.

Then snippets of a conversation between his concubines and Mirceo swirled in his brain. Instead of rousing Silt to fight the trespassers, they'd *propositioned* the vampire.

Perfidious females! He'd warned them not to hold any affection for him, but now he wondered *why* they hadn't involuntarily fallen for him. In that perfect window after smoking his pipe—and just before smoking some more—he'd once been a somewhat generous lover. He wasn't awful to them.

This princess would be half in love with him if he put forth any effort whatsoever. How badly it would hurt her—and therefore her brother—if she lost her heart to Silt.

Tempting. But he had no time to toy with her. *Nightside isn't through with us*, he thought as another quake rumbled. The stakes were life-and-death, and all he wanted was to smoke and blunt the impact of them.

Mina rose silently, readying her weapon. The sorcerer had fallen asleep without insisting on a vow from her.

His last mistake.

While she'd rested, the plague had seemed to gain a foothold. After dreams of a moonlit desert, she'd been inundated with red-hot scenes of blood drinking—with this male in every one.

And now a cold-blooded kill was on the table. Taking a life without a fight struck her as wrong—her parents were rumored to have been murdered in cold blood—but what wouldn't she do for Mirceo?

This cave's dying fire reminded her of that night Mina had asked him why they had no parents. Later, she'd awakened and crept silently into his suite. She'd found him staring at the flames of his bedchamber's hearth with blood-tinged tears tracking down his face.

Had he been struggling with the unimaginable responsibility of raising a child? Or missing his mother and father? Perhaps he'd also pondered Mina's last question, one he'd answered only with a tight smile:

Who will take care of you?

Though only four, Mina had dedicated herself to him as much as he had to her. They were connected by blood, by their past tragedies, and by devotion.

Tonight, Mina would prove hers. . . .

The sorcerer slept sitting up, his breaths deep and even, his heartbeat like a drum. She quirked a brow. So much for keeping watch. In the waning firelight, her gaze roamed over him. His face appeared chiseled, the shadows lovingly dancing over him.

Shadows. Shady. He certainly was that.

She stared at his mouth and ran the pad of her forefinger over her lips, imagining his kiss. Her inexplicable attraction to him dwarfed the longing she'd felt for Kristoff. The Gravewalker had struck her as the most gorgeous male Mina had ever seen, but this . . . this *ruffian's* pull was even more powerful.

Her gaze dipped to his laborer's build. With rest, he'd put on even more ripcord mass. The tattoos across his broad chest, visible between the lapels of his coat, drew her eye. She made out curious shapes, animals, feathers. What did those mean? Why had he marked himself so before he'd even frozen into his immortality?

She would never know, secrets lost to the universe. Like her foremothers before her, she stalked closer to make a kill.

Standing over him, she raised her weapon. Mirceo would never be safe as long as Silt Harea—and his ill-conceived vow—endured.

Good-bye, sorcerer.

Some unsettling hesitation tried to stay her hand. Love for her brother made her swing.

FOURTEEN

Castle Dacia

U h-uh, Leo. Not on your friggin' life," Ellie told Lothaire, her thick Appalachian accent pronounced. "When you breezily informed me that you want to vacay in a hellplane filled with the undead, did you think I wasn't gonna push back?"

Kristoff wasn't sure why Lothaire had brought him here to Ellie's sitting room to witness this conversation. Across the space, Balery, the court oracle, gazed on as well, her fey ears giving a twitch with each inflection in the conversation.

Lothaire took a seat beside Ellie, clearly unused to explaining his actions. "Before Nïx lightning-portaled away, she confirmed our suspicions that the Gaolers took Mina to Nightside. And she gave us this." He handed Ellie the journal.

She skimmed through, then set it aside with a shudder. "Feels as creepy as a two-headed snake."

"Yes. An evil wizard penned it." Lothaire had rapidly read it, the pages speeding under his fingers as if the journal were a flipbook cartoon. "Apparently his victims' blood had stained the pages, requiring witchcraft to clean. I suspect Nïx stole it from a coven. Finders, keepers, et cetera. What's important is that it contains directions to Nightside's portal. I've garnered enough information for me and Kristoff to try to breach that realm."

"And why would I go with you?" Kristoff asked, even as he knew he would have to.

"Don't play coy. You must keep me alive so my secrets don't die with me."

Keep alive the one I hate most.

Lothaire turned back to Ellie. "You did say you wanted our niece found."

"Of course I want Mina found!" she cried. "But you're talking about waltzing straight into danger. Again. And I've heard you yappin' about how to get *into* that plane—but not how to get out."

Good point.

"If an entrance exists, an exit surely must as well." Lothaire uttered this unreasonable statement in a reasonable tone. "And consider this: Nïx wants me there. She's set all these moves into motion. She would not lead me into disaster."

Ellie raised her brows. "Uh, are you serious? She's done it to you, like, ten times now. She got you sent to that human pokey, and she knew you were buried in the Bloodroot Forest for six centuries."

Lothaire's eyes deepened in color with that memory.

Kristoff had recently learned that Demestriu had planted Lothaire deep within the Horde's forest, for carnivorous bloodroot trees to feed on his ever-regenerating body. Part of the reason Lothaire wanted to control the Horde castle of Helvita was to raze the trees he'd grown with his blood.

His torment had probably been as hellish as Furie's, which made sense as they were devised by the same vampire. Known for his tortures, Demestriu had also burned alive the werewolf king for centuries.

Kristoff would almost prefer that over roots boring under his skin. Sometimes he experienced a flare of pity for his half brother. Then he pictured Furie at the bottom of the ocean, her fire wings extinguished, her mind possibly lost.

All pity morphed into rage.

Lothaire shrugged away Ellie's points. "If Nïx has undercut my aims on occasion, it's only because I veered off course. Each of those setbacks was for my ultimate benefit, leading me to you. And you know I would withstand them repeatedly to find you." Lothaire couldn't lie. He would go back to his bloodroot nightmare in order to share a life with his Bride.

Will I ever feel the same about Furie?

Ellie's expression softened. "Do you really believe Nïx wants you in Nightside?"

"She might as well have decreed it. And she knew I'd take my brother with me, so he's been marked by fate as well."

Debatable. And *half* brother.

"Nïx's foresight is exquisite, is it not?" Lothaire mused with excitement. "We are all leaves carried in a stream, and a mad Valkyrie directs the currents."

"Emphasis on *mad*, Leo. I care for Nïx, but she is fritzing in the head." And Ellie didn't even know that the Valkyrie carted around organs of unknown origin. "What if she got this wrong, and I lose you forever? If you have to do this, then take Mirceo, Caspion, and the entire Dacian army with you."

"No. Only Kristoff and I will go. The others would just get in the way of The Incursion."

Kristoff scoffed. "The incursion?"

Lothaire turned to him. "Any incursion that I lead is *The.*"

Ellie gazed at Kristoff with sympathy. She had been trying to influence Lothaire on his behalf. Her king seemed to give her everything she could ever desire, spoiling her human family with riches and protection, but he held firm on the secret of Furie's location.

Kristoff pointed out, "Mirceo will be furious that you are leaving him behind."

Ellie crossed her arms over her chest and nodded. "Madder than a rooster with its tailfeathers on fire."

"Exactly. He's too emotional," Lothaire said. "He attacked me, remember? Just because I lost his sister one measly time."

And Mirceo had paid utterly for that attack.

Balery finally spoke: "The other houses of Dacia suffer without the heart of the kingdom in the castle. Viktor is more warmongering than usual. Stelian is imploding. Trehan and Bettina are ready to level all the worlds to get Mina back. They each need to help."

"If Kristoff and I fail, then the others can try to salvage. Divulge this information to them only if you think we have no shot."

Ellie was wavering. "At least let Balery roll the bones to see if this is a good idea." Though the fey oracle and potions master could foretell much, she possessed only a fraction of Nïx's vision.

Lothaire said, "We stopped in Hag's laboratory before we came here. The becroned one rolled them there."

Balery had once been cursed to resemble a crone, dubbed the Hag in the Basement by the Sorceri who'd enslaved her. Lothaire refused to call her anything else.

He added, "Yes. I'm surprised you didn't smell the boiled eye of newt and sautéed spider web clinging to me. Not to mention the pungent scent of a fey's dreams gone to die."

Balery and Ellie glared at Lothaire's casual callousness.

Kristoff frowned. "Why do you stay in his service, fey? You were trapped by Sorceri before, but you're free to leave now." *As I long to do.*

She raised her palms, her hands glittering from some potion or another. "My lab here is state-of-the-dark-arts. And I like most of the castle's inhabitants. Besides, Lothaire is old enough to know the root of *hag* is *hagios*. Holy. And *crone* comes from *corona*, or *crown*—as in, crowned with knowledge. He's aware of this. He delights in trolling others. Not to be mistaken for *troll-ing*, because that involves a troll's brute force and club accessories. Not to be mistaken for *dance-club* accessories—"

"We get it, we get it." Lothaire's lips curled as if a light prank had been revealed.

Kristoff was yet again struck that he didn't know his half brother at all.

"Back to the subject at hand," Lothaire said. "*Hag* rolled her bones and advised us never to cross Nïx."

Balery canted her head. That hadn't been her exact wording. She'd gazed at the bones and murmured, "Nïx is not just an agent of fate; she's an agent of chaos. For whom does the Valkyrie act now? If you thwart the former, you invite the latter."

Ellie asked, "Did Nïx say anything about Mina's health? I can't see her getting nabbed because she broke the law. She must have the plague."

Balery said, "I can detect it in blood, but there's no guarantee I'll ever have a working cure."

Lothaire rose. "Nïx didn't mention much about Mina, was too busy wondering how we'd come by a giant heart—one that *she* had just brought with her to Dacia. But we'll cross the Mina-might-have-plague bridge when we come to it."

Ellie sighed in resignation. To Kristoff's surprise, she was going to allow this insanity. "When do you leave?"

"Now, Lizvetta." Lothaire patted his sword. "We go to meet our destinies."

No wonder he'd made sure Kristoff was armed tonight.

Ellie reached for Lothaire. "You come back from that place, okay?"

He leaned down and gazed into her eyes. "Coax me, hellbilly."

She cupped his face gently, but her words were steel. "You fuckin' return to me, Leo, or I'll be comin' to get your ass."

"My fierce queen, you delight me." He kissed her lustily. Then tenderly. Then he brushed his pale fingers over her face.

She looked awestruck.

"I'll return anon." He straightened. Giving a nod to Balery, he intoned, "Hag," then disappeared.

Before Kristoff could blink, Lothaire had traced across the sitting room, snared him, and teleported them to a forest cloaked in night.

Kristoff surveyed his new surroundings. Lichen draped towering trees, and ferns dotted the rich forest floor. Scents enveloped them. *Brooks. Stone. Bear?* "Where are we?"

"Canada."

"And how do we get to Nightside?"

Kristoff's hackles rose when Lothaire only smiled.

FIFTEEN

Nightside

Millennia of instinct made Silt lunge to his side when the air whistled. A blade sliced an inch above his head to clang against the cavern wall.

The vampire had swung on him! "You little leech!" He raised his own weapon—just in time to block her next strike.

He scrambled to his feet, managing to defend against a third hit. "Stealing my head while I sleep! After all I've done for you?" She was no better than his concubines. Perfidious women all! "I've protected you. I offered you blood. I made you a fire."

"Oh, in that case, feel free to kill my brother!" Their breaths were loud as they circled each other. "You said you would keep watch. I should skewer you just for falling asleep on the job."

"And to think I'd considered sparing you. You've earned my revenge all on your own."

"If only that frightened me. Empty threats from an empty sorcer—" She charged with blistering speed.

He parried, battering her weapon. "You really want to do this?"

"Quite. I won't rest until Mirceo is safe."

"And I won't rest until revenge is mine. I worship it, female. Vengeance is everything."

"It would be to a man like you, a cruel cipher with nothing else in his life." She struck again, feinting high, then aiming low.

He blocked, narrowly defending the artery in his leg. "You call me cruel? When you drink your victims, do you send them home with a bandaged throat and a pat on the head? No. Your eyes are red because you drain your prey to death, down to the very pit of their souls. Admit it."

Color high, she snapped, "*You* are the villain here! I've never harmed another living creature, except in self-defense."

She couldn't lie. "And your eyes?"

"A Horde vampire clawed me."

Plague. "You've never tapped a neck?" Had he brushed away that possibility because otherwise he'd have to admit he was tormenting a young innocent?

"Never! Most Dacians consider drinking from others a deviancy, a pollution of our rational minds."

No wonder Mirceo had been clear-eyed. "Don't vampires live to take throats?"

Kosmina kept her weapon up as they continued to circle. Tension ricocheted between them. "We would harvest too many memories, losing our revered logic."

Even if a vampire didn't possess that blood-reading ability—and most Horde vampires didn't—they still couldn't drink indiscriminately without madness trailing them. "That plague you landed is going to do a number on any logic you might possess."

She raised her chin. "Nothing could horrify me more. I'll greet dawn before then."

He fought against what might have been a kernel of sympathy. She didn't feel any for him, saw him only as a dissolute addict bound by a vow. And now he saw her as a clueless princess who'd bumbled into a shit fate. "If you plan to greet dawn, why are you fighting so hard for escape?"

"I'm not ready to give up. Once I get free of Nightside, I can consult Dacia's healer. If she can't cure me, then I'll seek out a magical talisman that grants wishes, a ring possessed by a powerful sorceress."

"You're *not* talking about Dorada's Ring of Sums." La Dorada, the Queen of Evil, possessed that talisman, a wishgiver with a twist: the more wishes one made, the farther off course one's outcomes went.

Kosmina slowed. "You know her?"

"By and by." Since Sorceri were relatively short-lived for immortals—they didn't enjoy the protective unity of a Lykae pack or the Horde's ability to trace—the older survivors tended to become aware of each other. "Heard she got mummified somewhere."

"She's returned. She now grants the use of the ring if one gives a vow of absolute fealty, but she only bargains with those who are good."

"Good, is it? The Queen of Evil can control all evil beings—that's her Sorceri power—so she must be looking to expand her reach." For what purpose? "Only a fool would swear fealty to that one. Beware the Sorceri."

"I do, especially you."

"Especially me, little princess."

"What if that ring is the only thing that can save my life?"

"I'd prefer death," he said, and he meant it. "You're just delaying the inevitable. She'll make you wish you were dead when she's using you to kill your loved ones, or some other waking nightmare."

A flicker of doubt arose in Kosmina's courageous gaze, and some long-buried part of him didn't like that he'd put it there. He commanded himself to muzzle this fascination he felt for her. Lips curving, he said, "I'd make your peace, sweet, and prepare to feel the rays."

"Loathsome man! Again, *you* are the villain here."

"Appears so."

"Look at you. My innocence changes nothing, does it?"

"You were about to behead me in my sleep! That's the closest I've ever come to death. You remain a menace." Besides, Revenge still commanded him. He would keep the vampire close in case her brother showed. But Silt feared that was not the only reason he wanted her next to him. Protecting her against those wendigos and saving her from the lava had felt . . .

Good.

As ever, the hedonist in him craved more.

She twirled her weapon. "I do remain a menace where you're concerned—a menace with a purpose to . . ." She trailed off, cocking her head.

"What is it? Your ears are twitching."

"Silence!" she hissed.

"Ordering me like a servant?" Like a fucking Inferi? Memories of slavery bubbled up.

Silt should have been the strongest in his homeworld, but he'd been defenseless against the Sorceri with their chilling abilities. And they'd despised Inferi—considered them a constant reminder of a hellish existence that could befall any of them. His hands glowed as he relived torments. "Princess, you are no longer in your gilded kingdom, and you're about to learn—" His diatribe was cut short when lumbering footsteps sounded in a tunnel parallel to theirs. "Even *I* can hear that."

To herself, she murmured, "It's immense, whatever it is."

"Do you detect a heartbeat?"

She shook her head.

"I was afraid of that."

Her eyes widened. "It's an undead basilisk."

SIXTEEN

No wonder Mina hadn't scented fresh kills. No wonder the wendigos had been so afraid. "It must have been hibernating before." Otherwise she would have heard the basilisk's scales crackling, its slightest movements.

"We need to work together to get out of here," the sorcerer said. "You think you can keep from attacking me?"

"You need my senses to escape this cavern system. I have no equivalent use for you."

"I know a lot about Nightside and about the plague. I'll tell you more on the other side."

He reminded her of Lothaire, withholding information for his own gain. But what if Silt held the key to her escape?

A loud roar trumpeted and pounding footsteps quickened in their direction. The basilisk had locked in on them.

"Fine," Mina said. "I'll refrain from killing you for now."

"Good enough. The creature probably knows of an intersection to reach this cavern. Let's go." They started running together—

Rock exploded just ahead of them; a giant head had burst

through the very wall!

Silt muttered, "Or it could *make* an intersection."

The mammoth beast had blazing green skin, and its slit-pupiled eyes were putrid yellow—the color of sickness. A true ghoul basilisk.

It seemed to be stuck in the rock, but its head stretched nearly the width of the cave. When it snapped dripping fangs, each one longer than her forearm, she buried her shock and readied to strike.

"Ah-ah." Silt shook his head. "We'll just anger it. To fell it for good, we'd have to hack through its meaty neck with inferior weapons."

"Speaking of inferior weapons—use your sand. Blind it." When he made no move to, she said, "Are you still drained from that paltry platform? That was days ago!"

"My powers are temperamental right now."

"So is the dragon, Silt." It lunged against the rock's hold, widening the opening around its neck, turning to them with a drooling snarl. "We should go back the way we came."

"Return to wendigo territory? Not a chance."

"There might not be another way out, and then we'll be trapped with a creature desperate to unleash its contagion." A single bite or scratch equaled doom. *Kind of like the vampire plague.*

"With your senses, we'll find our way," Silt insisted. "For now, move slowly against the wall. Don't even breathe."

After a beat, she muttered, "Very well." As she sidled along the wall, the dragon's nauseating scent threatened to overwhelm her.

It lunged again, couldn't quite reach her. Hindered by the rock, it jabbed its forked tongue out at her; she raised her arm to block the blow, striking the slime-covered tongue with her other hand. "Enough!"

The dragon didn't listen. It curled its lips outward like rotting pincers. A hair's breadth separated her from those dripping lips.

When it failed to snag her, it roared again, spraying her face with spittle. She gagged when its rancid breath wafted her hair all around to stick to her coated cheeks. Had some of it gotten inside her mouth? She spat frantically, reminding herself, *Bite or scratch, bite or scratch.*

The sorcerer read her fears. "You won't turn from that." He wasn't far behind her.

"How is this creature even possible?" She'd never read about animals being turned.

"It was transformed the same as we would be. The undead rule here. This is *their* realm."

She eased past its reach, earning another roar. Swiping her slimy hair from her eyes, she gauged Silt's progress. Halfway across.

The basilisk yanked its head side to side, breaking through more rock. Mouth wide, it struck with a serpent's speed—

At the last second, the sorcerer dove out of the way, just as the dragon's fangs snapped closed.

Silt muttered a curse at the near miss.

Mina heard the beast swat its tail in frustration, making rocks rain from the ceiling. Then it snatched its head back and started running in a cavern bordering theirs.

"Where's it going, sorcerer?"

"We need to get ahead of it!" Silt grabbed her hand, and a tremor of . . . something passed between them as they sprinted together. "Find us a way out of here, vampire."

She inhaled deeply, trying to ignore the foul spittle coating her. *Concentrate. Sort the threads.* She detected a welcome smell.

"I've picked up fresh air! But it's some distance away."

"We'll make it!" He squeezed her hand; she squeezed his back; then they scowled at each other and yanked their hands away.

The dragon pursued a parallel track. Intermittent roars spurred Mina and Silt as they sped around corners. At each cavern intersection, she selected a direction—while wondering if she was leading them right back into danger.

"You still think I should forgive your brother for putting me here?" the sorcerer said. "A ghoul dragon bears down on us, but *water under the bridge, Mirceo.*"

Never slowing, she said, "What's done is done. You made that vow, can't ever reverse it." *Illogical dolt.*

"If Mirceo's so wonderful, why would he let you go out into the mortal realm to get clawed and hell-bound?" Even as they ran, Silt frowned. "And why would you be there if not to hunt prey? You weren't worried about falling ill?"

She would never tell him about her mist, the mist that no longer worked because the plague was altering her, making her less Dacian. *I* am *turning into a monster.* "My uncle Lothaire dispatched me on a mission when Mirceo was away." And the entire trajectory of her life had changed.

"Lothaire? *The Enemy of Old* is your uncle? That explains a lot."

She paused at another intersection, heading right—only to backtrack left.

Silt's brows drew together, but he gamely followed. "Ages ago, Lothaire tried to get me to sign his ledger. He's a Horde vampire."

"Half Dacian." At the last second, she leapt over a hole in the cavern floor, trying not to think about the fact that she'd spied no bottom to it. "And now he's our king."

"I heard he got planted in the earth like a seed."

"Yes, for centuries." How Lothaire had retained any sanity was a miracle. "But he rose once more."

"You have a lot of nerve to talk about my stronghold's defenses. A red-eyed leech conquered you!"

"We invited him. He's the last of the House of Old, the traditional ruling house of Dacia. Now the other royal houses can finally know peace after ages of infighting for the throne."

"Invited?" The sorcerer glanced back, appearing satisfied by their lead. "Then your people were conquered by your own foolishness."

"We had to do something. You wouldn't understand." Fleeing a ghoul basilisk wasn't the time to explain three thousand years of Dacian history to this male, even if she were so inclined.

"Royal intrigues are beyond a lowly sorcerer's comprehension?" This seemed to incense him.

"Just drop it."

"How do you think your brother will locate you here anyway? Nightside has never been found."

"He has ways and powerful allies. My uncles—a cadre of warriors with many talents—will assist him. At the very least, Mirceo will get himself captured and condemned here."

"He'd do that for you?"

She nodded easily. "Just as I would for him. What people like you never realize is that devotion to others isn't a weakness; it's strength."

Silt disagreed. Devotion involved trust; trust was absolutely a weakness. "Still won't divulge how Mirceo breached my defenses? Since we're about to die and all."

With sudden insight, she said, "That's why you hate him so much. Such a young vampire bested your greatest efforts, and you can't stand it."

"I'm sure you like being bested. Enjoy getting outwitted, do you?"

"I wouldn't know—it's never happened!"

He grew quiet, and what looked like an involuntary smile curved his lips.

She dragged her gaze away when strobing light drew her attention. Bolts flashed from outside! "Look, sorcerer, we're close." The night sky called them forth. The rain had slowed to a drizzle. On solid ground, they could *gain ground*.

"I see it!"

They careened out of the tunnel into the night. Beneath their feet was a smooth black surface. Not soil. Not rock.

Craaack.

"Freeze!" Silt yelled.

She stilled, not moving a muscle. And yet . . . *craaack*. "It's shattering. It's some kind of crystal surface."

"It forms over lava tubes."

Pardon? "Are we above a boiling pit?"

"Likely. On the count of three, we each leap to the side." He held her gaze, his expression determined. "One, two, thr—"

The basilisk thundered out of the cave.

The crystal shattered beneath its weight, and all the world was shards, claws, and contagion.

SEVENTEEN

Silt, the princess, and an undead basilisk plunged down the tube. No lava awaited them.

Rushing water churned far below.

Midair, he snared Kosmina's wrist, arching them away from the flailing beast that plummeted beneath them. Its claws scrabbled down the sides of the tube as it tried to fly, but its rotted wings were useless. It landed first; displaced water exploded upward.

"Take a breath, vampire!"

They both sucked in lungfuls before crashing beneath the surface of rapids. The force of the current propelled them like a witch's hexshot down another tube. The pressure tore their weapons free.

The basilisk eyed them from its spot ahead of them and splashed, driven to infect, oblivious to the danger.

Coughing, Kosmina said, "The water's rising!" The tube's air clearance tapered, foot by foot.

"There must be a way out." He secured his hold on her. "Or the water wouldn't rush." No sooner were the words spoken than he spotted a drop-off ahead, the tube descending at a ninety-degree angle. The basilisk floundered for purchase as it went over the edge.

Then . . .

Our turn.

He and Kosmina dropped again, this time into a freezing pool. As they circled above a vortex, she cried, "Where's the basilisk?"

"It must've gotten sucked down—"

Supernatural suction snatched them beneath the water.

Clutching her wrist, he kicked his legs and grappled to swim upward against the force. Not a chance. One-way trip. The basilisk too was trapped in the water's grip as they all coursed down a never-ending tube.

He and Kosmina tumbled head over heels until equilibrium vanished. *No air. Can barely see.* As currents threatened to rip them apart, he caught her wide-eyed gaze through the turbid water, her expression flashing one question: *The end?*

He yanked her closer. More water. More force. They pitched end over end with no way out. He couldn't hold on much longer, marveling that she hadn't yet drowned—

She began to.

He clamped her body against his when her scream bubbled up with the last of her air. Water filled her lungs, and she seized. Again. And again.

Drowning in his arms. *Dying.* Was she old enough to revive? He couldn't save her if he lost consciousness. Judging by the burn in his chest, he wasn't far behind.

Somehow he kept his head, channeling Kosmina's unearthly focus. An outlet must exist. He struggled to keep her close, to *see.* Far below them were cracks that allowed the water to rush through, like volcanic grates. The basilisk would never fit. Would they?

When the creature slammed against the grates, it gave a watery roar, its claws raking the water. Its colossal body blocked most of their way out; a slight opening remained. How to reach it while dodging a claw strike?

With Kosmina in his arms, he conserved the last of his power, riding the vortex until he neared the tube's wall. He managed to kick against it, propelling them toward that tight opening—

Whoosh! They raced through, narrowly skirting past claws.

Yet the water only continued. Freedom *wasn't.* That burn in his chest morphed into agony. His eyes closed against his will, his grip on her weakening. The years of his long, wearying existence played out in his mind.

Time wasted. Opportunities missed. He'd indulged every impulse, and he'd had nothing but misery to show for it. And now all he wanted was—

Air.

Air?

It rushed over him! He pried open his eyes, gulped in a breath.

The tube had spat them out into the night! He clutched Kosmina's limp body tight against him as they free-fell once more within a cascade of water—a massive waterfall. He dared a glance over his shoulder, saw the ground rushing closer. Jagged rocks awaited.

Enfolding her, he twisted to take the brunt.

PAIN.

A dagger of rock pierced his side, but he'd preserved her safety. Sucking in breaths, he managed to rise and carry her out of the pounding water. Once he reached the shore, he dropped to his knees and laid her on the ground. "Kosmina!"

Her pale lips were parted, her limbs motionless, her heart

still. Lightning above reflected in her sightless eyes. Her clever mind and lively gaze were gone.

Realization hit. Connections fired in his mind. *Something mysterious binds us. I want to solve this mystery.*

Was it too late?

She would revive. She had to. He pressed his mouth to hers, blowing air. "Breathe!" He gave her air. More. *More.* He started compressions on her chest. "Breathe, damn you!"

She was so young, might not be fully immortal yet. Might be truly . . . dead.

Now his panic came, a fist that throttled. He'd seen untold faces of death over the years, so why was her demise eviscerating him?

She's gone. Incomprehensible loss tolled through him.

No. She couldn't be—not while he still had breath in his lungs. *And blood in my veins.* With a wild yell, he bit his wrist open.

EIGHTEEN

The Wilds of Canada

Racing against the coming dawn, Lothaire and Kristoff sprinted along animal trails for what must have been a hundred miles, following the vague directions outlined in the wizard's journal.

They passed the residents of the woods—elk, cougars, and, yes, bears—but not another Lorean or human. Kristoff struggled to keep up with his much faster half brother, would be damned before he asked to slow down.

Lothaire only did once they'd reached the base of a cliff wall. Quiet reigned here. No small creatures rustled, no night birds calling. Using his enhanced senses of smell and sight—honed over millennia—he investigated the area, stalking back and forth with a look of intrigue on his face.

Kristoff grudgingly followed. "What are you searching for? It's not as if there will be a sign to mark the entrance."

Lothaire dragged away some foliage from the cliff and pointed out an etched section on the sheer rock face. "Here." He brushed away grit, revealing cryptic symbols carved into the stone. "Why, I believe it's a sign marking an entrance!"

Kristoff scowled. "Then what does it say?"

"No idea." Lothaire didn't sound discouraged whatsoever.

"We need to find an expert who knows the language. We can return once the sun sets again."

"I'm going to sleep." Lothaire dropped to the ground and rested with his back against the rock.

"What are you talking about? Dawn approaches. We have no shelter."

"I'll wake before then." His eyes closed.

As Kristoff paced, fingers of sunlight loomed over the cliff, soon to reach them. Part of him was tempted to let those rays scald Lothaire.

Closer . . . closer crept the light, a phantom's hand ready to snatch a vampire's long life.

For the sake of Furie, he said, "Wake, Lothaire."

Nothing.

Kristoff wasn't as sun-paranoid as some vampires—he'd met many who couldn't even view a picture of it—but he also didn't court unnecessary burns. Again it struck him: *I can't abandon my nemesis, even to his own insanity.* "Wake *now.*"

Lothaire roused and traced to his feet. "That was a productive nap. I haven't always been able to pull up memories at will, but I continue to evolve—to your detriment."

With another glance at the growing dawn, Kristoff asked, "*How* was it productive?"

"I once drank another vampire, a thirsty sort who was filled with memories. *He* had drunk a wizard who'd mind-melded with a Gaoler. Anyway, while I slept, I accessed that vampire's memories of memories. It's all very meta, but I know the Gaolers' language now." Of course he did. "You forbade your Forbearers to bite others, but you're not truly a vampire until you consume another. You haven't *lived.*"

Kristoff could scarcely imagine drinking a victim. Before his heart and sexual impulses had gone dormant in his thirties, he'd sought pleasure like a male who'd known he was on borrowed time. Yet he'd never been tempted to bite another.

Lothaire returned to the panel. As he deciphered the symbols, he absently said, "Stolen memories hold power. And not just mental. They fuel my physical strength too."

As if a being his age needed help with strength. "You overindulged."

"Yes. No one can be a reservoir for so many memories and not dance along the edge of the abyss."

"How has your queen not gone mad after drinking from you?" Kristoff asked. "Shouldn't she have harvested all of your memories?"

"When I used Dorada's magical ring, I made a wish to ensure my Bride never took memories from my past, just my own going forward. Once she drinks from me again, she'll be able to witness all of my bravery within Nightside."

Comprehension hit. "You embarked on this trip to impress your Bride. You really are mad." Lothaire had struck a devil's bargain: power in exchange for lifelong madness. Would Kristoff have done the same if he'd had to contend with both Demestriu and Stefanovich?

"Only now realizing this?" Lothaire continued his translation. "The journaling wizard was right; this is indeed the portal to Nightside, the official entry into a mythic hellplane." He read aloud: *"Nightside, land of the forsaken, ruled by the dead. Woe to any be-lived who enter."*

"And *how* does this portal open?"

"The code to unlock these magics is . . . a puzzle." He all but vibrated with anticipation. "One must crack the Lore's most challenging puzzle, a conundrum that would baffle any creature short of a sphinx. Once begun, failure to solve it will bring"—his lips curled, revealing a flash of fang—"death."

"Sounds ominous."

Lothaire's grin deepened. "Did I ever tell you about the time I drank a sphinx?"

Seven minutes later . . .

The portal to Nightside opened, the rock face disappearing, leaving air in the shape of a large door.

Lothaire demanded of Kristoff: "Admit it."

Sharp shake of his head.

"Admit it. I'm *that* good." Lothaire fogged and buffed his claws. "Yet you refuse to acknowledge how alike we are? Some people can't take a compliment." He strode through the portal without a care.

When Kristoff hesitated, Lothaire turned back. "Best hope I don't perish—me, poor Furie's only chance."

With a muttered curse, Kristoff followed into some kind of cave. When the portal snapped closed behind them, leaving a seamless rock wall, he attempted to trace, but that ability must be bound here. "Congratulations, you insufferable ass. We're trapped. And weaponless." Their swords had disappeared. "How are we to save Mina if we're imprisoned in this land of the forsaken with her?"

"It'll come to me, I'm sure." Lothaire found an opening out the cave and headed into the night. He lifted his face and inhaled. "I already have her scent. Ah, and another one? A sorcerer is likely with her. Well, that's a bad break. Enchanters, right?"

Wouldn't know.

"She might not know up from down when he gets through

with her." At Kristoff's questioning look, Lothaire said, "I once played cards against the King of Lies. Took me a decade to right my mind after that."

"How do you fight an enchanter?" Was Mina in even *more* danger?

"Depends on what his abilities are. All I know for certain is that Sorceri are not to be trusted. This way." He strode onto a rocky path.

Kristoff trailed after him, surveying the area with a gimlet eye. Lava and misery. "I can't believe I followed you into this place."

Lothaire gestured around them. "I offer you an opportunity to learn about the Lore—*this is the classroom*—but you resist me."

"Didn't you say the same to Mina? That's what got us into this situation."

"You were raised by humans and lived among them for centuries. You're just as sheltered as Mina is and equally in need of education."

Born in Helvita, Kristoff had been smuggled out of the castle as a babe after his mother's death. He knew little about her, piecing together that she'd been stricken with the plague following his birth and then executed.

If the same malady had befallen Mina, would her king kill her?

Lothaire continued, "I'm not greater than you because of my age and earned strength, or even because I'm part Dacian. I'm greater than you are because of all I know."

"I started building my army hundreds of years ago. I've been immersed in this world."

"Yes, but since then, immortals have worked together to keep you—and your army of turned mortals—in the dark. They don't favor former humans."

"Perhaps so, but three of my generals have wed Valkyries, and they are learning much."

"Ah, the legendary Wroth brothers. But are those warlords passing on all they learn? If you think any one of them will choose you over the well-being of his fated Bride, you are laughably mistaken."

"They would never lie to me." Especially not the two oldest. Three hundred years ago, Kristoff had *made* them, dripping his blood into their mouths to revive their dying human bodies.

Lothaire continued forward and Kristoff kept pace, sensing information to be had. The Enemy of Old didn't disappoint: "If Furie rises, she'll likely sentence to death any Valkyrie who allies with a vampire. Those Wroth Brides will be fugitives from their own coven. Will your generals allow that? In your own power base, a family of warlords will be united by blood and steel against your female." With clear glee, he said, "You need to look farther down the board, brother. And all gambits lead to one eventuality: the fall of your queen."

His analysis was disturbingly on point. "You've said Furie will be my greatest asset, yet now you hint that she'll be the dividing wedge in my army. So which is it?"

"I said she would be an asset *if* you could tame her. It all depends on what emerges from those depths. One way to find out. Sign my ledger."

"I might as well sign Dorada's." The Queen of Evil had taken a page from Lothaire's book—in fact, she now *possessed* Lothaire's old ledger—and was supplementing it by making offers with her ring in exchange for a vow. "I could wish for Furie, my crown, and peace among my ranks."

"You fought Dorada not long ago. If she deigned to bargain with you after that, would you pledge your future to a former mummy who chums around with wendigos?" Lothaire added,

"And how do you think your Valkyrie Bride would feel about your being oathbound to a malevolent sorceress? Remind me: Aren't the Valkyries the 'good guys'?"

No one made a secret of Furie's hatred for vampires. She would despise Kristoff doubly.

Though he'd never met her, he knew exactly what she would look like because he'd seen her identical twin, Cara the Fair.

Beautiful—in an eerie, lethal way.

Lothaire tapped his temple. "Starting to put together the bigger picture?" Knowing how trapped Kristoff was in every sense, Lothaire said, "Your Bride's a Valkyrie born of a Fury. And more, she's an *arch-Fury*, with wings of fire. Hunting evildoers is in her DNA."

She'll consider me *an evildoer.*

"When I last met her six decades ago, she nearly incinerated me with those wings in a fiery embrace, right before I chained her to the bottom of the ocean." He sighed to the sky, *"Good times,"* and walked on without a care in the worlds.

Rage welling, Kristoff followed Lothaire, beginning to sweat in the increasingly hot air. They headed toward that plain of piping lava, the heat mirroring his inner turmoil as he seethed over his options.

Oathbound to one of two evil beings: Lothaire or Dorada.

Or let Furie continue to drown.

Unless . . . Kristoff narrowed his eyes on Lothaire's back as he devised another alternative. *What if I change the rules of the entire game?*

The checkmate of them all. He found his lips curving. *Yes, brother, maybe we are more alike than I'll admit.*

NINETEEN

Power coursed through Mina's body.

As if from a distance, she heard the sorcerer's words, commanding her to breathe and . . . drink?

Yes! Immortal blood dripped onto her tongue. It raced through her veins, heating her from the inside out. She managed to open her eyes; the sorcerer filled her vision.

Gaze glowing, he held his gashed wrist above her mouth.

More drops landed on her tongue. The taste quickened her plague madness, sharpening her fangs and dulling her resistance. She tensed to seize him—

Pressure rushed up from her lungs. She twisted onto her side and spat water mixed with blood.

He rubbed her back. "That's it." His voice was rough. "Easy, vampire. Easy."

Struggling for control, she sucked in breaths. "Wh-what . . . happened?"

"You died. It didn't take."

Get hold of yourself, Mina! Had she truly just perished? And nearly bitten him? His blood had been as full of life and magic as she'd suspected.

"How did we get free?" Submerged in that churning water, she had been certain the end had come for them both. Yet here they were.

"We found the end of the lava tube."

She sat up, swiping her hair out of her face. "And the basilisk?" Her gaze darted.

"Didn't." The sorcerer knelt beside her. "You need to drink more."

More of his nectar. She'd never tasted anything like it—liquid bliss.

When he held his wrist to her again, bloodlust welled like a leviathan inside her. "No!" She was a heartbeat away from biting him. The memory harvest from a male like this would be her doom. "No more."

"Why not?" He frowned from her to his wrist and back. "Did you not like my taste?"

"You can't be serious. You're concerned about that now?" She made it to her feet.

He did as well, staring down at her. "Then why don't you want more?"

"You give your blood away readily for one spending so much of it." Crimson seeped from his side as well.

He flicked a glance at that injury. Shrugged. "I'm already regenerating." Yet his magic-filled blood seemed to be everywhere. All over him. Their clothes. The ground.

To remove herself from temptation, she crossed to a puddle of still water. Kneeling beside it, she regarded her reflection in the smooth surface. Her irises were dark purple, the color of a bruise. Blue mixed with red. Soon they would match Lothaire's eyes. *I almost bit the sorcerer.*

So?

No!

From behind her, Silt said, "Was that a resuscitation or a resurrection? Are you even fully immortal?"

She patted her face, disbelieving her appearance. "I am immortal."

"You're not healing from those claw marks on your arm." Her sleeve had ripped, revealing her injury. "How do you know you've passed the threshold?"

When Loreans froze into their immortality, their senses grew even more amplified, intensifying their desires to a boiling point. "Because crossing that threshold is a very . . . distinct time." Understatement.

"Even after all these years, I recall that torment," he said in a husky tone. "Flesh aflame. Always aching, never satisfied."

As his deep voice washed over her, she recalled her fraught time of change—night after night of suffering in her bed, feeling alone and empty.

Having recently died, it seemed her body had bounced back and wanted *to live*—in all ways. And his luscious blood inside her was an accelerant fueling a wildfire.

"Did you not have a lover to see you through it?" he asked.

No, though I'd yearned for one! "That's none of your business." She rose to face him.

Appearing pleased, he said, "So you didn't. No lover, no mate." He struck her as keyed up over her revival, almost jubilant.

Ignoring him, she took in her surroundings, as harsh as everywhere else in this place. Not a single plant grew, and she spied zero signs of civilization. They had no food or weapons and no real reason to hope.

He'd asked her if she ever got daunted. She hadn't before, but *dying* had daunted her. She now knew what her future held once the plague forced her to greet dawn. And that was if

Nightside's creatures didn't get her first.

She frowned up at the sky. *Great plan to greet dawn, Mina, in a dimension with no sun.*

"How would a female vampire find her mate anyway?" he asked. "When a male vampire becomes immortal, his heart goes dormant, beating again when he finds his fated one. Your heart isn't dormant. Well, mostly not. Except for when you drown."

She almost flinched at the reminder. "A female vampire doesn't have those physiological changes."

"But you still mate for eternity. So how do you know who's yours?"

"We just do. Instinctively." Mina didn't have time for this distraction—her life remained on the line. "Why are you asking about this?"

"Because *I* just made your heart beat, princess." With a smirk, he added, "Seems you'll be following *me* all around Nightside now."

She cast him a cutting look.

"I'd say 'You're welcome' for saving you yet again, but you haven't thanked me."

What—if anything—did she owe this male? A few hours ago, he'd proudly told her, *Yes, of course I will murder Mirceo.* Silt's saving her life wouldn't make her spare his own, but she would no longer relish killing him. "Why save a dying vampire?"

"What can I say? I'm a hero." He checked his pockets, cursing to find them empty of sand. *Washed away.* "In any case, you don't believe you're dying. You plan on using Dorada's wishgiver."

Lothaire had used the ring but cautioned against its power. Kristoff had refused to bargain for it, even to find Furie. Would Mirceo use it? Despite this sorcerer's warning, would Mina?

Logic said no. Love said no. How could she jeopardize her

family and kingdom? But without the ring—or the sun—she would become a danger to others. Maybe she needed to be back in that water tube, trapped with a fellow monster.

Yet because of this sorcerer's strength, she was free. "You don't strike me as the type to risk yourself for another, but I know how you protected me. Even after I drowned, I somehow sensed your every struggle. You kept your head and got me to safety."

Was he developing feelings for her? Heightened circumstances heightened emotions. She would know. Fresh from these perils, the sorcerer looked like the hero that he'd deemed himself.

Determined jaw. Penetrating gaze. Bravely earned injuries.

Silt hiked his broad shoulders. "My bait is no good to me dead."

So no feelings for her. "I hate you so much."

"Good. Use it. That hatred will keep you going. I know this well."

He was right. But hatred wanted more than for her to keep going. Hatred demanded results. Though she had no sword, Silt's wounds and blood loss signaled this was the time to strike.

"Why do you think I worship revenge?" He turned to gaze at the horizon. "It provides much more strength than your idea of *devotion* does." As she silently collected a large stone, he added, "We need to put distance between us and that basilisk just in case it breaks through, so pull yourself together, you bleak wench—"

She leapt for the sorcerer and brought the rock crashing onto his head with all her might. A lesser immortal would've collapsed; he staggered around but shook off the hit.

Then he lunged for her. "Leech!" Tackling her backward, he knocked the stone free and covered her. "The thanks I get!" Seeming not to notice his bleeding scalp wound, he pinned her arms over her head. "I should throw you back to the basilisk."

She leaned up from the ground, sneering, "At least its motives are pure, *Silt*!"

"You don't have enough sense to be thankful." Lips drawn back from his teeth, he grated, "The plague is already rotting your mind."

"If I lose my sense totally, why, we could be mental equals at last!"

"*Bitch.*"

"*Fiend.*"

And then they were kissing.

How? Why? The pressure of his firm lips felt so good she moaned. He dipped his tongue inside her mouth, sweeping it against hers, shocking her with more delight.

Hate him! Feels so good . . .

Her arms went pliant beneath his merciless grip. When his hips maneuvered between her thighs, she spread them for him. Even with the wet clothes separating them, she perceived the heat of his stiffened penis rubbing over her mons.

It was hot—*with blood*. His heart thundered against her breasts as he thrust that generous erection atop her. *Don't stop, don't stop!*

Sorcery emanated from him like a tangible touch, caressing her skin. She traded moans for his groans; wanton sounds passed between seeking lips and tangling tongues. Despite all his experience, he was as lost as she was, his mighty frame straining over her.

When he released her wrists to pin her hips, she gripped his hair hard, and blood dripped from his scalp wound to her cheek, sending her into a frenzy.

Blood all around her. Sorcery enveloping them. His tongue and body arousing her as never before. *Blood and heat and magic and madness.*

Holding her where he wanted her, he bucked wildly, desperate to lose his semen. His rod rubbed her throbbing clitoris until she could perceive little else. She lusted for his length to fill her emptiness, piercing her wetness.

He broke the kiss to rasp, "You've got my blood inside you. My breath. And now you crave my seed inside you too."

She moaned at the idea. *I do! Crave it filling me up, marking me.*

"I'll own every inch of you."

The possessiveness dripping from his words sent her hurtling toward climax, and she whimpered. She needed to be owned, marked, mated. . . .

He took her lips once more, was about to catch her scream with his mouth. Yet her fangs sharpened again. As if he sensed her quandary, he broke the kiss and focused on her neck.

Sucking her pulse point. Flicking his tongue against her sensitive flesh. Thrusting his powerful hips. *So close . . .*

Yet something alerted her senses outside of this encounter. Danger? No, she had enough of that here with him. Somehow she murmured, "Wait. Just wait."

"What?" He raised his head, blinking glazed eyes. "I'm one thrust away from coming till my cock screams *mercy.*"

Really? His words were yet more titillation. Her attention zoomed to his lips, and her fangs grew even sharper. She was tempted to take another taste of him, of blood and pleasure.

No! Bloodlust and sexual lust were indistinguishable in Horde vampires. The plague gained ground. . . .

He exhaled a ragged breath. "You better have a damn good reason for stopping."

Hadn't she? Oh! "I smell something."

He shook his head hard, clearing his eyes. "What is it?"

"It's far away but definitely a new scent." Recognition. "It's *food cooking.*"

TWENTY

"Stay sharp, princess," Silt told the vampire as they followed the scent trail toward what might be their salvation. His balls still ached so badly they pained him with each step.

"I don't detect any threats so far," she said in an absent tone. After their cataclysmic kiss, the vampire wouldn't meet his eyes, her gaze bouncing everywhere but in his direction.

At least the earlier flicker of despair in her expression had vanished. The dauntless princess was back, and he sensed here to stay.

The area around the waterfall ascended to another range they would have to cross. They pushed on, ever upward through a rocky corridor. Though immortals like them could scale heights with ease, seamless marble made up the rock face on either side of this passage, too slick for climbing. Dense fog obscured even the vampire's vision.

Their damp clothes were in tatters, they'd lost their weapons, and their surroundings were grim. Still, Silt's injuries had almost healed, and food beckoned them.

Also on the plus side: they were alive.

As she'd pointed out, he'd kept his head and saved their lives. Maybe he was starting to get an idea of who he was. Based on his performance against that basilisk and the water, this drugged-out sorcerer might be a godsdamned death defier.

Now if only he could stop replaying the vampire's kiss. He'd almost come while clothesfucking her on the ground! The pleasure he'd felt with her had been like distilling into one act all the sex he'd ever had.

Then magnifying it.

A volcano on the sun produced less heat.

This hedonist wanted more. Now that drugs no longer sandbagged him, he coveted her as much as opium. Did she feel the same about him? He thought he could've made her orgasm beneath him.

"This might be a dead end." She squinted against the fog.

He had to clear his throat to say, "We'll just have to follow it and see."

"You promised me information. What do you know about the plague?"

A promise was a promise. *Except when it isn't.* "You're infected with a sickness that wiped out female vampires—if the Horde didn't destroy them first."

This didn't seem to surprise her. "Why would they murder their own?"

"Rumors were legion, but I saw some cases firsthand. Once the plague takes hold, you'll want only to kill, gorging on blood, worse than any red-eyed male. The Horde couldn't control those rabid females, so they were eliminated. If a female got loose among humans, the Gaolers would capture her to be quarantined here."

"You've told me nothing I didn't already know or suspect. Have you heard of a cure?"

"I haven't. Not in all my years." Silt had planned to demoralize the princess; so why did the stoic acceptance in her eyes make him need to smash something? "Doesn't mean there isn't one. Besides, if you're bent on using Dorada's wishgiver, I wager that would work on the plague."

"You made logical points about the ring. Perhaps I wouldn't sign over my life to her."

Then perhaps you're going to lose that clever mind of yours. And all of this was a moot point anyway if they couldn't escape.

Staring straight ahead, she said, "I thought you would have more information about my situation."

"Maybe I do. How did you get clawed?"

"I lost focus and my concealment for only a few moments, yet it was enough for a Horde vampire to seize my arm. We fought, and he sliced my skin."

"How much time passed between that wound and the Gaolers coming for you?"

"I roamed New Orleans for mere hours before they appeared."

"Hours, was it?" He had a suspicion.

She finally faced him. "Yes, so?"

"I'll tell you more if you answer some questions."

"Pose them, and we'll see."

"What's Dacia like?" He'd never met someone who hailed from a "mythical" kingdom.

She hesitated, and he could all but see her calculating the risks versus benefits of answering him. At length she said, "Our realm is located in a hollowed-out mountain range with a breathtaking black-stone castle in the center. At the top of the highest mountain is a diamond as big as a cottage that allows in filtered sunlight, so we have days of a sort." She slid him an unreadable look as she added, "Sometimes we even see a hint of moonlight." Then her gaze went distant. "Mist is constant, blanketing the cobblestone streets. Blood fountains bubble, feeding the populace. The kingdom is known as the Realm of Blood and Mist for a reason. My brother and I are all that's left of the House of Castellan, the castle guard. We're considered the heart of Dacia, tasked with caring for all those within its walls."

"What was your life as a princess like?"

He didn't expect her to answer that question, but she surprised him: "I appreciated what I had, but I often felt smothered. Mirceo and my uncles don't see eye to eye over much, but they all agreed I should be protected. Which meant sheltered."

Not sheltered enough. *You're in hell—with* me, *forgodsakes. Silt the Befouler.*

"Sometimes . . . it was as if I moldered in a grave, slowly dying. Though I understood the risks to me away from the kingdom, I burned to dig my way out to freedom. To never look back."

You dug straight into a plague-ridden prison sentence. "And here you are." *Fucked as fucked can be.*

She nodded. "Yes. On an adventure like no other."

Heh. "You said your parents died. What happened to them?"

"They were murdered—my father before I arrived, and my mother when I was three. Mirceo was just fifteen."

Silt cast his mind back to when he'd been the same age. He'd already been pledged to revenge for years by that time. "Who did it?"

"My uncle Stelian's father. He was then secretly murdered by another family member, most likely one of my other uncles. We might never know by whom. It's all a snarl of royal intrigues and backbiting," she said with a dismissive wave, again as if Silt couldn't keep up with such lofty matters. "The generations who came before mine nearly destroyed an entire family through grudges, and we were expected to inherit our line's vendetta, to punish Stelian and more. But Mirceo and I reject that. We've declined that inheritance forever."

Silt stared at her in bafflement. She was breaking the chain of pain? Ignoring vendettas? "You don't want to avenge your parents?"

"Mirceo told me that while they were loving to us, they were just as eager as the rest of the royals to deal death for power. Which meant other relatives might have inherited their own vendettas—against us. When Mirceo took over as my guardian, he was also my protector, always looking over his shoulder for danger. I'm more a daughter than a sister to him."

Then pain was heading Mirceo's way, regardless of Silt's moves. "I can't square the idea of your brother as some selfless protector." The vampire had seemed apologetic during Silt's handoff to the Gaolers, as if he'd had found a kindred spirit whom he'd been forced to screw over. *No hard feelings.* "He struck me as more of a hedonist."

"Once the danger lessened and he was assured of my safety, he partook of all the delights denied a young man."

"So you don't mind dissolution in general. Just when I do it."

"I believe there's a difference between indulging because of desire or because of necessity. The trick is knowing which is which."

And not *indulging in something that would readily own you body and soul.* As the thought occurred, he met this female's gaze. She peered up at him with her blond brows drawn, and a charge passed between them, like lightning.

Silt was reminded of when bolts struck sand and birthed glass. He felt equally electrified and brittle.

Breaking the moment, she said, "I've answered your

questions. Now tell me what you were going to say earlier. Why did you find it interesting that only hours passed before I was captured?"

"Because the Gaolers don't work that fast. Someone informed on you."

"I don't understand."

"You have an enemy with both foresight *and* the ear of the Gaolers. Do you know any oracles?"

"Yes, I'm close friends with one. But Balery is steadfastly loyal."

"Might want to rethink that."

She frowned. "My uncle Lothaire entertains a friendship of sorts with Nïx the Ever-Knowing."

"The most powerful soothsayer in all the worlds? You're caught up in her web, and you don't even know it."

"Then my brother is too—if not my entire kingdom." With a firm nod, Kosmina said, "I have much work to do and must return as soon as possible."

Moments later, Silt caught her gaze trailing over a loose rock beside their path. "Sand almighty, how many times have you tried to off me?"

She shrugged. "One too few. Logic dictates that I take you down before Mirceo arrives or before I succumb to another of Nightside's threats."

"True. If he somehow breaches this realm, his odds of survival would make even yours look good."

"Now, if only something could make your control of sand look good."

"I'll get it back, princess, then show you control as you've never seen."

She feigned a yawn. "If I use Dorada's ring, my second wish should be for you to enjoy all the cruelty you've ever delivered."

He enjoyed verbally sparring with her, found it a refreshing change from her braining him. "Why not wish for what you really want? More of my kiss. Of course, you don't need the ring for that. I can grant all your fantasies. I'll do it right now."

"How can you desire someone you want to hurt?" Judging by her expression, she wrestled with this question herself. "And someone who regrets kissing you in the first place?"

Her disdain rankled, reminding him of when highborn Sorceri females had shared his bed then refused to acknowledge him, an Inferi, in public. And they'd been better than the ones who'd simply demanded his presence in their bedchambers. Those females hadn't even treated him like a man, more like an animal.

Memories harshened his tone. "Desire you? I just need to get off. Before you flatter yourself, know that I'll sleep with anything, and you're the only quarry in this realm for all I know. You're not *preferred*, princess; you're just *available*." Giving a laugh, he said, "But *you*, ah, you delighted in my kiss."

"I'm going crazy from plague, remember? And I just died. Let's just say I'm not at my most discerning."

His lips thinned. She wouldn't have surrendered to him otherwise, and they both knew it. "That was your first kiss, wasn't it?"

Her cheeks reddened, burning through the blood he'd given her. "I don't want to discuss this."

"Come on, princess, are we not to talk about how you took my lips like a vampire starved?"

"Madman! *You* kissed *me*."

"Hard to remember, when you met me with such enthusiasm. You were so close to coming for me, aching for me to fill you."

Blushing to the tips of those ears, she said, "I desire more than an exchange of . . . culminations. I want a communion."

"Huh?"

She exhaled an impatient breath, as if he wasn't worth her upcoming explanation: "I won't make love until I'm in love. It's that simple."

"Don't knock an *exchange of culminations* until you've tried it, sweet."

"And I suppose you've tried lovemaking? If not, don't knock it."

"What do *you* know of it, then?" he countered. "Explain to me, young and impressionable female, what the difference is between sex and lovemaking. Be sure to include examples since you've experienced neither."

"I saw both during my mission to observe the New Orleans nymphs."

"Your mission was to observe the goings-on at the Tree of Delight?" Even Sorceri raised their brows at that notorious covey.

She nodded. "On my last night there, I came across a couple who were in love, and what they shared was unlike everyone else."

His curiosity demanded to know more, but his instinct cautioned him that this territory was best left unexplored. *Don't even dip a toe in this nonsense.* "How was it different?" *The hell, Silt?*

"Before, each act I'd witnessed had been about one aim— pleasure for pleasure's sake. With this couple, the aim was to demonstrate love, with ecstasy to follow. Two people in love *made love*. I knew I was in the presence of something transcendent, and it humbled me so utterly that I . . . I lost track of myself. Sorcerer, I beheld divinity, and I was forever changed. There's no going back for me."

Silt stared down at her as if she'd uttered an unknown language. For some reason, when he turned her words over in his mind, apprehension hit him.

Did she know something that he wasn't able to grasp, a mystery withheld from him? Did this romantic love she spoke of—an emotion he had ridiculed—hold power?

Mysteries usually did.

And she was privy to it. Right now she seemed like some preternatural, alien being—a creature so far removed from a man like him that they would never connect.

The princess and the befouler.

And he resented her for that.

The ground rumbled as if in league with his ire.

TWENTY-ONE

D ivinity is a strong word," Silt finally said, but he didn't appear as confident—or scoffing—as before.

On unfamiliar footing, sorcerer? "And yet it's not strong enough to do it justice."

Lothaire had been right; Mina's mission had tempered her feelings for the Gravewalker. But then Silt's kiss had obliterated them. And the sorcerer was even less of a possibility for her!

"Wait a second . . . the Enemy of Old dispatched you—an innocent—on a 'mission' to observe the most raucous nymphs in the Lore?" Silt gave a laugh. "At least that vampire has a sense of humor."

"You think he intended it as a joke?"

"Not a doubt in my mind. Immortals of a certain age find diversion where they can. I would know."

Initially she'd feared the same. No longer. "Joke or not, I learned much." Preconceptions about the nymphs had been overturned. Those females didn't live for revelry and the indiscriminate taking of bedmates; they lived for their coven and bedded only the most skilled lovers.

Males who brought no pleasure to a nymph took no pleasure from one. Mina didn't precisely know what "porn" was, but she'd heard more than one nymph telling a potential partner, "Don't return until you cut out the porn and read some romance novels." Those females knew what they wanted and set parameters.

They were also gifted spies, able to meld with many elements. They had an unmatched network for intelligence, and their wild fests harvested more.

From her observations, Mina had learned to value herself and the sharing of her body, and to never underestimate an unknown. She inwardly sighed. As everyone continued to do to her.

Was she underestimating this male? After all, what magic must he be using on her to affect her so deeply? She'd made a promise to herself to search for love and to honor it; at the earliest opportunity Mina had welcomed this rough sorcerer's attentions.

If they hadn't been interrupted, would she have surrendered everything to him? "I witnessed enough to discover that I want love from my future partner."

"Love?" He all but spat the word. "Love can end. It can get twisted."

"Then it wasn't true to begin with." She paused on the path. "Who hurt you, sorcerer? Who wounded you so badly that you never recovered from it?"

He stopped beside her. "No one. What are you going on about?"

"If only I could lie with such ease." The *rána* was an effective teacher—and punisher. Since falsehoods were so rare in Dacia, the concept of them had always fascinated her.

"Nobody's hurt me, because I don't give anyone the chance to," he said proudly, even as his golden eyes flickered with emotion. "Trusting another is like voluntarily wading into quicksand. You deserve to sink."

She felt sorry for him. How lonely his existence must be. "We'll have to agree to disagree. In the meantime, I remain a staunch believer."

"Are you sharing all these thoughts with me because you still anticipate killing me?"

"Yes." Plus, she remained unshackled by blushes and reticence. Here she was, conversing freely with an otherlander, as if she'd done so all her life. Bright side: she would never have known what this was like if she'd never caught the plague.

"You really are a piece of work, female."

"You're the villain here, sorcerer." She started forward once more, and he followed.

When another quake rumbled, they fell silent, each lost in thought, even as they remained on alert for threats.

The path descended, widening. As the fog lifted, no dead end greeted them—the corridor opened up into a plain with a long lake of black water. Far on the horizon loomed a steep hill, covered with rocks. The food scents came from that direction.

The sky was a black dome scattershot with yellow lightning. The lake lay still as slate, reflecting the scene above. Those flashes of lightning reminded her of senses firing during a resurrection—such as her own—or the finale before dying. Was this realm coming into being or breathing its last?

As she studied the sky, she pondered whether she was indeed in Nïx's sights. Had the Valkyrie wanted her in this place? Mina did find it odd that the Gaolers had been in New Orleans on the very night she'd been clawed. Maybe Silt's information wasn't totally useless.

She peered over at him, feeling a tightness in her chest as she took in his strong profile. Fighting beside him with their lives on the line must have supercharged their chemistry, sending it tumbling into less . . . deniable.

He was handsome and focused, a world away from her initial impression of him. Maybe her attraction grew apace with his own metamorphosis. She rubbed her tongue over a fang for a shot of blood—his still spiced her own, and she almost moaned. *He* is *inside me.*

"We haven't spotted any wendigos in this area," he said in that deep voice. "Not a single stray bone. Why aren't they following the same scent we are?"

Her survival instincts flared; thoughts of the past and the future grew muted. "Another imaginary line they won't cross?"

"Probably."

Yet again, she and Silt had likely stumbled onto a worse threat. Was some malign being using the food as a lure? "You mentioned that revenants and ghouls live here," she said. "I've read a bit about both. But I thought revenants were corpses reanimated by sorcery."

"Not here. The majority of Nightside's revenants are born, not made. They get nourishment from snuffing life, and they're brutally strong. A mystic told me she'd once seen a vision of a revenant attack. A single jabbing punch from one knocked an immortal's head neatly off."

The force that would take . . . "If the undead are born here, how do they multiply?"

"That mystic thought the ghouls reproduced like insects, in addition to an infected immortal here or there. Maybe the others do too."

"Insects, is it?" Mina shuddered at the thought of spiders' webs or egg sacs. "Ghouls usually move in large troops. That basilisk notwithstanding, why haven't we seen any?"

"Luck?"

She laughed without humor. "You believe in that but not in love?"

He slid her a look, his eyes hinting at tangled secrets. "No one expects luck to last forever."

With that, they continued on in silence, crossing the distance to that rocky rise. Side by side, she and Silt scaled the mound of stones.

Once they crested the top, Mina breathed in shock: "What sorcery is this?"

He bit out, "Exactly."

At the top of the rocks, a marvel unfolded before Silt and Kosmina.

Past a valley filled with vineyards was a classical castle on an island, surrounded by a sea of boiling water. Torches illuminated the stately exterior in welcome, yet no bridge or ferry offered to take them across the water to reach it.

The sight of this wonder in such a wasteland sent him tumbling back in time to that momentous day when he'd been six. He'd followed a desert deer's trail into the sands, far from home. Water pouch empty, he'd sworn that each hoof-marked dune he climbed would be his last. But he'd wanted to bag that game for his parents.

Picturing their relaxed smiles and the laughter that came only with a full belly, he'd pushed on with a mixture of excitement and wariness, kind of how he felt about this vampire.

Though he'd never caught that deer, he'd found an oasis filled with fruit trees. After he'd devoured his windfall and night had neared, he'd watched a wave of sand crest in front of the setting sun. In that moment, he'd first sensed his connection to it. *I saw everything in the sand.*

That oasis had been real; this *wasn't*. Feeling the magic thick in the air, he murmured, "Behold the lair of a very powerful Sorceri."

Kosmina faced him. "A good one or an evil one?"

"Odds lie with evil. Nature of the beast and such. And yet we're still going there."

"You said you give others of your kind a wide berth. Beware the Sorceri, remember?"

He had, even when fully empowered. Was he now to enter another one's domain at his weakest? He traced the tattoos on his chest. *Never again.* And the easiest way to make a sorcerer give up his power was to threaten something he valued. He glanced at Kosmina, his asset. *I know this well.*

Still . . . "We have no choice but to investigate. The food is there."

"We can't leap over an expanse of water that wide."

"He or she will probably test us before dispatching a ferry of some kind. Just stay on guard."

She quirked a brow. "What if we fail the test?"

"We can vow to the Lore that we mean them no harm. And the only thing Sorceri like more than isolation is carousing. New faces will be welcome." Novelty could revive a stale scene.

"Very well." She squared her shoulders. "Let's meet this Sorceri."

"Stay close to me—"

A pair of scents hit him simultaneously, two things that wanted to steal his life.

Behind them: the stench of revenants.

And from the castle: the vinegary spice of . . . *dragon's breath.*

TWENTY-TWO

"Stop." The sorcerer swallowed audibly. "Maybe we should avoid that place."

"Pardon?" His abrupt reversal baffled Mina. "You're starving and exhausted, yet you don't want to head to the one guarantee of food? Not to mention that even you must have smelled the foes that near."

"Revenants. I know. It's just . . ." His muscles coiled as tight as a bowstring. Had he started sweating? "There's no bridge, and that water would boil us alive. If one place has food, others might."

She sensed movement from all directions, didn't have time to analyze him. Besides, her thinking about this sorcerer continued to prove faulty. "I need information. You can search elsewhere on your own, but I am going." She'd just uttered the words when she recognized another scent, one relatively new to her. Guests at the Tree of Delight had smoked opium on occasion; the acidic smell of it trailed from the castle.

Ah. No wonder Silt hesitated. He feared a relapse; having lifted off the ground, he didn't want to crash once more.

Pang. Empathy tightened her chest with an unexpected tenderness. She inwardly sighed, *Complicated, shady sorcerer.*

What if Silt Harea wanted to be better but didn't know how? What if he regretted his vow?

She hardened herself against him, calling to mind how he'd looked as he'd threatened her brother. *Of course I will murder Mirceo—*

The rocks suddenly shifted beneath their feet. She whirled around as stones flew up into the air; revenants clawed up from the ground! "This isn't a hill—it's a grave!"

The massive creatures appeared lumpen, as if they'd absorbed stones under their skin. They had wild black eyes. Their mouths were slack, tongues dangling as they roared.

"We can't fight this many without swords!" Silt grabbed her wrist, and yet again they ran.

Sprinting toward the castle, they wound among grapevines. Behind them, undead monsters that hungered to kill trampled over the rows like a wave of locusts. "They'll trap us against that water, sorcerer."

"Then let's hope the castle's owner has something up their sleeve to ward them off."

As she sprinted, Mina willed some faceless magic practitioner to save them. "If something's going to happen, it needs to happen now." They were mere miles from the water's hazy edge, and the revenants were gaining on them!

Never slowing, she scanned for anything she could use as a weapon. Rocks? Wood? *Nothing but vines.*

A mile separated them from the water.

A quarter of a mile. The revenants' frenzied roars grew louder behind them.

"Silt . . ."

He slowed. "Yeah. We fight—"

A sudden banging sounded. Mina blinked in disbelief as a rolled-up bridge unfurled from the castle out over the water, like the curled tongue of some giant reptile.

When the end landed on the nearby shore, they hastened over to the floating bridge, and Silt shoved her onto it. "Go, go, go!"

They charged over the bouncing surface. Halfway across, she realized something. "The revenants aren't following." Standing along the bank, they pounded their hulking chests with rage, but none stepped atop the bridge. "Another sinister threat senses yet another sinister threat and decides not to pursue."

Silt muttered, "Welcome to Nightside."

The bridge bounced even more, twisting in place. Mina's steps crisscrossed as she and Silt fought for balance. She jerked a glance over her shoulder. Behind them, the unfurled bridge was *furling.*

Wide-eyed, Silt pushed her ahead of him. "Faster!" The sorcerer matched her speed, even when Mina dug in.

They couldn't leap into the piping water, had only one means of escape—the castle entry. Two towering doors opened wide like a ravening mouth. . . .

"Almost there, vampire. Dive!"

She tensed when he did, and they sprang past the doors, skidding bodily across a tiled entryway. The rolled-up bridge slammed shut behind them, just missing Silt. Air gusted over them.

Then stillness.

Their breaths were loud in the echoing chamber. Lying on the floor, Mina raised her head to see stiletto boots a couple of feet away. She peered upward, taking in gartered legs.

"Welcome, weary travelers," said a statuesque female with ebony skin, long black braids, and fuchsia eyes. She wore a red mask and a sophisticated headdress. Her golden garments covered little, the slits of her short skirt climbing all the way to her narrow waist. "I'm Entity, the Sorceri Queen of Dreams. And I'm here to make all yours come true."

TWENTY-THREE

I've been expecting you," the Queen of Dreams said. "Up, up, up. We can't be late."

At any moment, Silt expected this *Entity* to clap her hands together. But he didn't sense an acute threat from her. Nor did he scent that dragon's breath.

He levered himself to his feet, helping Kosmina to hers. "Late for what?"

"Our banquet starts in one hour. We keep schedule by the clock, because it's always night here. One could go batty without a schedule! Besides, I know you must be hungry. Running from revenants and all manner of creatures increases the appetite." She started off briskly, her bootheels clicking along spotless floors.

Chandeliers lit the area, and every fixture gleamed with gold. Rich wood panels covered the walls, adorned with collections of formal Sorceri masks through the ages. The large windows framed a view of a paradisical courtyard with more grapevines growing.

Of all the things Silt might have expected in Nightside . . .

He and Kosmina shared a look, then caught up with the sorceress.

"I'll show you to your rooms for baths and fresh garments." Tapping her mask, Enti said, "We dress for dinner here."

"I'm Silt—"

"Harea. I know! The great King of Sand. And she is Princess Kosmina of Dacia."

Kosmina said, "Are you a mind reader, Entity?"

The sorceress said, "Call me Enti, which is better than the other way I could have shortened my name." Broad wink. "To answer your question, yes, I read minds. I see your hopes, dreams, and more. Oftentimes I can make them come true. Within reason, of course."

Good luck reading his dreams. He didn't even know himself anymore—or what he might want. As soon as the thought occurred, he recalled how he'd felt as Kosmina lay dead.

Something mysterious binds us.

Enti eyed Silt, and her strange irises appeared to swirl like pinwheels in the wind. "You'll find everything you need here, every luxury to make your stay pleasurable."

Everything he needed? The food scents were stronger here, making his stomach knot with hunger, but he still didn't detect that dragon's breath.

"The revenants won't try to swim?" Kosmina asked.

Enti drew her gaze from Silt, her irises stilling. "No. Now they'll bury themselves back inside their rock grave, hibernating until they sense the living once more."

"Why didn't they storm the bridge?"

"In the past, we furled a number of them in it. An absolutely crushing way to go," Enti said dryly.

Anger flaring, Silt said, "Yes, we got that up-close impression."

"I apologize, but some of the revenants looked like they might try me once more, so I had to enact my best defense quickly to keep everyone here safe. Sometimes accuracy suffers."

Kosmina's brows drew together. "Why help us?"

"We welcome all living immortals in Castle Vitis, without judgment for how you came to be here." *Vitis*? Named for the vines outside?

"In exchange for what?" the princess asked, hunting for the angle.

"For not having ill-intent. I can read people's hearts, and you two hold no malice—at least not toward me. But my gods, toward each other? You, princess, dream of killing this sorcerer, and you crave to drink more of his 'magical' blood—not at the same time." Enti pointed at Silt. "You dream of killing her brother, and you're in a lather to bed her alone—also not at the same time."

Silt and the vampire spoke at once:

—"I'm not *preferred*, sorcerer? Just *available*?"

—"My blood is magical, is it?"

Kosmina craved him! Yet his self-satisfied grin faded. After their kiss, he'd hoped her resolve to murder him would have faltered. Despite Enti's words, his own plans to off Mirceo felt less pressing.

As they turned a corner into another corridor, Enti said, "Nevertheless, we have a peaceful existence here. I will maintain it." She turned the full impact of her smile on him. "Sorceri come along so rarely. We have just a handful here." As her steps matched his, her eyes indicated she was reading his mind again.

Then she would see his gravest secret: *my past as an Inferi.* He refused to glance away. Would she reveal his ignominy in front of Kosmina? Didn't matter. The princess would be lost soon anyway.

"What a pleasure it will be to know you," Enti said, hinting at layers of meaning.

And you. If her power proved gettable, would he change his view on sorcery accumulation? Maybe. "I haven't heard of you before, and I know of most."

"I believe you were already in Poly when I came into my abilities." She led them down another hallway.

Before he could drill down on her answer, a gaggle of scantily clad demonesses passed them. All of them looked well-fed and happy. Where had Enti found so many females among those condemned in Nightside?

Silt flashed them a smile. When they giggled and waved, he turned to see Kosmina's reaction.

Eye roll.

So he tapped his jugular with raised brows. *You know you want it.* And now Silt did too.

She gestured to herself from head to toe and mouthed, *Me alone.*

He liked this facet of her. Who knew saucy lit his wick?

As if she hadn't just made his cock swell, Kosmina asked, "How do you provision yourself here, Enti?"

"Sorcery works well in this plane. Not enough to leave, but our jail isn't so bad when I can produce shelter, food, wine, and *anything else* one needs for pleasure," she said, clearly for Silt's benefit.

She'd discovered his habit and was offering to create dragon's breath for him. His heart pounded at the thought of a never-ending supply.

With females everywhere and smoke at the ready, this castle varied little from his home. His plans to rebuild his power stores dimmed. . . .

When they reached a grand set of stairs and began to climb, Kosmina kept her head on a swivel, scanning for the next sinister threat.

Though she looked unsure of Enti, Silt didn't anticipate treachery. And why would Enti try to take out two immortals who posed no harm to her? With this castle's protections, the only issue facing the Queen of Dreams was boredom.

"Why are you in Nightside, Enti?" he asked.

"I meddled with humans, granting their dreams in return for their worship. I see that you did a variation on that theme as well. Delicious sport, isn't it?" She turned to Kosmina. "Why are you . . . ? Oh." Enti's gaze dropped to her arm. Were those wounds growing angrier? Seeming genuine, the sorceress said, "I'm very sorry about your illness."

Kosmina canted her head. "And if my dream is to be cured, sorceress?"

"I wish I could help you. But some things are beyond my abilities."

"I understand." That stoic acceptance returned, tugging at something inside him. Had she had a brief hope that Enti offered deliverance?

They climbed what felt like endless stairs. This castle appeared even larger from within. Silt perceived sorcery in every flickering lamp, every stone, every inch of the plush carpet lining the stairs.

Kosmina glanced out one of the airy windows. "Is this place . . . real?"

Enti chuckled. "What's real or unreal? It's all conjured with a wave of my hand, but it feels real to me."

When laughter broke out downstairs and a moan sounded from somewhere within these walls, Kosmina said, "With so many immortals here, you must know much about this realm. I'm eager to locate an escape."

"Unfortunately, there is none." Before Kosmina could argue, the sorceress paused and raised her hand. "I know you have many questions, and I will answer them all at the feast. But I never discuss business before pleasure—such as a warm meal—and I'm never late for dinner."

Though such a force in combat, the vampire hesitated before saying, "I can wait until then." Was he watching royal socialization at work? He could imagine her princess brain flashing a warning: *One mustn't insult one's hostess.*

They reached a landing and continued onto a new floor. Enti indicated two rooms across from each other. "You'll find clothes inside, and your baths are prepared. Silt, your room is to the right. Princess, yours is to the left. Unless you two prefer more space between you after your trials?"

He and Kosmina both said, *"No,"* at the same time.

He wasn't keen to let his asset out of his sight, and she seemed hell-bent on keeping her target near as well. He reminded himself that neither of them could leave without the castle's bridge.

Enti said, "I must warn you both: magic will prevent any violence inside my home."

Appearing put out, the princess eventually nodded.

He did as well.

When an unseen clock chimed, Enti said, "Oh, I must dash! Once you're ready, follow the sounds down to the banquet hall and bring a large appetite. Until then!" She hastened off, boots clicking.

"You get a reprieve," Kosmina told him. "Enjoy it."

"You couldn't kill me before. You wouldn't be able to do it here, even if allowed."

She gave him a smile with curving red lips and a hint of her little fangs. "Soon." That smile hit him harder than her knee to his balls. She turned from him and headed into her room, saying over her shoulder, "After thousands of years, you've finally met your ruination."

He rubbed his nape. *Starting to believe that.*

He entered his palatial suite, one even more lavish than the bedchamber in his stronghold. Would Kosmina's suite compare to the luxury of her home in Dacia? He found a steaming tub large enough to swim in, a basket of fruit and nuts, and a bottle of wine.

Sorceri were susceptible to poisons—*I would know*—yet wines that could mask such a taint were always on tap in their lairs. He shunned the drink but devoured the food.

It fueled his immortal regeneration, his frame putting on some of the muscle he'd lost during his withdrawal and Nightside's trials. His body had retained its resilience; why did his power still suffer?

Once he'd satisfied the worst of his hunger, he stripped off his clothes and sank into the steaming water. *"Great sand."* He rested his head on a waiting pillow and basked. . . .

Yet antsiness soon invaded him. Not surprising. His drug of choice was on offer here.

Would he accept and let down his guard? The only thing that could make a sorcerer more vulnerable than exhaustion was inebriation. And during his last binge, Silt had mistaken a cold street for a warm bed!

He traced the tattoos on his chest, a vow to defend his root power to the death. No, he'd never make himself vulnerable. Surely not. And so the cravings would continue. That must explain the unease.

His fingers paused. His need for opium wasn't all that affected him.

He gazed in Kosmina's direction. *I don't want to part from her. Not yet.* For the first time since his parents had betrayed him, he had another's safety on his mind.

My asset. My prize. His oasis memory remained fresh in his mind. *Should I follow that irritating vampire over the next dune and see what might be?*

He snatched up soap and quickly scrubbed himself, intending to dress and then harangue her again for trying to kill him. He'd just dunked his head a last time when half a dozen bath attendants, beauties all, sauntered into the chamber.

One said, "In a hurry, King of Sand? We're here to assist you with *anything* you might desire."

He swiped water off his smiling face. So Enti had sent in concubines to service him? He sensed that three were shifters, and the others were masked Sorceri of limited power. *I'm one to talk.*

"We've heard you're quite the ladies' man," another one said. "*Ladies* plural."

With their coy glances and wiles, they reminded him of his own harem. His smile faded. Why hadn't a single one of the females in his stronghold lifted a finger to help him?

His gaze flicked in the vampire's direction as he recalled all she'd done—and would continue to do—for her loved one. He dug into the idea of a bond like that, feeling like he'd spotted a hint of a wellspring in the deepest desert.

"Sorcerer?"

He turned back to the females. Pleasure was on tap here; all he had to do was surrender to it. But Enti was right—he craved Kosmina alone.

For now. Once sated of the vampire, that feeling would fade.

Had the sorceress been testing him with this offer of females? Gauging how long his preference would hold when his desires went unmet?

His eyes narrowed. Maybe Enti had procured males to help Kosmina with her bath. He shot to his feet with a curse, securing a towel around his waist.

"Sorcerer, we don't bite!" The females laughed. Feminine laughter was his aphrodisiac. It meant women were happy and more likely to bed him. These were guaranteed.

And yet he strode to the door.

He yanked it open and came face-to-face with Kosmina.

TWENTY-FOUR

Mina had heard pealing laughter in the sorcerer's room and thought, *He's wasted no time.*

She'd frowned at her bitter disappointment. Enti had said Silt desired Mina alone, but she'd learned at the nymphs' that a male could lust after a female and feel nothing in his heart.

No loyalty. No love.

No thanks.

Now he seemed to take up most of the doorway—a towering male clad in only a damp towel. He'd put on even more muscle, his physique brimming with virility. Droplets of water trailed over him. His smooth skin emanated warmth and his seductive natural scent.

"Your attire for the night?" she managed to ask without a quaver, though she was talking to a half-dressed man.

"Not quite. I thought you might do something stupid, like try to leave this place."

"Not without information. Unlike you and Enti, I still believe escape is possible."

"Because you have to." He leaned one broad shoulder

against the doorway. Corded muscles and tattoos flexed from the movement, distracting her.

She murmured, "What do those tattoos mean?"

"They're a secret that will die with me."

Nothing could make her more curious.

"You look spellbinding, by the way," he said. "Fancy, like a *princess*. I'll miss that T-shirt though."

She let him change the subject. Aside from the signs of her illness, she was pleased with her appearance. Having bathed, she'd found an array of clothing laid out atop the sumptuous bed.

Though she'd always dressed demurely in Dacia, she'd decided on fitted pants and a royal-blue tunic with a collar that dipped to the swells of her breasts. She'd left her hair loose to flow over her shoulders.

Since he'd complimented her, she supposed she should return the favor. "You appear . . . hale."

"I assume that means I look less *dissolute*?"

"Looks can be deceiving."

His eyes grew lively. "Still trying to match me to the descriptions of Sorceri you found in some library tome?"

By all the gods, the bruiser was sexy. "You prove unmatchable."

He clearly liked that.

"Are you going to tell me why you rushed out in a towel?"

"I also feared for my bait in our new surroundings. Just because you're a predator doesn't mean you can't be prey."

"I told you I've never drunk anyone."

"Wasn't talking about that. Attempts on my life—what are we up to now?"

She smiled coolly. "Still one too few."

His gaze fell to her lips, and his own curved. "You keep trying, but your heart's not in it." Flirtatious sorcerer. With his devastating grin.

He . . . might be right. Something had to have fouled her aim in the cave.

"Were you spying outside my door?" he asked.

"Yes. But I wouldn't begrudge a lecher his lechering. You may get back to it," she said with a queenly wave. "Enjoy what you can, while despairing of what you can't. *Me.*"

"I like a challenge, maneater. You want my 'magical' blood, and I want your luscious body. I still think we could have something meaningful." When he stepped closer, a larger drop of water caught her attention as it coursed down his chest, dipping between tattoos along his rigid torso.

When her focus wandered lower, taking in the places she'd kill to bite, he shifted on his feet. Before her eyes, the sizable bulge beneath his towel swelled.

She'd seen an outline of his member in his leather breeches, but the clinging towel revealed the edge of the crown and even— she swallowed thickly—a prominent vein. As she stared, her tongue flicked her parted lips, her fangs sharpening. . . .

"Kosmina?" His rumbling voice only fueled her stimulation. "Let's make another bargain: my blood for your kiss."

I want it from the tap. Want to punish that taunting vein. Fang it like prey.

No! That must be the plague rabidity, invading her thoughts and impulses.

More laughter sounded from his room, reminding her what a rogue he was. It'd taken him less than an hour to locate an orgy. She met his eyes. "Right now, I'd rather bargain with Dorada." Mina turned and headed away, sensing his gaze locked on her back until she'd passed from his sight.

Jealousy scalded her as she imagined him heading back into his room to find pleasure with others. *My first experience with jealousy.* Even when she'd pondered Kristoff and Furie's matehood, Mina had never felt it.

Her illogical emotions made her both wary and furious. She had an urge to go retrieve the sorcerer by his ear! But she reminded herself of what she truly wanted.

Love. Given and received.

An impossibility with Silt, and so she would waste no more thought on him. She descended the stairs, averting her eyes from a foursome kissing on the steps. On the main floor, she passed a den of wild-eyed demons playing dice. She wasn't versed in gambling beyond the theoretical, but they all seemed to be winning with every roll. In the next salon over, more demons drank from mugs and sang songs in rough Demonish.

She suspected most of the guests possessed wings; they could just fly over the lava and wendigos to land here.

"Wait, Kosmina!"

Mina turned to see Silt striding after her. Masking her surprise, she paused to let him catch up. He must've left those females directly and raced to join her. She curbed a thrill at the idea and took in his appearance.

He'd donned a pair of leather pants to encase his muscled legs. His tailored tunic, cut from a golden fabric, highlighted the expanse of his chest, his broad shoulders, and the color of his eyes. His air was commanding, a sorcerer king ready for whatever fate had in store.

Any woman would be proud to call such a male her own. Well, any woman who didn't know him. "What do you want?"

His lips parted and closed, as if he struggled to voice his thoughts. *No idea what that feels like!*

Though filling the silence wasn't her forte, she said, "You left your party *prematurely.* I understand that's common among some men."

"Heh. I sent those females on their way. Untouched, if you must know."

Thrill. Damn him. "Why?"

He lowered his voice. "Maybe because I need you." They stared into each other's eyes, the air between them charged.

She could pretend his words were romantic, but he only *needed* her to trap her brother. Silt had told her she had no idea how important revenge was to him; she was beginning to understand. Vengeance took precedence even over sex. "I won't let you use me—in any way. That's what you do, isn't it?"

"You'd never regret it." Somewhere in the castle, a female screamed her way to ecstasy. Then came another, literally. "That could be you, sweet."

She might have been tempted to kiss him again—if he hadn't made that vow to the Lore. "Considering everything you know about me now, would you make your same vow?" What if he said no? What if he said he'd been out of his mind with withdrawal symptoms and was sorry for it? It wouldn't change anything.

He ran a hand over his mouth. "It's complicated. You know how I feel about revenge, but you don't know why. And I have been wronged—though I'd never met your brother before, he put me in Nightside and stuck a target on my back, for what sounds like a joke to him."

"No target could be bigger than the one you put on yourself. Instead of working on revenge—you should be working on your powers. Make your foes too afraid to challenge you."

"It's not that simple."

Voices sounded from what must be the dining hall, reminding Mina of what lay before her. Bottom line: this male was oathbound. Why was she even talking to him? She started forward without another word, and he followed.

She would be polite to Enti to a point, following the sorceress's lead, but ultimately Mina would get the information she wanted. Considering she couldn't extract it at swordpoint, that might prove a delicate dance.

Shyness squeaked, *But you've got two left feet, especially around crowds.*

Mina straightened her shoulders. *So?*

She remembered when her uncle Trehan had decided to depart the kingdom for good to court his otherlander sorceress. At the time, that had meant he would be forbidden ever to return. Grieving, secretly longing for just such an exile scenario for herself, Mina had told him, "Do you want to hear something sad? Your leaving is the most exciting thing that's ever happened in my life."

No longer. Mina had survived wendigos, a basilisk, revenants, and a sorcerer's sinful kiss.

This dinner would be as nothing.

TWENTY-FIVE

Hostility bounced between Silt and the princess as they entered an opulent banquet room.

Seemed Kosmina was all out of patience with him. He mused darkly, *If I'm not careful, she might even try to decapitate me.*

Flickering chandeliers cast light over the roughly two dozen immortals seated along a lengthy table. Most were winged demons or shifters.

Lustful gazes swept over Silt—understandable, because he looked good.

Kosmina's elegant beauty drew just as many gazes, and her bearing screamed *royalty*, reminding him that she was far out of his reach. He might be the ruler of sand, but that was a powerless scepter at present. Resentment simmered.

"Our new guests!" Enti called from the end of the table, her ivory mask highlighting her fuchsia eyes. Her dinner dress was typical sorceress garb—revealing and heavy with gold. "Welcome to Princess Kosmina of Dacia and Silt Harea, the King of Sand. See, everyone? I told you more guests would come." Had that been under debate? She indicated two seats to her left. "Please."

Kosmina raised her chin and waited for Silt to pull out her chair.

"Do you figure me for a gentleman or a servant?" He sat, leaving her standing. "I'm neither."

She gazed skyward with a sigh, then took her seat. "Thank you, Enti, for your hospitality."

The sorceress gave them a warm smile. "It's my pleasure, princess." She gestured to a siren beside her. "This is Pearl, my right-hand woman around the castle. She inspired our boiling sea."

Pearl nodded civilly. She wore a crown of shells atop her chestnut hair, her hazel eyes kohled. A voice-box modulator collared her throat, standard for Sirenae. Without it, Pearl's raised voice or song would enthrall every unmated male within hearing range, a problematic ability sirens rarely used.

"And beside her is Xodin." Enti indicated a winged demon next to Pearl who inclined his horned head in greeting. "He's in charge of security. He's relatively new here but very capable. The rest you'll come to meet in time." In old Sorselan, she told Silt, "I trust you found everything"—she cast him a meaningful glance—"to your liking."

He answered in the same, "I did. My thanks."

Her little frown told him she knew he hadn't slept with the females she'd sent. When Enti murmured, "Sometimes what we dream of isn't actually what we need," he commanded himself not to look at Kosmina.

So the sorceress was attracted to the sorcerer. Did he reciprocate?

The owner of Castle Vitis was ravishing, with the kind of smile that made others vie to provoke it, just to be dazzled. And seeing another of his kind, one who spoke his native tongue no less, must be heartening. *This entire place would be*, Mina thought as servants delivered dishes.

The Queen of Dreams offered abundance, all with that beaming smile. He would surely want to bed her.

Switching to English, Enti asked him, "No mask?" A server set a platter of roasted vegetables before her.

"I only wear them when in pursuit or battle, like the Sorceri hunters of old."

"I see," she said evenly. Yet Mina got the impression that Enti considered his lack of a mask some kind of Sorceri gaffe.

Another server approached to pour blood into Mina's golden chalice. The sight of crimson across gold brought to mind the sorcerer's nectar and burnished gaze. She feared all feeds would taste like chalk compared to him.

When he covered his own goblet to decline wine, Enti pursed her lips. "You don't want to sample the vintage? It's sweet, a Sorceri favorite."

"I try to stay sharp in new situations."

"Indeed." Another Sorceri gaffe? "I would not have guessed that about you. *At all.*"

Mina didn't sense malice in Enti, but they would be wise to keep up their guard. She scented her goblet for poisons, as Balery had taught her. Finding none, Mina sipped, then tried to hide her disappointment. Though the animal blood was of good quality, much like that in Dacia's fountains, it *did* taste like chalk next to the sorcerer's.

Had she enjoyed Silt's so much because he was her first taste of an immortal—or because he was exactly to her liking?

He studied her expression with a smirk. "Not as *magical* as mine, is it, princess?"

How to answer without the *rána's* burn? "No. But it doesn't bray afterward about how good it tastes, so on balance"—she made a weighing gesture with her hands—"it's preferred."

Nearby diners laughed, and Enti and Mina shared a look of mirth.

Silt's glower was priceless.

In a casual tone, Mina asked the sorceress, "From where do you hail?" as if she'd never struggled to voice a thought. If she found a cure for the plague and removed herself from all danger, would her awkwardness return?

"I was born in the mortal realm ages ago," Enti said. "Before Nightside, I've made my home across all the worlds, as far as the Elserealms."

"That sounds exciting," said the sheltered vampire. *Previously* sheltered. "I'd like to see the Elserealms one day."

A pall seemed to settle over those seated near her. So everyone already knew about her malady? *Gods above, I'm not rabid yet!*

A platter appeared before Silt, breaking the moment. He inhaled its aroma, and his lids went heavy. "Desert-deer venison. My compliments, sorceress. With a power such as yours, I'm surprised books haven't been written about you."

"They *have*, but bookshops don't abound in Poly, and tales of my exploits haven't reached that dimension yet."

A beat of a pause with a micro frown. "News of the Lore is often delayed in exile."

Mina had been learning how to decipher the sorcerer, and his pause told her much. He was trying to remember something about this sorceress but couldn't bring it to the surface.

Silt Harea was a fascinating subject of study, especially now that his behavior had changed so much. Despite the tension at the table and the uncertainty of their situation, he exuded . . . steadiness.

Some devilish part of her wanted to provoke him, to watch

him unravel again. *I want under his skin*, she thought, which was a new experience for her. In the past, she'd only wanted to fade into the walls of court, silent and unnoticed.

When he took his first bite of food with a pleased rumble, Mina recalled his groan as he'd thrust between her thighs and squirmed in her seat. Provoking him would earn her another kiss. Was that why the prospect tempted her?

Over the rim of her goblet, Enti said, "Not a lot of Sorceri savor meat, but then you're unique in many ways. You possess so many talents that few others can lay claim to."

Was this innuendo? Mina couldn't tell.

Currents passed between the two Sorceri. He was taking Enti's measure and seemed unsatisfied by his progress. But he remained calm. "My root power is enviable."

"In Poly, yes. Yet Xodin informs me that he's found no sand in this realm."

Silt smoothly told her, "With a wave of your hand, you could gift me some, and I'd put it in service to you."

Behind her mask, her gaze shimmered. "I'm sure we can work something out."

Usually even-tempered herself, Mina felt annoyed with the sorceress. She peered down at her arm, could sense the plague heightening her aggression.

Or perhaps Silt's focus on another had rekindled Mina's earlier jealousy. . . .

Small talk flowed as he continued to enjoy his meal while Mina sipped her own and bided her time. Prolonged food courses and vampires didn't mix. Between leisurely bites, the sorcerer seasoned the conversation with intelligent commentary.

Xodin and Pearl contributed little, hanging on Enti's every word. Were the three a throuple? Had they each preyed on humans to earn their way here?

As Mina took it all in, awareness grew between her and the sorcerer. Casual touches felt electric between them. His leg would brush hers, eliciting a shiver. A mere bump of their elbows became a crackling connection.

She couldn't decide if the plague made her feverish or if it was *him*.

Yet Silt must be feeling the same. More than once, he cast her a look of puzzlement with hooded golden eyes.

Visions of him in that towel replayed in her mind, when his length had swelled for her. What would he have done if she'd reached beneath the cloth to explore, cupping and weighing? Or if she'd knelt before him for a bite . . .

She squirmed again, endeavoring to focus on the conversation. Having gotten a taste of passion, her body wanted more. She wondered if she would get the chance to experience it with someone she cared for before madness took her. What if Enti was right and no escape existed?

Mina thought of all the places she'd never gotten to see, the adventures and family she'd hoped for; she was in a castle of dreams and hers had never been more distant. Sadness swept over her, dousing her arousal.

Seeming to detect the turn in her mood, Silt glanced over at her, gaze searching. If he discovered her thoughts, he'd probably ridicule her predicament and threaten her brother some more, staying in form.

"Princess, you've been quiet." Enti turned her full attention to Mina. "We have other delicacies and treats."

Mina wanted to treat herself—to the sorcerer's blood. So how to answer without a lie? *I'm satisfied.* No. *My thirst has been quenched.* Absolutely not. "Thank you, but I've had my fill of this blood."

Enti inclined her head. "I've learned much from you about

Dacia, a realm I thought was mythical. And now you've got an infamous new king."

Mina regretted that Enti's mind reading threatened the secrecy of her people. But then, Lothaire planned to reveal Dacia to the Lore anyway. And really, if all Dacians were so committed to observing without engagement, then how had her brother even met Caspion in the first place?

Silt had stopped eating, seeming very interested in this topic. When the server made another try for his goblet, he covered it again. "For some reason, the princess doesn't see the Enemy of Old as an enemy. Spoke highly of him."

Not true; any unwarranted praise would have burned her throat to a crisp.

Enti said, "I see that Lothaire sent you away from the safety of Dacia to observe the nymphs of New Orleans. But I can't tell if he did it merely as a jest or in a bid to get rid of another royal. What say you, princess?"

Everyone at the table quieted to listen. Mina felt her cheeks heating, her old shyness stammering a hello. *No, begone!*

Xodin, the handsome demon, cast her a flirtatious grin. "There are no secrets in this castle." He waved a clawed hand at all the food on the table. "We each pay a toll for this bounty with our confessions."

When Mina still hesitated, Pearl leaned forward, planting her elbows on the table. "Do a deep dive on her, Enti. Plumb all her depths." Spoken like a true siren.

Before Enti could learn even more about Dacia, Mina hastily said, "Lothaire sent me away because I . . . I had an unsuitable infatuation."

TWENTY-SIX

Infatuation?" Silt grated. For someone so unfamiliar with jealousy, he recognized its stranglehold immediately.

Enti's irises swirled as she read the princess's mind. "Ah, you call your crush the Ideal. With very good reason."

The *Ideal*? Silt wanted to howl. "Who is he?"

The color in Kosmina's cheeks deepened even more. "King Kristoff, the legitimate heir to the Horde throne. He is Lothaire's half brother, but no relation to me, of course."

Enti said, "I've heard of him. The Gravewalker."

Having accepted his . . . partiality to this female, Silt had never considered her heart might be set on another.

Inane thought: *Could've pulled out her godsdamned chair, Silt.*

Kosmina favored royalty; he was as far from a vampire king as he could be—the son of two Inferi. He'd been born into slavery then betrayed out of the one thing that could have delivered him from those bonds.

"It's of no matter," Kosmina said breezily. "Lothaire trundled me off before I could make a fool out of myself."

She was desperate to escape from Nightside because she needed a cure. Did she also long to return to the *Ideal*?

With a questioning look, she glanced at his hands, and he was shocked to find himself making fists. Silt didn't do jealousy. He'd always considered it a sign of insecurity or immaturity.

A wiseman had once told him, *the more sand has escaped from the hourglass of life, the clearer we should see through it.* But Silt didn't. Despite his age, he had a young man's confusions.

Desiring this vampire warred with his honed instincts. She filled him with doubt and made him think ridiculous thoughts.

Was he becoming obsessed with her?

He again commanded himself not to look at Kosmina. Didn't work this time. His gaze was already on her lovely face.

Obsessed? *Hell.* He feared that deed was done. And for what? Did the object of his desires want only another? What if the Gravewalker was her fated one . . . ?

The sorcerer beside Mina vibrated with new tension as he pointed out, "You told me a female vampire would simply *know* who her mate was."

"Yes, well, I got that one wrong." And she was obviously still far from the mark because she felt a pull toward Silt that she couldn't explain—a compelling draw, some kind of tether between them. She had scant experience in a situation like this, but she could swear he felt something deeper for her as well.

"Why do you believe it was only infatuation?" he asked.

"Because Kristoff is destined to another, and I didn't awaken his heart." *Stop getting sidetracked, Mina.* "Enough about my schoolgirl ridiculousness. I'd like to know more about Nightside. Enti, are you the only source of food and civilization?"

The sorceress clearly debated keeping her in the hot seat but relented, her irises stilling. "Yes, we're the sole source."

"How many live here in the castle?" The sounds of gambling and sex continued from all corners of the place.

"Just under fifty. Though fewer have arrived of late." Had tension stolen over the table's occupants? "Yet Xodin has scouts who fly over the realm, and they've reported two immortal males recently arrived. Maybe vampires, but the scouts had trouble seeing through the haze and geysers."

"Did one have black hair? It might be my brother!"

Silt too tensed at the possibility, his vow like a shadow over him.

Xodin shook his head. "Neither did."

Oh.

Both Mina and the sorcerer seemed to stand down.

Enti said, "Be glad your brother isn't one of them, princess. Their survival is doubtful. They got sidetracked even before the wendigo hunting ground." She added in an *it-happens* tone, "Pursued by the undead hellhounds."

"We missed those."

"To your fortune—there are few things as disturbing as their howls carrying across the wasteland. That pack was chasing the newcomers straight toward the revenants' bog. While we have a couple dozen of their ilk lying in wait outside the castle, *thousands* inhabit that bog. The two immortals will be doomed. Probably already are. Time moves differently there."

"Within the same realm?" Silt asked, sounding distracted, his smooth steadiness from before gone. "I assumed that time varied between Nightside and the mortal world, but not within a single plane."

"A week at Castle Vitis could equal a day in the wendigo hunting grounds. When poor Xodin first started flying over the realm, the time changes used to confuse him terribly." Enti patted his horns, an erogenous area in demons, and those lengths straightened as his lids grew heavy.

Well, then. Mina only drew her gaze away when she sensed Silt's eyes narrowed on her. She shrugged. Xodin was an attractive demon, and, unlike some people at this table, he'd made no murder vows against Mina's family.

Enti lowered her hand, growing serious. "Nightside is a cruel prison, which makes Castle Vitis a place of refuge. I wanted to extend a formal invitation to you both to stay here as long as you like. We can all pass our sentences . . . until the Gaolers parole us."

Silt's head swung around to the sorceress. "Parole?"

TWENTY-SEVEN

Enti smiled. "Correct. We're each to serve a minimum of five hundred years, but the Gaolers only release prisoners during an Accession. Sadly, I'll be here for half a millennium more till the next one. Yet it's not so bad."

Silt had never considered the possibility of a release! If Enti spoke the truth, then all he had to do was survive here for five centuries, and this plane wasn't much worse than Poly.

Yet Kosmina looked suspicious. "How do you know about paroles?" Despite burning to secure her "information," she'd been on her best behavior during dinner. Royal etiquette must be ingrained in her.

"When I was captured, I read the minds of the Gaolers," Enti said. "I know their intent. You earn your freedom through survival and learn your lesson never to offend again."

"I find that . . . illogical." The vampire pushed aside her goblet. Setting aside her royal socialization as well? "If the Gaolers released immortals, then every Lorean would know about this place. And what am I meant to learn since I never broke a law?"

"Unfortunately, you are in an unfair quarantine situation.

Of your other point, perhaps the Gaolers will make us forget about this place and that's why none speak of it."

"How is a lesson to be learned when the punishment is forgotten?" Were Kosmina's eyes reddening more?

"I have no idea. But the fact remains that we will be released."

Silt frowned. The sorceress sounded like a zealot, determined not to entertain contrary arguments. Still, that didn't mean her belief was wrong.

Kosmina said, "I appreciate your offer to stay, but I will continue searching for an escape."

Enti sighed. "Your plague might not progress to the end for years. You can remain here in safety, or you can court death out there or worse—for no reason."

Silt would much rather be dead than transformed. "Why are you so certain there's no escape?"

Xodin answered, "Because my demons and I searched almost every inch of Nightside looking for one. The only place we haven't explored is this realm's most deadly heart—the hive of the ghouls."

Kosmina leaned forward, as if she'd just received *good* news. "Then that's where my chance lies. Tell me about this hive."

The demon said, "It's a mountain teeming with ghouls. They dig tunnels throughout it, dumping rock all around. We don't know why."

"No one has ventured inside?"

"Whenever we get too close, their sentries spill out like a kicked ant mound."

"Silt and I contended with a legion of wendigos in unfavorable conditions," she said. "Ghouls shouldn't prove more difficult. If enough of us unite, we can take that mountain. We have strength in numbers."

Silt glanced down the table. These libertines weren't about to abandon their lair. Kosmina's drive was like a shining beacon, separating her from those who'd learned not to *dare*.

Have I *learned not to?*

Enti said, "There's one other problem. If you somehow got past the ghouls in their favored habitat, you would then face one best avoided. What do you know about the primordials?"

"A bit. They're the strongest and oldest of a species, either because they were born first or because they've outlived all others. A firstborn primordial can spawn child terrors—monsters—with their blood."

Rumor held that Sequara, Silt's scorpion, had descended from a child terror. Though she'd been a loyal creature, original child terrors were vicious, arising from a single drop of blood to defend the primordial to the death.

Kosmina asked, "Are you saying the primordial ghoul lives in that hive?"

"One of them." At her frown, Enti explained, "Everyone thinks that the ghoul king of the mortal realm was the primordial of that species, but he shared an egg with his queen and mate. She rules Nightside's hive."

"Twin primordials," Kosmina murmured, deep in thought. "So who laid the egg? Wouldn't *that* be the primordial?"

Silt had to say it: "We're debating which came first, the ghoul or the egg?"

Enti shrugged. "There's no debate. When I read the Gaolers' minds, I learned that all of our immortal species were seeded by gods. The answer of all answers: the egg came first."

Silt raised his brows. "So who created the gods?" Perhaps with her mind-reading ability, she'd come across that information. The Gaolers might have known.

"No idea. Nor do I know who created the worlds. That line

of thinking will drive you either to insanity or religion. Like the hive's primordial, it's best avoided."

Her advice got his back up. Avoid certain thinking? Yet hadn't he done that through his habit?

While he processed this new and startling information, Kosmina's focus was in full force. "Can we get back to the topic of the hive? Chiefly, an incursion into it?"

Xodin's wings fluttered against his chair. "My demonkind and I will pass on any incursion. We'll be here, enjoying the perks"—he raised his mug of demon brew—"until the Gaolers return for us with a parole in hand. You should stay here as long as you can, princess."

Enti tilted her head at Kosmina's undeterred expression. "The prospect of facing the mother of all ghouls—who can spawn even more and varied monsters—doesn't give you pause?"

The princess lifted her chin. "My uncle Trehan killed the primordial demon in a bloodsport contest, without creating a single child terror. Part of my sword training was under his tutelage." Her uncanny eyes glittered with determination. "I like my odds."

Pride swelled Silt's chest. *Fascinating female.* Still, that didn't mean he was going to head out with her and share those odds. For argument's sake, he asked, "Enti, how many are we talking about in that mountain? Do you have an estimate?"

"We do. If I could convince everyone here to fight, the ghouls would outnumber us a thousand to one."

Even Kosmina's confidence appeared to take a hit. Then she rallied: "The seismic activity here is unmistakable, and the quakes are intensifying. Our choices are simple—fight or perish."

Enti adjusted her mask. "It's just a cycle. Nightside is a world still in the throes of birth."

"Or death."

"I've been here for a century. The realm always quiets. I understand why you would want to leave—and I'm sympathetic—but others don't feel such pressure."

Silt didn't. A parole offered him hope he hadn't felt in memory. No more exile in Poly. No more hunters breathing down his neck. Hell, he could behold his Sorselan oasis once more.

Kosmina glanced at him, then back to Enti. "I will take my shot."

"Very well," the sorceress said. "If you give me a list of provisions in the morning, I can try to outfit you, and we will wish you all the luck in the worlds." She turned to Silt. "What about you? Will you continue on with your travel companion?"

Leaving this place would be lunacy. But if Kosmina was set on going, he couldn't force her to stay. He'd have to send her on her hopeless way.

Forgo her. Forgo revenge. Break the chain of pain.

The idea felt like reaching for a handful of sand and gripping ash instead. The only other option would be to follow her. He stared at Kosmina's resolute gaze. *Something mysterious binds us.* "I will—" A scent hit him, and his muscles went rigid.

Demons had retired to a nearby balcony to share a pipe. Smoke slithered up from the bowl, curling in the still air like a viper's trail over sand. "Stay." Silt cleared his throat. "I will stay." Not because he planned to relapse, but because he simply didn't share Kosmina's urgent need to leave.

The princess flashed him a look of confusion, but what else could she expect? Revenge couldn't outweigh survival.

"Then we should welcome you to your new home in style, sorcerer," Enti purred. "Perhaps with an after-dinner smoke? Our opium is the finest in all the worlds."

He'd decided not to let down his guard near another

powerful Sorceri. A decision had been made. But one small inhalation didn't mean instant ruin.

Fucking does! A hit would turn into oblivion, and he knew it.

In a challenging tone, the princess asked, "Yes, Silt, will you smoke?"

He narrowed his eyes. He'd been proud of matching wits with her. He'd been proud of the erection he'd thrust while cradled between her soft thighs. Opium would rob him once more.

But could he remain here for his entire sentence and never falter again? How else would he pass the years? Maybe he ought to follow the princess to the gallows—

More smoke wafted over him. It wove a tapestry in his brain, promising to temper all his unfamiliar emotions—so many of them centering on the vampire.

Just one taste. To find my footing . . .

Though he hadn't answered, Kosmina looked disappointed in him. She rose and told Enti, "Thank you again. I'll draw up a weapon plan tonight, and we'll talk more tomorrow."

"Of course. Sleep well, princess. Ring the servants if you need anything."

Silt stared at the doorway long after she'd strode out of sight. Then he turned back to face yet another threat within Nightside.

Himself.

TWENTY-EIGHT

So I'm going to die even sooner than I expected.

Mina's shoulders fell once she'd exited the banquet hall. She'd disguised her anxiety about her future in front of the others, even when it felt like tiny needles stabbed her chest from the inside.

Her options were all dire. Disaster awaited her in the ghoul queen's hive. Should Mina somehow survive without being turned—and escape Nightside—then a barter with Dorada awaited her.

No, Mina could never surrender her freedom to that sorceress. So without the wishgiver, how long would she have to search the worlds for a cure?

How long?

How long?

What if she escaped this place only to become a danger to those in the mortal realm? The tiny needles were back in force. Seeking comfort, she reached for her sword but grasped air.

Maybe *she* should embrace the mindlessness on tap here. As soon as the thought occurred, she grew ashamed. In fact, she felt as if she'd betrayed the sorcerer by leaving him behind—as if she'd abandoned a wounded ally in hostile territory.

The feeling confused her. His impairment could only help her protect Mirceo. And more, she *liked* Enti and her crew. If they needed pleasure-seeking and parole fairy tales to get through the nights, then maybe Mina shouldn't judge them.

A sudden vibration rumbled beneath her feet. Surely, she couldn't be the only one concerned about these quakes.

When she reached the stairs, the foursome on the steps had escalated their pursuits in number, nudity, and intensity. She veered around the growing orgy, trying to ignore them, but the desperation in their touches struck her. She *wasn't* the only one concerned. They sensed this place was on borrowed time, yet they didn't dare fight for a different ending to their story.

Hampered by fear and ruled by pleasure. She pitied those immortals, thought them tragic, but if they met her halfway, she would help them.

She'd just made it to her door when footsteps sounded behind her. With his broad shoulders back, a sober Silt strode down the corridor.

Relief swept through her, but she made her tone bored. "I thought you'd be imbibing."

"Maybe I'm just enough of a contrarian prick to walk away. Of course, the night's young."

"When we were outside this castle, you smelled the drug from afar, didn't you? That's why you hesitated to come here."

He gave a shrug that belied how conflicted he'd been. The fact that this sorcerer *desired* to change made her heart twist. "If you truly don't want to smoke again, what do you think will happen here? And if you give in, then another Sorceri could take your root power from you."

"That's true, but I doubt anyone wants it. As you've

noted—repeatedly—my ability suffers, and sand sorcery is hardly an asset when there's none around."

"You need to leave this castle. Just keep moving. I can tell the cravings are gripping you even as we speak."

He stabbed his fingers through his hair. "Because without smoke everything is . . . askew. Everything feels jagged and raw." He looked more frustrated than she'd seen him, even over the last few days as they'd faced such hardships. And he peered hard at her—as if *she* were the source of his struggles.

Was he feeling more for her? Her attraction to him refused to fade. What would have happened if they'd met under different circumstances?

"Enough about this," he said. "I want to know if you're seriously considering an incursion."

"Planning one as if my life depends on it. Have you changed your mind about going?" Her hopeful tone embarrassed her. But he *had* saved her life. At times, their partnership had worked—

"Not a chance."

Good, she rushed to assure herself. His staying in Nightside would defuse the danger he posed. Unless Mirceo showed up here.

"Vampire, as I said before, if an escape existed, then those ghouls would have overrun the mortal realm."

"Maybe the exit requires a toll—like a blood sacrifice or reciting an incantation—that the ghouls aren't sentient enough to understand. No matter, I'll soon find out."

"You're not short on courage, are you?" This seemed to trouble him. "With a sword from Enti, you can get through those revenants outside the castle, maybe even a number of ghouls in their hive, but a primordial—one that must not bleed—is going to prove tricky. How did your uncle kill one anyway?"

Since an arena full of Loreans had watched Trehan's match,

Mina saw no reason not to tell Silt about it. "He stole a magical scythe with a flaming blade from the Vrekeners, then got a mystic to superpower it. The blade's unnatural heat cauterized as it sliced, preventing blood loss."

Silt looked impressed. "Good for him. The Vrekeners are no friends to my kind."

That demonic clan had long punished Sorceri for magic outlays, had even attacked Bettina. "I'm going to ask Enti if she can create a similar scythe for me. When I leave, I go to war—I'm going to give myself the best chance of winning it."

"And if there's no escape? Just because the mountain is unexplored doesn't mean it holds what you seek."

"Then I'll die fighting, won't I?"

His gaze flicked over her face, as if he were reading an indecipherable text. "I can understand your drive—you have no choice—but others will never follow you."

"Because they believe in the parole myth, and they want to believe Nightside will endure. It's easier that way. But if they dug deeper"—*if* you *dug deeper*—"they'd understand they don't have a choice either. This ship *is* sinking. The swim is long. The more we hesitate, the farther away the shore is getting."

His brows drew together, his gaze fierce. "Are you even real?" he murmured as his hand shot out to grasp the back of her neck. "Your will is glittering sand. I wish I could steal it like a Sorceri power." He dragged her closer and leaned his head down.

"Exercise your own will, and you can have the same." She leaned up, helplessly drawn to him. "Sorcerer, what do you want from me?"

Bafflement crossed his face. "I fucking do not know. All I know is that our kiss was not enough." He grazed his lips across hers, the slight contact sparking a bombardment of pleasure.

Not enough? On this . . . I agree.

Maybe she should enjoy a bit of play with him—up to a point—before she departed. *Before I am departed.* Another graze of his lips convinced her. She gripped his shoulders and squeezed to encourage him. *I won't let it go further.*

Between kisses, he reached behind her and opened the door to her room. They stumbled inside, and he managed to close them in.

He pressed her against the closest wall, nuzzling and licking her neck until her head fell back, offering him more flesh to taste. "I think you've been sent into my life to torment me." He tongued her pulse point, sucking it with a groan.

She moaned, her senses drinking him in like blood down her throat. His scent. His voice. The heat from his body. "And you've been sent to madden me."

He was only getting started. He reached for her tingling breasts, fondling them.

"Yes!" She arched to his touch, shimmying for more contact.

Against her neck, he rasped, "I've wanted to play with these since I saw them bouncing in your wet T-shirt. I crossed a wasteland as hard as granite for you."

She tried to marshal her thoughts enough to speak. "You look good in a towel." *So sexy, Mina.*

He gave a rough laugh, a puff of air against her damp skin. "Admit it, you've wanted your hand on my cock since you saw me half-dressed earlier. You wanted to stroke me. Suck me."

His spicy language shocked and aroused her. She couldn't lie. "During dinner, I pictured scenarios."

He tweaked her nipples with light plucks that nearly put her on the ceiling. "Did you, then? Had my own imaginings." One of his hands descended past her navel to the waist of her pants. He held her gaze, a question in his eyes.

Her throbbing nipples urged her to nod.

He eased his hand into her pants, into the heat of her silk panties. "Will I find you wet, princess?"

Yes! Even as her hips wantonly rolled, misgivings arose. "I shouldn't allow this."

"Should. I'm going to bring you off hard, make you wonder how you've lived without me."

Could he? She breathlessly admitted, "I-I *am* in need of climax."

Pained chuckle. "I'll take care of you, sweet." He flicked his tongue against her throat as he strummed her jutting nipples, and reason fled. Lodging his knee against the wall, he hooked her leg over it, parting her to his hand. He cupped her sex and groaned, "So *wet*. Gods, you please me." Her soaked flesh blossomed against his hot hand.

Lost, she nodded and moaned, "Take care of me . . . bring me off."

"You need this as badly as I do!" Clever fingers played with her arousal, spreading it all around.

Those caresses weren't enough. She shifted, undulating to get his touch on her needy clitoris.

Yet he centered on her entrance. "I want inside you. Want my cock . . . *here*." His finger inched into her channel, delivering revelations of pleasure—sensations only hinted at when she'd touched herself alone in bed. "*Tight*. Are you a virgin, Kosmina?"

"Guh . . ." The sultry pressure made her head loll. "I . . . yes . . . *yes* . . ."

With his other hand, he clasped her nape to keep their gazes locked. "I want it. I want your innocence. You're going to give it to me."

The fog cleared enough for her to say, "N-no. Just touching. And I'm rethinking that as I speak—"

He rubbed her bud, stealing her words more than shyness

ever had. She jolted in his arms, nearing the precipice.

But he kept her there, returning his attention to her entrance. "So close to coming for me. Let me inside you." He slowly thrust that finger into her channel, mimicking sex. "You need me filling this, the hungry core of you."

She bucked on his hand. "Go back to where you were! Just a little more . . ."

"You'll have what you want. For now." He pumped his finger, grinding his palm against her clitoris. The tension mounted, sharpening to a diamond point.

Just as a frisson of fear arose—how much pleasure could she withstand?—she reached the very brink.

Teetering . . . resisting . . . wanting this to last forever . . .

"That's it. Let it happen, princess."

His voice broke her, broke the wave. She toppled over into rapture. Each slippery clench around his finger wrenched another cry from her lungs. *"Ahhh . . . ahh . . . Silt!"* Her head thrashed against the wall as ecstasy overwhelmed her.

"You're coming for me so good." At her sensitive ear, he said, "I feel you. You'll grip my cock like that, won't you?"

"Ah! I would," she breathed, out of her mind. "I'll take you so deep inside me."

"Each squeeze drags me further under your spell. That's it, beautiful." Once he'd wrung every molecule of bliss from her, he rested his forehead against hers. While he played with her climax, she caught her breath and tried to recover cognition.

A satisfied sigh had just left her lips when his other hand yanked at the opening of his pants. "Wh-what are you doing?"

"What do you think?" His jaw muscles bulged, his lips thinned. "If a dripping-wet vampire needs me deep inside her, then that's where I want to be."

Mina's body tightened at the thought of sex with Silt, his

penis entering her as he caressed her face and murmured adoring words. She pictured the two of them making love like the couple in the clearing.

But it wouldn't be like that. With him, it would *never* be like that.

No thanks.

"This is going to be mine." Silt cupped her, giving a shudder when her orgasm soaked his palm. *"Mine."* That word sounded foreign on his lips.

Gold was his. Revenge. But never another person.

No one belonged to him, and he belonged to no one.

He had those thoughts even as he hovered on the edge of coming, even as he wrestled to drag his pants down with one hand. This innocent vampire with her tender kiss had done something to him, making him feel like he'd been hexed with a desire spell.

"Wait." She tugged his hand away and twisted from him. "I don't want more."

"If you're worried about someone like me getting a babe on you, I have this, remember?" He flashed his cuff.

"That's not it."

"Then what? You might not know this, but your immortal body's just getting started."

"*We* aren't." She finally met his gaze, appearing disgusted with herself.

That look sent him right back to thousands of years ago, when females had never wanted anything beyond a fuck. Probably because he'd had nothing more to offer. He'd been just a befouler.

"This was a mistake."

"A *mistake.*" He wanted to rage. "Where have I heard that

before?" What would it take to find someone who didn't regret more with him? For once, he wanted a female in his bed who looked damned happy to be there—with no gold or transaction between them. Roiling inside, he fastened his breeches over his still hard shaft.

"Before you followed me up here, I'd been processing certain facts," she said. "Any distraction would have appealed at the time."

"You realized you're going to die, and so you decided to slum it with the sorcerer?"

"In a moment of weakness, I succumbed to someone I should detest."

He sneered, "Someone you came hard for."

"I see what this is. I learned from watching the nymphs that males can attach strings to sex acts. I'm glad I didn't allow this to go further."

"*Males* attach the strings?"

"Yes. Considering how we've both reacted to this touch of pleasure, our joining would be fiery and life-changing. You would never want to let me go, and that, sorcerer, would be a problem."

The nerve of this leech! "I've had some *fiery joinings* in my long existence, and never have I attached anything, much less strings." He was like sand—impossible to pin down, escaping any confines. Yet this arrogant waif thought he would change for her?

A part of him whispered, *She's aroused you like nothing before. Careful.* "Over and over, I've met your type. Thinking you're better than I am, but in the end, we're all just animals looking to scratch an itch."

"I've never met your particular type, and I hope I never will again."

Cruel laugh. "The odds of that are good, princess."

She exhaled a small gasp.

Low, Silt. Even for him. But her contempt got his back up.

In a quiet voice that somehow rang with strength, she said, "You—so rich in years and having squandered so many—continue to mock my likely death." She softly added, "You don't worship revenge, *Silt.* You revere grievances from the past, because you have even less of a future to look forward to than I have—and you know it."

He pointed his finger at her, about to unleash his frustration.

But the denial wouldn't come.

Seething, he gave her his back and stalked across the hall into his room, fighting the urge to destroy everything in sight. He paced, cursing the day he'd met that princess. His cock remained an iron bar of pain.

Another bath might help. He would call for the attendants, get this taken care of. Yet even now they didn't tempt him. He hungered for only one thing.

Her. Kosmina Daciano.

He *was* obsessed.

Head still swimming from their encounter, he glanced down at his hand, and his gaze narrowed. The scent of her orgasm lingered on his palm. His length flared even harder, his body strung tight for her.

He brought his hand to his face to inhale her essence, his lids growing heavy. Covering his mouth, he . . . licked.

His eyes rolled back in his head. *Sand almighty, yes.*

With a muffled growl, he shoved his pants to his knees. He gripped himself with his free hand and almost spilled from the contact.

Shuddering, he cleaned his palm to the fantasy of tonguing her entrance . . . sucking her plump little clit . . . eating her till she came on his lips and her tight core squeezed. . . .

As her taste filled his senses, he fucked his fist, his cock burning from his callouses. *So good. So good.* He wanted to edge himself and wallow in this, but a merciless pressure mounted.

He dropped his hand from his mouth, readying to catch his seed. With a stifled roar against his shoulder, he spurted one heavy jet after another into his palm to mingle with the last remnants of her orgasm. . . .

Body gone limp, he collapsed back on a couch. Legs sprawled and mind thunderstruck, he caught his breath.

The fuck was that? He must've forgotten how good a sober release could feel.

But if he were honest—he really wasn't—he'd admit that ejaculation had been the most explosive he'd ever known.

How? He hadn't even taken her!

And yet.

He cast a scowl in her direction, confused as ever. Even post-release clarity wasn't working for him. Clarity was in short supply all around.

As he washed off, he glanced down in disbelief. He'd hardened again. Hating Kosmina for that, seething with some foreign feeling of wrath, he left his room and charged downstairs to do what he should have done as soon as Enti had offered him all the delights in Nightside.

TWENTY-NINE

"Good morning, Enti!" As the clock struck ten, Mina delivered sketches and a description of her dream weapon to the sorceress. She'd already gone down twice to find her, but few had been awake. The stair orgy had still been at it, which had made Mina worry about their poor backs.

Blinking at the stack of papers, Enti sipped coffee with her mask askew, looking like she too had enjoyed a long night of leisure. "*Is* it good? And is it *morning*? I suppose we'll have to take the clock's word for it."

Bleary-eyed guests now milled in the dining hall. Once they'd recovered from their excesses, Mina would question them all, digging for more details about Nightside. She'd expected to see Silt sooner or later, but he wasn't eating, nor was he among the smokers on the balcony.

She still couldn't believe what had happened between her and the sorcerer last night. And he'd expected to take her fully! Though Mina had made decisions about her future, she'd been about to throw everything away in the heat of desire.

Enti skimmed the first page with a yawn.

Mina herself had experienced a fitful sleep. Dreams of making love to Silt had besieged her. Yet then those dreams had turned into nightmares of stalking him, slamming him to the ground, and piercing his neck.

She'd awakened with her fangs buried into her wrist, her blood covering the sheets and filling her mouth. Gods help her, she'd still been able to taste his crimson spicing her own. With the shimmer of magic heating her body, she'd climaxed from one graze of a blood-drenched finger.

Yes, indistinguishable lust and bloodlust was a red-eyed vampire's trait; the plague continued to gain ground within her. The sorceress had said she might have years, but Mina no longer believed that.

Enti blinked up at her and said, "You want me to create a scythe with mystically cauterizing heat?" She blew out a breath. "It's awfully early to be thinking about complex weapons, is it not?"

The ship is sinking, and no one can feel the water rushing in. "Do you think you can do it?"

"I will try, princess."

"Try? You derive power from delivering dreams, right? This is mine."

"And I'll do my best." She adjusted her mask. "But it could take some time."

Mina's least plentiful resource.

"In the interim . . ." Enti waved her hand, and a sword and scabbard appeared at Mina's side.

She unsheathed her new weapon, a curved sword of polished metal. "Dacian steel. I'm impressed, dream weaver." She tried not to get too excited. As easily as the sword had appeared, it could disappear. Though she liked Enti, Mina didn't trust the sorceress, not even a little.

"Perhaps practicing with that will occupy you until I can get back to you on the scythe."

"Thank you." Mina planned to drink her fill of the blood available here while training her body, getting as strong as possible for her next mission. Yet even as she thought of strength, she succumbed to weakness, glancing around for a glimpse of Silt.

He'd probably bedded down with another female—or females—in his room.

The pain in Mina's heart couldn't be ignored any longer. She tried to convince herself she suffered from another wayward infatuation. But she knew it was more.

Defying all sense, she'd . . . developed feelings for Silt. Undeniable ones.

Yet he held no real regard for her. Only lust. And she could never have him anyway, because of something he'd said in the spur of the moment.

"Looking for the sorcerer?" Enti asked.

Even if Mina could lie, the sorceress would see the truth. "Yes. I have an interest in him, one that must never pass beyond *interest*." Just because she had certain feelings didn't mean she would act on them.

"Wise. A trifling between a sorcerer and a vampire could never become more."

Though Mina had no intention of *trifling* further with Silt, she pointed out, "Our species aren't natural enemies." Not like Kristoff and Furie would be. "One of my uncles wed a sorceress and is overjoyed by the union."

"She must be the exception. My kind don't seem to form lasting attachments outside of our own. And of course, we don't have a fated mate." Most immortal species mated for life. Not so with the Sorceri. "If a vampire female like you accepted Silt in your heart, you would for life. Yet in time he would stray, devastating you."

Yes. Exactly.

"So what will you do, friend?" Enti asked.

Was this girl-talk? Mina was unsure, having never done it. As ever, she wished her mother had lived and that they'd been close. They could have bonded over blood tea, her mother sharing womanly wisdom.

Mina had a mysterious aunt she might have talked to, a princess Lothaire dismissively referred to as *the sixth cousin*, but the poor vampiress was a shut-in who never left her wing. No girl-talk for Mina there.

She'd thought about discussing males and such with Ellie and Balery. But revealing her disastrous crush to them would've come with pitying looks—much like the one Enti was giving her now.

"No devastation for me," Mina said firmly. "At least, not from him. I envision other things for my future."

"Do you? Let's see." The sorceress read her mind, her irises appearing to spin. "You dream of what that couple experienced in a moonlit clearing. What a sight. I wish I could give that to you. Hell, I wish I could give it to *me*," she said with a sigh. "You refuse to settle for anything less than devotion. And, princess, I don't blame you."

"No, I won't settle, especially not for someone who vowed to kill my brother." She was almost thankful for his rash words— if not for them, she would do something ruinous like fall completely and utterly for Silt Harea.

Enti parted her lips to say something, then must've thought better of it. "Yes, he did. By collecting that bounty, Mirceo crossed a powerful Lorean. I remember the first time I saw Silt's wanted poster. I had the thought that he would prove a formidable outlaw to meet."

An outlaw sorcerer. Mina almost groaned. Her taste in males wanted refinement.

And more, her focus needed work. She should be concentrating on survival—not golden-eyed enchanters. "When Xodin explored the realm, did he map his findings?"

"Meticulously. He can show you detailed renderings of the dimension. He'll rise soon enough."

"Thank you. I'll reconvene with you on this"—Mina tapped the papers on the table—"later today."

Enti raised her brows. "Checking on my progress? You're lucky I like you, vampire."

Mina cast her a wink over her shoulder, which made the sorceress chuckle.

Yet as Mina walked away, vibrations shivered beneath her feet. She turned back a last time and found Enti with a studiously benign look on her face. But perspiration dotted her upper lip. . . .

THIRTY

*F*uck sand." Silt exhaled a frustrated breath, returning his new grains to the pouch on his belt.

Enti had gifted him pure quartz the other night, and he'd spent these last three "days"—or whatever this time period might be—alone in his room, training with it like some absurd Sorceri monk.

Training. Almost as if he were leaving.

Which he was not.

So why had he made Enti promise to alert him if Kosmina left? Why would it matter if the princess departed on a whisper?

He had no answers, his mental state worse than when he'd smoked himself into oblivion. Despite practicing with his favorite medium, he hadn't reconnected to it, unable to think of anything but that vampire.

He'd kept looking at his palm. Replaying the feel of Kosmina. Her *taste*.

Silt couldn't escape her, not even in sleep. Whenever he managed to doze off, he'd been visited by feverish reveries of her feeding from him. More than once, his dreams had turned wet—

he'd awakened to his own groans as hot semen had spurted over his torso.

Only one thing to do: convince the princess to stay here with him for a time. He could bed her and get her out of his system. She was a novelty; all novelties lost luster eventually.

He headed to her room, determined. His crude attempt at seduction the other night had only gotten him so far. He was no charmer—unusual for a sorcerer—but females weren't immune to him. He could close this one. And if she still proved ungettable, he had a card to play.

He raised his hand to knock but hesitated. All was quiet. Was she resting or downstairs among the libertines? Hastening to the stairs, he ignored the ongoing orgy on the steps, though they reached for him and moaned his name.

Looks uncomfortable to me. They reminded him of the quicksand traps he used to position on well-trod paths, ever ready to snare the unwary.

He passed the manic gambling in the dens and the decadent spreads of confections. Immortals gobbled up food as if it were about to run out. Gorging, gambling, and orgies—were these the dreams of demons and shifters? He supposed so.

He didn't find the princess in his search of the castle. A young vampire like her would probably be asleep now, during this "day." So he meandered to an unoccupied balcony, in no mood for other company. Gazing out over the boiling sea, he prickled with misery.

Sober. Antsy from the smoke that clung to every corner of this place. Halfway hard for a vampire he hadn't seen in days.

The princess I'm obsessed with, who haunts even my dreams.

Without his usual shroud of dragon's breath, his thoughts were too piercing, and all of them centered on Kosmina. Time passed—he had no idea how much without a moon, a sun, or stars. Still no sign of her.

Though everything in his demeanor said *back off,* Enti and Pearl approached him at the railing. The sorceress looked tired. "We despaired of seeing you again. You and the vampire both cloistered yourselves. Antisocial, if you ask me."

"She hasn't been down?"

"No, she's been taking blood in her room and getting updates on the weapon there." In a conspiratorial tone, Enti said, "Our princess isn't a fan of some of the more lascivious scenes on display. That first morning, she questioned our guests about the realm and the Gaolers, but few were sober enough to give her any information. Or they were only interested in sleeping with her, making her promises in exchange for a place in her bed."

He cast a murderous glance in the direction of the banquet hall, wondering which ones had propositioned her. The stair orgy alone . . .

"Now, now, sorcerer," Pearl said with a laugh. "Remember, no violence is allowed in the castle." At his look, she said, "I don't have to be a mind reader to interpret that scowl."

"No violence planned." *Liar.*

Enti waved to a nearby table. "Sit for a moment?"

No, he didn't want company, but he also didn't want to cross this female unnecessarily. Silt had doubts about her, like a vague memory that wouldn't surface. So he sank down into a chair. "What?"

"I feel like I'm failing in my duty as a hostess." Enti signaled to a passing wine bearer, who hastened over with a bottle and three goblets. The buxom female poured, failing to elicit more than an indifferent glance from Silt before she sashayed away.

This clearly puzzled Enti. "I'm supposed to make your dreams come true, yet I know you're more unhappy than you've ever been. Your pacing would have worn a hole in the carpet of your room had I not used sorcery to repair it," she added pointedly.

Even after his parents' treachery, he hadn't been this miserable. Revenge whispered, *Because I gave you hope. Will you abandon me?*

Enti's eyes appeared to swirl as she read his mind. "Have you set aside your quest for vengeance?"

To break the hallowed chain of pain? "It's complicated." His answer of the week.

Revenge had made him chase Kosmina across Nightside. It'd spurred him to barrel headlong into a pack of wendigos and made him fight to save her from drowning.

But what if it *hadn't* been revenge? Chills erupted over his skin. What if all along it was . . . some kind of connection?

"Have you changed your mind as well about going with her?" Enti asked.

No matter how much Kosmina affected him, she wouldn't be worth dying over. "I'll never follow her into that hive."

Relief flickered over Enti's expression. "Yes, I can see that now. Sometimes reading you is difficult." She tapped her temple and said, "Everything inside that head of yours seems conflicted."

Apparently. Self-reflection must not be his strong suit—he felt unpracticed with it. The investigation into *Silt Harea* continued.

Pearl sipped her wine. "You just need to bed that vampire to get her out of your mind. But you had better hurry. She will likely leave tomorrow."

He glanced over at Enti. "You finished the weapon?" Then the princess might have a shot.

"No. I failed to create it. It's not in my wheelhouse."

Pearl said, "She set our room on fire last night. Xodin had to use his wings to put it out. After that, we made her call it quits."

Enti raised her palms and shrugged. "I'm going to tell Kosmina after dinner."

The princess had dreamed it; Enti should be able to *will* it into being. Unless the sorceress was weakening?

He considered making a play for her tempting sorcery, but she would detect his plans before he ever got a chance to strike. "Aside from that weapon, is there anything else that can neutralize a primordial's blood?"

Enti nodded. "In theory, the magic of an entire coven of witches should do it. Nightside is one coven short. Without a weapon or witches, I think one's best bet is never to fight a primordial. Evasion is the only hope."

"Let me inform Kosmina about the scythe in a few days. If she asks, tell her you're still working on it."

"To give you time to seduce her?" Enti adjusted her mask. "That sits ill with me. The princess doesn't have much time left. When I said she could last for years more, I hadn't considered her young age. She will succumb quickly."

Bile rose in his throat. "In a year? A month?"

"Days. Already her eyes are reddening more, and her aggression is getting worse. Though her chance is billions to one against the primordial, she has zero chance against her illness. I will have to exile her soon. She'll become a threat, and I take very seriously my promise of a haven here."

"Your powers can't help her retain lucidity?"

"Maybe outside this realm I could attempt to stabilize her, but not here." Seeming dispirited by this, Enti slid his goblet closer to him. "Things fall apart, don't they?"

"Without fail." Tempted by the drink, he mined for fortitude—actually coming up with some. This surprised him considering their topic of discussion. He pressed the goblet away. "Have you ever heard of a cure? She's considering Dorada's ring."

"Assuming Kosmina escaped, the ring could save her. Yet bargaining with that sorceress would be as good as a death sentence."

"Why?"

Enti shared a look with Pearl then leaned in. "When Xodin arrived, he brought news from the Lore that Dorada had risen and was amassing an army. Sorcerer, this is the prophesy. She's going to use all her new oathbound soldiers to attack against her ages-old foe Morgana. It will happen this Accession. Thank gold we'll be safe here!"

"Sand almighty." Morgana was the Queen of Sorceri in two senses. She was their monarch, and her power was to control all Sorceri. All of them except for Dorada. Those two colossal powers had been prophesied to destroy the mortal realm, ushering in an apocalypse.

"And apparently Morgana has harvested even more powers of late," Enti continued. "Anyone sent to fight her will be annihilated like cannon-fodder."

Pearl adjusted the modulator at her throat and said, "If the ring is the princess's hope, will you tell her about Dorada? Maybe right after you tell her no magical scythe is coming?"

Demolishing all her hopes. "I'll come clean about everything when I find the right moment."

Enti said, "If she drinks from your flesh, she could see us discussing this very plot."

"I won't let her."

"That might prove difficult, considering you've repeatedly dreamed about it." The glimmer in her eyes told him she'd seen his memories of ejaculating all over himself. *Fantastic.* "It's nothing to be ashamed of, Silt. You're a hedonist faced with a new temptation. Our kind don't change."

Yet he hadn't always been a hedonist. As the years had come

and gone, he'd hunted and built strongholds. He'd warred and meted retribution. He'd made mistakes and tried to learn. *So many interminable years.* "I can handle it."

Enti gazed deeply into his eyes. "And once she's gone, you'll enjoy all we have to offer here."

It wasn't a question, but he said, "Exactly." Once Kosmina was gone, she'd be . . . gone. He recalled how he'd felt holding her lifeless body—that incomprehensible loss. His leg jogged beneath the table, his palms flickering erratically. He clenched his fists to conceal the light.

I stay. I surrender revenge. The vampire dies out there alone.

She was doomed anyway!

"Very well." Enti quaffed her wine. "You and I will keep her hopes alive, while allowing her to deteriorate—so that you can sleep with her and then cast her off like so many women before."

Pearl looked shocked by Enti's words. "Castle Vitis is all about merriment and sport, isn't it? Let the sorcerer have his."

Yes. I want what I want, and damn the consequences.

"You're right." Enti adjusted her mask yet again. "The merriment of many over the gloom of the few."

Undercurrents passed between the two females.

"What is it? What aren't you telling me?"

Pearl said, "If you want the princess, you'd better hurry. She isn't alone."

THIRTY-ONE

Silt stalked away from the balcony and charged up the stairs.

"Not interested," he snapped at the stair orgy when they reached for him.

Pausing outside Kosmina's door, he heard grunts and groans. Cut-off bellows. She'd already been seduced by one of the wastrels here!

A thud pounded against the wall. Then another. It sounded like they mauled each other. Jealousy seethed, and that weird feeling of wrath shaded his thoughts, swelling his muscles.

The thudding died down, and Kosmina said in an exhilarated tone, "That was amazing!" She was out of breath.

Silt quaked as much as this realm continued to do. He should be in there, taking her body and accepting her praise. She would've fallen for him. Why hadn't he just told her the truth about his powers?

Because there's no future. A princess like her didn't want more from him. He didn't want more from her. So why couldn't he just walk away?

"Where did you learn to move like this?" Kosmina

exclaimed. Then another thud sounded. "You've impressed me."

Silt's hands clenched, and the sand in his pouch churned.

"Lots of practice," a male said. *Xodin?* Fucking Xodin? "But I think you are simply a natural at this." A natural!

"Time for another go, demon."

Xodin's hands on her . . . making her moan . . . his wings wrapped around her body . . .

Enough. Silt backed up a step. With a yell, he booted in the door. He launched himself at Xodin before the male could defend, and they went flying across the room.

"What are you doing?" Kosmina cried.

Before they crashed into a wall, Xodin sculled his wings and changed the trajectory. So Silt swung a fist with all the wrath inside him.

Xodin's head whipped around, wings juddering.

"Stop this, Silt!" Kosmina's voice sounded far away against the pounding of his heart.

He dimly noted the two were dressed. Had Xodin been training with her? Atop a table were maps and a pitcher of blood next to a mug of demon brew. How godsdamned cozy. He unleashed another hit.

Xodin growled, horns and fangs lengthening. "Though violence is forbidden, I will defend myself! Your next hit will be your last, sorcerer."

"No violence? But you got an exception to train in this room, right? So let's do this."

Kosmina snatched a sword from a nearby scabbard and rushed between them. "Enough! What is wrong with you, sorcerer?" When Xodin extricated himself from Silt's grip and backed away, she told the demon, "I can handle him. Please go."

He swiped blood from his lip. "I don't want to leave you like this."

"I'm fine"—she twirled her sword—"but I'm about to blister his ears."

"Very well. Then I'll let you have at it. Tomorrow, princess?"

"Unless Enti succeeds with my weapon before then."

"Exactly. It might be soon." Xodin knew the weapon wasn't possible.

Seeing the demon dissemble with such ease made Silt a little less proud of his own lies. *Want nothing in common with that wastrel.*

Giving Kosmina a courteous bow—and Silt a rude gesture with one wing—Xodin turned toward the rapidly repairing door.

Silt stayed on guard, gaze locked on the demon until the door shut behind him, then he rounded on her. "How much time have you been spending with him?" Her eyes *had* reddened—which just upped Silt's agitation.

She glared. "That's none of your business. What gives you the right to attack my friend?"

"Xodin's not your friend. He's using you."

"Using me? By going over maps of Nightside, bringing me updates on the weapon, and helping me prepare my body for battle? How could he?"

"Battle's not the only thing he wants to prepare your body for. He's seducing you."

"Don't be absurd." Then she thought for a moment, glancing at the door with interest. "Do you really think so?"

Venting that wrath, Silt snapped, "You're not Xodin's. You're not the Gravewalker's. Vampire, you belong *to me.*"

"Belong? Are you hearing yourself?" Silt's behavior harkened back to the time in the cave when he'd been so crazed. A mere week ago!

Yet this seemed . . . different. Before, he'd appeared to be ruled by his habits and his past; now by jealousy. Or by his heart.

Hers stupidly clamored for him.

Over these last three days, Mina had willed herself to concentrate on her mission. She'd tried not to picture him indulging in all the debauchery here. She'd tried to ignore her worsening nightmares and growing thirst for him.

But her concentration had been wrecked when Xodin had let it slip that Silt wasn't indulging—at all. *Why, why, why?* She kept thinking, *What if he cares for me?*

Now the sorcerer paced before her. "That demon is not for you!"

Silt's possessiveness made her chest twist, her body already responding to him. This man—so flawed, so wounded—called to her, a clarion call as strong as fate's. But it was too late for anything more between them. "Are you always so jealous?" She set aside her sword and drew a breath to give his ears the blistering she'd promised.

Yet her words died in her throat when he rasped with bewilderment, "*Never.* Do you understand me, princess? You've done something to me." His tension was like a force in the room. "Do you want that demon?"

"I don't want him, and I don't want you—ahhh!" The *rána* scalded her throat on that lie. Cupping her neck, she gasped, "I don't *want* to want you. But, gods help me, I do," and the burn eased.

Silt looked as if the sight of her pain was too much to bear. He strode over and leaned down. "You can't lie to me." He kissed her neck, soothing her there, while making the rest of her body burn. "I don't want to want you either. But you're inside me like sand in an hourglass. I don't know that I'll work without you."

What would have happened if they'd met under different circumstances? Didn't matter; they hadn't. "Your rash words will always stand between us. One sentence destroyed any chance we might have had." Voicing that truth aloud brought stark comprehension. Tears welled, and she whispered thickly, "You're so far away from me that you might as well be a ray of sun." A blood-tinged tear tracked down her face.

His eyes went wide. "Shh. Don't cry, sweet."

"This could have been something. You and I both know it. We're each drawn to the other, more than we ought to be."

He didn't deny it.

Another tear spilled, embarrassing her. "That's why this hurts so bad. And I've already got enough hurt coming my way. The last thing I need is more pain, and that's all you offer."

He cupped her cheeks. "Kosmina, I won't harm your brother."

"You'll have to. Your vow will force you to!"

He thumbed her tears away. "Then it's a good thing I have the power to break it."

THIRTY-TWO

What are you talking about?" Kosmina gazed up at him with what might be *hope* in her heartbreakingly beautiful expression.

Silt noticed with puzzlement that his hands shook on her face, as if he held something so precious he ought not to be trusted with it. He dropped his hands and drew himself up.

"Silt?"

Now that he'd started his confession, he wasn't sure he wanted to finish it. *Yes, Enti, everything inside this head of mine is conflicted.*

His glanced at the table of maps and back. Kosmina was leaving this sanctuary; he was staying. She was dying; he wasn't. He had a momentary twinge of guilt, getting her hopes up about something more with him, but he had to have her for a time. "I can break a vow to the Lore. I'm known as the Oathbreaker. It's my secondary Sorceri power."

"Oathbreaker? Then why should I believe you now?" She looked like she needed to.

"I'll prove it." He thought up some ridiculous conditions to convince her. "I vow to the Lore that I will stab my eye out. Whenever it regenerates, I'll stab it again," he said lightly.

"Madman!" She didn't breathe, her heart distinctly racing.

"See. Nothing happened." What terrified all the Lore was inconsequential to him.

Her lips parted on an exhalation. "Why wouldn't you have told me that before?" She narrowed her gaze, getting that analytical look. "You wanted to keep me at arm's length."

"Maybe."

"It worked. Although I had started to wonder if you might have some means to neutralize that vow."

"How?"

"When you decided to stay here, I had a shiver of suspicion. That oath should've forced you to do anything to keep it—even try to escape from this place."

"Clever princess," he said, a touch unnerved. Was she *too* clever?

"My uncle was once bound by a vow. He even tried to kill himself to escape it, but it wouldn't let him. Yet you . . . you are free from that unbreakable hold. Extraordinary." Her brows drew together. "Why tell me now?"

I don't want loss. I do want access to you so I can extinguish this obsession and prove that you aren't everything. Voice gruff, he said, "I don't know."

Her gaze searched his expression for more—that he couldn't give her. Yet whatever she found there made her say, "This changes everything." She caressed his jawline with her tender hands. *Gentle. A communication.*

The dimension seemed to spin. With a single gesture, this vampire was making him imagine an oasis growing amidst nothing. Off-kilter, he searched for solid ground.

Before he could find it, she murmured sadly, "But it's still not enough."

Mina allowed herself to truly look at Silt without the stain of his vow. She'd reached a watershed moment, the mountain of this new information separating two rivers.

The river of hating the sorcerer.

The river of deeper feelings for him.

Much deeper. She accepted that this would be the course and flow she followed forever.

Before, she hadn't allowed her own possessiveness. Now, imagining him as hers alone brought on a wave of arousal. As she gazed up into his eyes, she comprehended three things.

One: If she was going to reach the divine, it'd be with this man alone.

Two: He might not ever be capable of love.

And three: Even if he learned to love, that didn't guarantee a successful relationship.

So? She would still make a gamble on this male—which meant she needed to raise the bar with him. Mina wasn't going to settle for his initial offer of *won't murder your loved one.* She had some ideas for how he could prove himself, but they'd get to that. "No, it's not enough," she repeated. "Yet for tonight, it will do."

He exhaled a pent-up breath and moved even closer to her, his scent making her lids heavy. "I want you. Been thinking of nothing else but you for days."

Wanting to get lost in him again, she said, "Then kiss me, sorcerer. I'm aching for more of what you gave me the other night." Would she be able to control her thirst for him? Her nightmares gave her pause, but this new development spurred her optimism. Right now she felt like they could do anything together.

"The thought of you aching for release lights a fuse in me." Yet then his eyes gleamed with jealousy. "Did you burn for the demon? Or the *Ideal*?"

She smiled up at him. "Make me forget them, enchanter."

Silt moved his hips against her, letting her feel his hardness. "Once I'm done with you, you won't remember your own name."

When he pressed his mouth to hers and groaned at the contact, she believed him.

THIRTY-THREE

Kosmina's lips called to Silt to deepen the kiss. His tongue dipped between them, seeking hers.

She gave a muffled cry as she met him with an eager lap, so clearly out of her element. *Innocent vampire . . .*

Yet what he experienced with her was so different from what he'd known that *he* might as well be a novice. Pleasure mingled with confusion, both heightened in turn. So he channeled all his jagged new emotions into this kiss. Slanting his mouth across hers, he took and gave.

Her arousal soon melted away any inhibition, and she met him stroke for stroke. She fisted his tunic, her hips grinding against him in a tantalizing dance.

Too good. Between her response and her sensuous curves, his cock surged precariously, and he drew back.

Her lustrous gaze locked on his mouth. "Don't stop. Why are we stopping?"

Voice unrecognizable, he said, "Trying to pace myself here." Not a customary issue for him. Buying time, he leaned down to run his chin over the tip of one of her ears, back and forth, wondering if she'd be sensitive—

He found himself shoved back on the couch, a wild-eyed vampire atop him.

"That felt electric!" She ripped at his shirt, his lusty female demanding more. "I like this *very* much."

He snatched the garment off. "Getting that impression," he said, his tone sounding thrilled even to his own ears.

With heavy lids, she ran her hands over his chest, her palms smoothing over his tattoos. "You're such a beautiful man." The chest she rubbed swelled with pride. "I want to see more." She yanked off his boots, tossing them over her shoulder. His pants were all but clawed away, leaving his cock to bounce before her.

"That's what I've wanted to see," she all but purred. "It's even better than I fantasized."

Her enthralled gaze was like a touch. Moisture beaded the tip, as it hadn't done since he'd been decades old.

"Does it feel good when the head grows wet?"

Guh. "*Yes.* Talk about it *more.*" Her sultry voice alone could get him off!

"I'll bet the slit across the crown is sensitive." She leaned down and puckered her lips to blow a breath.

Air ghosted over it; his hips shot up to chase sensation. "Fuck!" Who had the magic between them? She could make him a thrall for her.

When her soft hands seized his length, his rod swelled even harder for her, and he gave her more pre-cum. With the pad of her forefinger, she rubbed the slickened head until his mind blanked, his knees falling wide.

Rubbing . . . rubbing . . . while he ground upward to her touch.

"I didn't expect it to be so hot."

He blinked to attention. "You've really never touched a male?"

A blush crept across her cheeks as she gave him a tentative stroke that had him twisting on the couch. "I've only had a furtive kiss or two."

Infuriated that others had taken her lips before him, he tossed her to her back, intending to make her forget those kisses too. He clutched her blouse in his fists and tore away the material, but not quickly enough; she wriggled out of the garment remains.

He hissed in a breath at the sight of her breasts. Cherry-red nipples tipped pale mounds of flesh. "A mirage?" His imaginings hadn't done these justice.

That blush returned to spread from her cheeks down her chest, but instead of covering herself, she sought his gaze. The expectancy in her eyes leveled him. She wanted him to tell her tender things, a language he simply did not know. So he would show her.

He bent down to remove her boots. Kisses across her sensitive ankles made her gasp. He tugged off her pants and underwear, then sank back on his haunches to behold her unclothed—like witnessing a new magic he'd never encountered.

She'd hungered to feed from his body; now he fed his senses from hers, drinking in her scents and these sights—every detail from her glossy hair spread out on the sofa to her impudent nipples to the plump folds of her blond sex.

A sensual medley that stupefied him. "Kosmina . . ." Lowering his head to one of her breasts, he kissed the flesh all around her nipple. She tunneled her fingers through his hair to guide him.

Determined to set the pace, he somehow resisted her. This teasing couldn't be rushed. He alternately wanted to bind her tightly to him and send her flying. Lips above her nipple, he rasped, "Shall I suck it? Or graze it with my teeth?"

She arched her back. "ANYTHING!"

He grinned, descending closer . . . closer . . . When he exhaled an awed breath around the point, she murmured in Dacian, words that even he could tell dripped with arousal. "What are you saying?"

"Any shyness has burned away. I feel like I was made to be with you like this. I am nothing but need, sorcerer!"

"Good. That's how I want you."

"I *ache*. Suck me."

"Soon." He touched his tongue to her nipple, then swept it across the straining tip. More licks followed to toy with it, readying it. . . .

Plaintive sounds spilled from her lips.

Taking pity on her, he sealed his mouth around it. Tongue flicks turned hungry, and he took that nipple as if her body contained the secret of life. He only released her to blow on it.

Her body shivered, breasts quivering. "Silt!"

He turned to her other nipple, hardening that point as well, suckling it with a snarl. He edged the tip with his teeth, just shy of bringing blood to the surface.

She gripped his hair roughly, an aggressive vampire in the throes. Between breaths, she demanded, *"More."*

"I'm going to torment you first." He spoke with all the arrogance of a practiced expert, yet everything about this interaction continued to feel unfamiliar.

Kosmina's pleasure was paramount—vastly more important than his own. Not for the first time with her, he had to wonder: *What's happening to me?* Uneasiness simmered but was overrun by need.

Lids heavy, she said, "Then show me where this swagger comes from. You promised to take care of me. To make me wonder how I ever lived without you."

Bold claims, but based on her initial responses to him, he

said, "As good as done." He descended her body, planning to eat her up then claim her fully. He frowned as he tongued her navel. *Claim* sounded permanent. Immortals had to tread carefully with permanence. "You're about to benefit from my extensive experience."

"Demonstrate. Please." She parted her trembling thighs, revealing a glistening pink heaven.

Her scent swept him up; only the pain in his cock kept him tethered to this plane. He leaned down and inhaled her soaked curls, gone lightheaded. "Stunning female. With her sweet pussy." His length dripped for it.

He bent his head, and his lips met hers. Pliant folds greeted his tongue, coating it with dew. A lost groan rumbled from his lungs as he drank from a spring of perfection.

She writhed. "Sorcerer . . . your tongue is wicked. Make me climax with it."

He palmed her breasts to hold on, pressing her down into the couch. He wanted to build her pleasure. She demanded it *now*. So he flicked her little clit.

"Ahhh!" She dug her heels into the cushions and bucked to his mouth. Slippery flesh parted even more for his kiss.

"Mina!" He buried his face between her thighs and rimmed her tight entrance as he'd fantasized. But no fantasy could come close to capturing this. With his stiffened tongue, he claimed her core. Soon to claim her completely. *Mine.*

Stray thought: How could any pleasure exceed what he experienced now? Would he surrender revenge for more of it? Surrender smoke for more of it?

Yes.

Every night of the millennium.

Light drew his gaze upward as sorcery danced in the air. Whorling power enveloped them as his power sparked—not as it once had, but maybe this marked a beginning. The connection between him and Kosmina was like air and tinder, combining to feed a flame of magic.

He returned his kiss to her clit and replaced his tongue with his finger. Supple tightness gloved it as he slid it home. He added a second one, increasing the fullness.

"Release me, Silt! *Please* . . ."

He couldn't deny her anymore. He thrust his fingers, screwing them inside her. When her channel tightened around his plunging fingers, he met her shocked eyes. Pumping his hand, he leaned down to suckle her clitoris, but he kept his gaze on hers.

"*Ahhh!*" Expression staggered, lips parted, she wouldn't look away . . . holding his gaze . . . holding it . . .

Ecstasy seized her. She screamed in abandon.

He tongued and thrust, wringing her orgasm and snarling for more. *He* was the vampire, frantic to devour her.

Her eyes rolled back in her head when nothing could hold her anymore.

THIRTY-FOUR

Mina's body slowly returned to her control, altered forever by Silt's bone-melting kiss. As she lay sprawled, he slid his fingers from her.

Seeming unable to help himself, he sucked them clean with a shudder. Noticing her riveted attention, he avoided her gaze.

"Sorcerer? What is it?" She was amazed by how steady she sounded when he'd just delivered even more revelations.

He kissed her thigh, grinding his shaft against the bed. "Nothing."

"Have I done something wrong?"

"No!" He raised his head, brows drawn. "You're . . . *no*."

Ah. "It's different with me, isn't it?" His hands had shaken when he'd touched her, and even *she* had sensed the magic in the air. After thousands of years feeling one way, the sorcerer now dealt with a new experience—and it was spooking him. "It's okay. We'll figure it out as we go." And so far everything was marching along to her plan. . . .

"Figure out what? The next step is clear," he said, his manner businesslike. Trying to make this encounter similar to all the others? "You're ready. I need inside you." He rose up between her thighs and fisted his swollen length.

"I'm not ready for sex." They weren't in the presence of the divine. Not yet. And she wouldn't settle for mere intercourse for her first time. Mina had made herself a promise about this. If she couldn't keep a promise to herself, how could she keep them with others? "But that doesn't mean we can't continue to break new ground." She yearned to explore other acts she'd witnessed.

A flare of interest lit his gaze. "I'm listening."

"I want to reciprocate. Unfortunately, I won't be very skillful—not like you were with your kiss. You must have practiced on a million females. I can tell."

"Thanks?"

She sighed. "I'm not saying the right things. Sexy things. Pleasure has confounded me."

His gaze softened. "Good."

"So you didn't deny it when I guessed you'd had a million lovers?"

"Princess," he said warningly.

"Very well. Trade places with me? And I'll stumble through what I can."

Expression filled with curiosity, he allowed her to steer him until he reclined on his back.

Primed from her orgasm, her senses felt even more alive. Inhaling his mouthwatering scent, she let her gaze roam from his golden eyes . . . to the muscles of his rippling torso . . . to the pulses of his magnificent rod.

Filled with life, his length pointed toward his heart. In a trance, her gaze followed that taunting vein. Would she be able to keep herself from punishing it as she'd fantasized? Maybe she shouldn't chance this.

"Do not second-guess yourself, princess. Our course is set."

She nodded, not sure how to embark. Then his testicles tightened, drawing her attention. She reached to fondle them, and he groaned as if this was a special delight for him. At last, she got to cup and weigh them until he grated, "No more stalling, female. I want your mouth on me."

That mouth pouted. "I could play with these forever."

"Or as long as I could withstand this onslaught." He made her attentions sound like a battle offensive, which pleased her.

She might not have experience with this—not like his millions of other partners had—but she knew moves and countermoves. She could adjust her campaign based on his reactions. Logic would dictate how she proceeded. And she had seen the act plenty of times at the Tree, although seeing and doing weren't the same. . . .

"Relieve me of this"—his lips were thinned—"or I'll do it myself."

She debated between these two appetizing possibilities. Deciding on one for now, she took his length in hand once more, her pale skin stark against his blood-filled shaft. It throbbed in time with his heartbeat as she dipped down to lave the crown. His sublimely salty taste greeted her. *"Umm."*

He gazed on with his lids hooded, but his chest heaved.

She kissed the contours of the proud crown. Under the ridges. Up to the tip. She licked that sensitive slit, dipping her tongue for more saltiness. Logic receded as she lovingly kissed him. "You taste like magic."

"Sand almighty."

She'd felt feminine power when sword training and when acknowledging her intellectual capabilities. Now as she moved down his shaft with butterfly licks and little sucks, she felt a different kind of feminine power. His mounting groans told her she could make this sorcerer crazed, could enchant *his* will for a time—

He sucked in a breath. "Bite?"

She jerked back. Peered down in shock. One tiny globe of crimson was rising from just above that vein. "I didn't mean to nick your skin! I didn't taste it." Her fangs had sharpened beyond her control. "I feared this would happen, but I got so carried away."

He leaned up on his elbows, gaze inscrutable.

Rushing to fill the silence, she said, "When you fed me blood at the waterfall, the urge to bite you nearly overwhelmed me. Vampires can learn to govern their fangs in time, but considering my affliction . . ." She trailed off, attention back on the flawless globe of that drop. It'd grown. Firelight reflected in the liquid. Transfixed, she murmured, *"Life."*

Wicked impulses arose within her. Vampiric impulses. She wanted to steal his blood, his seed, steal into his every waking thought like some nightmare creature. *I want to haunt him.*

Whatever he saw in her face made him say, "Fuck it all— pierce me." If anything, his shaft was harder. "You have fangs to tap my flesh. We both want you to do it."

It'd be like tapping into the very heart of him! "It's taboo." Yet how could she possibly resist sinking her fangs into his meaty length?

"Only a matter of time before you draw my blood again."

Could she handle the influx of his many memories? Anxiety replaced awe; she was already on borrowed time. "I'm losing control, and I don't want to drink straight from the flesh."

He gave his head a shake. "Okay, you're right. It's not time."

"Maybe you should go. I've dreamed of attacking you, biting you, and the bloodlust makes me stronger—"

He flipped her onto her back, trading places with her. "I can handle you." Maneuvering his body over hers, he pinned her wrists above her head. With his other hand, he held his rod above her mouth.

That nick welled crimson—its pendulous drop hanging suspended above her lips. . . .

"Do you want it?" he asked, a challenge in his tone. "I'll feed you like this."

"Yes, yes, *feed me*." She held her breath as his blood fell.

Falling.

Falling.

Contact. The smoldering drop hit her bottom lip; starbursts exploded behind her fluttering lids. "More!" She licked her lip, sucking it. Overcome by his taste, she twisted beneath him to get free. *Bite him. Drink him down, down . . .*

But he was too strong for her, mastering her body. The sight of his flexing muscles and the feel of his grip only added to the sensory overload.

As he peered at her eyes, his widened.

"What is it?"

"My vampire needs more blood"—he stroked his member, and another drop fell to her lips—"from the fountain of me."

Taboo!

So?

As his lifeblood coursed through her veins with molten intensity, more magic swirled around them.

"You crave my taste like it's the finest wine. You always will." He stared down at her eyes. "I've ruined you for all else."

He had. He had! She writhed beneath him, about to climax again. Magic. Sex. Man. Everything about this sorcerer melded to pleasure her. This infusion of him couldn't be denied much longer.

He's in my heart. He's inside me. She squeezed her thighs and undulated. "Ah, ahh!"

"You're going again?" He gazed at her frenzied hips. "Lusty piece."

Once she hovered on the very brink, a stream of blood met her tongue directly. He'd somehow cut his length to drench her mouth. She might as well have kissed his heart. As she drank him down, rapture tumbled her over the edge, her core contracting with each wave of it.

No logic. Just sensation and starbursts.

His brows furrowed, his body a mass of tension. "You've robbed me of control. Can't fight this any longer." He aimed his big shaft down, gave his fist a pump. The muscles in his neck and chest went rigid, his arms bulging. "Going to . . . *come!*" He threw back his head and bellowed as his semen erupted.

Scalding lashes took both of her breasts. Her straining red nipples peeked up through whipmarks of white seed.

He yelled over and over until his voice broke, till he could scarcely utter a stunned, *"Sand almighty."*

Her tension ebbed in time with his, her movements slowing, breaths easing.

Spent, he gave a last husky groan. "Look at this." Pure masculine satisfaction lit his face as he stared at his seed upon her. "I'll never come again. You've drained me, princess." He released her and collapsed against the back of the sofa. Between breaths, he said, "And you've shocked me. Do you know how difficult it is to shock an immortal like me?"

"Hmm?" His pearlescent semen was slashed through with a thread of red. Unable to help herself, she dabbed her finger in both and brought it to her mouth. Her tongue darted for a taste.

"Oh, fuck me," he muttered in shock, and the madness began all over again.

THIRTY-FIVE

After several more bouts of bed sport, additional food for Silt, and a bath for both of them, he and the princess lay in bed, bodies fitted together. Their appetites—matched as if he and she had been cut from a single grain of sand—were sated. For now.

He still hadn't claimed her, but it was only a matter of time.

The fire crackled as Kosmina rested her head on his shoulder and traced his tattoos. He threaded his finger through her hair, taking its irresistible scent into him. His thoughts were clear, and yet relaxation stole through him. *That's new.*

He still puzzled over who he was and what he ultimately wanted—just knew it included more of this. He'd thought smoking was bliss. Yet nothing could compare to this *connection.*

He frowned down at the intoxicating vampire. Had he traded one drug for another?

Over the night, she'd confided to him that she used to be tongue-tied and shy. At times, he'd seen hints of that bashful princess when she blushed to the tips of her pointed ears at some new pleasure he introduced, but mostly she'd struck him as a femme fatale he'd barely kept pace with.

Now she'd grown quiet, and he didn't like that he had no idea what she was thinking about. "What are you musing in that clever mind of yours?"

In a wry tone, she said, "Tell me, did you feel as if we were eleven females short?"

He raised his brows. "I can hardly handle just you, Kosmina."

"Who?" She languorously stretched beside him. "As you foretold, enchanter, I forgot my own name." She laughed. Feminine laughter was his aphrodisiac, but hers was different. *I can* feel *it.*

Her levity faded too soon, and she grew serious. "I shouldn't have taken your blood. I'll only get accustomed to it. And eventually I will lose control and bite you."

"When those drops first hit your mouth, your eyes cleared for a moment, the red receding." Their true color was light azure ringed with gold, the color of that Sorselan oasis he'd found. The spring lake had been all the more vivid against the expanse of sand surrounding it.

This princess was as otherworldly as his home realm. If he possessed her, then maybe never going back wouldn't hurt as much. "My blood temporarily muted the sickness. With enough of it, you could beat the plague."

She looked like she didn't dare to hope. "How could that be?"

"Do you remember when I told you the sand hisses at the sun? It does at the rain too, warning it off. But then a shock wave of energy gets released, and the sand welcomes it with opened arms. I felt something shift like that when you consumed those drops."

"A shock wave is exactly how I'd describe it."

"Sorceri often possess unknown powers. What if one of

mine is to fight this plague in vampires? To test out my theory, I'll need you to feed on my blood often."

The gratitude in her expression as she gazed up at him jabbed his conscience further. Her smile returned, but it was sad. "Can I depend on that? Have you forgotten I'm going soon?"

"Considering what you've found with me in this bedroom, perhaps you shouldn't plan so easily to leave it."

"I don't want to leave you, but I can't remain here indefinitely. And not just because of the plague. Something isn't right with Enti."

He'd had the same feeling. Her hedonism, though typical for a Sorceri, seemed to carry an edge.

Kosmina frowned. "Everything she says makes sense, and she is trying to help me, but . . ."

"But . . ."

"I can't figure her out, and I can figure out most."

Not me, little princess.

"The sorceress gives generously, so why do I feel she's even more of a reaper than the Gaolers? And more, why do I *still* like her?"

You wouldn't if you had truly figured her out.

Kosmina leaned up. "Do you believe her about a parole?"

"I want to. I long to do my time and be free of this sentence. Escape sounds great in theory, but exile in Poly is all that awaits me." The thought depressed him. What was the point? Why keep enduring?

"You could come to my realm. The Gaolers might not ever find Dacia."

"Your brother would love that." Silt's face flushed as he remembered the scene in his stronghold that Mirceo and Caspion had stolen upon: Silt, naked and drugged out of his mind, surrounded by an army of monsters and an uncaring harem.

In the history of first impressions, I take the prize.

Mirceo would disown Kosmina over her dalliance with Silt. And she would never choose a condemned, powerless sorcerer over the brother who'd raised her.

She didn't push the idea of Silt's coming to Dacia. It was ridiculous—but he still wished she'd insisted upon it.

Changing the subject, she said, "I still can't believe you were born with the ability to break vows."

He rubbed a hand over his mouth. "I wasn't. I stole the power off a sorceress who'd stolen it off another."

Kosmina stiffened. "You told me you'd never stolen a power."

"I lied. I didn't feel I owed you the truth."

"But you do now? No more lies, please?"

"Of course. No more lies." Once she'd relaxed back against him—seriously, why did she keep believing him?—he said, "I'm curious why you denied us sex, even when you were in the throes. If you thought what we shared was divine, the pleasure will only grow."

She had never lost that last inhibition. In fact, she'd seemed more interested in taking his blood than in taking his shaft. But as promised, he'd kept her from drinking from his flesh. He would do so until she was ready, and until *he* was ready. For now, his memories must be kept close.

She sat up and pulled the cover to her breasts, as if the sight and feel of them wasn't emblazoned in his mind forever. "It wasn't *divine.*"

He chuckled at her joke. It'd been so worlds-shattering that he might as well have been numb all the times before.

Then he realized she was *not* joking. "Kosmina?"

"You brought me ecstasy. More than I ever imagined. But we've higher to climb."

The most pleasure he'd felt by realms—and she thought they had room for improvement. His bafflement must be written on his face. *Shocked again.*

Defensive, she said, "I'm sure you haven't always been an incomparable lover to every woman you've taken."

He sat up as well. "No complaints, vampire." No partner had scored him on his performance and declared room for improvement. She parted her lips, but he cut her off: "I didn't pay *every* female, princess."

"You are surly once again. But I know what I want."

He recalled her explanation of the divine. *Does such a thing really exist?* "You want love. Love*making*. But what if I can't give you what you want?" Where to even start? Love involved trust, right?

Could he learn to again, despite grueling lessons of betrayal? Allies had betrayed him. Almost all Sorceri. His own family! Since then, he'd resolved never to dive into that quicksand, and he'd never regretted it.

The point was moot anyway. *She* couldn't trust *him.* "I can't give what I don't possess," he said with such surety.

Yet *something* had happened over these hours. He relived that day in Sorselan when he'd traversed over dunes before coming upon his oasis.

A bounty found. A discovery made. All because he'd kept going.

Am I cresting a dune even now?

If he was ever going to trust, it would be a direct female, one who could never lie—one who had no problem informing him that he alone had touched the divine this night.

"I'm not asking you for forever, Silt. I'm just telling you that the man I fully give my body to will be mine—forever. It's very simple: if you can't give me that, then you're not *him.*"

Him. The idea of some future male claiming her . . . claws must be raking him on the inside. Would she return to wanting the Ideal?

She chuckled at his obvious unease. "Forever, sorcerer."

"And where does that leave us now?"

"You can only give what you can give. That doesn't mean we can't enjoy each other, up to a point, until my weapon is complete."

The weapon that was never coming.

She ran her nails down his chest. "While we wait, I'll give you ample opportunity to sexually spellbind me. Give it your best shot, short of intercourse."

More bed play with Kosmina. Repeatedly pleasuring her. She offered him almost everything he'd wanted, what he'd schemed to get. "Your terms are acceptable." He cleared his throat into his fist, working to shake off his guilt, an emotion he had little experience with.

"Be careful that you don't lose your heart in the process."

"I've pursued women for eons, and my heart remains mine." He was convinced he had none.

"But, Silt, you've never met anyone like me," she said with a vulnerable smile, demonstrating that directness mixed with sweetness—a unique blend that made his chest tighten and proved her statement.

He would figure all this out later, when sleep wasn't calling him and when his balls weren't pleasantly sore from the night's activities.

She nibbled her bottom lip. "If we do grow closer, you will grieve as this plague worsens." She sounded more worried about him than herself.

"It won't worsen. You'll gorge on my blood the way those demons downstairs gorge on delicacies." But could he say for certain such a plan would work? He'd be betting with her life. Just like that, thoughts of sleep vanished.

She looked unconvinced as well. "I can sense the plague closing in on me. I might be weeks out from losing control. Maybe mere days." As Enti had predicted. "If your blood doesn't forestall it, I'll become a danger to you. I've read about vampires who channel unstoppable strength in a bloodlust. I could hurt you, Silt."

He gave her an indulgent look. "You can never overpower me." He lay back down and dragged her to him with the ease of lifting a feather. "I'll be fine. You worry for nothing, female."

"Hmm." In time, relaxation returned between them. "I want to know something about you, something you haven't told me." She was likely angling to discover what his tattoos meant.

Which he would never reveal. Had the transactions between them already started?

She surprised him by saying, "Tell me your real name."

"You assume it's not Silt?"

"Your parents didn't name you that."

True. Millennia ago, in a major battle for territory, he'd caused a tidal wave of silt to choke a crystalline river that had once given life to thousands. He'd dammed it forever.

Not entirely on purpose.

His enemies had called him Silt. He'd let the name stick. Afterward, he'd lived up to his reputation as a befouler. "Why would you want to know this?" He resisted revealing his name but couldn't say why.

Yet then she gazed up with those eyes of hers. "Please?"

"My name is . . ." He hadn't uttered it in eons. "My given name is . . . Adham."

In a dulcet voice, she repeated, *"Adham."*

Chills raced across his skin, and his shaft swelled yet again.

"I like that." She ran the softs pads of her fingers over his tattoos. "I want you to know that no matter what happens with me, I'm glad we've spent this time together."

So she didn't regret him. But then, she didn't know his history or his lies. Still . . . "You're in my bed from now on, Kosmina. Mine alone."

"*From now on*, he says." She gave a gallows laugh, and a flashback hit him—of lightning reflected in her sightless eyes.

Roiling from that memory, he bit out, "Listen, you bleak wench, if my blood doesn't work, then we will find another cure somewhere." What the hell was he saying? Yet he kept *godsdamn talking*. "You're going to enjoy a long, immortal life."

"We?" She'd pounced on that one word like quarry.

Now what? The more he'd considered his options, the more he'd accepted that staying here was the only path that made sense.

A billions-to-one chance at escape—versus a curtailed idyll with this female, his favorite one so far. They didn't even know a way out existed! *Unknown* did not equal *windfall*.

Clever Kosmina had to have determined their two options.

One enters the hive to die. Or two enter and die.

And yet he knew what her next question would be. . . .

"Adham, when the weapon is ready, will you leave with me?" She held herself still, as if his next words would be monumental. As if they'd be *true*.

Staring into her eyes, he lied, "Yes."

THIRTY-SIX

The Bog of Revenants

Use your mist!" Kristoff yelled over the pouring rain as a foot slammed down on his back, brutally shoving him deeper into the mud. Lothaire had used his mist to take them across a field of lava but not in this fight for their lives. *Why?*

Nearby, massive revenants dragged Lothaire to the ground with inconceivable strength as he tried to defend himself, but he was too weak. Kicks and punches battered his prone body.

Exhausted from fending off undead hellhounds, he and Kristoff had then battled revenants for what must be days.

"Damn you, Lothaire, fight!" Blood dribbled from his nose and ears in the rain. A kick to the temple made his head recoil and his mouth go slack.

A kick to Kristoff's own head followed, and consciousness wavered. As he dimly watched, half a dozen revenants shoved Lothaire's face into the mud to starve him of air. Hands atop hands. So much strength.

His half brother thrashed, grappling . . . grappling . . . a last flurry of movement . . . His suffocated body stilled.

A pair of the brutes seized Lothaire's shoulders. Another

gripped his head to twist it free.

After three thousand years of life, the Enemy of Old was about to meet his end.

Furie's location would die with him. "No, no!" Kristoff was next, and then his Bride would truly be lost. "Damn it, wake. Wake!" Mustering his last reserves, he bellowed, *"FOR LIZVETTA!"*

Tremors rippled through Lothaire's frame, then muscles flexed. Suddenly he threw off the number holding him and shot to his feet with a horrifying roar. Red eyes crazed in his muddy face, he snatched at the closest revenant and pulled apart its hulking body like gossamer. Bloodlust of a different kind had overtaken Lothaire.

Kristoff used the creatures' shock to fight for his own freedom. Making it to his feet, he threw punches, watching out of the corner of his eye Lothaire's flood of madness. Being facedown in the muck—breathing it—must have sent him back to his burial in the Bloodroot Forest. He'd relived that torture.

Now Lothaire laughed in the rain as crimson sprayed, clearly didn't feel his many injuries. Using his bare hands and fangs, he tore revenant flesh from their bones.

This is the Enemy of Old. Madness wed to savagery. *This is why so many fear him.* Lothaire hadn't used his mist, because he'd wanted this fight—because he was *insane.*

As he annihilated his way through the throng, the revenants' howls changed tenor. Their maniacal eyes held fear. One turned and fled. Then another. Soon a stampede of them barreled over each other to escape the frenzied vampire.

He's their monster. Would they have a primal memory of him passed down throughout time? They crawled back into their underground hovels and mounds until silence reigned. The swamp was still. Only puddles of gore gave evidence of what had happened here.

Lothaire swiped his face with a sleeve and cast him a rictus grin.

Sucking in wet breaths, Kristoff sensed he was about to impart more information. Kristoff also sensed he would not want to hear it.

Lothaire didn't disappoint: "When I had no breath, do you think I was dreaming of air? Or *fire?*"

The unspoken question felt palpable in the storm. *When Furie rises, what makes you think she'll be saner than me?*

Lothaire shook his head, sending blood flying from an array of wounds. "Come along, little brother. I suspect we were driven farther away from Mina. We have work to do." Brushing off his coat with a casual mien and a mangled arm, he added, "And also those rascally hellhounds from before are returning in three . . . two . . . one . . ."

"Ahh-wooooooo."

THIRTY-SEVEN

Silt held Kosmina as she slept, moving not a muscle, wanting her to rest and heal.

As if it promised all the answers, he stared at the ceiling above the bed. He'd memorized every inch of that expanse, had watched as minute cracks appeared after a rumble, only for sorcery to repair them.

Despite ceding his blood streams to Kosmina over the last six days, his body grew stronger. Despite partaking, she might be . . . weakening. When they'd trained together tonight, had she lacked her usual stamina?

He refused to believe that. Her eyes weren't getting redder, and her wound hadn't worsened. He told himself his blood tamped down her illness and would forever.

He told himself this a lot. Seemed lying was all he did these days.

Apparently, Silt could abandon revenge. He might even be able to forsake smoke. But he could never jeopardize his own survival to go with her—even though he'd told Kosmina he would.

Why did she keep believing him?

Because a sheltered young female like her was no match for a deceiver like him.

He wasn't the only one wearing a figurative mask. Kosmina joked about her illness, but earlier he'd seen her glance at the mirror and avert her gaze with a look of disquiet. Another time he'd caught her on the balcony, staring with foreboding at the ghoul's mountain, visible in the distance. She'd quickly recovered and donned her stoic expression. . . .

Though everyone in the castle knew about Silt's ruse, somehow they'd kept the secret from her, and it weighed on them all. Enti, Xodin, and even Pearl had looked guilty whenever the princess accompanied Silt on his arm to dinner.

Enti's irises no longer swirled when she was around Kosmina. Was it because the sorceress refused to read the mind of one so doomed and betrayed? Or because Enti herself was weakening?

Weirdly, Silt's lie weighed on him—the Oathbreaker—the most.

Each time Kosmina expressed delight with him in bed.

Whenever he forgot their situation and found himself laughing with her.

Every hour they spent training, her with her sword and him with his floundering sand, for a trip he would never make.

Would she feel embarrassed or enraged once she discovered he'd duped her? He had a lot of time to think about this. He held her whenever she slept, wanting to be there if she woke amorous or thirsty. He always sent her drifting back to sleep with a satisfied sigh, *"Adham."*

Though their bed play continued to astound him, he hadn't taken her fully. The glimmer of an oasis on the horizon grew closer, but she withheld the last of the mystery from him. . . .

Now as he held her, his musings tangled: the pleasure of her in his arms versus the torment of his thoughts. He himself slept little.

She'd told him that whenever he did, his sorcery spilled out over into the room. So why couldn't he channel it while awake? He felt as if a dam of silt blocked his sorcery, the way he'd once choked that crystalline river. How to explode the floodgates when he was awake?

If his powers returned to full strength, could he take on a hive of ghouls and a primordial to save this female from her fate? He gazed at one of his hands, willing it to light. *Sputter.*

With a silent curse, he returned his gaze to the ceiling. A builder like him recognized the stress fractures above as a systemic issue. Didn't he suffer the same?

At dinner last night, he'd asked Enti, "Have your scouts uncovered anything about those immortals who entered Nightside?" If the two had somehow survived, they might have information or unexpected powers to help with Kosmina's situation.

"The pair escaped the revenants, but then the hellhounds descended upon them in numbers unseen before." Seeming saddened, Enti added, "Some beings simply aren't meant to survive out there in the wasteland." *More reason to stay here.*

Kosmina sighed in her sleep and nestled more closely to him. He pressed a kiss to her hair before he'd even meant to.

Damn it, no union could be more hopeless than his and this female's.

And yet . . .

A former Inferi didn't belong with a princess. The King of Sand didn't belong with a vampire who could never behold the desert sun.

And yet . . .

Even if they surmounted all the odds against them, her

family would never allow them a future together.

And yet—*no, no, no.* This was all moving too fast. He'd known Kosmina for less than two weeks.

He'd confessed to her at least some of what he'd learned here: Dorada's agenda.

Kosmina had said, "I'd decided I wouldn't use the ring anyway. Short of that, what could cure an illness that can sicken even an immortal?"

"Somewhere out there, an answer exists. We'll escape this place and comb the worlds for it. Your brother will expect you to persevere."

Had Silt played the role of caring lover so deeply that he was becoming one?

To a point. But he still wasn't leaving with her.

Fuck. Even he hated Silt Harea.

Waking to streams of sunlight must be like this.

A glow bathing her eyelids roused Mina. Before she opened her eyes, she luxuriated in the sorcery surrounding them, experiencing it as a warm embrace.

Adham—she couldn't refer to him as Silt any longer—only slept an hour or so a night, but when he did, he dreamed. As his eyes darted behind his own lids, the light from his palms would illuminate the room, while the sand from his ever-present pouch levitated above them to form images from his reveries.

Tonight the quartz glittered as it formed sand spheres to populate a floating galaxy. Then the shimmering sands crested and danced like the dunes of his childhood.

No wonder he longed to reconnect with his beautiful power. Yet during the day he struggled to move even a grain. He'd told her, "Maybe I extinguished my conscious control of it for good.

I've met other Sorceri who'd sublimated their mastery and never got it back." But that didn't stop him from training hard with it.

In between their mission preparations, they treated themselves to decadent bed play. He'd made no secret of wanting to claim her, but she'd somehow resisted.

They released a measure of the sexual tension between them, yet they couldn't alleviate it. That force continued to grow, like a volcano waiting to erupt—like *this realm* waiting to quake.

He hadn't pressed again for her to drink him—probably didn't want her to discover all his many secrets—but he repeatedly dripped his lifeblood into her mouth and urged her to heal. Those streams had seemed to quell the worst impulses of her plague. She hadn't bitten her wrist once as she'd slept. Progress!

Deep down, she knew it wasn't a cure though, and she had moments when despair set in. But she had a goal in mind—a way to have everything she'd always wanted—and she would try to accomplish it.

Silt had told her about Dorada's plot against Morgana, but Mina had already decided not to use the ring. With no blood cure and no wishgiver on the horizon, every night here lessened the odds of a favorable outcome. Mina needed to be out searching for a solution, but the chance of more with him beckoned her.

Though she and Adham rarely spoke about the future away from Nightside, she often pictured their existence together. What would her family and friends think of him?

Ellie and Balery would welcome him, but Mirceo, well versed in decadence himself, would never bless whatever was between her and Adham. And Mina feared her uncles would react . . . violently.

If she presented Adham as her male, Viktor would give a bellow and target the sorcerer's head for a mounting on his wall. Coolheaded Trehan would tell her something like, "Your aim in this area lacked accuracy; recalibrate," then strike Adham. Stelian would say nothing, drink more, then secretly hunt the sorcerer as if he were a trespasser across Dacia's boundary.

She knew this, yet her feelings for Adham continued to deepen—despite all the currents she'd detected around him. Was he shady? Very. But Mina came from a land of shadows. She could handle shady.

She glanced down at her chest. Her vampiress heart beat for him alone. *He's mine.*

A wave of pain made her arm ache. She could imagine an existence with Silt all she liked, but unless they escaped, her existence would end. She no longer believed her brother would arrive to save the day. He would have been here by now. Her worry that he would reveal himself to humans remained, but she figured the Gaolers had stopped sending new prisoners here—for a reason.

Mina had heard others in the castle whisper that two or three immortals used to arrive every night. None had made it here over the entire last week, and that absence seemed to be affecting the sorceress and all the beings here.

Any laughter in the halls felt forced, the sounds of pleasure rote. Even as morale was abysmal, everyone pretended otherwise.

Uneasy, she lost herself in the sand eddying overhead. In time, she drifted to sleep once more, hoping to dream about Adham showing her a moonlit desert.

Instead, nightmares arose of leaping atop him, wrestling to get to his jugular. Her fangs dripped, sharper than they'd ever been. She snapped them greedily.

He yelled, "Kosmina!" trying to startle her out of her bloodlust. "Kosmina!"

When she opened her eyes again, she was atop Silt, her nightmare a reality.

THIRTY-EIGHT

Kosmina, wake up!" Silt gripped her shoulders, holding her at bay. "Mina!"

"Adham?" Her reddened gaze slowly grew focused. Then she twisted away from him, scrambling across the bed. "Oh, gods, what did I do?"

"Nothing. It's fine. We're fine." He'd discounted her worries when she'd told him that vampires grew stronger in bloodlust; she'd just stunned him with her strength. If he hadn't awakened when he did . . .

She sat against the headboard, curling her knees to her chest, her eyes welling with tears. Kosmina Daciano was such a courageous female, yet she still reminded him of a fragile desert rose. "The thought of harming you is like a blade to the chest." She'd spared no worry for herself. Only for him. "We can't go on like this."

Whenever she'd expressed doubts, he'd given her the same assurances, the same lies: *You just need more blood . . . the weapon might be ready tomorrow. . . .* Gazing at her like this, he admitted, "The benefit of my blood seems to be wearing off." The plague was resurging, and Enti would soon exile Kosmina. She would have to. "Princess, you're succumbing."

"You would know all about that, wouldn't you?" she snapped, then looked aghast. "I'm so sorry. I'm not like this. Why would I ever try to hurt you? You who mean so much to me?"

Guilt was worse than a thousand years of withdrawal, made him just as nauseated.

"The plague is already changing me. I used to be shy. No longer. Logic once ruled me. Now emotions do. It's a very uncomfortable situation to be in. Which you must understand very well since you're living in a den of opium."

Every minute was a struggle. If he hadn't been so preoccupied with her . . .

"I should have known this would happen," she muttered. "My nightmares of biting you keep returning because they're a warning. It's time I heed it."

"And what if you did bite me? Maybe that's exactly what should happen. We've both dreamed of your taking blood from me. Could be for a reason." Would it buy her more time? *For what? Who is coming to save the day?*

"Are you ready for me to know everything about you?"

He swallowed, and she clocked the movement. Just before her attack, he'd dreamed that she shared his memories and became one with him—but dreams differed from reality. He was the last person who needed to offer up his past. Still . . . "It's what we must do."

"And what if it backfires? Your memories could send me over the edge. I might attack you again."

"I won't let that happen," he assured her. "Just think about it, all right?" Because no other scenarios existed for her here.

"I'll give Enti another day or two. In the meantime, you can't sleep around me anymore."

Did Kosmina have that kind of time? He almost came clean about everything then, but she looked so tired. "Very well." He took her in his arms, and they lay back down. "We'll revisit this tomorrow," he said, feeling as if his tongue were barbed.

"Hmm. Distract me, will you? Talk to me."

"What do you want to talk about?"

She traced one of his tattoos. Though she didn't understand their dark meaning, they'd seized her attention. With her little licks outlining each, she'd learned them with her mouth, making him twist in a mix of bliss and unease. The idea had struck him again that nothing was pure for him, all was sullied. Delight and disquiet forever battled inside him, just as they had when he'd smoked.

She murmured, "Tell me about these."

"Maybe in the future. But not now." He hadn't uttered the word *Inferi* in centuries.

"*In the future*, he says." A soft laugh.

"Damn it, Kosmina."

"Oh, come on, you can make jibes about my death, but I can't?"

He did *not* make jibes any longer. "You act as if you know me so well? Then you tell me what the tattoos mean."

"They have to do with your past as an Inferi."

The fuck? He leapt from the bed, snatching on his pants. "Enti told you."

"No. She didn't." Kosmina was so calm in the face of his burning shame, he felt as if he'd been transported into some kind of horror tale where no one reacted as they should. "I deduced it. You're a Sorceri, so it makes sense. Will you tell me about it?"

He began pacing. If Mina knew, then why had she proudly accompanied him to dinner? He pictured her with her chin up, her arm linked in his. "I'm not going to do this . . . this spilling of secrets between new lovers—the ritual exchange of woe. Other men do that. Not me." Like that Ideal. The vampire king would surely do the ritual. "Why should I peel off my skin just to show you what lies beneath?"

"Because we are friends. Friends share their pasts."

"Friends?" Kosmina Daciano coursed through him like his very lifeblood, but she wasn't godsdamned sold on him? He stalked to the bed and palmed her nape. "To hell with your friendship! You're not my *friend*. You fucking belong to me." *Until I'm done with you.* The words might as well be hanging in the air.

Instead of agreeing with him and declaring herself his, she said, "You explained to me about the mechanical breakdown of stone into sand, but you won't tell me about your woe?"

He dropped his hand and straightened. "What are you talking about?"

"Those processes aren't unalike. They both *shape*. But at heart, we—and stone—are still the same. Can you not reveal what shaped you?"

Using his element to convince him? His very language against him? "You have no shame, and so you can't understand it. But that won't stop you from prying mine out of me."

"No, it won't—just as I would draw a sword from your side and give you relief from pain." Like some kind of catharsis?

Wait, if she'd known his secret, then had she kissed his tattoos for . . . succor? To communicate acceptance? The idea sent him spinning. He began to sweat, palms flickering.

And now she expected him to recount his history when he was blisteringly sober. He glanced to the door—

"Adham?"

That fucking name. A sandstorm must be pummeling him inside. He'd never wanted to smoke more than he did right now.

"If I do this, you'll tell me you belong to me alone. You'll say the words." He wanted her to tell him that he was her mate. Or would she get over Silt as effortlessly as she had Kristoff?

Her gaze never left his face. He could all but see her calculating her way through this interaction, while his jagged feelings were a coil of razor wire around his heart.

"I will say something to you that I've never said to another."

He made a sound of frustration. "Fine, Your Highness. You'll have your way tonight." Swiping a hand over his chest, he said, "This reads, *Upon pain of death, I will never be parted from my soul again.*"

"How did you lose it?"

Dare, Silt. Just dare. "When I was a young boy, my own parents conspired against me to break my connection to sorcery forever."

THIRTY-NINE

"T ell me about them." Mina and Adham hadn't committed to much of a shared future, but perhaps they could share his past. "Tell me what happened." Right when she wondered if she ought not to have pushed him, he appeared to resign himself.

"Over the years, my mother and father had both been robbed of their powers, then enslaved by other Sorceri. The three of us shared a difficult life, but we found some measure of happiness. And I was a good son, a genuinely good child."

She imagined Adham as a golden-eyed boy, and her chest tightened.

"Some of my earliest memories are of hunting game for them, keeping our larder full. In the market, I stole things they enjoyed, anything to brighten their harsh existences. I thought they loved me in turn." His gaze grew distant, his complicated mind awash in memories.

"Please, go on."

"When I was six, I wandered out too far into the desert, tracking a deer. I discovered my power over sand among those mysterious dunes. My sorcery was so absolute, I knew I was the king of that element. A slave like me was the King of Sand, and in a desert realm like Sorselan, no ability could be greater. I expected my parents to be thrilled when I told them. Yet they looked at me . . . differently. I felt the love they had for me change as if it'd been cleaved with a sword."

Adham paced once more, the firelight silhouetting his tense frame. "I think that's why my mind turns to that fateful day in the dunes so much. It was truly the last day of my childhood. Of innocence." He glanced up with an embarrassed scowl.

"What happened then?" Mina asked, though she could guess the ending of the story. That fateful day had been his last day to be *loved*.

"From then on, both coveted my soul, manipulating me to give it up. Especially my father. Even at that age, I knew I couldn't part with something so important, but they were relentless. He told me he would use my ability better than I could and protect us with it—we could leave the slums and have all the food we could ever eat. Ultimately I trusted the two of them more than myself. I was eight when they persuaded me." He stopped and faced her. "I was so young and gullible that I handed it over to him with love."

Mina's heart was breaking for the boy he'd been. "Did your father deliver on his promise?"

"No." Bitter laugh. "With my sorcery, he took control of Sorselan with ease. He left my mother and me in slavery and married again, fathering another son he genuinely cared about."

Mina bit out a curse. "Were you able to forgive your mother for her part?"

He shook his head. "I can't explain to you what it feels like for a Sorceri to lose their root power, that soullessness, and she *knew* what it would do to me. They'd been tricked out of theirs, and they visited that same torture onto their child. In a chain unbroken," he added almost to himself. "After my father left us, she grew unstable. I was on my own from about nine years old. I later heard that she drank a cup of wine with enough poison to end a Sorceri."

This was his childhood. No wonder he'd grown hardened. "What happened to you then?"

"I endured. I grew tall and strong, so I was assigned duties as a laborer. Every day I was forced to dig sand, me, the former king of it."

Mina imagined how she would react if she lost something so intrinsic. It would be like someone stealing her logic. She cast a glance at her arm wound. Someone basically *had*, setting her on a path to insensibility. Thank the gods, Adham's soul had been returned.

"My existence was one of the deepest misery, interrupted only by rage. But nothing that happened to me during those years—no outrage, no violation—could compare to the treachery that had come before."

Mina could guess what predatory Loreans had done to this male. Her heart ached for him, pain like a physical wound. She believed one day he might tell her all the details about his past, but not tonight. "When did you get your sorcery back?"

"For years, I plotted, waiting for a chance to strike. Decades trudged by before I could abduct my guarded half brother. I threatened to kill him, unless my father returned my soul." Adham ran a hand over his face. "The bastard readily surrendered it. To save his other son, he gave up all his power—a move that fucked with my head worse than anything else he could have done to me. The man wasn't a monster; that would've been easier to take. He could, in fact, feel love. He just hadn't felt love for *me*."

Gods. She'd once asked Adham who'd hurt him, imagining a capricious lover. It'd been so much worse.

"Think about it: if my own parents didn't value me enough to safeguard my soul, then either no one is to be trusted—or I wasn't worthy of protection as a child." Looking weary, Adham sank down on the edge of the bed. "Both scenarios are grim."

"Of course you were worthy." She eased closer to him. "What they did was horrible. But maybe your father gave back your power so readily because he regretted his actions."

Adham's gaze went distant. "I suppose it's possible."

"What happened to him?"

"Those he'd crossed when he took over Sorselan learned he was an Inferi once more. They assassinated him and his second family. My half brother was destined to die one way or another. My father should have kept the power and let me kill my brother."

"But you wouldn't have."

"No?"

"No." Over these days, she'd studied him and probably knew him better than he knew himself. "What did you do with your reclaimed ability?"

"Revenge became my mistress once more. I targeted all those who'd conspired against my father. *I* could hurt him—no one else should dare to and live. I hunted them in spectacular ways, mistaken for a vengeance deity. Then I took control of the realm. Doing so was child's play. After a millennium of ruling, I grew bored. I left for other dimensions with sand, seeking a challenge, finding none."

"And so you meddled with humans, becoming a god to them."

He shrugged. "Why not? No deities were present. Few other immortals challenged me."

"Were you happy? If the Gaolers hadn't targeted you, would you ever have left that life?"

His brows drew together, as if she'd posed a question no one had before. "No, I wasn't happy. But what else could I work toward? What was my purpose? I think people who are satisfied know something I don't. They've solved a mystery I've just scratched the surface of. I want that mystery to be revealed." He gazed at her face, parting his lips to say more, but then he must've thought better of it.

What he called a *mystery* might be what she called *divinity*, and maybe they were both right, seeking the same bond—the thrum and glow of alchemy.

At length, he murmured, "I would do a lot of things differently. Starting with never trusting my parents."

"Is that why you've never had children?"

"I have it on good authority that I'd be a horrible father."

"Who told you that?" She was livid on his behalf.

"No one in particular. Just a consensus over the years. And they weren't wrong. After my parents' treachery, I never put another's needs before my own. I know little about fatherhood, but I believe you must put a child before yourself."

"I'm so sorry yours didn't."

Resentment crossed his expression. "I don't want your pity. I had enough of that as an . . . an Inferi." The scars ran so deep that he could barely say the word all these years later. "Which is why I didn't want to tell you."

"I'm not pitying you. I'm feeling for you. Your pain has become my own."

He studied her face, must be searching for a lie—one she could never give him.

Catharsis.

Was bullshit.

Silt had said the words aloud, giving Kosmina what she wanted. For better or worse, he'd acknowledged what had made him the man he was today, and she'd accepted it.

But he didn't feel any better. A secret like his wasn't steam to be released from a valve; it was a bruise best left untouched.

Uneasiness rippled through him at this vulnerability. He'd sworn to never again open himself up to the possibility of betrayal—yet he'd just dropped his shield and bowed his chest. Comprehension hit him: if Kosmina betrayed him too, he would not recover. . . .

He reminded her, "Now it's time for you to keep your end of the bargain. You're to tell me something you've never said to another."

"Very well." She held his gaze with unblinking eyes. "Sorcerer, my heart is open to you forever." Such simple words—accompanied by an innocent caress across his cheek—fucking *felled* him.

He pulled her closer, inhaling the scent of her hair and relishing her breaths on his marked chest. While he'd been so mired in retribution and then conquest, he hadn't seen what was right before him—the most remarkable female he'd ever encountered. And he was winning her heart.

Yet nothing was pure. She felt this way because she didn't know about his latest lie. He'd taken something beautiful—her own trust—and tainted it.

Silt sullied. That was what it always did. What *he* did. What he would still do.

He stared at that ceiling and knew: *I'm no better than my parents.*

In time, she drifted off once more, wrapped in his arms. Considering her attack earlier, he remained awake. Drinking from his flesh regularly was the last viable option open to them, with all the risk that entailed.

He'd always envied Kosmina's focus, but now focus only illuminated a shit situation. *Fucked as fucked can be.*

FORTY

*O*ut of time.

Awakening alone, Mina had risen and stared in horror at her reflection, at her eyes.

Fully red.

And stabbing pains had begun to shoot across her injured arm. She couldn't stay here another night.

Where was Adham? She'd asked him not to sleep around her, but when she'd roused outside of his warm arms, her disappointment had been shaped a little like grief. Her first thought? *Better get used to this, Mina.* He'd been distant for the last two days, ever since she'd pressured him to recount his past to her.

Or maybe since her attack on him.

She gazed out of the window of their room at her next destination: the hive. In the distance, lightning struck all around that mountain, an ill-omened backdrop. She imagined that lethal queendom readied for her. *Brace, fiends. Here I come.*

Mina had no choice. Her gamble of staying here hadn't paid off. She rose to ready for her one-way trip, had just belted on her sword when a knock sounded at the door. She called, "Come in."

Enti entered, looking as tired as Mina felt. "I sensed you would leave soon. And now I can see it in your eyes." She added, "Perhaps your sorcerer senses it too."

His first clue: I tried to force my fangs into his throat. Mina canted her head at the sorceress. Though Enti smelled wonderful, her neck didn't beckon a bite. Why hadn't Mina had the urge to drink her, or anyone else in the castle? The only one she wanted to consume was Adham. "Have you seen him?"

"He cornered Xodin downstairs to grill him about dimensional vulnerabilities and the hive. Preparing for your trip as usual," Enti finished brightly.

Once Adham realized that his questions still had the same dismal answers, he'd stop asking them. "I see."

"Xodin hasn't updated you about the weapon lately. And you haven't asked me at dinner about my progress."

"No. I haven't." Mina had tired of playing games.

Enti's lips parted. "You *knew* I couldn't make it. How?"

Shrug. *You tell me much when you tell me little.* "I know whenever the sorcerer lies to me. He told me you were still working on it, and that he intended to leave with me. I've known all along that both were falsehoods."

Enti blew out a breath. "I'm impressed. Silt is a practiced deceiver. One of the best."

The name still struck Mina wrong. When she could forget about his lies, he was more *Adham.* "And I'm an observer. You read minds for answers. I deduce them."

"Why would you stay an entire week with no weapon coming? And why would you show up at dinner, so happy to be on his arm?"

Because she'd thought he would change. Fall in love. Leave with her. "The downstairs gatherings were fascinating to me, since everyone knew about Silt's ruse. You each danced like you were invisible and I couldn't see your movements. So many lies were spilled, I was able to learn everyone's tells."

Enti nervously adjusted her mask—her tell. "You seemed so optimistic."

"That's my nature in general, and I believed I could drag him over the finish line." She'd begun to accept that she couldn't—because he didn't *want* to reach it with her. "I thought he might surprise me."

Something unsettling flashed in Enti's eyes. "I've waited eons for a male to surprise me."

Even after Mina had figured out the sorceress's part in Adham's deception, suspicions about this place continued to whirl. Mina still sensed something wrong. No surprise, this Sorceri lair wasn't as it seemed.

Smoothing her hair, Enti said, "Your extra days here weakened you. You rolled the dice harder than the demons downstairs—and with far more at stake."

"Yes. But I hesitated to go for other reasons." *Hampered by fear and ruled by pleasure.* She'd pitied the denizens here, but she'd been just as pitiable. She'd feared losing Adham—and her life— and the pleasure she'd found with him had ruled her.

Tragic.

"I can imagine what kept you here." Enti fanned herself.

Another shrug. "No gambler can win all the time."

"Debatable, young princess. You hold no anger toward me for my part?"

Mina tried to muster a smile. "I was warned. Beware the Sorceri."

A quake rumbled, shaking the castle, rustling the vines outside and sloshing the sea.

When the vibrations stilled, Mina said, "Sorceress, leave

with me. Tonight."

Instead of answering, Enti moved out to the balcony, and Mina followed. "Sometimes you can hear the ghouls roaring from their mountain." The sorceress's gaze narrowed on it. "I try to muffle the sounds for everyone here. Nervous guests don't dream as much."

Chills rose on Mina's arms.

Enti turned to her. "My powers won't help me one bit away from Castle Vitis. This is where I'm safest. Besides, it's getting even more dangerous out there. Revenants, wendigos, and hellhounds have started roaming outside their normal territories. The undead continue to hunt, but unpredictably now."

"And still, I'm going." Mina inwardly repeated, *All the worlds should fear me.*

"Courageous princess. Silt would be lucky to have you, but he doesn't appreciate you, so you wouldn't be lucky to have him."

"What would you do with a male like that?"

Enti shrugged. "Steal his sorcery, then leave him behind in the dust."

"Will the sword you gave me remain?" Mina had decided not to request anything else, figuring another weapon would just get in the way. Besides, maybe fate would smile on a lone Dacian with a sword taking on a horde. What an epic battle it would be!

"It will remain anywhere in Nightside. I'll make sure of it, as long as I have power." Holding her gaze, Enti said, "I don't wish you ill, princess. I very much hope you succeed."

Mina still sensed deception in the sorceress, but she believed those words. "Thank you," she said, puzzling over the woman. Enti had tried to trick her. *Yet I still like her.*

Adham had tried to trick Mina. *Yet I might . . . love him.*

"I still can't believe you played the player. I'm glad you spent this time with him with open eyes. In thousands of years, he's never formed a bond with a lover. Not once. He gazed at others in perplexity over their attachments."

The mystery. He'd craved the answers. This only made Mina want him more! She ached to imagine how lonely his existence must have been all these years. *But I can't force him to want me as desperately as I want him. I can't force him to leave.*

"When the hottest fires fade, one can hope for ever-molten gold," Enti said. "But you are logical. I'm sure you've *deduced* that isn't possible with Silt." The sorceress turned to go, saying over her shoulder, "Good luck, Kosmina Daciano, and gods-speed. I do hope we meet again someday. . . ."

FORTY-ONE

What the hell are you doing?" Silt had entered Kosmina's room to find her on the balcony, dressed for travel.

Over her tunic and pants, she wore a coat, her sword belted around her waist. When she turned to him, he nearly flinched to see her eyes. Over the night, they'd turned completely red.

"I was waiting for you to return."

"Listen, I've thought about things, and I'm convinced you must drink straight from my flesh. We've both dreamed about that because it might be a cure."

"I don't believe it will work, and I don't have a few days to wait and find out. I've already stayed too long. Tonight, I'll meet my fate head-on while I've still got some fight—and sanity—left in me."

She'd readied to leave without him? He asked slowly, "Why are you acting as if I'm not going with you?"

"Why are you still acting as if you will? I've known for days that you were lying about leaving."

He scrubbed a hand over his mouth. "I did lie. I . . . regret that."

"Have you changed your mind about coming with me?" she

asked with that expectancy in her expression. Even after all his lies, part of her wanted to believe in him.

"No." The word was like a death knell. But he was tired of deceiving her.

"So you let the days go by and had no intention of fighting alongside me. These were probably my *last* days and you played with me?"

"I didn't lie about wanting you. Under different circumstances, we'd be starting something together."

"So where does that leave us now?"

"We have to try this last step before *anyone* leaves," he insisted, his words punctuated by a quake.

"That's the second one today. The pressure is escalating."

"The quakes could end tomorrow."

She rolled her red eyes. "Come on, sorcerer, talk about burying your head in the sand. Do you think the gases of this realm will outstrip your oxygen first? Or will the lava make it quick? We're nearing world's end. Staying here is illogical."

"But trying to defeat a primordial ghoul with a sword makes sense? We're not even certain an escape exists. You value logic so much? You're ignoring it now."

"I'm not setting out filled with false bravado, and I'm not underestimating my foe. Facing the queen will be horrific, but I'd rather fight than surrender."

"Then give yourself a chance." With difficulty, he formed a blade of sand from his pouch and slashed his wrist. "Drink from my flesh. It's not a request."

Kosmina's fangs went sharp as she stared at his blood. She looked ravenous but also . . . wary, like an animal scenting a trap. Heartbeats passed before she broke her stare. "I have to go. Now." She hurried to the door.

Why would she not listen to him? *Maybe because you keep*

lying to her. And she knows you do. Pocketing his sand, he hastened after her into the hall. "Can you just stop for a moment and discuss this?"

She didn't slow when she reached the steps and hurried past the never-ending orgy. "I won't rehash the same arguments. And it's not like I sprang this on you."

"Why won't you *try* to drink me? What would one bite hurt?"

"The time for that has passed. Besides, right now, I'm not sure I *want* to know you that well."

A mace blow to the chest would've hurt less. But he deserved that and more.

Downstairs, banging sounded as the bridge unfurled. *She's actually leaving me?* "Another Lorean with more information might arrive. Your brother might. Xodin just told me that those two immortals somehow survived the hellhounds and will close in on the castle soon. We only need to maintain until then." He raised his regenerating wrist.

When she refused to look at it, striding on toward the foyer, frustration sharpened his words: "You're ready to get both of us killed out there. You're selfish! A typical princess. Nothing matters beyond *your* illness. You've given no thoughts to what *I* need to survive."

She finally slowed and turned to him. "That's not true. If you want to survive, you must leave this place. Can you trust me enough to do that? Please, Adham."

Adham. Fists clenched, he stalked over to stand before her. "You'll never be satisfied with me! You expect me to bend and bend. This reed will break."

She raised her hand to his cheek. "I hope the reed will grow. And I'll grow right beside you."

He just stopped himself from leaning into her touch. But

tonight was not the night he planned to lose her—or to die.

She murmured, "Fight for me." The words were part question, part command; directness mixed with sweetness. "Fight for us?" Her palm trembled against his cheek. So much expectancy . . .

He gritted his teeth, then snapped, "Give me something I *can* fight! With you, it's fucking plague and primordials. You expect too much from me."

She lowered her hand with that gut-wrenchingly stoic look.

Grasping for calm, he rasped, "If you want to punish me for lying to you, this is not the way to do it."

"Yes. So many lies." Her brows drew together, her expression crestfallen. "You said we would comb the worlds together for a cure."

He held up his wrist again. "Yet you won't even try the one on offer right here!"

She wasn't looking at his injury, just stared into his eyes. Hers welled with tears.

Unable to bear her grief, he raised his face to the sky and loosed a roar. *"Ahhh!"* He met her gaze again, not bothering to hide all the turmoil inside him. When she gasped at what she saw, he gripped her nape, his hand shaking on her. "If there's nothing I can say to change your mind, then you lied too! You told me your heart was open to me. Forever."

"It is!" she cried. "Which is why this hurts so much. Sorcerer, I stayed here *for you*. Even as I got sicker, I stayed to give you a chance to see what is right before you. But you haven't. And I don't think you can." She drew back, freeing herself from his grip.

"Don't," he bit out. "You cannot leave me."

Voice breaking, she said. "I have to, because even now, I'm tempted to give you more time." She dashed the back of her hand against her eyes. "Time I don't have." Clasping her sword handle as if for comfort, she whispered, "Good-bye, sorcerer," and stepped out onto the bridge.

In disbelief, he watched her putting space between them, watched her form grow smaller as she reached the other end of the bridge and picked up her pace. Self-preservation warred with undefinable emotion. *Go with her. Live—or perish—with her.*

He'd just taken a step when Enti sidled up to him.

"Let her go, friend. In her heart, Kosmina wishes to meet a heroic end, and in your heart, you wish to remain in the comfort of my keep. She doesn't belong here, but you do."

As Kosmina passed out of sight, he said, "I belong with her." He'd just taken another step when dragon's breath enveloped him like a miasma. His lids went heavy.

At his ear, Enti murmured, "The Silt Harea of old would not follow a woman he'd known for such a short time into a nightmare."

True. And he must still be that man. Kosmina had coaxed him, warned him, offered her partnership and maybe even her love. But he hadn't committed to her. Of course she'd felt like she had to go without him. *She* was the reed that had bent and bent.

Enti continued, "That ghoul queen won't kill you; she'll *keep* you. What purpose do you think you'll serve for her as a new slave? A sentry or a common drone? Perhaps you'll dig tunnels in her hive, laboring like you used to. As we Sorceri often say, 'Once an Inferi, always an Inferi.'"

That word still carried a blade's bite—yet all he cared about was Kosmina's fate against the primordial. His princess needed him. She needed his blood from the flesh. His protection. Him.

Yet he stood, immersed in that smoke, making no move to follow her.

"Now that the vampire's gone, you can return to your previous existence. Pleasure is here for your taking, Silt."

Kosmina called him Adham. If *Silt* belonged here, maybe *Adham* didn't. "That vampire moved me like a desert of sand. There's no going back for me. She believes this is the right course, and I *trust* her."

How . . . *monumental.*

"I trust her," he repeated, tasting the words, finding them right. "So either you are not seeing what's in my heart, or you're lying about it." He dragged his focus from Kosmina's direction to Enti and found her irises swirling. "Why are you sweating? You're using some kind of power on me!" He shook as he resisted it.

At last, that memory he'd struggled to recall surfaced. Hadn't he heard tales of an infernal sorceress who fed on the fall of her victims? One who could conjure anything needed to entrap them?

He swept his gaze around his surroundings, seeing Castle Vitis anew. *Vitis* was the root word of *vine*, but also of *vice*. "You don't read others' dreams. You read their *sins*. You're the Queen of Vice." The gambling, gorging, and orgies here had been by design. She was feeding on sin, enabling it. "You lied about the parole, the Gaolers, everything."

She sneered, "And you *never* lie." Reining in her temper, she asked, "Are dreams so different from vice?"

"Yes!" That was why Enti couldn't create the scythe; the weapon would have been used for virtue.

She smoothed her hair. "Well, I had to lie. Vice has gotten a bad rap. *Vicious* used to mean full of vice, now full of cruelty. People got suspicious of me, so I opted for a rebrand."

"You feed your powers when people surrender—but you can compel them to as well. You're compelling me right now."

"Because without that vampire, you will fall!"

"So *with* her, I won't?" He managed a step away from Enti. "You know I'll be true to Kosmina. You know I'll never smoke again. It doesn't matter to you!"

She ran her forearm over her damp brow. "Your potential for vice is greater than that of anyone I've ever known. For the better part of a millennium, you worshipped it like gold. You could empower me as no one before."

"Never."

"You already have been. You gave me wrath with Xodin, and even some with the princess. And so much deception. That was good, but I need you at your peak—all your lust, your weakness, your jealousy. And, of course, your habit."

"I won't be some mindless host for you. I'm going after Kosmina, will follow her to the end of the worlds." Yet he remained rooted to the spot as Enti's power battled his willpower, a muscle he'd left unused.

"Do you know what that princess's vice is? *Pride.* And she will never allow you to injure hers again with more lies."

"Did you work on her too? Making her leave, so I'd get back to feeding you?" His jaw clenched as he fought Enti's influence. But the smoke swept him up as never before—until nothing could compete against that pull.

Nothing.

Almost nothing.

Kosmina's pull was greater. The princess with her oasis eyes. He squared his shoulders. "I'll never lie to her again."

Desperation crept into Enti's voice. "Why do you deserve another chance with her when you've squandered all you've ever been given?"

He had no answer. Only Kosmina could answer that question. He pictured the way she already reached for him in sleep, and calm filled him.

"You belong here, Silt!"

He hated that name now. "That's not who I am any longer."

At last, he'd discovered himself. "I'm Adham." He was Kosmina's protector. He hadn't only lied to her; he'd lied to himself, because he'd *always* been going on this fateful journey. He'd trained with his sand to give him a shot at defending her.

He would reach his princess before she faced the revenants, then take on hell beside her. If he died giving his life to defend hers, then that would give meaning to everything that had come before. "I'm going to fight at Kosmina's side." With no guarantees, he would cross the desert for her, one dune at a time.

"Just wait! Without you to empower me, everyone living in this dimension will be in jeopardy. Don't abandon us." A quake rumbled, the third one tonight. Enti's eyes swirled hypnotically, and she gave a cry—as if with effort.

"You've been masking the quakes. The Gaolers stopped sending in prisoners because this place is done, just as Kosmina sensed."

"I can handle the quakes until they ebb. And they will!"

He'd said much the same. No wonder Kosmina had lost patience with him. "Listen to me, Enti. The quakes won't end, but Nightside is about to. Your only hope is to come with me. Sound the alarm and evacuate this place. We'll storm the hive together."

"It can't be won!" She ripped off her mask. "You said I lied about everything, but I didn't. I read the Gaolers, and everything I said about that primordial is true. We must make the best of our situation here. Besides, this is my home. I have nowhere else to go."

"Then you'll die here." Finally he could turn from her, taking his first step toward his future. "You have no control over me."

"I might not be able to control you any longer," she said from behind him, sounding less desperate. "But *she* can."

A sinking suspicion gripped him as he glanced over his shoulder. Pearl now stood beside Enti. Her kohled eyes were black as the sea on a moonless night.

And she'd removed her voice-box modulator.

"No!" He sprinted to escape her all-powerful song. But the bridge began to furl once more, trapping him . . . until the ringing notes of Pearl's voice washed over him.

FORTY-TWO

Come after me, Adham. Come after me.

Had Mina hoped he would be jarred into seeing reason, declare his undying devotion, and come running?

Maybe.

Having seen her uncles Trehan and Lothaire evolve in miraculous ways once each had discovered love, she'd believed Adham could as well. She must have counted on too much too soon. *Or too much period.* She'd forced his hand—as hers had been forced—and he'd balked.

Damn him, he'd made all of this bearable. The team of them had made even hell bearable.

As the miles grew between her and Adham, she tried to draw on her logic, but conflicting emotions tolled inside her. Her throat felt tight, and more blood tears threatened. She couldn't afford to lose any blood now that she was in a fight for her survival.

Alone.

No heartfelt yells sounded from behind her. No hectic footfalls as he raced to catch up with her before she faced those revenants on her own. If any of those creatures landed a single hit, a young immortal like her would be done.

Yet Adham had decided to stay within that castle, immersed in what must be his true dreams. She glanced back, could barely discern from afar a last flicker of light. Was he smoking even now? In such a state, would he succumb to all of the castle's other temptations? If so, then Mina would simply have been one female in his endless lifetime of them.

How could she have been so wrong about him? Her chest squeezed, and she stumbled. *Focus, Mina.*

As she neared the edge of the revenants' stony rise, rain began to fall, then pour. Hoping to meet her foes on flat ground, she drew her sword and called, "Hello, there! Does anyone want to come out of their grave and play?"

Rocks shifted, slowly at first, then faster, just like her shifting emotions. Self-pity morphed into outrage. She'd been good to Adham! She'd forgiven his faults and granted him every chance to do better by her. If he didn't have the sense to follow her, then good riddance.

Monsters boiled up from their lair. When the first roar reached her, she squared her shoulders and spat rain. In her current mood . . . *I'm going to lay waste to every last one of them.*

Dozens of them shucked off stones and lumbered down to attack. As they reached her preferred terrain, she sped into the throng. Her sword flashed out like some possessed talisman to sever heads from thick necks.

When a large one launched an anvil fist at her, she ducked under the displaced air and yelled, "I expected Adham to leave"— *slash*—"with me." Its head tumbled as she pivoted to another foe. "We were supposed to do this"—*slice*—"together." Another down. "He promised me"—*strike*—"a future together!"

She surrendered to the riot of her emotions, leaning hard

into fury. *Slash. Slice. Strike.*

Too soon, only one monster remained to hear her venting. She waved it closer. "Come then, and I'll tell you a secret you can't take back to your grave." It careened forward, tongue lolling. "That sorcerer is a . . . a *fucker*!" Her sword arced and took yet another neck. The force of the blow sent the creature's head sailing through the rain. "I said what I said!"

There she stood in a field of twitching bodies, disbelief billowing through her. She sheathed her sword and told the nearest head, "That fucker really isn't coming."

With leaden feet, she trudged past the carnage. She almost stopped herself from glancing back at the castle before it passed from sight. Almost.

Forcing herself onward, she reached the foothills leading toward the hive. Setting upon a stony path, she ascended between rock faces as she searched for an entrance into the mountain, toward what would likely be her final battle.

Would Mirceo ever know that his little sister had bravely met her fate? Maybe Balery could see it all in a roll of her bones. Would Adham regret his choice if he sensed Mina had died?

And still he hadn't come running.

Her brows drew together, and she slowed. Logic finally spoke loud enough for her to hear over her anger. *You didn't imagine the bond between you and the sorcerer.*

Yes, Mina was good at observation, and every signal indicated that he cared about her, maybe even as much as she did for him. He should have followed her. If he remained behind— in a *sorceress's magical castle*—instead of pursuing Mina, some other power must be at work.

But logic also said, *Unless the enchanter truly played you and is now right at home.*

She couldn't believe that. Her heart still clamored for him

alone—because he was hers. Her . . . *mate*. Would that be the lonely one-way street Enti had described?

Possibly. But Mina wasn't ready to give up all hope on Adham.

Turning back toward the castle, she increased her pace until she was sprinting through the pounding rain. What could she say this time to convince him to join her? She couldn't force him to go.

Wait. Yes, she could. She was a Dacian. *I'll take him by swordpoint.* If Mina believed the realm was dying, then she couldn't leave him behind. She ran faster, raindrops pattering her face, blurring her vision.

"Kosmina!" A booming voice carried. "Where are you? MINA!"

"Adham?" He'd come for her! He'd proved himself, risking everything. *Or else he's come to escape the quakes as well.*

She mentally waved that away and quickened her steps even more. Down the stony path, she caught sight of him.

He sprinted toward her, looking huge and frenzied. *"Mina."* His burnished eyes were wild, his lips parted around breaths. He ran full speed until they were upon each other. When she skidded to a stop before him, his hands shot out to grip her shoulders. "You're safe."

"You came!"

He clenched his jaw, as if to hold back the words she could all but see burning in his expression. He finally managed: "We do not part. I never want to separate from you again."

Better! "But what changed?"

"This: I realized I'd rather die beside you—than survive without you."

She made some breathless sound that couldn't decide between *oh?* and *ah!*

"I would have come sooner, but Enti struck. She's the Queen of Vice. She feeds on it and can force others to surrender to it."

Mina had sensed Enti's deception, but she hadn't thought the sorceress would lie about her very identity! Not daring to breathe, Mina asked, "Did you surrender?"

"No. I fought like hell. They tried to keep me from you. Nothing could." He looped an arm around her lower back and dragged her against him. Leaning down, he took her lips.

She gasped, her hands flying to his damp chest. His heart pounded furiously beneath her palms, awakening her bloodlust, her sexual lust. When her fangs sharpened, she jerked back before she nicked him. "Be careful. You see my eyes—*I* am a danger to you."

"You must drink me. You asked me to trust you and leave that place. Eventually I did. I need you to trust me in this. At the very least, let my body make you stronger for the trials ahead."

Was she convinced that this move would cure her? No. But his unwavering certainty kindled a small hope. Yet then she shook her head. "I can't weaken you. You'll need your blood just as much."

He wiped rain from his face. "Pearl sang to me."

Mina's eyes widened. "The siren tried to ensnare you?"

Nod. "When I shed Enti's sorcery, she got Pearl to remove her voice-box modulator. Her notes should have captured me, but I'm immune."

"A Sorceri power?"

"No. Your hold on me is greater than theirs. When they couldn't control me, they let me go with their blessing. Enti even gave me a sword." He waved at the scabbard next to his pouch of sand.

"I don't understand. A siren can enslave any unmated male."

His golden eyes were fierce in the rain.

She whispered, "Sorceri don't have mates."

"Do we not, then? I dreamed about your drinking me because on some level, I already knew what you are. Mine. So I want you to take my blood, whatever strength I can provide, and my memories—because they are already *yours*."

An avalanche of emotion fueled her desire. "We're mates. Found."

He looked so proud as he said, "Delivered to each other by fate."

"Adham, you're *him*."

"Him." He swallowed thickly. "Always."

The rain ended with a gasp, so suddenly it felt like a nod from the gods—like permission that they didn't need. The abrupt silence magnified their shallow breaths, the rustle of their clothes as they shifted even closer to one another.

Voice a rasp, he said, "In the beginning, I viewed you as a desert rose that didn't know the sands were about to destroy it. Yet a part of me wondered, what if the desert gentled its touch? What if it learned to protect instead of destroy?" Light emerged from his palms, and the sand in his pouch rose to float beside them, resembling a silken scarf caught on a breeze.

Her lips parted when it flowed to caress her cheek, the warm embrace of his sorcery made physical. Then he raised his flattened palm, and the sand collected above it. Before their eyes, grains coalesced into a shape. . . .

"It's a rosebud!" A desert rose. "Your power is so beautiful."

He made the twirling bud blossom, as if illustrating what had happened with their feelings. *I love him.* And that love was bound up in the heat that already pulsated between them. The divine had never been closer.

Sorcery reflected off the sparkling quartz in pinpoints across their faces. Eyes rapt on her, he murmured, "I was born to protect you, Kosmina. I will tonight and for all my days after." He returned the sand to his pouch. "You must feed."

"Then I want you inside me at the same time."

He surveyed their surroundings. "We can't do this here. I need to be on guard and get you to safety—"

"You're talking as if this isn't already written in stone. It is."

He wavered but shook his head. "You were right before; we have to escape this dying place. And for your first time, you need a soft bed, time, and a gentle touch. Inside, I'm all chaos. I can't give you what you've dreamed of."

"You told me to follow my instincts. They're screaming at me *to mate* until I can't think. And if I can't think, I can't fight. If your instincts are half as loud as mine, how will we concentrate on our incursion?"

He hesitated. Then he exhaled a pent-up breath. "Your point is sound."

Nothing could stop this now. "You're ready to give me what I want?" Love.

Grave nod. Intent eyes.

She gripped his hard shaft, making him shudder with pleasure. "Then why isn't this inside me?"

FORTY-THREE

*G*ood *question.*

Adham had been immune to the siren's voice because his soul was given; denying Kosmina's own allure simply wasn't possible.

As she peered up at him, he sensed some primal feminine knowledge within her. Was she about to teach him the mystery? She rubbed his shaft, blanking those thoughts, then released him to undress. She stripped off her sword and clothes until she stood naked before him. Though she straightened her shoulders and lifted her chin, his princess trembled.

"Exquisite." *My mate.* As he gazed at her, he had difficulty processing how brightly fortune had shined on him. Now he must be worthy of her.

She backed up to a wet rock face, as far from a soft bed as it could be. "Be with me." Part question, part command.

"Always," he repeated. He dumbly followed, tearing off his belt and yanking free his rain-soaked clothing. He was so stiff that his length slapped against him with his movements. As his eager steps took him closer, the realization struck him that he was about to claim his virgin mate. *It's really going to happen.* He needed to prepare her untried body, sparing her pain.

When he stood before her, he leaned down to kiss her supple breasts, each in turn. She cradled his head to her when he sucked, but her sex's sweet scent drew him lower.

He knelt before her and hooked one of her legs over his shoulder. Burying his face, he inhaled his woman's ambrosia. *My mate's.* The idea tightened his chest as much as it swelled his shaft.

Everything felt different as he spread her with his fingers, baring her pouting clitoris. She was eager too, her folds plump and ready. *This sorcerer's paradise.* He gave her little bud a flick of his tongue. . . .

"Oh, Adham, yes!" She petted her breasts, molding those ravishing mounds to his delight.

He delved a finger into her slickened core. "So *tight*," he grunted against her clit. "Luscious." Burning need besieged him. More than desire. Everything with Kosmina was *more*.

When she pinched her red nipples and jolted, he groaned into her curls, nearly spilling his seed on the ground. Somehow he kept control. He wedged a second finger inside her, thrusting them.

In a wanton voice, she murmured, "I float atop your fingers."

Sand almighty! He pumped them; he licked. Switching hands, he gripped her taut ass and teased her moisture between her cheeks with a blunt fingertip.

"Oh!" She clawed the rock behind her, thighs quivering. "*Ohhh . . .*"

Fingers filling her everywhere, he sucked at her little clit at the same time. She gripped his hair and mindlessly rode his mouth and hand.

As her cries rang in his ears, one thought replayed: *She's mine. She belongs to me.* He set back in to finish her, commanding, "Give me your come." That belonged to him too.

Throwing her head back, she screamed, *"Adham!"* and offered herself up to his lips. Her channel squeezed his fingers, more torment for a man awash in it—until her wet climax almost stole his.

Adham kissed her thighs, then rose to take her mouth, sharing her taste.

Mina gave a cry against his lips, her arousal rebounding. Which meant her fangs were sharp. When she drew back, he understood her hesitation.

Leaning his forehead against hers, he said, "It's time for you to drink, love."

He was ready. Was she? "If this goes the other way—"

"It won't. You've already robbed me of my godsdamned heart. You'll take my blood as I take you. Just follow your instincts."

They'd never been clearer. She hungered for him in every way possible. Yet her gaze dipped to that taunting vein.

"Mina?"

When she peered up at him, his pupils were blown.

"Yes! That. We . . . *Yes.*" He hastily palmed her head and guided her to her knees.

She gripped his length. He bucked with readiness, so she gave him a praising stroke. "Are you sure?"

"Utterly. Certain." Voice husky, he ordered her, "Now."

He asked for it. She leaned forward, licking his flesh in greeting. His taste ruled her, until logic held no sway. As she widened her jaw and suckled the crown between her lips, he didn't breathe, his chest still.

She slowly sank her fangs into his meaty rod behind the head, and that vein gave up its elixir, no punishment necessary. *Homecoming.* A direct channel to the sorcerer's thundering heart.

"Gods almighty." His head fell back, his body whipcord tense as he bellowed to the sky. *"Yes!"*

Blood shot so hard down her throat, she didn't have to suck. She still did, hollowing her cheeks as she consumed him. Her lids slid shut, a canvas for more starbursts.

Life. Magic. Adham.

She'd been born for this. For this sorcerer.

Drinking him so might be a taboo, but it wasn't a danger, and it wasn't wrong. *Nothing this right can be wrong.*

When she opened her eyes again, he was gazing down at her in disbelief. He cupped her face with glowing palms. "Mina. Mine. I'll feed you well for eternity." His erection swelled even more, tightening around her throbbing fangs, as if to hold them there forever.

With each pulse of his mighty shaft, blood surged throughout her body, heating her from the inside. She gripped his narrow hips with her claws, a ravenous vampire glorying in her mate's nectar.

Yet anguish marked his face. "I give you my blood freely, but you're stealing my seed too soon."

A seasoning to go along with her feast? She sucked harder and fondled his tightening sac to milk it from him.

"Can't hold on, beauty." He sounded in agony. "Will spill beneath your bite!" His back bowed as he offered up his rod to her. *"MINA!"* he roared to the night.

His seed pumped from his body into her hungry throat, each contraction of his shaft massaging her fangs and muffling her greedy cries.

"Fuck . . . fuck . . ." he grated in shock as he watched her consume him. Once he'd emptied himself, he groaned, *"Mercy."* His muscles shuddered, so she took pity on him, reluctantly releasing her bite. Boneless, he fell back against the rock.

As she stood before him, her nipples rubbed his sweating chest, her skin tingling with sensitivity and wonder. Magic bubbled like a cauldron in her heart. Her claws met his tattoos, digging into flesh. *Mine.* She felt powerful, wise, *loved.* She was shocked that the cataclysm of her emotions wasn't echoing throughout the Lore, toppling bloody kingdoms.

"Mina," he groaned. "I miss your dark kiss already." Still staggering from his release, he peered down at her face. His adoring look was replaced by a wince he tried to hide.

FORTY-FOUR

No change, huh?" The stoic rise of Kosmina's chin gutted him.

"I . . ." Adham worked to marshal his thoughts. His ejaculation—the hardest a sorcerer had ever come—had left him feeling like a brainless revenant. "Your eyes didn't clear." Though her lips and cheeks were blooming with color, her eyes were somehow . . . redder.

"It was a long shot. Maybe in time."

He gazed down at her arm. He'd imagined those marks regenerating before their eyes once she'd fed from his flesh. If she could be stoic, he could try. He leaned down and kissed her wound. "This brought you to me; I won't let it steal you from me. I will take on hell to get you to safety."

"That's the most arousing thing you've ever said to me." Her ruby nipples jutted in the night air, her hips rocking. And she still looked hungry. *Sand help me.* As if she'd devour him in one gulp.

His lust reignited like a lit wick, his cock bobbing.

Her lips curved. "I have your blood and seed and magic

inside me, but I need more, sorcerer. Show me the divine."

"No pressure, though?" A quake rumbled to mark his words, yet there was no turning back now. He clamped one of her thighs and positioned it at his hip, spreading her for the taking.

"We're already halfway there." She grasped his shaft, tucking the head against her soaked core.

"Woman!" Everything he could do not to shove home! He had to remind himself that she'd never done this before—even when her vampire's gaze was eating him alive. Gnashing his teeth, he tilted his hips to nudge the crown inside her tightness. He'd just come; he struggled not to again. Every detail about Kosmina—from her hungry eyes to her gripping pussy—conspired to undermine his control, just like her bite had. *Don't think about that. Don't think about the initial puncture . . . the first suck . . .*

Stop.

Thoughts of her bite were overrun when he delved deeper. "You'll show me the rest of the mystery. I want it. I want your innocence. Want it all."

She nodded slowly, a promise in her expression.

When he withdrew with a shudder and inched inside her again, her eyes widened. "I can feel your erection throbbing inside me!"

Because it was about to explode. As he seated himself as deeply as he could, his brave princess grimaced.

"Don't hurt." He leaned down to press kisses across her forehead, her nose, her thinned lips. "I'm sorry." Her pain tempered his drives, quieting the voice inside him screaming, *Fuck her hard, fuck her hard!* He held himself still so she could adjust.

"It'll be fleeting," she assured him. "Already it feels better. Probably because of all the blood you gave me." She shifted atop him, getting accustomed. "I think I can take more."

"I'll go slow." He worked his hips, unhurriedly withdrawing and easing back inside her. "We have time." He amended the lie: "We'll make time."

"Better!" She moaned, flashing fangs. "The throbbing is back in force!"

Oh, that it is! Yet he never quickened his pace, just gave her measured thrusts.

She started to meet them, greedy for more. "This is *fantastic*," she cried with the thrill of discovery. "How will we ever stop ourselves?"

His lips curled, another new experience. Her pleasure rendered him light-headed, their connection surpassing any high by magnitudes. Surely he soared.

Sorcery sparked in the night air as the mystery revealed itself. *I've been searching for this my entire life. Have been waiting for her.* "I've found you across worlds and time. I'm never letting you go, princess." He palmed the globes of her ass, pulling her up.

She wrapped her legs around his waist, settling atop his cock. "Hold nothing back! You've made me even stronger." Clamping his shoulders, she leaned back with straightened arms, giving him free rein to plunge as he needed.

Lashed by her cries, he pounded between her thighs, his sweat-dampened skin slapping hers. Quakes rumbled as sorcery swirled. Shock waves were tame compared to each flex of his hips.

Pressure grew inside him, overwhelming his earlier euphoria, until he felt like the geyser that had shot him into the sky.

Out of his mind, he rasped words in the old tongue of Sorselan, praise for his female. As he stared at her, his eyes glowed so brightly they reflected in hers to infinity.

Sorcery whispered all around them, binding her union to Adham. She tasted his magic; she pulsed from his blood. Both sent her skyward.

When warm light from his eyes bathed her, she raised her face, basking in him as she might the sun. "You are magic, Adham. I can see it." She tightened her legs around him, chasing relief.

"You spark it." He reached between them to rub her clitoris. "I'd give it all to you," he said, despite his tattooed vow.

When her head lolled, he gripped her nape, forcing her to meet his sunlight eyes as he thrust harder, *harder*. He widened his stance, his muscles sharp with relief as he obliterated her with sensations.

Despite his force, he was making love to her. Another epiphany struck her as her body tensed to climax. If two souls were in love, then any intensity—no matter how raw or wicked— was lovemaking.

The bond between them thrummed and glowed; even in this dying place divinity existed.

Right when she was at the precipice, he rasped, "I told you I saw everything in the sand. I think I even saw *you* there." Holding her gaze, he bit out the words, "I've waited so long for you, Kosmina."

She tried to answer him, but emotion engulfed her, blinding rapture about to consume her.

With each wild surge of his hips, he propelled her heavenward. "You are everything." He plunged with all his might, his big body straining. "I don't fucking exist without you."

Quakes. World's end. Control's end. They surrendered to transcendence.

He came with a roar, pumping heat into her, his brilliant eyes filled with awe.

Just before ecstasy ripped an answering scream from her lungs, she whispered, *"I knew you could take me here."*

FORTY-FIVE

D ivine?" Adham muttered between breaths, still buried inside her.

"Divine," Kosmina answered, sounding as thunderstruck as he felt.

It wasn't every night one crested such heights. Yet he knew with her, it *would* be. His chest swelled and so did his shaft—even though he'd come till his legs had buckled.

When the ground shuddered again, harsh reality returned, but he was finally—*finally*—ready for it. Clarity followed, and he embraced that as well, seeing through the hourglass at last.

She *was* the reason he'd endured, and now he had a job to do—one he'd been fated to complete since his birth. As he withdrew, she gave a moan of loss.

"Soon, love."

Though doubt flickered in her expression, she said, "I'll hold you to that." They swiftly found their clothes and dressed. Yet before they set out, she murmured, "I don't want to give up this moment in time."

"I don't either. But we have work to do."

"Work, said my pleasure-seeking sorcerer." Her small smile faded. "You were right—this is a suicide mission with no guarantees."

He'd been thinking about that. "I want to leave you here, search the hive, then return for you."

"Your sorcery is growing—I saw it just now—but it's not enough to take on countless ghoul sentries. Not yet."

His magic had simmered earlier, but he couldn't depend on it. He raised his palm, producing a faint light. "Damn my power."

"Enti told me the wendigos, revenants, and hellhounds are roaming farther afield. More danger would likely find me anyway." Another quake vibrated beneath them. "They're coming faster now."

"Enti muted our perception of them, disguising them as if with a Sorceri's mask. For whatever reason, she's stopped affecting them. Without the promise of my vice to fuel her, she must be rethinking her decision to stay."

Kosmina gazed in the direction of the castle. "They were only trying to survive. Do they deserve to die for their actions?"

"I urged her to come with us. She made her choice, and she made it for all of them."

"I asked her too. Apparently, not everyone has the mettle to fight ghouls. I scent them already." Kosmina drew her sword. "We're not far from the hive entrance."

"We'll be ready for them." He'd just drawn his own sword when she went still. "Kosmina?"

She raised her face and frowned. "Huh."

"What is it?"

"I've caught something . . . another scent. An unexpected one." She inhaled deeper. "Cold and sap?"

"Mina?"

Her lips parted. "I smell evergreen trees and snow!"

"Then you've picked up the mortal realm. Where is it coming from?"

"It's faint, the tiniest thread, but it's emerging from within the hive. The quakes may have opened a new rift. Adham, we're so close."

"Just like you said, our escape lies there. With your senses, we could find the exit—perhaps without even facing the primordial." Would the other undead creatures throughout Nightside pick up that same thread? "But we need to hurry."

She nodded breathlessly. "Let's go home."

As they sprinted toward the hive, another quake rocked the realm. He helped her along the shuddering path. "And where will home be? We'll be safest from a recapture in Poly. Will you live with me there?"

She veered around a mini landslide and gave a warm laugh. "I'll live anywhere with you, sorcerer."

"Not to be the heart of the kingdom any longer?"

"I'll be the heart of another kingdom."

That earned her a brief but fierce kiss, their swords clinking against each other before they pressed on.

The path ended at a large plateau. The mountain rose on the far side, skirted by giant rock folds resembling draped cloths. He said, "Any one of those coves could conceal the entrance. What are your senses telling you?"

She scented the air. "It's that one." She pointed with her sword to an area at two o'clock.

"Are you sure?"

"I'm sure," she said wryly as ghouls began to pour out of the opening like ants from a kicked mound, just as Xodin had described. Their green skin blazed in the blustery night, yellow eyes aglow. Their claws and fangs matched those eyes, and they bared them with menace, dribbling infection. "These sentries are meeting us on advantageous ground? They underestimate their opponents."

"They must not understand that they're all that stands between us and our future."

She grinned. "Let's educate them!"

When those sentries charged, Adham and Kosmina met them with their swords flashing. He fought like a man possessed. Well-timed blocks helped him evade claws, while his blade felled one after another.

Between her own inspired sallies, she noticed his moves. "Motivated?" She used a shoulder to brush hair from her face, then skewered a ghoul in the eye. She'd been good with a length of crystal; with a sword she was a marvel.

"As never before. I suspect I can be very hardworking"—he mowed down a trio with one concentrated strike—"when I have the right incentive." Green blood sprayed like a fountain.

"I believe it." She finally could.

"We're making inroads." The ghouls had noticed; their howls grew deafening.

"Almost to the entrance! We need to reach that rift in time—" A crevasse suddenly ruptured beside them, splitting the plateau like a cracked plate. Ghouls bowled against her as the ground shifted. "Adham!" Kosmina evaded their claws but teetered at the edge, nearly horizontal.

He lunged for her, snatching her sword arm before she fell. The drop couldn't be more than a couple of dozen feet, but ghouls had tumbled in to fill the ravine below her.

As Adham yanked her up, they sprang into the air and seized her hair, dangling from it!

"Ahh!" Her head snapped back, neck arcing.

He gripped her arm tighter. Tug-of-war; she was the rope. He slashed his sword behind her, lopping off the ends of her hair.

The recoil flung her into him. *Safe.*

Yet then she screamed. A ghoul had slipped up from behind. Before Adham could defend, Kosmina shoved her free arm between its claws and Adham's neck.

Five new wounds gaped across her skin.

"Kosmina?" Adham backhanded the creature so hard it didn't rise, then pulled her against him. Blood rushed from her arm to soak her slashed sleeve, but he spied the green contagion already spreading.

She'd known she would get clawed! "Why? Woman, why?"

She swallowed, stoic look in place. "What's done is done." As more ghouls welled from the entrance, she freed herself from his grasp, rushing into the fray. "I'll get you inside. You'll pick up the scent of the mortal world as you get closer."

Burying his shock, he charged after her. He would kill every one of the ghouls, get her to freedom, then secure that wishgiver ring. Kosmina would turn within three days at most, but it could be hours. *I'll save her before then.*

Another quake almost sent him to his knees; she was flung feet away. The ghouls, used to this, maintained their footing and attacked him in number. As he carved with his sword, he kept his gaze on her.

She'd leapt to her feet—too late; a sentry swung a rock, bashing it against her temple.

"Noo!" Adham roared when she crumpled to the ground unconscious. Sword slashing in a frenzy, he barreled forward.

But a pair of sentries snatched her up and sprinted inside the mountain with their prize. Others guarded their escape.

He fought headlong. "Mina!" Another quake reverberated. Just before he reached the hive's entrance, a massive landslide rained down.

He dove to follow his mate into the hive—

Boulders caught him, bulleting him back into that new ravine. The force was unstoppable; stone ravaged even his immortal body. Sword and sand lost. And then the ravine closed on him like a giant mouth, swallowing him and a troop of ghouls.

He had to reach her, had to fight! He thrashed with all his strength; exposed bones flayed open his ragged skin. His mangled limbs couldn't budge the rocks. Without moving the rocks, he couldn't regenerate. Pain warred with panic. Air grew scarce in this tomb.

A glow appeared in the dark, a ghoul buried right beside him. It dug its green hand through the rubble toward Adham's trapped arm but couldn't stretch enough to reach him. Desperate to infect, it extended its forefinger until scant inches separated him from a dripping claw. Wriggling closer. Closer. A worm burrowing . . .

Immobilized, Adham couldn't flee. Couldn't fight. Couldn't save Kosmina.

He struggled to sense his pouch of sand, tried to connect with the silt these rocks had created. But suffocation threatened. Would he die and resurrect over and over until Nightside's end? Or until his ghoul neighbor made contact?

Thoughts faded with his air supply. His princess's name carried on his last breath. *"Mina . . ."*

FORTY-SIX

For the love of all that's unholy, will you shut up?" Lothaire snapped as he and Kristoff limped farther away from the first sign of *living* life they'd found in this godsforsaken place. "I tire of your constant complaining. I have Mina's scent, and I will continue to track it." Lothaire's insanity remained piqued after his near death against the revenants and the return of those hellhounds.

Yet Kristoff needed to reach him. "Of course we will follow her, but that castle you passed up back there would've had food." The holding, amid a sea of boiling water, had looked like a lifeline. "We could regenerate and ready ourselves for other foes."

"There was also sorcery in that castle," Lothaire pointed out as they climbed to a rock-strewn plateau beside a mountain. "You failed to learn from my earlier wisdom. Lesson two thousand and twenty-nine: Beware the Sorceri." He inhaled the misty air, frowning. Had he lost the trail?

Probably. They were too depleted to be effective. "You might be able to feed on a reptile's leisurely schedule, but I need blood every day. I could bite my own neck right now."

"Those revenants we passed earlier were beheaded by a lone fighter with significant sword skills and speed—Mina might as well have left a calling card. She was at that castle, but she left it and challenged those creatures for a reason."

Kristoff frowned. "Because of the sorcery?"

"Could be that. Could also be because the world is coming to an end. These continuous quakes tell a story, and the ending is a tearjerker."

"*What?*" Kristoff gazed around in horror, feeling as if they were trapped in a collapsing tin can. "You said an exit would exist. We've been all over this realm and have found none!"

"Perhaps Mina did," he said with an unconcerned shrug. "I scent a mass of ghoul blood buried beneath these rocks, but not her. Though I do smell a sorcerer. Ah! It's the one who accompanied Mina earlier. Where are you, sorcerer? Come out, come out." Lothaire climbed atop a mound of boulders, repeating, "Where are you?"

Still dumbstruck that this world was ending, Kristoff gazed on in silence. Did Lothaire have enough sanity left to answer his own question?

At length, the Enemy of Old peered down at his feet.

Mina burned in the hive of ghouls, with no idea what had happened to Adham.

Her fever raged as it hadn't done since she'd been a child, held securely in Mirceo's arms. As she fought the contagion, her body flailed on the ground. Lucidity waxed and waned. She was transforming.

No, not transforming.

I'm dying, soon to be reborn a monster.

Regaining consciousness, Mina had found herself on a

raised shelf of rock inside a hollowed-out cavern that must be several miles wide. Green slime coated the towering walls, giving off a sick-tinged light. A rudimentary stone throne stood nearby.

At least two dozen sentries circled her.

She tried to rise, but the infection had set in with a vengeance. She had to get away from these creatures and find Adham. *He's still alive. He must be.* She longed to guide him to freedom. At least one of them could be saved.

More quakes hit, the stone vibrating beneath her. She again detected that thread from the mortal realm. After all their struggles, she and Adham had been so close to deliverance.

She mopped sweat from her brow. This couldn't be happening. The worst fate for an immortal had befallen her. A Lorean's body lived through almost everything—oftentimes even death.

Yet she didn't regret saving Adham from that ghoul. Logic said, *You were succumbing to plague anyway. Best to sacrifice for him.* Her heart said, *That's not why you did it.*

She loved him.

But her actions had likely been for naught. If her fate was a nightmare, what was his? Clawed as well? Trapped in Nightside until it imploded into nothingness?

They'd been so close. . . .

Tears coursed down her cheeks. She held onto her love for him, wanting to cradle something so precious as her fever intensified, marking her end. She would cradle that love until cognition left her.

Adham.

The ghouls began to sway in unison. In her delirium, she felt linked to all the monsters in the mountain, as if she shared a collective hivemind with them.

She sensed these sentries were excited that their contagion

burgeoned in another host. Drone ghouls labored away in their tunnels, searching for an escape from the realm. Somewhere in this cavern, the primordial queen longed for her mate and brother. Ages ago, she'd dispatched him through another rift to the mortal world to explore new territory and to infect. But the rift had closed behind him.

The queen was frantic to reach him and to escape this dying land. She had laid eggs for others to seed, but she wanted her chosen king to sire their future generations, passing on his strength and sentience—

Mina shook her head hard. She wanted no shared thoughts with them, ached to scour her mind clean of the illness they'd inflicted upon her.

Even as the last of her strength faded and her lids grew too heavy to keep open, she bared her fangs at the sentries.

Though she'd provoked them, none would attack. Because she would soon be one of them.

She closed her eyes and dreamed of a sorcerer with eyes like the sun.

FORTY-SEVEN

Adham resurrected to waves of pain. He comprehended where he was and his lack of air. Soon he would suffocate again, only to be resurrected.

He would accept this fate if he could save Kosmina first. How much time had passed since she'd been taken? *Must reach her.*

How? Mangled body. Withered power.

He shoved against the stones trapping him. His futile efforts only brought him closer to that ghoul claw. Had it eked out another inch closer?

Consciousness faded once more. *Need air. Need—*

Air?

For the second time in Nightside, it washed over him to fill his emptied lungs.

Over the sound of his hacking coughs, he heard other immortals. Two males were arguing as they dug him out. He tried to yell, *Mind the ghoul!* But his jaw was shattered.

Hands clamped his limp body. As they lifted him from the last of the rubble, he narrowly missed that still-buried claw.

Someone managed to prop him up against a boulder. Through the blood in his eyes, two shapes grew visible. He blinked until he made out appearances: one had dark-blond hair and blue eyes. The other had red eyes, pale hair, and a fierce countenance.

Vampires.

The red-eyed one crouched before Adham. "A burial in rock, huh? Not as lengthy as my burial was, but it probably got your attention. If I weren't on a mission, I'd have gotten you to sign my new ledger for your freedom."

Ledger. As Silt's sight cleared, he recognized the Enemy of Old from their last meeting ages ago.

"You're the sorcerer I scented with my niece," the vampire said. "Do I know you from somewhere?"

Adham tried to answer, could barely move his broken jaw.

Realizing the problem, Lothaire's attention dipped to Adham's chest, to his ripped shirt. He reached forward and tore away the bloody cloth to reveal tattooed skin. "I never forget a tattoo. You're Silt Harea, the Sandman. Where's Kosmina? Just nod in her direction."

An immortal as old as Lothaire could possibly save her! Adham managed to nod toward the hive entrance, shocked to find the landslide had blocked it. He grunted, "Ghous . . . too . . . er. Save . . . er!"

"Aww. Has little Mina made a conquest?"

"In ountain. *Dig!*" They could get through those boulders quickly enough.

Lothaire followed his gaze, then turned back to assess Adham. "You wouldn't have separated from her unless tons of rock had covered you. So that landslide must have struck before you could get to her. It probably happened during that big quake last night." An entire night had passed? "Which means she's been captive of the ghouls at least since then.”

Yes, yes, go fucking get her!

“Well, that is disappointing.” Lothaire stood. “Kristoff, the mission has changed.”

Kristoff? The one Kosmina had wanted was here for her. Adham didn’t care as long as the Gravewalker saved her. “Changed to what?”

“The assassination of a Dacian princess.”

Noo! Adham thrashed his wasted body again.

Lothaire said, “The ghouls will have infected her. She’s even now one among them.”

Adham had two immediate foes: ghoul contagion and these vampires. If he didn’t regain his sorcery, he’d lose Kosmina to one or both.

He glared down at his frame, at the compound fractures and crushed bones. He was more helpless than he’d been as an Inferi.

No sorcery. No Kosmina.

Her earlier words whispered through his mind: *You are magic.*

He hadn’t imagined that spark as they’d claimed each other. His sorcery had simmered, just untapped. If he could create a desert rose, he could bring a reckoning. *As with a building, the only difference is scale.*

Kristoff scowled at Lothaire. “You went straight to assassination? You never even considered the Ring of Sums for her, did you?”

I did!

Lothaire said, “As you remember, Dorada already controls me. And my new ledger isn’t yet big enough to tempt her.”

“You *have* thought about it, then.”

“Attributing decency to me is the foremost mistake of my fallen enemies,” Lothaire said. “Will you join their ranks?”

"You didn't deny it!"

While they argued, panic filled Adham, supplying him with enough adrenaline to shove his dislocated shoulder against the rock behind him and work it back into place. Function returned to one hand. He used it to grip a leg bone. Choking back pain, he manipulated his splintered femur back under the skin and muscle to speed along regeneration.

Lothaire asked, "Do I look like the type of vampire who would bargain his soul away for a distant, inconsequential relative?"

Kristoff paced. "Use all your knowledge to figure this out!" He must truly care about Kosmina.

"Wendigo toxin responds to salt. Nothing in my memories hints at a similar weapon against ghouls."

As the realm spun, Adham cobbled together his other leg. Somehow he stayed conscious. Even with regeneration, he wouldn't be able to walk, much less fight, for hours. Unless . . .

Could his atrophied power compensate for his broken body? He needed substantial amounts of sand, yet none was here for the taking.

You're the King of Sand—it's there for the making. All he had to do was conjure millions of years of mechanical force and energy.

Lothaire and Kristoff's argument faded as he concentrated. Kosmina needed him; she needed a reckoning. *You are magic.*

Instead of trying to force his sorcery to obey his commands, he recalled what had occurred whenever it had sparked on its own.

Bonding with Kosmina. Dreaming of her.

The divine. The mystery. She was both.

He'd realized that he was a protector, born with one job: to keep Kosmina Daciano safe. He'd been equipped with a sole power. He stiffened as recognition hit; pain made him dizzy, but he held on to the thought. *This sorcery is as much hers as it is mine.*

Instinctively, he knew that if he allowed it, his power would grow to match his love for her. No time to waste. Once more, he dropped his shield and bowed his chest, opening himself up to her. To them. To everything.

His hands began to glow. He clenched them, concealing that light from the vampires. For now.

Sorcery burgeoned inside him infinitely, the wellspring in the desert, the oasis just waiting for him to find. In the deepest recesses of his mind, he could see his power overrunning all obstacles, bursting through a dam of silt. Crystalline—

Light beamed from his eyes. Sorcery sparked his regeneration, his heartbeat thundering to pump magic and blood to injuries.

All the while, the vampires argued over Kosmina's fate, never knowing that they would have no bearing on it.

When his jaw healed enough to speak, he said, "I won't let you hurt her."

Lothaire turned to him with a laugh. "And what are you going to do about it, Sandman? It'll take you hours, if not days, to regenerate your limbs." He told Kristoff, "I've made my decision, and quarrelling with you no longer amuses me." Lothaire turned to size up the landslide.

With a curse, Kristoff followed. Still sniping at each other, they began moving the boulders that divided Silt from Kosmina.

Those rocks should pay a price for that. He waved his hands, deploying sorcery until the stones glowed gold.

The vampires leapt back.

With a yell, Adham levitated the boulders. *You are magic.* In midair, he crushed them down to rock . . . crumbled them to pebbles . . . pulverized them like gritty fireworks.

At last, silken sand flowed into an immense pile on the ground beside him. He had tons of it to work with, and it fueled him in turn.

The vampires gazed on warily, ready to attack. *Try it.* They were no longer a threat to Kosmina. Nothing would stand in Adham's way now, not even his wounds.

He directed the finest sand to pour over his body, then stiffened it, forming a suit of armor to scaffold his bones in place and to help him move. Biting back agony, he rose—a hybrid king, half sand, half man. Sand masked his face like the Sorceri hunters of old. He spun two tornadoes of it to flank him.

With cold intent, he addressed the two vampires. "This doesn't concern you."

"She's a ghoul by now." Lothaire flashed his fangs. "Princess Kosmina is a proud female, worthy of her line. She would never want to go on like this."

"*I* will use Dorada's ring to turn her back."

"Will you then? Long ago, I read your tattoos with interest, considering those Sorselan words a challenge. You marked yourself with a vow never to lose your root power. Dorada will demand one thing of a sorcerer like you—your very soul."

"Yes."

Lothaire clearly hadn't expected that answer. "You'd become an Inferi for Mina?"

"Anything."

"Even if you secured the ring, it can't undo death. As soon as the sickness took hold, the Mina we knew was lost. You'll have to do what's necessary. Or we will."

"Stay the fuck out of my way. Try to harm her, and the last thing you'll breathe is sand."

Instead of attacking, Lothaire's expression glimmered with interest. He hiked a thumb at him and remarked to Kristoff, "I've got to see what this Sandman can do."

Ignoring his pain, Adham rushed through the cleared entrance to the hive, vaguely aware of the vampires following him. A storm of more sand trailed them.

Man-made—or ghoul-made—tunnels opened in all directions. Figuring they'd each lead to the hive's heart, he chose one and charged in.

A troop of dozens of sentries met him. He waved his hands, directing focused grains until a wall of sand hardened. He wielded it against them like a giant cudgel, liquefying them to the soundtrack of Lothaire chuckling and Kristoff telling him, "Shut up and let the sorcerer concentrate."

Nothing could distract Adham; nothing could mute his godlike power.

In Nightside, one threat after another had attacked him and Kosmina. Now *he* was the sinister threat—the King of Sand.

Body healing with each moment, he vaulted over the puddled remains, heading into hell. From deeper within the mountain, untold groans sounded. What must be thousands of ghouls teemed upward to greet him.

He sent another wall of sand at them. It splattered the ghouls, one row of them after another.

The world was glowing green blood and sand.

Blood and sand. A reckoning.

From behind him, Lothaire muttered to Kristoff, "Beware the Sorceri."

Yes. Fully empowered now, Adham was unstoppable. He would rescue Kosmina from this place, get her to the mortal realm, then call upon Dorada.

He knew that old witch would come for his soul.

Especially when it produced power like this. She would be the Queen of Evil and of Sand, and Adham would call it a bargain because he would have Kosmina back.

Blood. And sand.

FORTY-EIGHT

The fever dreams ebbed, and the fog burned away. After hours—or nights—had passed, Mina's eyes opened. She blinked and brought things into focus; those sentries still circled her, yet now their mouths were slack.

What happened? She didn't feel like a ghoul. Maybe none of them did. She still had cognition; did they? She knew certain facts. She'd been scratched. Infection had spread. She had burned with fever and suffered delirium.

She was afraid to look at her shaking hands. Would they be green?

Summoning all her courage, she glanced down. Her skin remained the same! She ripped at her slashed sleeve.

Smooth flesh greeted her. Not only had the ghoul scratches disappeared; so too had her plague wound. How was this possible? Energy filled her, and she felt like her old self.

The ghouls around her hissed and shifted threateningly, tightening their circle. The hivemind link she'd experienced had disappeared. She leapt to her feet and swept her gaze about, seeking a weapon. She'd somehow escaped their contagion once;

she didn't hold out hope for a second time.

"Kosmina!" Adham's deep voice carried from inside this mountain. He'd survived!

"I'm here! I'm in trouble!"

"Hold tight!"

As the ghouls closed in on her with bared claws, she scented Adham—and sand. *A lot* of sand. He was accompanied by . . . Lothaire? Yes, and Kristoff too.

They must have been the two immortals who'd faced such hardships here! Somehow they'd breached this realm and located Adham, and now the trio fought their way toward her.

Their footsteps sounded in the tunnels, accompanied by the screams of ghouls. A louder roar echoed from deeper in the mountain, raising chills on her skin. *The primordial.* Faster and stronger than any of the rest.

But Mina couldn't worry about the queen right now. Ghouls closed in. She had no weapon, couldn't use her speed to break through the crowding line of them without risking another scratch. They were close now, mere feet away. She pivoted, baring her fangs.

Before her eyes, sand flooded into the chamber like a swarm of bees. It solidified into a straight line, hovering. . . .

"DUCK!" he bellowed.

She dropped to the ground. "Now!"

The sand sliced through the air like an enormous scythe mowing down blades of grass. Heads rolled all around her. As bodies crumpled one by one in a dance of spasming limbs, she skirted their claws and kept herself safe.

"Whoa." Adham's sorcery was magnificent! How had he reclaimed it? She told the decapitated head closest to her, "The King of Sand is back!"

He charged into the chamber, eyes gleaming with magic and

emotion. Kristoff and Lothaire followed.

She grinned at her sorcerer, who looked like a desert god. Sand made up a suit of armor and formed a mask around eyes like the sun. Two funnels of sand stood guard beside him.

He did a stutter step at the sight of her. "Kosmina! What happened to you?"

"I don't know. I lost consciousness a couple of times, but I woke feeling great." Her attention drifted behind him. "What are you two doing here?"

"Rescuing you, obviously," Lothaire said. "Or euthanizing you. It all depended on how much ghoulness you retained. After excavating the sorcerer from a landslide, we've been unneeded as he annihilated countless bogeys to reach you."

"A landslide?" What had happened to him? And why wasn't he taking her into his arms?

"Woman, your . . . your eyes are clear!" His were wide with shock. "The red is gone."

"So she *did* have the plague too!" Lothaire said. "Buried the lede there, no, sorcerer?"

Mina ignored her uncle. "Look, my arm has healed completely." She held it up.

"How can this be? That sentry sliced your skin. The infection was spreading."

"I had a raging fever." Her brows drew together. "But I felt like a battle also raged inside me, as if one contagion fought the other, but neither won."

"Miraculous."

Lothaire told Adham, "Assuming Mina drank from you— and I do assume that—your blood probably helped that battle. Nothing like a sorcerer to make opponents so crazed they both lose all."

Mina said, "However it happened, I've been delivered from two horrible fates. Am I ghoul-proof now?"

Lothaire shrugged. "One way to find out."

"Which we will not risk." Adham started toward her. "We'll have time for shock later. For now, let's leave this foul place behind. Do you still detect the scent of the mortal realm?"

"I'm struggling to pick it up in the midst of all the putrid slime." The cavern walls seemed to ooze more sickness, the rocks weeping it. "But I think we need to head deeper into this cavern." She glanced at Lothaire for confirmation—the king's senses were strong—and he nodded.

Adham took her hand, and the group hastened onward. He kept his sand at the ready, his tornadoes tightening.

Gaze alert, she said, "I sense other sentries concealed all around us. Yet I can't see them."

Lothaire muttered, "Stay sharp, and do not run if you can help it. Running just makes them frisky."

As they passed an opening, Mina cast a glance into another soaring cavern, and her steps faltered. "Oh, gods."

A multitude of huge greenish-yellow eggs covered every inch of the ground and walls, and more sacs dangled from the ceiling. The quakes had dislodged a number of those. As the group watched, one sac plummeted to the ground to burst in a splash of slime and half-formed limbs.

Lothaire gave a thrilled laugh. "How *refreshing*. Just when you think you've seen it all!"

Another quake rumbled, intensifying. Boulders crashed all around them before the aftershocks quieted. In the dust and confusion, Mina had to yank her hand from Adham's—to grasp the monstrous one that had clamped her neck.

Comprehension struck, and Mina swallowed against the chill pressure. Camouflaged in sickness, emerging as if from the very wall, the primordial had struck.

And she has me in her clutches.

FORTY-NINE

The mother of ghouls stood behind Kosmina, a nine-foot horror.

Adham's sand was useless when this female could rip off his mate's head without blinking. A single graze and Kosmina could succumb again. Her eyes, now so clear, were stark, but she somehow held herself still.

More sentries skulked from tunnels into the cavern, readying for a battle. *Standoff.*

Adham was crazed to defend Kosmina. Yet this queen was no ordinary monster; only cold logic would prevail here.

Movement out of the corner of his eye.

Lothaire tensed to attack with his bare hands.

"She's a primordial. Do not dare," Adham commanded him. He would take Lothaire's own head before he allowed anyone to jeopardize Kosmina.

"What does she want, sorcerer? She's sentient. To a point." That earned Lothaire a hiss from the queen.

Yes, Adham spied something *knowing* in her gaze. At length, she nodded at his palms.

Kristoff murmured, "She wants your sorcery. For what . . . ?" He trailed off as another quake rumbled. The mountain groaned and seemed to adjust its position. "Ah. I finally scent what she's after."

Lothaire turned his attention to a spot in the distance. "A couple of miles away, there's a crack in the far wall of this cavern." Adham could barely make out a fracture about two inches wide. "I scent the mortal realm just beyond it, but it's too small for a monster and her army to escape. She must know what the sorcerer did to those boulders and wants him to pulverize her way out of here." Lothaire added, "See, Kristoff, as I said: if an entry exists, then an exit will as well."

He snapped, "Is this really the time?"

Adham grated, "Will you two stop bickering?"

Kosmina dared to whisper, "She wants to reach her twin brother and mate. He went to the mortal realm, but he got trapped there."

"Yeah." Lothaire sucked his teeth. "About her mate. So a certain witch broke into a certain wizard's haunted house—"

"*Ahh-wooooooo,*" sounded from somewhere within the hive.

Lothaire's head swung around. "We know that sound. The hellhounds are crashing this party." Growls joined those howls to make an undead chorus. "Revenants and wendigos too. I think everyone's gotten the memo that Nightside has been canceled— and that there's one way out."

With a wave of her free hand, the queen sent a number of ghouls to beat back the invasion.

A steam vent shot open beneath one sentry, flash-cooking green skin from yellow bones. The smell of gore and sulfur filled the cavern.

Adham addressed the queen: "We all need to leave *now.* Give the vampire to me, and we can resume this on the other side.

But if you claw her, I will scour you until you're not even a memory."

Another quake. More boulders whistled through the air as they rained from the ceiling, pounding to the ground and flattening the queen's guards.

The primordial hissed again with frustration—until the cavern shifted like a house of cards.

That cracked wall in the distance ruptured, the fracture forking down like a growing bolt of lightning. Within moments it had stretched to a couple of feet in width, a new rift. The nighttime sky of another world became visible. The land of mortals.

The queen's yellow gaze darted to the opening; Kosmina swallowed; the vampires froze; Adham didn't dare breathe—

Kosmina suddenly twisted from the queen's grip and dropped like a blur, kicking backward from the ground to strike one of the ghoul's knees.

I recognize that move, he thought as he swarmed the primordial with sand.

As Kosmina scrambled out of the way, he unleashed his power. The queen shrieked with fury and fought his sand with her monstrous frame. Baring fangs and claws at them, she charged through the tornadoes. *Fuck, she's strong.*

Voice strained, he said. "Were you scratched, Mina?"

"No, I'm okay."

"Watch yourself," Lothaire warned. "You must not make that creature bleed."

He bit out, "I've got this." But the primordial kept coming, digging in against him.

"Uh, Adham?" Kosmina said from beside him.

With another wave of his hand, he used the cyclones to sweep the queen off the ground, taking away her momentum.

Wrestling against her strength, he funneled the thrashing creature back to the other side of the cavern, toward the throne of her doomed queendom.

"Good show, Sandman," Lothaire said. "And with nary a drop of blood spilled."

"I can only hold her suspended there for so long. Let's go." He kept his sorcery focused behind him, and they all charged toward Nightside's sole exit. Already the rift had started to rebound, the weight of the mountain pressing down on the opening.

Having just emerged from rubble, Adham would now face another gauntlet of stone. If it closed, could he somehow pry it open? Probably not without bringing the entire hive down upon their heads.

More howls sounded. Throughout the mountain, undead factions met the ghouls, fighting each other to reach the rift. Other tunnels would lead them straight here.

"Go!" Kristoff yelled from behind Adham and Kosmina. "Faster!" The vampire had realized the same problem. "If we miss that opening, an army will descend upon us."

As Lothaire brought up the rear, he said, "Are those friends of yours?"

Adham narrowed his eyes at a sight far ahead. Enti, Pearl, Xodin, and several castle dwellers had just emerged from a side tunnel and were sprinting toward the opening. "Not exactly," he replied.

The sorceress and her inner circle must've sneaked into the hive right behind Adham and ahead of the undead. No wonder she'd stopped masking the quakes—she'd been running across Nightside at the time.

Over her shoulder, Enti blew them a kiss as she passed through the rift. "I took your advice. And more! Turns out, the realm *is* dying." She added something, but more boulders fell, drowning out her words.

And then they were gone.

FIFTY

Without slowing, Mina exclaimed, "Enti and company used us as a distraction! She always said it didn't make sense to fight the ghouls."

The mountain gave another lurch. Howls and dust followed them as the four closed in on the rift.

Still directing his sorcery back at the queen, Adham paused in front of the opening. "I'll keep the ghouls pinned down. Out you go." He pushed Mina.

"No, Adham, I'm not leaving without you!"

Kristoff shoved them both. "We need him to seal this once we're through. Just fucking go."

Lips thinned, Adham followed Mina. Would his control of the sand inside the hive waver?

Kristoff twisted his body to sidle out. Lothaire would be right behind him.

Free at last, Mina scented the night air. They'd emerged onto an expansive shelf of rock overlooking an evergreen forest dotted with snow.

Enti and the others had already disappeared, no doubt

teleported away by the demons.

The stars and a waxing moon were out, luminous to Mina's vision. Her distant dream of visiting a moonlit desert with Adham could come true—

"Blyad'!" Lothaire yelled when the rift suddenly slammed shut. The rock had snared one of his legs, bringing him down to the ground. To Adham, he said, "Crush the stone holding me. Quickly."

Kristoff said, "And risk opening this barrier to all those undead? Trace or use your mist."

Lothaire looked as if he'd attempted to do both. "I can't when I've already been trapped . . ." His words died down, his face like granite.

"What is it, Uncle?" Mina asked.

"On the other side, something seized my leg, clawing it. From the strength of that grip, I'd say the queen ghoul has broken free of the sorcerer's sand and is merrily infecting me as a last *fuck you.*" He yelled back at her, "I have it on good authority that a nasty witch killed your mate recently!" Then he looked at Kristoff. "Take off my leg, and quickly. Or lose Furie forever."

"I should let you rot from the inside out." Yet he scouted the clearing for something to sever Lothaire's leg. "Too bad you don't have the plague too. Then you could drink the sorcerer and battle the ghoul contagion, as our Mina has apparently done."

"The Sandman's even older than I am! All his memories would trip me into full-blown madness for certain. Mina's got that to look forward to."

Nothing that right could be wrong. She shared a look with Adham. He'd been spot-on about their instincts; drinking his blood *had* saved her, just in a way they'd never imagined. "I remain optimistic about our future, Uncle."

Finding a rock with a sharp edge, Kristoff returned to

Lothaire. "This will hurt. You. But I will enjoy it." He raised the rock. "On the count of three. One—" He smashed it down, driving it a foot into the ground, severing Lothaire's leg.

"Ahhh! You brute!" Blood spurted from Lothaire's new stump, painting the rift behind him. "Lesson number two thousand and thirty: Learn to count." Then he yelled at the rock face, "Have the leg for a chew toy. Enjoy it!"

"Up you go." Kristoff yanked him upright to stand on his remaining foot.

Leaning against him, Lothaire snatched off his belt. Once he'd fashioned a tourniquet to stem the flow of blood, he made a tamping gesture with dripping hands. "Everyone, please, stop with your concern. I'm fine. Please, enough. The contagion didn't reach my heart or brain."

Kristoff muttered, "Do you possess either?"

Lothaire ignored him, inspecting his new injury with dawning excitement. "I can't wait to show this to Lizvetta and garner sympathy. The night is *mine*."

Adham turned to Mina. "Are you sure you weren't scratched?" He checked her neck, relieved to find smooth skin.

She smiled up at him. "I'm good." She even sensed her mist was returning, like a blood fountain slowly refilling.

"Princess, I'm pleased you're safe," Kristoff said.

When she faced the Gravewalker, Adham tensed beside her, delighting Mina. "Thank you so much for breaching the realm to help me."

Adham grudgingly added, "And thank you for digging me out. I couldn't have reached her without your help."

Kristoff inclined his head. "Be worthy of her, Sandman."

Aww.

Adham nodded. Then his gaze flicked past her to the rift. "Give me a second." He hastened over to place a hand on the bloody rock, sensing it. "I think the mountain has settled into its current position for a time, but we'll need to post guards here to make sure Nightside's monsters never emerge." That egg cavern must be on everyone's minds.

Paler from blood loss, Lothaire said, "I'll dispatch a contingent of Dacians. Remain in place and guard it with your sorcery until reinforcements arrive." He beckoned to Mina. "Come."

"I'll stay. Adham and I don't separate."

He arched his brows. "You and your brother with the unsuitable mates. First a demon, now a sorcerer. Unbearable."

"So Mirceo and Caspion are together?"

"Mirspion? Yes, you could say that." With that, he and Kristoff disappeared.

Her brother must have finally won over the reluctant demon, and the two of them were mated. Her smile widened.

Adham returned to Mina. "I still can't believe you beat the unbeatable." He took her in his arms, seeming stunned that she was within them once more.

"I did with the help of your blood."

"All that matters is you came back to me." He brushed his knuckles along her cheek.

"I always will," she promised him. "And now we're free."

"You were right. Escape existed."

"And you were right when you said it hadn't. Only that quake opened the rift." Their window of success had been minuscule.

"I'm ready to start our lives . . ." His words faltered, his eyes darting. He released her and stepped back to scan the shelf of rock.

"What's wrong?" she asked. "Are you sure *you* weren't scratched?"

He gripped his temples. "I'm sure. But something isn't right—"

"Mina!" Mirceo had appeared not thirty feet from her, with Caspion by his side. Both had their swords raised, and Caspion's amber horns were straightened with hostility.

"What are you doing with this filth, sister?" Mirceo demanded.

"Brother, drop the sword and talk to us. Didn't Lothaire tell you what happened?"

"Lothaire? He's been missing for months. Balery directed us here." Mirceo and Caspion stalked closer. "Get away from the sorcerer."

"Put the sword down, Mirceo. I mean it. I will never forgive you if you hurt him."

There was no risk of that. Eyes aglow, Adham raised his burning palms with a yell and lashed out with sorcery.

Time seemed to slow, events happening too fast to process.

A shockwave exploded beneath their feet; the cliff surface morphed into a mass of sand. Adham molded a swell of it into a razor-sharp whip and launched it at Mirceo. *"I'll kill you!"*

Caspion tackled her brother—too late? Blood spurted from Mirceo's severed neck, his head tilting at an unnatural angle from his limp body.

"What are you doing?" Mina screamed in horror, vaulting for Adham to protect her brother. She'd felt that strike as if the sorcerer had done it to her.

Wild-eyed, Adham blocked her attack and shoved her into the hungry sand.

Mina scrambled to her feet, but the ground sucked them all down, trapping them in place.

With a roar, Caspion used his demon might to power himself loose from the sand's grip and break Mirceo out. Freed from the quicksand, he traced her brother away. Only a demon desperate to protect his mate could have broken this hold.

And now Mina was left with a sorcerer she barely recognized. She'd learned to read him so well, yet nothing in his expression made sense—as if he'd been taken over by a malevolent stranger.

As she grappled against quicksand and shock, she cried, "Have you lost your mind?" The warm sand that had caressed her cheek and saved her life might have killed her brother. "What is happening?"

He didn't answer, just kept his hands raised to direct his power. The welcome embrace of Adham's sorcery had turned dark.

She struggled to free herself, but the sand was sucking her down . . . to her knees . . . to her waist . . . "Stop this! Why are you doing this to me?"

He gazed on with murderous intent as the sand reached her chest.

"Are you going to drown me? *Me?*" The male she loved was about to kill her. When sand circled her throat, she gasped for air and screamed, "Adham, no!"

"You're going to take me to Dacia," he finally grated. "Or I'll put you under again and again." Just before she sank beneath the surface, his sand lifted her up into a tornado cage of spinning grains. "I'll torture you until you do."

Trapped within his sorcery, she couldn't even trace. Her mist ability hadn't renewed yet. Over the buzz of the tornado, she cried, "How could you do this? *How?*"

"I will find him and kill him. I won't stop until he's dead."

Suddenly a claw-tipped hand breached the scouring sands of her cage. Caspion? A roar sounded as the sand abraded his skin away, leaving ragged meat and bone up to the elbow. What was once a hand still managed to clamp around her arm. Somehow Caspion locked onto her—to trace her away.

As they disappeared, the sorcerer lunged for her, bellowing, "Kosmina!"

Caspion teleported her into Dacia's court. Eyes black with emotion, he released her and traced to his mate who lay on the stone floor. Her brother was unconscious, his head hanging on by a tatter of flesh. Would it be enough to regenerate? Lothaire had recovered from a similar injury, but he was ancient and strong! Mirceo was barely older than Mina.

Caspion knelt beside Mirceo with a bellow of anguish, his own pain forgotten.

Lothaire traced into the court then, half-dressed and balancing on one leg. "What the hell happened?" He looked from Mirceo to Caspion to Mina.

Her lips moved but devastation rendered her speechless.

"Ah." Understanding shone in the depths of Lothaire's eyes. "Beware the Sorceri."

FIFTY-ONE

Kosmina, nooo!" Adham sank to his knees, fists clenched around sand. He cursed it, cursing his renewed power. His sorcery had launched beyond his control, his words and actions not his own.

How? Why?

Eyes wet and mind on fire, he threw back his head and roared to the sky, *"Believe in me, Mina."* One last time.

Compulsion struck; he morphed his sand into a dagger— and stabbed his own eye out with it.

FIFTY-TWO

Castle Dacia

Intervention, vampire-style.

The goal: getting Mina to drink.

And maybe to sleep.

All her family and friends had gathered at sunset in Dacia's court to "talk some sense into her"—because they'd failed to do so in their succession of one-on-one visits with her over the last week.

Lothaire and Ellie sat upon their thrones decorated with gilded skulls. Mirceo and Caspion leaned against the edge of the dais. Her uncles Stelian, Viktor, and Trehan, with his sorceress mate Bettina, stood nearby. Beside Ellie's throne, Balery looked on with a pensive expression.

The one person missing was Kristoff. He'd believed his presence would be an intrusion, but Mina also thought he was even more preoccupied with Furie than usual.

Caspion's hand had finished regenerating. Lothaire's leg had. A bandage still circled Mirceo's neck, but at least he'd regenerated enough to leave his bed.

Mina had fully recovered from her illnesses. Balery had

tested her blood and believed she was now immune to both the plague and ghoul toxin.

Yet my heart remains broken. Worry for Mirceo, Caspion, and even Adham fogged her brain, but she knew she was forgetting something critical. If she could just rest her eyes for a moment, she could figure it out. She hadn't slept since she'd returned.

Lothaire intoned, "We've called you here this eve because some people are concerned about you."

Mina gazed from face to face, taking in her loving uncles: steady yet fierce Trehan, combative Viktor, and hidden-depths Stelian, who sipped his bloodmead flask. Their love for her united these disparate beings. Looking at them now, she could scarcely believe that their lines had warred for centuries.

"I decreed them not to be concerned," Lothaire added, "but they persist—like your obvious feelings for the sorcerer."

All eyes on me. Mina was back at the very place where her shyness had taken root in her youth. Her king's words echoed in her mind.

. . . so socially inept . . . in my court . . . pains me.

A thousand visits here in the past had given her no hint of this coming night—the night she would stand before all her loved ones with her heart a bloody mess and her emotions in ruins.

Now that the plague no longer bolstered Mina, her shyness should reappear in the fertile ground that had once made it thrive.

In a pained voice, her brother said, "I still don't understand how you fell for someone who was sworn to kill me." When Mirceo rubbed his throat, Caspion's eyes flickered black with feeling, still haunted by how close he'd come to losing his newly found mate. Despite Mirceo's incredible recovery rate, the demon flinched every time her brother adjusted his bandage.

Mina had shared Caspion's vigil over Mirceo, had bonded

for life to her brother-by-fate. She'd once asked Mirceo who would take care of him, and she had taken it upon herself to do so; the two of them hadn't known that in a different world, a young demon had already been born to fulfill such a sacred duty.

Lothaire rubbed his own throat and muttered, "I know that feeling, boy." Ellie patted his hand sympathetically, though *she* had been the one who'd nearly beheaded him during their courtship. That had been an accident; Adham's strike hadn't been.

Mina had already been over this with Mirceo, but she quietly said, "Adham told me he had the ability to break vows."

Muffled groans all around.

"The enchanter lied about being able to lie?" Mirceo said. "Sounds legit."

With a laugh, Lothaire told her, "You got duped. It happens to the best of us Dacians. Literally, the best of us—me. A goddess of vampires played me for a fool. But fortunately I was not in love with her whatsoever."

Through her haze, Mina had tried to analyze every interaction, every word, every smile between her and the sorcerer. "You and Kristoff saw how Adham fought to reach me. Why doubt his devotion? Kristoff doesn't." As he'd absently said, "The Sandman loves you. Something else is at work."

What could explain Adham's actions? If Mina could only think . . .

Caspion gently asked, "Did Silt tell you he loved you?"

Adham. "Well, not precisely. But he said other things just as heartfelt, and he followed me to the hive, against all odds."

Expression sympathetic, Ellie said, "Didn't others go there too? When they all realized Nightside was dying?"

Mina admitted, "That's true." Though Enti had planned for Adham to stay and for Nightside to stabilize, the wily sorceress had prepared for other outcomes. She'd even attempted to make a scythe—for a Dacian swordswoman to clear a path through the hive so others could follow. Mina didn't blame her. *All's fair in love and Lore.* "But the fact remains that Adham and I are mated."

Lothaire said, "I have it on good authority that Sorceri don't have mates."

"I beg your pardon?" Bettina stiffened beside Trehan, who took her hand.

Lothaire waved negligently in their direction.

Caspion, Bettina's childhood friend, flashed her a look of sympathy.

This court was never going to believe Mina. The stout case against the King of Sand—including his past behavior with her and for the millennia before her—provided only one conclusion: a serial deceiver had repeatedly deceived her. Worse, he'd done exactly what he'd sworn to do from the beginning.

Hurt Mirceo to get revenge.

Her best guess was that he'd lied about being able to break a vow to the Lore and had meant to confess later. Maybe he hadn't grasped how much control that vow would have over him. *At his age, though?*

Those rash words, said in the rage of his withdrawal, would curse them for the rest of their lives. One single instant—a spur of the moment—really had been like a metal spur jolting him into an action from which there was no known return.

Unless he was actually evil and had played her.

As soon as those doubts rose, she recalled the adoration in his eyes when he'd made love to her. She couldn't have reached divinity on her own—and she hadn't mistaken that destination. Mina softly said, "If we're not mates, then why was he going to sacrifice his root power to Dorada? To become an Inferi for me?" Kristoff had told her about Adham's plan.

At the rim of his flask, Stelian muttered, "That's what he *said*. What he *did* was dissect my nephew's neck."

Actions spoke louder than words with this group. Mina could reveal all the sentiments that made her believe in Adham, but her family would never get past Mirceo's head hanging on by a thread. *Can I blame them?*

"You look like you're about to drop," Balery said, not looking much better after her extended efforts to find Lothaire, Kristoff, and Mina. At great personal cost, this oracle had rolled her bones over and over for weeks, until she'd been able to direct Mirceo and Caspion to that exit from Nightside. "You need to drink."

Mina didn't want to dilute Adham's blood. *He's inside me.* She'd taken him into her, and they'd become one body, one blood. Though she no longer had the plague, her hunger for him proved unrelenting.

"And I can give you something to help you sleep," Balery said, brows drawn over her doe-brown gaze. "Or are you worried about dreaming the sorcerer's memories?"

"She should be worried!" Mirceo exclaimed. "I still can't believe you drank straight from *Silt Harea*. Do you know how old he is, how many memories he's transferred to you? Your eyes might still go red."

Mina muttered, "You're one to talk about drinking straight from another."

His cheeks flushed, and Caspion pulled up his collar. With sudden interest, Trehan and Bettina both studied the ceiling. Lothaire and Ellie shared a smile. Seemed more than one Dacian practiced this "deviancy."

Viktor sighed. "Degenerates."

Stelian raised his flask. "Cheers to them."

Mina said, "I might not even see his memories."

Stelian took a swig. "One way to find out, niece. Face the coming onslaught with your usual bravery. You can't stay awake forever."

Ellie added, "Sweetie, this anvil's gotta drop."

Mina knew that, but . . . "If Adham attacked Mirceo because he was bound by a vow he barely remembered making in the first place, it will break me. If he *wasn't* bound by a vow, it will break me." Either way, she could never be with him again.

Yet wasn't there another alternative she couldn't quite put her finger on? She needed to think!

"You still want him?" Mirceo pointed to his injury and said, "I would shake my head with consternation, but it still might fall off!"

She winced.

"If you witnessed Silt as we did during his capture, you would not feel this way." He looked at Caspion. "Tell her."

The demon ran a hand through his shaggy blond hair between his horns, then reluctantly said, "It was a scene. Even by our former standards of . . . high-living."

"As you two have changed, so has he." Or he *had*. Maybe.

"He nearly killed me. He screamed that he was going to do it!" Mirceo cleared his regenerating throat. "He told you he'd torture you to get to me. Why won't you believe he's evil?"

Because he made me a rose. For what reason would he have created that token for her other than love? Which meant he was suffering somewhere right now from what he'd done. "I know in my heart he's not."

Mirceo blew out a breath. "When your arm got clawed, I *felt* it. I feared you had the plague the whole time we were searching for you." He and Caspion had worked tirelessly to find her, never giving up. "But you beat it on your own. And then you beat ghoul contagion! Why can't you defeat these feelings?"

Gazing at her boots, she said, "Because I *wanted* to defeat those other things."

Sounding as if she'd struck him, he said, "Talk about a loyalty conflict. You're so innocent that you can't understand what he is. He was only using you. That's what his kind does."

"I'm not innocent. And I wasn't used," she murmured, but no one seemed to be listening.

Caspion said, "Even now Harea is out there hunting both Mirceo and Mina, like some killing machine." According to the demon's bounty hunter network, Adham searched for Dacia, spending a fortune on spies and informants. If the kingdom hadn't been mystically hidden, he might already have found it.

Lothaire sat back in his throne. "Hag, what do your bones say?"

"I can't get a read on him," she answered. "He's empowered as never before, using his sand to travel, and such a constant sorcery outlay cloaks him from my sight."

That would explain how Adham had escaped so quickly from that cliff. By the time Dacian sentries had arrived to apprehend him and guard the opening to Nightside, Adham had already vanished.

"You're no Nïx, are you?" Lothaire said, earning a glare from everyone in the court. "So two options exist: either the sorcerer is bound by a vow he didn't mean to make—which I can empathize with—or he's evil and bent on revenge. Which I can also empathize with. But in the end, his motives don't matter. The sorcerer won't stop targeting Mirceo, so I hereby decree Silt Harea's death."

Mina jerked her head up with a gasp. "You would kill my fated one, Uncle? As I told everyone, a siren sang for him, and she had no effect on him. He and I *are* mated."

"Did you see the siren do it?" Caspion asked. "Or did he tell you that happened?"

"I . . . didn't actually see it."

Groans.

Lothaire said, "Did I ever tell you about playing poker against the King of Lies? You can't trust Sorceri."

Bettina put a hand on her hip. "I'm standing right here." Trehan's gaze darkened.

As if she hadn't spoken, Lothaire continued, "One thing I know for certain: a sorcerer assassination is a splendid spectacle. You never know what you're going to get with those fonts of magic. Kind of like different fireworks. Most go boom."

Bettina rolled her eyes behind her Sorceri mask. "Still right here."

Trehan cast Lothaire a warning look and protectively drew his Bride against his side. "Watch yourself, Enemy of Old."

"Often. My reflection entrances even me."

Dizziness swept over Mina, and she pitched on her feet. Exhaustion and grief had undermined her logic almost as much as the plague had promised to. Maybe she should sleep so she could regain it. "Adham made the vow to me. Why can't I release him from it? That can happen under certain conditions, right?"

Lothaire, an expert with these vows, said, "If he vowed to do *your* wishes by killing Mirceo, then you could."

"What about searching the worlds for a way to break such an oath?"

Lothaire's low-level amusement faded. "You think I didn't try that, girl? You believe I simply failed to come up with that idea when my Bride's soul was on the line? I had no option other than facing dawn and incinerating myself—which I tried to do. To answer your next question, no, not even Dorada's ring could relieve me of that vow."

Ellie reached over to pet his arm until the tense line of his jaw eased.

Caspion said, "Mina and Mirceo won't be safe from a sorcerer with that much power. He must be taken out. I volunteer to do it." Caspion was a death demon and a hunter; Mina took his words very seriously.

"Then it's settled," Lothaire said as she gaped. "Caspion will kill the Sandman. Let me know when you close in." He rubbed his hands with relish. "I do love a good sorcerer decapitation."

Bettina bit out, "Must you?"

Mirceo frowned at Caspion. "Wait a second—*I* want to take his head. None of this would have happened if not for my initial recklessness with Harea's bounty."

The demon answered, "Not a chance, leechling."

Viktor's hand already hovered over the hilt of his sword. "I'll do it."

Trehan said, "I am the leader of the House of Shadow. It's my job to assassinate threats to the royal family."

"Correction: it *was* your job, Trey," said Viktor, the head of the equally powerful House of War. "Now that you're busy running the kingdom you share with Betinna, I've been stepping into your position."

"*Mina* should do it," Stelian interjected. "She'll never get over him otherwise."

Warming to that idea, Viktor said, "Yes. She could strike from her mist, and that cretin would never see it coming. Not as valorous as battle, but it would get the job done."

As they blithely discussed Mina assassinating Adham, she felt as if she'd been caught in quicksand again, screaming into the void. . . .

"This is my little sister we're talking about. It's not happening, not on my life," Mirceo said with all the arrogance of a Dacian prince. "The sorcerer is mine to kill. I started all this madness with Silt's capture."

Ellie snapped her fingers. "Capture—now, that right there's a good idea. Let's nab him instead of droppin' him. We can *always* kill him."

Lothaire scratched his chin thoughtfully. "As good a point as ever."

But having lit on the idea of a murder, the majority in this court had no interest in anything less. They all argued their positions—at the same time.

Mina gazed from one face to the next. She should feel lucky that so many loved her enough to care about her future. Yet they all treated her like she was the same princess—the *old* Mina—who would welcome their guidance, squeak her compliance, and surrender her will.

Surrender my will. The fuck?

Yes, her shyness should have rebounded in the fertile ground of this court. But she refused it. In its place bloomed something different, something like a desert rose boldly spreading her stalks across the dunes and winking at the sun.

The *new* Mina yelled, *"Everyone, enough!"* Her outburst startled them into silence, all except for Lothaire.

With a sigh, he muttered, "Finally."

"I am *not* innocent. I have *not* been duped." *Blooming, blooming.* "And when I tell you Adham's my mate and that he loves me—I mean it." She addressed Mirceo: "Is it so ridiculous to believe the sorcerer lost his heart to me? Do I have no merits that might have earned his love?"

Eyes wide, Mirceo hastily said, "Of course you do, my precious sister! He just might not have had the sense to appreciate them."

Clapping her hands after each word, she snapped, "My—merits—are—undeniable."

Double takes all around.

As Mina said these words, she knew them to be true. Her *rána* burned not at all. "No one's going to kill my mate. I'm going to save him. Somehow . . ." She trailed off as her mind fired with logic at last, and that third alternative hit her with the force of a geyser: *Beware the Sorceri.* She turned to Caspion. "When your sources reported back on Adham's movements, did they mention anything unusual about his appearance?"

The demon frowned. "Yeah. Actually they did."

She cast her mind back to that night when Adham had told her he didn't have to kill her brother. She'd been so overjoyed that she'd barely registered all his words—or his *other* vow. He hadn't been bound by it then, but he was now. So what had changed?

Mina's fatigue disappeared, her thoughts sharpening as another mission took hold of her mind. She told the court, "I know what happened to Adham. And I know how to get him back."

FIFTY-THREE

All the worlds should fear me. Now it's Poly's turn.

"You two ready?" Caspion reached for her and Mirceo, taking their hands to teleport them. Balery's rolled bones had indicated that if they left now, they would arrive in the Plane of Lost Years on the night of the Cold Moon.

Mina gave Caspion a firm nod. "Ready."

Mirceo answered, "I was born ready, sweetheart."

Caspion was still shaking his head ruefully when they landed in Poly, just beyond the dunes bordering Adham's valley.

As a sandstorm raged in the freezing night, Mirceo created a bank of mist to conceal them. He gazed around with disgust as they floated up one of the dunes. "Poly is a place you don't have to *try* in order to *knock*."

Every grain of these shifting sands reminded Mina of how formidable Adham would be in this dimension, and by all accounts, his power already brimmed.

Her first instinct had been to bring an army with her on tonight's mission—her family had certainly wanted that—but too many people crowding Mina's trap might put Adham at risk. Yet then, too few might put Mirceo at risk.

So she'd decided on this trio, and for once, her decisions were binding. She'd refused to tell anyone what she'd figured out until they'd each agreed that she would oversee Adham's recovery.

Now she gazed at her brother's barely healed neck. What a danger this was! She would have liked to spring her trap on a more advantageous battleground, but one of the components she needed now lived here. . . .

As they neared the top, Caspion said, "The storm will dwindle up there, and you'll be able to see the stronghold. From that very spot, I watched hundreds of hunters attempt to claim the bounty on Harea. They all fell to his traps in gruesome ways."

"What would make you two try for that job in the first place?" Would she ever have met Adham if they hadn't?

"Yes, Mirceo"—Caspion raised his brows—"tell her what could possibly have moved us to such folly."

Straightening his shoulders, Mirceo said, "Well. It's like this . . . I wanted to show support for my mate's line of work, and I was angling to spend more time with him to win him over with my irresistible wit and charm. So I took Harea's bounty notice off the wall in a hunter's den, thinking *date night*. I didn't know that taking the notice meant I would be forced to capture the notorious King of Sand, or I'd be slain by other hunters."

"Oh, Mirceo." He wasn't perfect, but Caspion was very patient with him. Mina told her brother-by-fate, "You must love him very much."

Helpless grunt.

Mirceo grinned. "Did I mention my wit and charm? I could mention it again."

The two were perfect for each other. Fate knew what she was doing. "Will you continue bounty hunting together?"

Mirceo shared a look with Caspion. "We got burned out."

"I'm sorry. Ellie told me about all your rescue efforts." They'd apprehended the Gaolers' bounties one after another, planning to capture the demigods and force Mina's release, but the Gaolers had used time manipulation to thwart their attempts.

"I decided to out myself on live TV, but *somebody* said he'd be right there beside me." Mirceo hiked a thumb at Caspion. "This fucker—sorry, I mean—"

She waved away the spicy language, surprising him.

"Anyway, this lout swore he'd follow me to the ends of the worlds, and all that romantic drivel."

Caspion flashed his demon fangs in amusement.

"I figured you might pull exactly that stunt," Mina said. "And I worried you might use Dorada's ring."

"It was our next play. But then Balery told us she thought she had a lead. So we held off."

"You must have been furious to learn that Lothaire and Kristoff left without you."

"They rode off without so much as a word to go riddle-solving and sundry bullshit, and they landed in the one place we'd fought to get to. That stung. But it sounds like you wouldn't be here if they hadn't."

"True. And I wouldn't be here without Adham."

Mirceo rolled his gray eyes. "Say this trap of yours works. Say Silt's not totally evil. That doesn't mean he's become a good man."

"Brother, do you really want to go down that road?"

Even Caspion raised his brows at that. "Can people not change?"

Mirceo glowered. "I won't tangle with both of you. There's little sense to that. Let's just say that Silt isn't good enough for Mina."

"Fate thinks he is." Enti had been right; Mina wouldn't

settle for anything less than utter devotion. But sometimes a vampiress had to fight for it.

Mirceo exhaled. "He's not your mate. When you finally find the one for you, you'll understand how far off the mark you are about Silt."

"*Adham.* And let's agree to disagree." As they crested the dune, anticipation pricked her skin. Finally she would behold the structure he'd built with his own hands and sorcery. The sandstorm eased; below them lay a valley cradling a gigantic pyramid.

Caspion blew out a breath. "Whoa."

"*Whoa,*" Mirceo and Mina echoed at the same time.

"Lot of changes here since the last time we saw it," Caspion observed. "Of course, decades have passed in this realm."

Mirceo said, "The defenses are all gone." Instead of the multiple deadly traps Mina had heard about, the fortress was wide open, and revelers lined up for entry, an actual red carpet welcoming them in. Bowls of fire danced in the winds, and light spilled from the pyramid's slot windows.

According to Caspion's sources, this stronghold was *under new management.*

While Adham had been out searching, Enti had moved in and made his home into the Lore's hottest den of fleshly delights. Exiling herself in Poly, the one place the Gaolers never went, she'd resumed her moniker of the Queen of Vice and had leaned all the way into it.

Just then, one of Adham's scyllas thumped its purple tentacles against the pyramid. Answering that call, someone poured spirits out of a narrow window into the creature's gaping maw. Its tentacles flailed with drunkenness.

When it vomited in the sand, Mina, Mirceo, and Caspion all chorused, "*Whoa,*" again. Its tentacles fell limp, and it sprawled like a wet mop.

"Can you imagine how Silt will feel when he sees this?" Mirceo asked with glee at the prospect. "His hallowed haunt with all its security, turned on its ear. That'll stick in his craw."

Ignoring him, she asked, "How did Enti get past his defenses in the first place?"

Caspion said, "I heard the Sandman's concubines opened the doors wide for her."

Mirceo cackled. "That had to smart."

Mina pursed her lips and turned to Caspion. "Are you sure he'll be here?"

"He probably already is." The demon had put out the word through his network that Mirceo, renowned as a rake, was attending the rout of the century on the full moon tonight to celebrate his regeneration and his sister's return.

Mina surveyed the crowd, seeking Adham. Many of the attendees wore masks, and not just Sorceri. He would be in disguise as well, wouldn't want to spook a target like Mirceo who could just trace away. "Anonymous indulgence must be a draw." She was one to talk from the cover of mist.

Mirceo and Caspion exchanged looks, had probably attended countless of these fests in their time.

"I'll need eyes on the inside." She checked her new sword and inhaled a steadying breath. "You two, remain up here on standby, in case I need you." Keeping Mirceo and Caspion away from Adham was logical, decreasing the risk to all parties.

Except me.

Mirceo sputtered, "You really expect me to let you face him alone? I just got you back and barely survived losing you the first time."

Caspion's face was grave. "He suffered as you suffered, Mina."

"I am so sorry for that," she said with her whole heart. "But this is my mission."

Mirceo rubbed his forehead. "I can't do this."

She clasped his shoulder. "Brother, if you believe that I am smart and capable, then you must let me go. You raised me with such care and did an amazing job, but I'm not a child anymore."

Mirceo looked to Caspion to fix this, to help him make Mina fall into line once more. Whatever he saw on the demon's face made him mutter, "Not you too." Exhaling a breath, he said, "Fine. We'll stay up here. Just don't lose your mist again, okay?"

The mistake that had brought her to this exact point in her life. "I'm not planning on it."

"Sister, what if you *are* wrong about this wastrel?"

She shrugged and smiled. "I've never been so right."

FIFTY-FOUR

Where is he? Mina thought as she misted into the pyramid's crowd of what must be a thousand Loreans.

The masked crush filled this impressive structure from wall to wall, spilling out of all the rooms. She scanned faces for the male she loved, still surprised that Mirceo and Caspion had agreed to hold back and let her go on her mission solo.

By the light of mesmeric torches, immortals sampled sex, drugs, and gambling. The Queen of Vice must be harvesting a feast of power tonight.

Next to low tables with large opium pipes were rows of dice games. In darker corners, naked bodies writhed. Their screams of ecstasy were an alternating drumbeat to the yells of the dice winners.

Opium smoke hung so thickly in the air it must be embedded into the fabrics, the very stone. How would Adham tolerate it? She tried to imagine him living here but couldn't. How many centuries had he lost within these very walls?

He wasn't the only Sorceri she needed to find. She also searched for his nemesis, Enti—the sorceress who'd stolen his future and even this part of his past. Mina was here to change all that.

She'd expected the sorceress to be up on a stage somewhere, the center of attention. Instead she found Enti in a back room, enjoying what must be a game of poker.

Several drunken demons sat at the table, their mugs making rings on the surface and dampening their cards.

Enti's eyes were bright behind her red mask, her golden ensemble shimmering. She looked fully recovered from her trials in Nightside, her smile even more dazzling. When the time was right, Mina would have to strike quickly with her.

Enti laid down her cards and told the demon across the table from her, "You win again!"

The demon slurred, "Don't know how you can keep losing. And you, a mind reader!" He hugged the pile of gold between them and dragged it closer.

"Because when you win, *I* win. Another game?"

He laughed. "Play you all night!"

Sorceri gleam. "Won't you just?"

With Enti's position stationary, Mina returned to the main hall, scanning the throng. *Where are you?* What if he didn't show? Despite Caspion's reports, she worried that Adham might be killed fulfilling any other vows he might have made over the ages—

There.

Out of the corner of her eye she spied a tall figure, a male who towered over even the immortals here. He wore a domino mask, but she would recognize that bold stride and laborer's build anywhere.

Her fangs sharpened for him, her predator instincts rising. She almost smiled. The plague alone hadn't made her thirst for this male. The fated bond between a vampire and a sorcerer had.

He wore gloves to conceal his palms. One of his eyes was alight, the other regenerating—because a vow compelled him to stab it. He would be bound by it until Enti returned his oathbreaking ability.

According to Bettina, two Sorceri must be within sight of each other to transfer sorcery, so Mina needed to lure him to Enti. But to do so, she would need to do the one thing she ought not to. . . .

Kosmina.

Adham thought he'd spied a female with long blond hair amidst the crush, but she'd disappeared. She couldn't be in this place; her brother would never allow it.

Must be imagining things. Anguish coupled with lack of sleep had warped his mind. His eyesight suffered, but his right eye was almost regenerated. He had a blade in his belt, ready to stab it. This saved time—time he needed to complete the vow that would destroy everything.

He hoped Kosmina was safe in Dacia, far from his befouled reach. All he wanted to do was protect her, and now *he* was the greatest danger to her.

She wouldn't know what had befallen him, would think he'd deceived her yet again. After all the times he'd puzzled over her believing in him, now he desperately wanted her to. But he'd given her no reason to trust him.

He scanned the crowd. No sign of Mirceo yet. Why would that vampire abandon assured safety to come here? *To come to my own godsdamned stronghold?* Kosmina had admitted that Mirceo could be a touch arrogant. That trait would get him killed tonight.

At the thought, panic gripped Adham, but he knew he

looked outwardly calm, an automaton running on vows. He hastened through the mass of Loreans, their antics calling to mind his own past behavior.

He passed what used to be his library. *Orgy.*

What used to be his den. *Gambling hall.*

What used to be his smoking room. *Well, that remains the same.*

Without interest, he recognized some of his former concubines, had heard they'd opened the doors to Enti. His thinking on them had changed. He no longer harbored ill will, could understand why they'd shown him no loyalty. He clearly hadn't been worthy of it.

But Enti . . . he boiled with wrath toward her for all her thefts. When he'd first heard that the sorceress had wrested control of the haven he'd intended to share with Kosmina, he'd been furious. *Yet more stolen from me.* But seeing it like this, he knew he could never bring his mate here.

You can't anyway! He was cursed to forfeit her forever. *I cursed myself.*

The remembered horror of striking against Mirceo and Mina continued to gut him, but he would do it again. Most of his old vows were null and void because he'd made them to Loreans who'd died over the years. He'd been forced to carry out a few Sorceri assassinations, yet now only two vows remained: to stab his eye and to kill his brother-by-fate.

Adham couldn't pay an assassin to take himself out of the game, couldn't even utter the words: "Gold for my death." He couldn't use his sand to travel to the pit of mystical flames where immortals went to die. *I tried.*

Though Silt was in Enti's proximity and fully empowered, he couldn't force her to return his sorcery because that would counteract the aim of his vows.

No way out. Despair was a vice, one the Queen of Vice

amplified in this lair. It wrapped around him as absolutely as smoke had. The barren soullessness of being an Inferi was nothing compared to this.

At last Silt knew what he was and what he wanted, yet he had no control over his future. His dreams were a vanishing mirage.

He drew up short at another flash of blond. *That* is *Kosmina!* On the heels of dread and yearning, shame flushed his cheeks. She couldn't be here, seeing this desecration of his home. His own vices had been a facet of this cesspit.

Compulsion struck yet again. He shoved past immortals, yanking off his gloves. He pulled sand from the realm to follow him inside. It churned for a capture as he pursued her. He couldn't warn her away, couldn't leave to spare her.

Despite how much he loved Kosmina, nothing could break this curse—until his actions had broken *her*.

FIFTY-FIVE

H e's on the hunt.

Mina used her mist once more and hastened back to the poker room. The plan was simple: put a sword to Enti's neck to force her to return Adham's power as soon as he'd followed her inside.

As she misted through the doorway, the demon poker players were leaving. Why would Enti send them on their way? The sorceress sat alone at the table, tidying it with her powers, and she seemed to be looking right at Mina.

No time to rethink the plan. Mina drew her sword and zoomed behind her—

"Kosmina Daciano," Enti murmured, though she couldn't see her. "I thought I read your mind in the crowd. I sent the demons on their way, so we could chat. I've awaited you for so long, wondering if you'd ever show."

Mina placed her sword above the sorceress's golden collar. "It's only been a week since I last saw you."

"Your time, not mine. After years of vice here, I'm stronger than I've ever been." She tapped Mina's sword blade with an unconcerned nail. *Ting, ting, ting.* "Are you sure you want to make an enemy of a friend?"

"Friend? Are you jesting?" Curbing her fury, she said, "You know why I'm here. Adham's about to enter, and when he does you'll return his power."

"Or what? You won't behead an unarmed sorceress. You're *good.*" She said the word like an insult. "Well, except for your pesky pride." Voice vibrating with sorcery, she commanded, "Join us in vice, prideful princess."

Enti clouded Mina's mind, embittering her thoughts. *Why should I be the one to risk all? Why should I chase after a man who hurt me and my brother so badly . . . ?*

Mina shook off the sorcery. "I'm here for love, Enti, the greatest virtue—and my defense against you." She pressed her sword harder.

"You would never hurt me. You like me, have from the beginning. Princess, I just wanted a home."

"Then why take his oath-breaking power?"

Shrug. "I was going for the other one, but he had that one locked down."

"You went for his root power? Enti!"

"For the love of gold, it's what we do. I knew we'd have to settle here, and sand sorcery would increase our chances of survival until my own abilities recharged."

"Stealing a power wasn't enough for you, so you stole his home?" Mina heard a dim buzz from outside the room—the sound of a sandstorm approaching. *He's coming.*

"His concubines opened up the place and welcomed me. I started over from scratch here, didn't even have enough power to build a siren like Pearl the sea she needed to survive." Sounding bereft, Enti said, "So she and Xodin deserted me when I was at my weakest. I have nothing left but this place."

Mina's gaze darted to the door. Her sympathy was getting the best of her, but Adham would be here any second.

"Exactly," Enti said, reading her mind. "He's about to stalk in here with a storm raging, and you'll disappear inside it."

"Just do as I've told you!"

"I'm not returning anything, princess. Being able to break vows comes in handy at times, and I'm not keen to fulfill all the ones I've made."

"You're leaving me no choice. You think I'm bluffing, but the stakes are life and death. I will do anything to save my mate and my brother, and you know I can't lie."

Enti quickly said, "If someone like you takes my head, Silt's power will leave my dead body to be reincarnated into another Sorceri babe somewhere in time. How will you find it?"

Enti was right. Bettina had warned of that. That buzz grew louder, grains of sand tumbling over the threshold in advance of a storm. They felt cold—pitiless.

Out of time. *Think, Mina!* "If you return his power, we'll give you this place, and it'll be your home from now on."

Enti feigned a yawn. "Give me the holding I already occupy?"

"You'll officially own it, and he'll never come after you." Mina was almost sure he'd agree. But then, he had built this monumental structure with his own hands. "Don't get greedy, sorceress. Otherwise I'll have my uncle's army of Dacians level this place to the ground. You'll have to start over again, beginning from scratch once more."

After a beat of hesitation, she said, "Deal, princess." When Mina released her and sheathed her sword, Enti threaded her fingers together and cracked her knuckles. "Tonight, we play at virtue!"

Sand flooded in, scouring the doorway to the stone, the

sound deafening. Adham entered behind the storm, yanking off his domino. A king in all his glory, he wore sand armor over his muscular physique, and more grains hovered behind him like a cobra's hood. "Where is she, Enti? Where is Kosmina?" Sand clouded the room, waves of it seemingly searching for her.

The sorceress murmured to Mina, "You might be able to see through that sand, but I can't. And this won't work until I catch a glimpse of him, princess."

"On it." Mina misted to Adham. Because he was her mate, she should be able to extend her cocoon to him and turn him into air as well. As her powers wrapped around him, she imagined him as formless like her, glittering ether.

Fulfillment swept through her when he became mist—because he was her mate. There they stood, face-to-face, and it felt like an eon had passed. Or seconds. "Uh, hi!"

He was so shocked that his sand faltered, plunging to the ground. "Why are you here?" He gritted his teeth, sweat dotting his brow. "I have you now. You'll tell me where your brother is," he said with a barely perceptible wince. And all the while he'd been raising a dagger from his belt to place at her throat.

"No, Adham!"

Though she grabbed his arm to stop him, he struck, flipping the tip toward himself and stabbing his eye. He didn't even register the pain, just stared at her with what she could see was utter hopelessness.

"That's the last time, love." She allowed her mist to fade, and they grew visible once more. "Now, Enti!"

"Fine," the sorceress grumbled. "Take it, then."

Sorcery arced across the room like a monochrome rainbow. Adham's remaining eye glowed even brighter for a split second, and he jolted upright with a yell.

She didn't dare breathe. Had her plan worked?

"Kosmina?" he murmured in confusion, sagging against her. "Mina . . ." His heaving exhalations seemed to carry away a lifetime of frustration and sorrow.

She wrapped her arms around her sorcerer. "I've got you, Adham. I've got you." The sand that piled all around them now felt warm again.

Against her hair, he rasped, "You knew." He drew back to face her. "You *knew*. How did you figure it out?"

She cradled his face in her palms. "I believed in you."

His brows drew together, and he kissed her.

"Enough already!" Enti cried from behind them. "Too syrupy."

They broke their kiss. Then Adham turned to Enti. The weariness in his frame disappeared as his resentment welled. "You did this to me—to *us*. You knew I had vowed to kill her brother. I should annihilate you for stealing my sorcery from me."

"Like you didn't think about robbing mine!"

Sand rose ominously. "Thinking about it *right now*." The sorcerer who'd revered vengeance had just cause for it.

"Adham, wait," Mina said, only wanting to leave this place. The background cacophony of music and raucous laughter must be needling him. She didn't believe Adham would imbibe again, but breathing the smoke had to be uncomfortable. "Let's just go."

His menacing gaze remained locked on Enti. "You tried to make me a siren's mindless puppet to trap me in a dying world and keep me from my mate forever. When that didn't work, you gave me a sword as a parting gift, so that I could fight the hive for you and your friends. My power cleared the way for your escape, but that wasn't enough for you. You turned back and stole my oath-breaking ability. Why would you go for that one?"

Uh-oh.

But Enti didn't take the bait, changing the subject instead.

"If not for my resources at Castle Vitis, you and the vampire would've perished in Nightside. So what will it be now? Your mate has promised me ownership of this place. All you have to do is walk away and you'll have almost everything you've ever wanted. But *can* you? Or is Revenge still your mistress?"

Mirceo and Caspion traced inside the room at that moment, both looking incensed as they climbed over sand.

"You tossed a fucking *sandstorm* at my sister?" Mirceo swung a fist before Caspion could restrain him, pummeling Adham's face.

FIFTY-SIX

Adham simply took the blow. Though Mirceo's fist had felt like a cannon shot, he deserved that hit and more.

Then he realized what could have happened to Kosmina. "I could've killed her! You two were here the whole time and you let her confront me by herself? Why weren't you with her?"

Mirceo shook out his hand, seeming surprised that Adham still stood after that powerhouse punch. "Fuck if I know how she convinced us not to be."

"Hey, hey, everyone," Kosmina said. "We won the day. No one got hurt. . . ." She trailed off with a frown at Enti. "Wait a second. You could have forbidden violence in your lair."

Enti's dazzling smile threatened to emerge. "I usually do. Wrath is good, but not nearly as good as all the other vices put together."

Kosmina gasped with realization. "You knew Adham would be a threat—and you knew I would make some concession to avoid hurting you. You plotted all this to get his stronghold!"

She examined her nails. "Had enough time to."

"Another ruse?"

"There's no such thing as too many." Broad wink.

When Adham tensed beside her, Kosmina said, "What's done is done. Tempers are flaring. We should go."

Go. Break the chain. Yet he stood with his palms glowing. Could a Sorceri who'd lived for payback let his adversary go unpunished? Adham peered down at his mate's clear eyes, her gaze so full of concern. *Everything I want is before me.*

He turned to Enti. "I'm going to follow my mate's lead and let this vendetta go." He added icily, *"Once."*

Enti adjusted her mask. "Until we meet again, sorcerer."

With a last look around, he said, "I hope this place does to you everything that it did to me."

"Come, love," Kosmina said, hastily tracing him to the front entrance.

Sand blew over the structure, a storm approaching the valley. With a wave of his hand, he quieted it, revealing the full moon.

"Oh, Adham." She smiled up at him with a proud look, and his shoulders straightened. "You gave up revenge for our future."

"I'd do anything for you." Despite what had happened or what would happen, he'd somehow earned her love. And his ever-stalwart princess, unbending in her loyalty, had saved him from his curse. She was as magnificent as the greatest desert; like a desert, she'd claimed his heart whole.

Nothing else mattered. Which meant he had work to do toward their future. When Mirceo and Caspion found them outside, Adham told them, "I apologize for hurting you both."

With an expression of surprise, Caspion said, "An apology to the ones who got you sent to Nightside? Holy shit, the player really is in love."

"Yes. I am." He took Kosmina's hand in his, earning a scowl from her brother. "And if you hadn't dispatched me there, I never would have met her." Adham gazed back at the stronghold warily. *I would still be back there within those walls.* He faced them again. "So I can only thank you for delivering me to hell." Words he never would've believed he'd say. But the true hell would be not having her.

Mirceo appeared nonplussed before his scowl returned. "You cut off my head! Nearly!"

"I had no control. I tried to warn you, but my actions weren't my own."

"Now what? We'll have to do this every time you get high or sloppy and lose your power."

"I'll never get high again, and I'll never lose it again. I only did the first time because I'd just killed tens of thousands of ghouls and warded off a primordial. Plus, no one's ever made a move for my secondary ability. I'll lock it down like I've done with my root sorcery, and that hasn't been stolen from me in eons."

"But it was once stolen?" Caspion asked. His friendship with Bettina meant he was familiar with the Sorceri. "You were an Inferi?"

Kosmina's grip on Adham's hand tightened in support, yet the word had no sting. Everything was relative.

From inside, Enti yelled, *"Guess who won at poker tonight, people? This sorceress! Drinks all around!"*

Kosmina nibbled her bottom lip. "You're not angry that she has your holding?"

"I never want to see this place again. I'll build you a new castle in this realm. A fresh start." He pressed his forehead to hers and could almost *hear* Mirceo's deepening glower.

"You still might get red eyes, sister. You only drank him once. You can quit."

She laughed. "I'm going to drink him this very night!"

Adham went ramrod straight. After her bite, his body had prepared for future ones, creating more blood for her. His veins felt thick with it. "I concur." Wonder rippled through him at the turn of his fortunes.

Mirceo's jaw muscles bulged as he obviously bit back choice words. At length, he said, "I'm trying hard not to strike right now. Just . . . Cas, help me out here."

Sounding resigned, the demon said, "She's not a child. There's nothing we can or should do. Except for one point. The sorcerer just said he'd build her a castle *in this realm*, which is—"

"—not fucking happening," Mirceo finished for him.

These two hadn't yet been a couple when they'd captured him. Now they appeared bonded for eternity. "The Gaolers won't give up," Adham said. "They'll find another jail and come for me again. And possibly Kosmina as well, now that she's escaped."

"She no longer has the plague," Caspion said. "She'll be fine. And we can protect her in Dacia."

"Adham and I will live here in Poly," she said. "We'd already planned to."

"Sister, no. This place is unequaled desolation."

"Which is what I would suffer without him. Would you rather live with your new mate in Poly or live without him?"

"That sorcerer is *not* your mate. How can I convince you?"

"You can't. But I can convince you, quelling this topic forever . . ." Kosmina grew hazy, forming a mist—and she enveloped Adham in it as well. Their skin grew indistinct, their outlines glittering like sun-struck quartz. She told Adham, "I can share it with you because we're connected by fate."

He marveled from within her bank of vapor. "We're truly like air. I scarcely believed it earlier. You're a vampire of many talents. And suddenly I understand how those two breached my stronghold."

"Weakhold." Kosmina grinned up at him, her oasis gaze

merry. "Our new castle had better be an improvement."

"Oh, it will be. Can they hear or see us?"

"Not unless they enter our mist."

He drew her close. "How long I've searched for you—even when I didn't know what I was looking for." He pressed his lips to hers in promise. The kiss intensified, the fuse about to light . . .

When he reluctantly pulled back—her brother stood feet away and was still fuming—her expression was soft. She understood the pledge in his kiss.

Solidifying them once more, Kosmina told Mirceo, "You know I couldn't include a non-Dacian in my mist unless I was connected to him by fate. He's mine."

Caspion shrugged. "You can't argue with mist. Welcome to the family, sorcerer." He elbowed Mirceo.

"Not so fast!" The vampire paced in tight circuits. "Even if I can somehow accept this sorcerer with my sister, I can't accept Poly's time differential. If we trace from Dacia here twice a day, she'd still go decades without seeing us." He told Kosmina, "Should you two—I can't believe I'm about to say this—have children, Cas and I won't know them until they're grown. Our family would be torn apart."

Kosmina softly admitted, "Mirceo's right. It wouldn't be fair to them."

Adham told her, "I'll live in Dacia. For myself, I'd do this without a second thought." But for her . . . she'd once confided that she'd been slowly dying down there.

"I don't want to live in Dacia, but I can't go without seeing my family either." She was now faced with two unacceptable options: reside in a place she'd yearned to leave or miss her loved ones. Then her eyes widened. "There is another place. Would you take me to Sorselan?"

Mirceo: "Source what?"

Caspion muttered, "It's the Sorceri origin realm. Abandoned now. You should know it's a desert realm."

Mirceo halted his pacing. "A desert? We are *vampires*. Nothing is more horrifying than a blank canvas beneath a blazing sun." He shuddered. "We like dark. And cold. And underground. For a reason!"

The corners of her lips curved as she gazed at Adham. "I've heard the moon over the dunes is wondrous. And I do have my mist for the daytime."

Adham's heart pounded. Could he be hearing her right? "I'll take you anywhere, but are you sure?" Excitement hummed inside him at the thought of starting a life with her there. He could already imagine the castle he would build her—and the site.

"I'm positive. But would the memories be too much?" She frowned. "You might not want to return—"

He waved his hand and shaved flat a nearby dune, smoothed as if with a razor. "We'll wipe that slate clean and make new memories."

Her expression grew elated. "Then it's settled."

"Tell us about security," Caspion said with typical hunter pragmatism. "Assume the Gaolers keep coming."

"My sorcery is fully restored"—as boundless as his feelings for Kosmina—"which means that each grain of sand would be a sentry. I could detect anyone who arrived in the realm."

Mirceo wasn't sold. "What if the Gaolers just appear in your home and use time manipulation?"

Kosmina said, "I sensed their presence before they arrived, and my breaths condensed. Now that we know what to look for, we can trace to Poly at the first sign of them."

Adham added, "The sand scyllas are rumored to repel time manipulation. It's why I lured them to this holding. They were my backup in case the Gaolers ever breached Poly. With your help, we could transport the creatures to Sorselan."

Kosmina grinned. "I promised Enti *zero* scyllas with the transfer of this property." As if to punctuate her words, one of them belched loudly from the base of the pyramid and sand puffed up into the air.

"Rumored to repel? Rumored?" Mirceo's patience frayed at the edges. "There's still too much risk."

"I'm willing to take some risk in order *to live*," Kosmina pointed out. "Besides, since I've met Adham, I've dreamed of the desert. I think for a reason." Squeezing his hand, she said, "We've decided we're going to reside there. Wish us well."

At that, Caspion said, "We do, Mina, and we'll help you two in any way we can." He addressed his mate: "Come on, leechling, give them your blessing, and let's get to it. We've got drunken scyllas to wrangle."

Tense moments passed, and Adham felt as if his future hung suspended over a sand trap.

Then Kosmina said, "Brother, while I would prefer to have your blessing, I do not *need* it."

Adham checked a smile. His princess, shy no more, would live only on her own terms.

"Well. You really are different." Mirceo threw his hands up in surrender. "Fine. No hard feelings, Silt."

She firmly said, "His name is Adham."

FIFTY-SEVEN

Sorselan
Months later . . .

S he could not be any cuter," Kosmina said from her spot on the floor. Hearts in her eyes, she rolled a ball across the carpet.

"Or more mischievous," Adham said fondly from his spot beside his mate. "She pincered another pair of my boots."

"Naughty, stingerling," Kosmina cooed to their baby scorpion as it fetched the ball. Mirceo, as a token of goodwill, had apologized about Sequara and sourced this one for them. "Our wittle Sequaret must need more toys."

Adham raised his brows. Scorpion toys already covered an entire floor of their new home.

Unlike his former stronghold, he'd built his mate a vampiric castle in the style of Dacia's, with flying buttresses, arches, and Gothic turrets. Diamond windows filtered the sunlight during the day, and a blood fountain bubbled in her spacious salon.

He'd situated the structure on the banks of his oasis amid all the fruit trees and dunes, using sand to move blocks. Constructed in record time, it was the most spectacular thing he'd ever built.

Sequaret tired of chasing her toy and trundled over to her bed, all but purring. As the creature nodded off, Kosmina sighed, her gaze besotted. Though she'd begun to dream snippets of his memories, her irises remained blue. "I never liked arachnids before her."

"They grow on you."

As the sun set, the evening breezes roused to stir the castle's many windchimes. Recalling today's blistering sun, he rubbed his palm over the back of his neck. At some level, it must unnerve her to be here. "You know, we won't always be exiled. We will fight the Gaolers." Those phantasms had placed another bounty on Adham and also on Kosmina, which meant he would soon discover how to annihilate them.

With her by his side, he was strong. Still, he'd always be on his guard against power theft and their foes.

Aside from his sentries of sand and their growing guard-scorpion, he'd implemented more traps. And with the help of Mirceo and Caspion, they'd teleported the drunken scyllas here to inhabit the grounds around the castle. The fraught drying-out period for the creatures had proved eye-opening, but lessons had been learned, and everyone had grown from the experience.

"We will fight them. Yes," Kosmina said. "But I don't consider this exile." She rose and took his hand, leading him out onto their large observation deck to watch the rising moon. She lifted her face to the gentle kiss of wind, seeming enamored with the breezes here. Little wonder. When Mina had traced him to Dacia to pack her things, not even a wisp of air had disturbed the ever-present mist.

At the railing, they admired the scene before them. Palm fronds rustled and waves lapped the clear water. The globe of a full yellow moon peeked over shifting dunes. "This is home." She'd just said the words when a purple tentacle curled around a baluster. Then came another tentacle of a slightly deeper color. Used to this nightly ritual, she pulled jerky from her pockets and treated their scyllas.

With sounds of beastly delight, they took their prizes to the base of the castle. When more tentacles reemerged, she emptied her pockets with a chuckle. "Greedy scyllas." Kosmina truly did love it here amid all the sand and sun and monsters.

Marveling at his mate, he had to say, "Still . . . do you not miss being the heart of Dacia?"

She turned her face to him, her pale skin bathed in the moonlight. "Mirceo and Caspion are the heart now," she said easily. "Did I tell you they're coming for dinner tomorrow night?"

"Must they?" Adham asked, though he didn't mind. He felt only gratitude toward them, often wondered what would have become of him had a young Dacian prince not swiped a random reward poster.

Kosmina's brother and brother-by-fate made her happy, which made him happy. Plus, the pair weren't nearly as bad as he'd thought they'd be.

In fact, all the members of her family continued to trace over, forever debating the best defensive measures to keep their beloved Mina out of the Gaolers' reach.

The Dacians were indeed a contingent of talented warriors. With that much skill and might united, Adham and the Dacians could take on the Gaolers in a preemptive strike. He intended to broach his new plan for war during their next gathering.

He wouldn't rest until he'd neutralized that threat and plucked Kosmina's heirloom sword back from their grasp. Not for revenge. Simply because his mate wanted it.

"They must," Kosmina answered with a grin. But it faded as she said, "We're going to plot how to get Furie's location out of Lothaire." She'd explained to her uncle that she herself had drowned and couldn't bear the idea of Kristoff's mate suffering like that again and again. She'd beseeched him to help. Maybe with Queen Ellie's assistance, they could make inroads with the Enemy of Old.

Whenever Adham replayed Kosmina's drowning, he didn't understand how Kristoff was still sane, considering his mate's plight. Whenever Adham replayed his own burial, he understood why Lothaire *wasn't.*

"My uncle must reveal that information sooner or later. As my mate likes to say, it's as good as done." She leaned against Adham, sighing when he looped an arm around her shoulders, and relaxation stole over them.

They still didn't know if Nïx had targeted Kosmina—the soothsayer's intervention with Lothaire and Kristoff leading them to Nightside indicated so—but if this life of theirs was the result of the Valkyrie's meddling, then he was a fan.

"When you were out checking the traps earlier, I had some company," Kosmina said. "Queen Ellie traced Balery over."

"If only this place had more visitors," he said wryly, dropping a kiss against her hair.

"It is a little like a teleportation station, isn't it?" She chuckled. "But this was a business visit as well. Balery wanted to test my blood again just to be sure all my markers were holding steady."

He tensed beside Kosmina, turning her to face him. "And?" he barked, all relaxation vanished.

When worry filled Adham's expression, Mina quickly said, "No illness remains." Though Balery had pointed out that drinking from a sorcerer like Adham had given her potent levels of magic.

Mina spied traces of it everywhere, shimmering like the gold dust over the dunes of their lands. She could even see him radiating magic whenever he gazed at her.

"Good. Good." He exhaled, tension leaving his body. "Good," he repeated, as if he recited a spell to ward off ill-humors.

"I'm fine. I'm safe." She leaned up to press a kiss to his lips that swiftly grew heated. When she drew back, his expression promised wicked lovemaking, and she could hardly wait to experience the divine again. Her bite mark on his neck from earlier had healed, and he'd be eager for her to renew it in various places all over his body.

Afterward, they might explore more of the desert or frolic in the spring. And at moonset, as the windchimes and wavelets soothed her like a lullaby, she would drift off in his arms.

Each day as she slept, she experienced his memories—vague sensations of sun on her face, foods she'd never eaten, wines she'd never drunk. The woozy swim of opium. Her favorite was his recollection of tracking a deer across hoof-marked dunes toward what would eventually become their home. . . .

Yet now he frowned down at her. "Had you been worried about this, love?"

"Not really, since I'm able to return at will past Dacia's boundary. But I wanted to make sure about my health before I talked to you about this." She tapped his cuff. "You won't always have to wear it if you don't want to."

His tension returned. "You want children?"

"I've always dreamed of a family, but I had no specific urge before I met you. Yet now . . . yes. I want our children."

His brows drew together. "My first thought is that we're fugitives, so we can't plan for our future. But fuck that. We live on our terms together."

Her lips curled. "I thought you'd say that, my optimistic, hardworking sorcerer."

"You really would start a family"—he cleared his throat into a fist—"with me?"

"Adham, you're *him*. And they'll be *them*."

Nodding, eyes a little wild, he yanked off the cuff and tossed it away.

As he took her lips, she surrendered to his magic. She'd once hoped for molten gold with this man, but she now knew the hottest fires between them would never cool. Those flames thrummed and glowed, their bond alive with heat. They enjoyed nothing less . . .

. . . than heaven.

FIFTY-EIGHT

Dacia

"My queen continues to make a compelling case for me to help you," Lothaire told Kristoff as they sat on the villa balcony once more. The table that Nïx had destroyed had been replaced in the ensuing months. Chessboards, a pitcher of bloodmead, and chalices awaited their play. "Mina's heartfelt pleas for Furie did have some effect on me as well. Perhaps you will win tonight."

Though Kristoff churned with excitement, he forced himself to say casually, "Then let's begin." He opened with his white knight.

"You wouldn't believe where I've just been. We have a new visitor to the kingdom. You'll meet him soon."

When an enraged roar sounded from the dungeon, Kristoff observed, "An involuntary visitor."

How many lives Lothaire toyed with! He moved a pawn. Fitting.

Any sympathy Kristoff had mustered in Nightside for his half brother had been crushed under the combined weights of impatience and resentment. "My old dungeon cell?" he asked, voice scathing.

"No. We needed one with a bit more . . . unique security." He grinned as if at an inside joke, so Kristoff resolved *not* to ask him about it.

Instead they traded several moves, settling into their strategies.

Lothaire observed, "The taste of victory teases you. You must already be picturing your future. Yet your imaginings aren't in the realm of reality."

"Yes, yes. I've heard all this before. Furie is a crazed she-devil everyone should fear."

Lothaire sipped his bloodmead. "Here's something you might not be aware of. Rumor holds that she knew she would fail when she set off to assassinate Demestriu. Surely Nïx would have warned her. But Furie's rancor toward vampires drove her to hunt him regardless—because she would do anything for even a chance to kill a Horde king." With an attempt at an innocent expression, he said, "Isn't that the position you are currently applying for?"

Kristoff ignored that. "How did she go from assassin to captive?"

"Demestriu happened. She got the better of him and slew him, but he rose as if from the dead."

"How is that possible?"

"Our uncle was old when *I* was young. Very old immortals develop interesting powers; basically they're the pesky exceptions to all those fallible rules."

Kristoff narrowed his gaze. "You admired him."

"We had a complicated relationship. He ended up being more like Stefanovich than even I had anticipated. In a word: diabolical."

"I discovered that when I exerted against him." Seventy years ago, Kristoff had tried to take Helvita, but his Forbearer army had paid dearly, their numbers decimated.

"To be fair, you did better than most believed you could. No one predicted you would have the courage to take on Goliath." Again Lothaire gave him that measuring look. "And five years ago, you seized a Horde castle. Perhaps you're not utterly beneath my notice." He poured more bloodmead.

Kristoff didn't drink his own, wanting to stay sharp. Victory might or might not be here for the taking, but information certainly was. He starved for what Lothaire had in excess.

They exchanged a few moves; then Kristoff nonchalantly said, "Demestriu was known for his tortures." Wanting to distract Lothaire, he asked, "What did you do to earn a burial in the Bloodroot Forest?" *A burial that still torments you.*

Lothaire's eyes went hazy. "Nothing. I did absolutely nothing to him. But he wanted my vow to serve his interests forever, which I would never normally give. When he dug me out of the ground after centuries and threatened to plant me once more, I did anything he asked."

"A vow took you off the board? Then he did to you what you're proposing for me."

"Yes." Lothaire sipped his chalice. "Now that he's been assassinated, only you stand in my way."

"Not Cousin Emmaline?" Against all odds, their faint-hearted vampire/Valkyrie cousin had slain her own father, Demestriu.

"I'm not worried about Emmaline. She doesn't want the crown, not like you and I do. I wonder if there's a lesson to be learned from her?" Lothaire grew quiet in thought.

After a moment, both brothers spoke at the same time: *"No."*

They glared at each other.

Kristoff didn't want anything in common with this fiend.

And yet, Lothaire was the closest family he had.

As they exchanged more moves, Kristoff realized he'd never hung on for this long. He conceived of a complex gambit that Lothaire would never see coming. *Control your excitement. He can sense it like an animal.*

"Uncle Demestriu did so love his cruelties," Lothaire mused aloud. "He once smuggled a plague carrier into Stefanovich's royal chambers in Helvita, where his Bride and heir slept under guard. One little scratch later . . ."

Kristoff's jaw slackened. "Then Demestriu as good as murdered my mother? He was the one who did it?"

"It would seem so."

"But someone sneaked me out as a babe. Who hid me among humans—"

"Checkmate."

That word. It'd come from nowhere. *I thought . . . I thought I was winning.*

Lothaire hadn't tempered his stance, had only been toying with him. More games, more time, more sanity flowing away.

Checkmate. That *word.*

Wrath exploded. Speed and strength filled his body as he lunged across the table to overpower his brother. He had his fangs in Lothaire's neck before the fiend could blink.

Blood. From the flesh.

With a bellow, Lothaire yanked him away, hurling him into the far wall.

Kristoff collided with stone. A bone snapped. Skull fracture? Didn't matter. He'd already fed from the source. Even more power flowed through him, the transfer complete. He scrambled to his feet and bared his bloody fangs. "How's that for a killer instinct?" He'd decided against this course after witnessing Lothaire's insanity in Nightside, but rage had other ideas. "You're right. We are very much alike. Especially now that we'll share so many memories." *From all Lothaire's victims and Lothaire himself.*

"You fool, take them, then." Pressing a palm against the gash on his neck, he stared at Kristoff's eyes, which must be reddening. "You'll choke on them. My memories will madden you worse than I ever could. Like our father, you are lost."

"But she'll be found."

"Does Furie dream of air or fire? You have no idea what you're about to bring to the surface."

"My future." With that, Kristoff traced away from Dacia forever. . . .

FIFTY-NINE

Cheap Thrills Drive-in Theatre
Fayetteville, Arkansas
Months ago . . .

"How do you hunt the unhuntable when the unhuntable is hunting you?" Nïx murmured to her coalition in the theater's projection room. "You become"—she paused for the reveal—"*unhuntable.*"

Emberine, the Sorceri Queen of Flames, yawned. "Enough, Valkyrie. Just tell us where to *fire.*"

Portia, the Queen of Stone, nodded in agreement. "I've been levitating a mountain around in the clouds above us for an hour. It's not a clutch. And I want some of the mortals' popcorn."

Other allies—Valkyries, witches, and Furies—shared the Sorceri's impatience. But the witches were sober for once, and the Furies hadn't slain anyone off-target yet. No glittering stones had transfixed the Valkyries.

We are so on tonight!

"Fine. I'll curtail my pre-melee pep talk." *Boo-hiss, no fun.* Even Bertil screeched his disappointment, glaring from his perch on her shoulder. "Our prey for tonight is using his invisibility right now. The dragon-shifter primordial lies curled up in front of the drive-in screen." With a combination of her pastsight and foresight, she could all but see Uthyr, with his metallic-blue scales, mammoth body, and eyes like a pair of gold coins.

He was the Møriør's most potent member after their leader, Orion the Undoing. In his dragon form, Uthyr could create portals across realms or burn the world with a fiery breath. He could even time-travel. As a primordial, he had scales said to repel all weapons.

Uthyr was here in this random place solely to enjoy tonight's showing of *Godzilla.* The first big battle of the movie loomed, and his heart accelerated with gleeful anticipation.

Alas, dragon shifters didn't belong at mortal drive-ins. His vast arsenal of powers was undercut by a weakness: hubris. Tonight it might be his downfall.

When Nïx's allies turned in that direction, she surveyed the assembled females. The witches would fight to the death for Nïx. The Valkyries as well. The Furies had awakened from their nests for this battle, driven to stamp out evil. They'd deemed Uthyr evil. *Bummer for Uthyr.* The Sorceri . . . ?

Well, they were here.

Portia said, "Are you sure about attacking him in front of mortals?" The parking lot was filled with them, their trucks lined up for the show. "They'll film everything, and then we'll get clipped for revealing ourselves to humans."

"Needs must and all that. This is our sole shot at him." They would deal with the fallout later. Besides, Nïx had it on good authority that the Gaolers were dealing with a lack of prison space.

Portia's lips thinned. "You promised Ember and me a primordial *giant* to kill if we temporarily allied with you. We're not rent-a-help for other Møriør."

"Uthyr's quite large. Does that count?"

Emberine's red hair sparked at the ends. "You also said we would probably perish in battle. Is this our last night, soothsayer?"

Her concern had merit. Nïx had predicted much of the battle this eve, but she hadn't seen the ultimate outcome. And anything could happen when fate had a habit of sticking her nose where it didn't belong.

Yet if ancient Valkyries, a nest of Furies, a coven of witches, and a pair of evil Sorceri couldn't get this job done, who could? "I can promise you that no one will die tonight unless they die. Now, does everyone remember my brilliant plan? Because I do not."

Sighs all around.

Cara the Fair's violet eyes were solemn. "We remember. We're ready, sister."

"Such a sweet girl," Nïx murmured as a memory from long ago teased her mind. She couldn't quite pull it up, so she got back to business. "Okay, off you go. Don't stop until you bring him down, or the Lore will be lost forever."

As the coalition left Nïx behind to position themselves all around the drive-in—and above it—the witches held hands and softly chanted oothspeak, channeling magic to remove the dragon's camouflage.

Uthyr grew visible by degrees, a marvelous sight. Nïx's gaze swept from his gleaming eyes to his horns and fangs, then along the length of his sinuous neck. She admired his leanly muscled dragon frame down to his spiked tail. His blue scales shimmered like a half-remembered dream.

Remembered. Memory. That teasing one surfaced, and she was transported into the far-distant past to Valhalla, the Valkyrie origin realm.

Furie and Cara, twin girls born of a Fury mother, stood hand in hand before Nïx as waves of purple, green, and white aurora danced overhead. Seven years old, already bonded for eternity, they had hair the color of a raven's wing and their mother's violet eyes.

One twin burned to fulfill her Fury instincts; one already hid secrets, more Valkyrie than Fury. Their wings would emerge soon, which meant Valhalla wouldn't hold them for much longer.

Behind Nïx's vision, the battle against Uthyr commenced. Furies executed their attack, dive-bombing from the sky. Witches hurled hexshots. Valkyries charged, swords raised. In the clouds, Cara the Fair hovered with her fire wings, waiting to strike using an infamous weapon.

Yet Uthyr defended valiantly, bringing Nïx back to the present.

We're . . . losing? She dashed from the projection room down amidst the carnage.

Faced with bedlam between a dragon and other "myths," Arkansans abandoned the interactive flick, flooring their four-wheel drives away from a real-life Godzilla. Too late for some; groaning metal sounded when the dragon accidentally stepped on trucks, kaiju-ing mortals.

Weaving through the mayhem, Nïx sprinted across the battlefield. Puddles of blood splashed up over her and Bertil. "Fly away, friend." He did so with a screech.

Catching her gaze, Uthyr chuffed laughter and smoke, that hubris on full display. "Is this the best you can do, little Valkyrie?" He pounded his chest with his clawed paw.

"Honestly? *No.*" She spun in circles until lightning formed a shield around her. Bolts sizzled in every direction, and she shot them from her palms at him.

He roared with pain, rearing up in front of the screen just as Godzilla reared up to lay waste to ships. Uthyr inhaled a deep breath and exhaled a stream of fire at the screen. A portal opened at the end of the flame. He charged on four legs toward the new exit.

"Don't let him reach that portal!" Nïx cried as she shot more lightning at him.

Shrieks sounded as the winged Furies dove with their swords, hacking at his head. They targeted his eyes, but his scaled lids protected him. Forced to slow, he butted the angels of death with his horns.

Nïx waved to another contingent—the Sorceri. Portia rolled her eyes, still disgusted she was cooperating with the good guys, and dropped her mountain atop the screen, blocking the portal. As the dragon scrambled to stop, Emberine lit up the creature, who roared with frustration.

Baring his fangs at Nïx, he raised his gaze to the sky and spread his immense wings to fly away.

His chest was unprotected. His heart ready for the taking.

Cara dove from on high, her fire wings sparkling. Air whistled from her supernatural descent as she barreled into the dragon.

His back hit the ground, the momentum driving him across the dirt. His wings plowed a trench, with Cara along for the ride atop his expansive chest. He met gazes with her and froze for a critical moment—which was all the witches needed to mystically bind him to the earth with their spells.

His heart. *Her* heart. Cara.

Nïx's vision of the past returned. A blink of an eye ago, Cara had been a somber little girl. . . .

She asked Nïx, "What is our future? Will Furie and I always be together?"

Nïx swallowed. "You shall both do what is expected of you."

Furie said, "Of course we shall. Our kind are warriors, born of fire, desperate to return to it in the course of our duties."

"You were born of lightning, dearest ones. It's a bright sort of fire." In her next breath, Nïx spoke her inner thoughts aloud: "I love

you both so much, and yet I will let you suffer."

Watchful gazes. They asked as one: "Why?"

"I see songs in my flesh and hear stars in the daylit sky. Is that madness? Or delight?"

They weren't to be put off, repeating, "Why?"

"Because," Nïx whispered. "That is what I do—"

"Sister!" Cara called.

The vision faltered, and Nïx blinked back to the present. "Yes?"

"He's bound." Cara swiped blood from her emotionless face. It must be hers. Or a mortal's. The dragon hadn't lost a drop.

Nïx took in the felled beast. He thrashed against the witches' invisible bonds, but this coven was crushing it tonight, and didn't those sassy Wiccans just *know* it?

Standing beside their foe with a plain wooden staff, Cara asked Nïx, "Do you want to do the honors?"

She tapped her chin with a claw. "No. He is all yours, Carafina."

"What madness is this, Valkyrie?" he yelled. "You can't kill me. I'm a dragon."

"Poor creature." Nïx tsked. "You've been in this form so long you've forgotten that you aren't a real dragon. You're a *shifter.*"

"My scales are impenetrable!"

"They *were*," Cara said as she held up the staff, empowering it. A blade of jet-black flames emerged, transforming it into a scythe, one that had already felled the primordial demon. Though the flames were dark they somehow emitted light.

Uthyr's eyes went wide, his struggles increasing. "I'm still a primordial. One drop of my blood will annihilate you all. You can't kill me!"

"Relax," Nïx said. "Cara doesn't want to kill you. She just

wants your heart."

Uthyr's rows of fangs glinted in the light of the weapon, his pupils narrowing even more. "Do not do this, or you'll face hell. The Møriør won't just retaliate—they will punish you beyond imagining." Uthyr thrashed harder.

But the witches intensified their oothspeak to sedate him.

Without blinking her cold eyes, Cara stabbed the blade deep into Uthyr's chest, sinking past his supposedly invulnerable scales. The flame cauterized as it cut, and the coven's incantations neutralized any drops of primordial blood that might escape.

Convulsing in agony and shock, Uthyr gasped out the words: "What . . . are you . . . doing? *Why?*"

"We're making sure you can't shift into this form again." With Nïx's help, Cara dragged the weighty behemoth of a heart from his chest. "Isn't this the key to a dragon shifter's shifting?"

"No, nooo!" He began to transform, his scales disappearing, his body shrinking to become human in appearance. His dragon fangs and maw morphed into the face of a mortal man. "Why not . . . kill me?"

"Oblige him," Emberine demanded, her palms full of fire. "He's an enemy of the Lore."

"He's much more valuable to us alive," Nïx said. "He's a leaf on a current. You all are."

Emberine exchanged a look with Portia and muttered, "Whatever you say, Nucking Futs Nïx."

Uthyr bit out, "I'll never . . . help you."

"You will just by existing. Your leader, Orion, is said to be able to see the vulnerability in every being. So how did this attack on you come to pass? Either he can't see every vulnerability, or he lied to you about yours. Regardless, you'll return to your alliance as a grenade with the *pin*"—she patted his massive dragon's heart—"pulled."

Chest gaping, he crawled for his heart, clawing the ground for it.

Nïx snapped her fingers, and a witch tossed her a huge satchel. Nïx and Cara loaded the heart inside.

With exquisite timing, Bertil landed atop Nïx's shoulder for their dramatic exit. "You'll recover soon, my leaf. In the meantime, give Orion my regards." Together, she and Bertil lightning-portaled to Dacia with the prize—and a wizard's journal she'd just nicked from one of the witches—in hand.

This heart would change the entire war.

If I remember not to throw it away. . . .

ABOUT THE AUTHOR

Kresley Cole is the #1 *New York Times* bestselling author of the Immortals After Dark paranormal series, the young adult Arcana Chronicles series, the erotic Game Maker series, and five award-winning historical romances. She lives in Florida with her family and too many pets.

KRESLEY CAN BE FOUND ONLINE AT:

Facebook.com/KresleyCole
Instagram.com/KresleyCole/
KresleyCole.com